THIS is the story of the days when great adventure lay in conquest of the prairies. In the eighties, when Minnesota was well settled and farmers prosperous, David Beaton left his home and started off with a pair of thoroughbreds and his young bride to make good his claim of three hundred acres of grass land in Dakota.

He was nineteen years old and made of bone and muscle. He knew farming and he had a thousand dollars, but he did not know the rigors of Dakota weather and that he was to experience arctic snows, prostrating heat, misery, and hunger.

As he drove west with his little wife, he had his first sample of a blizzard. Later, he was to learn the nature of cyclones, droughts and snows that isolated them for days in their sod-house shanty. In the spring, he came to know the tenacity of prairie grass.

The transcontinental railroads were spreading their tentacles over the country and David's land lay along their prospective route. Over its rails, the scattered settlers hoped to transport from back east the food they needed until their farms were fruitful. But no engine of the eighties could plough through the worst of winter's snows.

The story of David's dangerous adventure, of his desperate fight against the elements, of his struggles to make habitations for his family and his stock is told with such force and such a wealth of detail, the publishers believe *Free Land* will be added to the classics of American frontier life. In this story of a stubborn pioneer, the author has surpassed her previous novel, *Let The Hurricane Roar*.

FREE LAND

Rose Wilder Lane

FREE
LAND

New York · Toronto
LONGMANS, GREEN AND CO.
1938

"But everything is changed now; there's no more free land."

A FEW facts about free land : The United States began as the only American government that gave no land to settlers.   France, Spain and Mexico offered free land ; the United States offered freedom to men, and sold its land to rich speculators.   When wages were 25 cents for a 12-hour day, our government was selling land in blocks of a thousand acres at $5.00 an acre.   American land was the rich speculator's gamble, causing huge bull markets and crashes.   After the fertile lands were settled, when only arid plains remained and the gambling was in railroad stocks, the Homestead Act was passed in 1862.   It was repealed in 1935.

The great period of homesteading was 1913–1926, when homesteaders took title to nearly 101 million acres of the total 276 million acres homesteaded during the whole period, 1862–1935.   In the 1930's, homesteading was continuing at the same rate as in the 1860's.   Homestead title was given to more than one million acres in 1934. Homesteaders held approximately six million acres in 1935, when the Act was repealed and 197 million acres were withdrawn from homestead entry.

R. W. L.

New York City, 1938

FREE LAND

FREE LAND

THE doctor came into the barn while David was milking. In the August evening the wide doors and windows stood open. The meadows had yielded heavily that summer; the mows and the hay-bay were stuffed and David's father was feeding from a surplus piled in the barn alley. He thrust the pitchfork firmly into the loose hay and came along behind the cow-stalls to meet the doctor.

"I've got it, Beaton!" Dr. Thorne sang out. "Straight from —" He stopped.

"Nobody here but Dave," James Beaton said. Nothing excited him. He sometimes remarked that a farmer got his fill of excitement early in life. Now he stood solidly planted, his thumbs in the belt of the old-fashioned farmers' smock which he still wore. He was past sixty, but young men had to hustle to keep up with the pace he led in his fields.

"My brother Ben got it straight from the railroad offices," Dr. Thorne continued. "From the President's clerk's own mouth. It cost me a pretty penny, they aren't supposed to talk, but it's authentic, Beaton! Not a doubt of it!"

Fumbling with a letter, the doctor hooked steel spectacles over his ears. His trimmed beard tilted jutting from his chin. Gazing at David's father over the steel rims he said accusingly, "It's my boy I'm thinking of. A start for Gaylord."

What James Beaton thought of the doctor's only son he kept to himself. Silent, he followed the doctor out to the fading daylight.

David finished stripping and hung up the milk stool. Stockily built like his father, he lacked an inch of six feet in height, but he was solid bone and muscle. He had begun to do a man's work when he was seven and had to stand on a box to harness the big workhorses. Nineteen now, he owed his father two more years of labor and obedience.

From the barn door he looked at the two men standing by the buggy under the maple trees. Dr. Thorne was arguing earnestly.

Alice stepped over the high threshold of the henhouse, carrying her gathered-up apron full of eggs. Forty-three today, she called triumphantly, shaking back yellow ringlets. The curls slid forward again across the blue filet and her hoopskirts swayed toward the picket gate. Beyond the white pickets, the big white house and the elms stood against a rosy sunset. In the pump house young Perley rhythmically swung his weight on the iron handle, keeping the spout gushing into the mossy watering-trough. David called him to carry the pails of milk to the house. In the barn, Whitefoot was whinnying imperiously.

David filled her manger and hung the pitchfork in the rack by the fanning mill. Going into the South Barn, he saw that his father had fed the calves. All the young steers had come up to the shed and their hay-rack was full. David swilled the hogs from the sour-milk barrel and in the corn-crib he shoveled the last ears of corn into a bushel basket. From now on until winter husking-time, he must strip the hogs' daily corn from the shocks. But the sleek Chester Whites would fetch a lump of money.

2

He dumped the corn before them, and leaning over the pen he scratched the jostling backs with a cob. Comfortable hogs put on fat ; well scratched, they get the full good of their feed. The white hogs grunted with pleasure, quirking their curled tails and wrinkling the pink hide along their spines while they rooted chanking over the corn. The old ewe was impatiently jangling her bell.

David opened the sheep-fold gate for her and woolly backs flowed by him. His mother used to card and spin the wool ; David remembered her protests when his father paid out cash to have the fleeces carded for her at the carding machine in Malone, back in York State. Now they sold the fleeces and she bought machine-woven cloth to make their clothes. Yet James Beaton refused to admit that times had changed. Railroads, factories, telegraph, machines of all kinds had changed everything since the war, but after being a very leader of progress in taking his fleeces to the carding mill, now James Beaton was an old fogy. David could not understand it.

Beyond the narrow meadow, trees almost hid the white houses and red barns of the town. David grinned at the church spire. On All Hallowe'en five years before, he and Gaylord Thorne had taken Banker Holcomb's new buggy apart and assembled it, unscratched, astraddle of the church roof. Half the men in town had worked with ropes to get it down intact, and to this day it was a wonder how it got up there.

He latched the sheep-fold gate and walked around the three big barns, making sure that no open shutter was left unfastened to slam and rack its hinges if a wind rose in the night. Times enough, his father's voice had routed him out at midnight to fasten one. The quadrangle made by the barns and the tight north fence was almost solidly full of corn shocks ; a great yield of corn, two and three

3

heavy ears to a stalk. Now that David was the only big son left at home, it would be a winter's work to husk that corn. Another crib was needed, too.

Darkness was rising from the land. The buggy, the old mare, and the two men were shadows against the pale road, where the doctor's voice was still talking. The white house seemed even larger than in the daytime, with a yellow blur from the buttery window behind the lilac bush, and the kitchen window lighting the back stoop. Eliza's voice was vehement in the kitchen.

A fashionable figure in the French calico she had worn to town that afternoon, bangs frizzed above her narrow forehead and earrings swinging, she smacked plates onto the blue tablecloth.

"I was never so mortified in all my born days !" she asserted.

"Eliza, go look it up in the dictionary," their mother said placidly, beating mashed potatoes.

Eliza's thin mouth set. She was naturally bossy, and teaching school for seven years had made her more so ; she was on the verge of disobedience. Mother glanced at her and quietly said, "N,a,nay ; b,o,b,bob. Nabob."

Eliza bit her lip and walked into the sitting room, angrily jerking her hoops through the doorway. The slam of the big dictionary amounted to wooden swearing. Alice looked round-eyed at David and he grinned, asking, "What's that word, mother ?"

"Cut the apple pies and get down a fresh cheese, Alice," his mother said. "And sugar some cream and grate nutmeg in it ; use the blue pitcher ; we'll finish up the blackberry betty. It means an East Indian potentate, rich beyond the dreams of avarice and living in the lap of luxury."

Sparrows reminded David of his small, neat, quick

4

mother. He had never seen her idle and rarely known her to be silent except in church. Reversing the creamy potatoes into a dish she continued while scraping the pot, "I stepped into the bank this afternoon to deposit the egg money, and Mr. Holcomb come out of his office taking extra pains to be affable." Dropping butter onto the potatoes, she glanced at the clock, whisked away a lid and speared dumplings from the steam. " 'And how be you all, these fine days, Mrs. Beaton?' says he and says I, 'Why, Mr. Holcomb,' says I, 'we're living like nabobs.' Eliza was with me, and no sooner on the sidewalk than, says she, the word's outlandish. I mortified her, says she. Be that as it may be, according to Noah Webster we're living like nabobs."

David filched a ruffle of piecrust and ate it. In the sitting room the big dictionary shut but the doorway remained vacant. It framed the spindled whatnot against gilt striped wallpaper, a corner of the tall secretary, the curved base and an arm of the spring-rocker, and the striped ragcarpet drawn blandly smooth over its padding of straw and newspapers.

It was true that you could not think of a Beaton without thinking of fat land well farmed, of big barns, sleek horses, good clothes, plenty to eat. Even the first James Beaton had not left Perley Manor in England until the Plymouth colony was firmly established. His mother continued, "Let the cheese alone, David, you'll spoil your supper. Alice, the big platter and the gravy boat. Go wash up, David, supper'll be on the table in two shakes of a lamb's tail. I wonder what's keeping your father?"

The wash-bench stood in summer on the back stoop, handy to the rain-water barrel. David smacked the water with the basin to drive the wigglers down, and dipped quickly. Rolling up his sleeves, he thrust his hand into soft soap slippery in the pannikin. He heard the doctor's nag clopping down the road and the wheels turning in the dust.

2

James Beaton stood watching the pale road lengthen behind the buggy. Lighted windows in town shone among the trees. He looked at the stars and remembered a thing his grandfather had said, long ago in York State. He had paid little attention at the time, but now he could almost hear the old man speaking and see his patient eyes and the long gray beard, icicle-tipped. They were loading logs on the bobsled in the wood-lot. The old man's strength was failing then ; inch by inch he worked his end of the log to near the top of the skids. It slipped, came crashing down and buried itself askew in the snow. Mildly, without rancor, he said, "My life has been mostly disappointments."

James Beaton wondered why the young never see old people. There, plain before them, is the end of the road they are starting out on. You'd think they would look at it. But they never do.

The stars burned unflickering ; there was no wind in the sky. Tomorrow would be clear, a good day for stacking the beans. He latched the barnyard gate and paused, folding his arms on it. None of his sons saw things the way he did. Young James had gone to St. Paul, Raleigh had followed him ; now David was set on going west. All summer, there had been that deadlock between them.

It was true that everything had changed since the war. Still, he remembered his grandfather's saying that everything had changed after the war of 1812. It seemed to him that in one way everything always changed, and in

6

another way, nothing did. In his time, he had stuck to a few basic ideas through a good many changes.

His wife said that his pride set him against David ; there might be some truth in that. He had not voted for Lincoln. They called him behind the times, then, back in '59 and '60, and they voted him down. But he was still opposed to giving public money to the rich and public land to the poor. He did not believe in giving, or getting, something for nothing. He believed in every man's paying his own way. The Beatons had always done it. The Beatons, men like them, had paid for that public land, had worked and paid taxes to buy it from France and Spain and to settle the war with Mexico. It belonged to the people who had worked to pay for it ; it should be honestly sold to lighten their taxes, as they had thought it would be when they paid for it. He objected to the Government's giving it away to rich railroad builders and to men who had not even earned farms for themselves.

"Who supports the Government ?" he had asked, in the grocery store in Malone on Saturday afternoons. "We do, don't we ? the people ? Well, then don't it stand to reason the Government can't support the people ?"

It did hurt his pride, now, to think that a son of his would take some of that public land. But there was another side to his objection. He did not believe that the boy would gain by it.

There had been plenty of government land in Minnesota when he moved west. There still was. He had reasoned that a man would do better to pay for land near a market. What had become of Rutger, who had rasseled most of this very farm from the forest and put the first mortgage on it ? He did not know ; the title had passed six times, twice through the bank. It had been a tussle

7

to pay off the mortgage, but he had never repented his judgment. He had a good property now, all clear and well stocked, and money in the bank. Most of the homesteaders he knew about had been starved out ; some were still starving.

The trouble was that young men nowadays were not willing to start out empty-handed, as their fathers had done. His own boys were not ; two of them working in offices in St. Paul, hired men, obeying orders, dependent on a boss for their very food. They wanted quick money, good times, good clothes, cigars and carriages. The truth was, they wanted such things, quickly, more than they wanted independence. James Beaton heard himself sigh. He straightened up quickly ; he had noticed how old men sigh, and he was not old yet, not by a blamed sight !

He walked heavily along the picket fence and through the sagging gate. The hinge had loosened from the nails ; in the press of harvest work it was not fixed yet. No man could keep up with all there was to do — everything lapsing, decaying, falling to pieces. He said harshly, "Chores done ?"

David's head lifted with a start from the towel. "Yes sir."

James Beaton disdained the steps. He set a foot on the stoop and lifted himself into the light from the window. Flinging the soapy water to the roots of the lilac, he refilled the basin and lathered his hands. "Doc wants me to let you drive Gaylord down to Yankton, to file on a claim. His old mare can't make the trip quick enough to suit him."

David waited.

"Seems as though he'd got it straight, where the railroad's put the end of the division."

David ventured, "A town's bound to build up there,

8

fast. Somebody's going to make that profit, father. Somebody'll take up claims out there and make a big profit."

All that had been said before. His father disregarded it. "Well, you know my opinion. Your mother don't think I ought to stand in your light." He paused. "I always tried to treat you fair, son. You got your own money in the bank, your hogs, a share of the corn crop." Nothing like that had been done for him ; he had started out, at twenty-one, with nothing but his freedom. Maybe he had been too easy on his boys, spoiled them. Whatever happens to a man is his own fault, somehow. He went on heavily, "The Nelson forty's a good buy. You can handle it with what you've got. Right here in the neighborhood — "

That had been said before, too. David was baffled by his father's obstinacy, urging him to pay for a run-down forty, when a hundred and sixty acres of rich, virgin land, sure to be worth town-lot prices within a few years, could be had for nothing.

The silence locked between them. Abruptly, James Beaton gave in. "All right. Do what you want to. I give you your time."

Unable to speak, David went on combing his wet hair. This sudden victory, freedom, stunned him. He managed to mutter something about the farm work. "How'll you manage without me ?"

"I can get along," his father said dryly.

3

At supper his mother chattered, commenting and advising, pleased and worried. Alice and Perley wriggled,

9

suppressed, still so young that they must be seen and not heard. Eliza announced that she would go with him and Gaylord to Yankton. She would take a claim. She could still teach her school, winters. "Summers I'll go out there to hold down my claim and look after David."

"You won't do any such a thing," David told her. "I'm not going to have you on my hands out there."

"I'm old enough to take care of myself," Eliza replied. She was twenty-four and made no bones of calling herself an old maid. Everyone knew that she had had offers. She added with meaning, "I am over twenty-one."

She had always been able to make him helpless. A bachelor under twenty-one could not legally file on a claim, and he was nineteen. He could hardly believe that Eliza would denounce him to the Government, but he had never been quite sure how far she would go. Since he was a baby she had known or guessed every crime he had committed; all of them now were in her narrowed, smiling hazel eyes. She had never betrayed him, but she would not let him escape from being the brother she could boss.

"That's a real good idea, Eliza, seems as though." Their mother went on talking about it. David promised himself that, in the west, Eliza would find him more than a match for her.

James Beaton said nothing. By nature he was a silent man. He pushed back his plate, drank his tea, and put his napkin in its ring. At the door he turned. "David."

"Sir?"

"I'm starting you out with Whitefoot and Star, and the wagon I traded from Porter. You can borrow the two-seated buggy for the Yankton trip. Sack up two bushels of oats, tonight, to take along for feed." He went out.

Whitefoot and Star were matched Morgans, full sister

10

and brother, the best team in the county; James Beaton had refused six hundred dollars for them.

"David!" his mother cried. "Go after him! Run after him and thank him. Go, hurry, right this minute and tell him how much you —"

Outdoors there was a scent of crushed white clover. The darkness cleared from David's eyes and he saw his father standing on the pale blossoms beyond the elms. He was looking at the stars as if judging tomorrow's weather. He must have heard David on the stoop but he walked on, past the corner of the house.

David went to the barn and sacked the oats. He looked Whitefoot over, slapping her satin shoulder with an owner's hand, and stroked Star's nose thrust jealously over the box-stall partition. He had raised them from colts.

Horses, wagon and harness were worth all of eight hundred dollars. He had six hundred and nine dollars in the bank, not counting six months' accrued interest. His five shoats would sell for eight dollars apiece, and he had two hundred bushels of corn, worth in cash thirty dollars. As he stood, he was worth near fifteen hundred dollars, and Uncle Sam would give him a quarter-section of the best land on God's green footstool.

"By Jiminy Christmas!" he said. He could lick his weight in wild cats.

His mother, Eliza and Alice were in the kitchen. He stole through the side door into the dark sitting room and went upstairs three steps at a noiseless stretch. In the big, square room where he slept alone since Ral had left, he changed hurriedly to his second-best suit, putting on a boiled shirt. Anxiously he trimmed his mustache and combed bay rum through his hair. He tiptoed downstairs and opened the stair door with caution. Eliza pounced.

11

"My, Davy, how fine we are!" She sniffed the air. "Bay rum! Well I'm sure Mary —"

Furiously he said, "I got to go roust out Banker Holcomb and get some money. You wouldn't think of that, oh no! The bank's closed, but we got to have mon —"

"He'll be smitten," she declared. "Banker Holcomb'll be utterly smitten. I am gratified, Davy, to see you have a high regard for the finer sensibilities of Banker —"

"Stop badgering me!" he shouted. "You stop it, or —"

"David." Their mother sailed in smoothly, undeterred by the practiced jerk of her hoops through the doorway. She dusted her palms on her apron, twitched his cravat, and gave it a pat. "There. Seems as though Mary's name might be mentioned without you flying off the handle. I'm sure she's a capable girl and sweetly pretty, and I see no call, Eliza, for you to badger the boy. There now, David; run along."

He struck rapidly through the orchard, piling the tree-tops between him and the house. Apples and quinces scented the dewy air and on starlit patches of ground some fruit was scattered, dropped from the loaded boughs. The stubble field glimmered pale beyond the trees. When he reached it he saw the Lathrop's wood-lot beyond the curve of road. The dark mass hid the Lathrop barns, but a corner of the tall house and its white porch pillars held the starlight.

The road was velvet underfoot, the air was cool, and the sky remarkably full of stars. It was a fine, large night, in which a man grew big and calm.

At the Lathrop gate he heard the stillness of the un-lighted house. Skirts flowed from the rocking chair on the porch and he saw a pale blur of face, but he reached

12

the steps before he was sure that he was looking at Mary. Halting, he asked, "Where's all the folks?"

She stood up. "They all went over to cousin Laura's. Johnny come for help, their prize Hereford calf's choking on an apple." Her voice was flustered and one hand fussed with her hair. She was upset because he found her, at this hour, in some old dress and an apron, without her hoops. "I been finishing up the preserving."

He went up the steps in a bound. This was not the first time they had kissed; he could not have counted their kisses since he had stolen the first one behind the big oak at a Sunday School picnic. But none had been like this one. She was soft and disheveled, still warm from the cookstove; she smelled of fruits and spices. She began to struggle for breath; he could not have released her if he had wanted to.

They laughed a little while she looked up at him, her arms around his neck. She kissed him again.

"You've been making apple butter," he said. She began to twist up the loosened knot of her dark hair and he put his palms to the porch ceiling and pushed, lightly; he could have lifted the house. "I'm going west, homesteading. Father's given me my time."

That simple impressive fact sounded good to him. He reached toward her, exultant. "Molly! And Whitefoot and Star! He gave me Whitefoot and Star."

Her head was bent, her mouth full of hairpins. She pushed them one by one into her hair. "That's nice."

"Let's go out to the hammock," he said.

She went down the steps quickly, leaving his arm empty. He glanced at the curve of her cheek in the starlight. When she smiled, her cheek threatened to dimple but never quite did. She was not smiling now.

13

"Tired?" he asked.

"Oh no. I was straining jellies mostly. I only finished off a boiling of apple butter."

In the side yard the grass was worn away. Hen-pecked apples lay scattered on the bare ground. The hammock was in shadow under two apple trees. David had helped Jay Lathrop make it from a hopelessly leaky barrel, weaving hay-bale wire along the ends of the wooden staves to hold them spread out evenly.

He said, sitting down, "I can't stay long, I've got to see Banker Holcomb before he goes to bed." The trees quivered and some apples fell smashing, then harder ones pelted separately down. "I'm starting to Yankton tomorrow to file on a claim."

"They're going to waste, cider apples, best we can do," Mary murmured. She asked hospitably, "You can stay long enough to sample the new cider?"

He leaned and hooked an arm around her, crushing her skirts into an armful at her knees. A tug would plump her into his lap. She said quietly, "No, David."

His hand retreated to his knee. Trying to see her vague face, he could not make out what was wrong. He asked desperately, "Mary, what's wrong?"

"Why, nothing," she said as if surprised. "I'm sure I'm happy to hear your good news, we'll all be, and I hope you prosper in — "

He cried out, "Don't you want to go west?"

Everything changed. The dusk trembled. She gasped as if she were smothering, "Do you — I'm sure I don't know what you — mean — "

He gathered her onto his lap, apples hailing around them. Lips met trembling and became an intoxication beyond space and time. The silky mass of her hair, prickly with hairpins, was deliriously fragrant. She mur-

14

mured against his shoulder, "You mean — get married ?"

Jubilant he sang out, "What the dickens you think I meant !"

4

Doing the chores before dawn was no novelty, though the season was early for it. Cows must be milked at the regular hour, but he cleaned the stalls and did the feeding before his father came. They wheeled the two-seater out of the carriage house and hitched up, then blew out the lantern. A thin light revealed the shapes of buildings, trees and fields.

"I appreciate the team and wagon, father," David said.

His father made an effort and gave him his first word of praise. "You know how to take care of horses, son."

Eliza, tying a veil over her bonneted head, pestered him to hurry. Deliberately irritating, he ate two more stacks of pancakes. Dawn was clear when he drove out of the barnyard.

Never before in his memory had he been free at milking time. Perley trudged to the barn with the pails ; David was living now on his own time. The hoofs of his glossy Morgans broke the dust film on the road, their legs moving in perfect rhythm and their heads proudly high. He swished the whip in air, and flashed along Main Street past startled early clerks.

"Stop making a spectacle of us !" Eliza shrilled from the back seat. Beaton's Morgans went like Thoroughbreds when you let them out. He pulled them up with a flourish at Dr. Thorne's gate and yelled for Gay.

Dr. Thorne came out, in his linen duster and carrying a carpet bag. In a manner which did not permit ques-

15

tions, he said that Gaylord couldn't make it. "I guess I'm elected. How quick can you make it down to Yankton and back, Dave?"

David spat over the wheel. Beyond the hollyhocks, the stable door stood open to an empty stall. This would not be the first time that Gay had taken the buggy and failed to come back when he was supposed to. With disapproving envy, David thought again that it beat all, what Gay Thorne could get away with. He said, "Hundred and fifty miles each way; three hundred mile trip. Takes good horse flesh to keep up forty miles a day with a loaded rig, doctor."

Dr. Thorne thought his patients could get along, nothing was likely to come up that the young doctor could not handle till he got back. He put his carpet bag under the seat and climbed in beside David.

The Morgans sprang forward, so fresh and willing that David let them trot an hour before he slowed them. Already they were beyond the farms he knew. Sunshine spread across woods and grass, thousands of birds fluttered chirping, and Eliza raised her parasol.

They passed the last shanty, the last fence. The glossy brown horses skimmed over prairie swells, black manes and tails blowing, their shadows flying across the grass pursued by shadowy buggy and parasol. Mile after mile, the land was empty. The Pipestone road dwindled to a trace, more clearly seen in the grass ahead than under the wheels. So much unsettled country in Minnesota was incredible. No one had questioned that they would find farmhouses along the way.

At noon, not a house was in sight. They stopped in a grove. There was not a speck of lather on the horses, but David let them cool off before he led them to the creek. He tied on their nose-bags and sat down to the

16

lunch-basket. Since midmorning they had not seen a
farm. The doctor said, "I presume there is a settlement
between here and Pipestone ?"

David did not know. They must find some shelter
where Eliza could spend the night.

At sunset they had not seen a trace of settlement. The
horses were still willing. They went on while the sunset
faded and twilight slowly left the sky. A sickle moon
sank in the west. The earth became a black rim against
paleness sprinkled with stars. The road was two faint
shadows constantly appearing before the horses. They
now fell into a walk without urging, but after a short walk
they began without urging to trot again. Hour after
hour, there was not a glimmer of light on the land.

David pulled up at last and the doctor started out of a
doze, asking what was the matter. David replied that he
was not going to drive his horses to death. "Here's
where we spend the night."

"May I ask what we will do for water ?" Eliza inquired.

David did not answer. They had not brought even a
lantern. He unhitched Whitefoot and Star and let them
roll, then rubbed them down. The heavy dew on the
grass would give them water. He tied the lines to the
halter ropes and picketed the horses to the buggy.

Eliza settled herself on the back seat. The doctor
dozed, slumped in his linen duster. When David judged
that the horses' thirst was satisfied, he tied on their nose-
bags. He feared that if he slept, he would not wake to
take the nose-bags off, so he stayed on his feet while the
horses ate their oats. He had never before seen such a
large sky.

The change of light before dawn awakened them.
Eliza bitterly stated that her hoops were ruined and that
she was thirsty. They were all thirsty. If the Govern-

17

ment had any sense, David said, it would put the Land Offices where folks could get at them without driving three hundred miles or paying railroad fares around Robin Hood's barn.

"Well, I must say!" said Eliza. "It comes with a pretty grace from you men, finding fault with what you do yourselves." If women had the vote, she stated, things would be run differently.

"That shows how much you know," David retorted. Somebody in Washington decided where to put the Land Offices. "If you think voting has anything to do with it, you've got a bee in your bonnet."

"Women in their homes don't put things where they can't get at them," Eliza continued. "If justice was done — "

"Oh, shut up!"

"Your manners are a sin and a shame," Eliza declared.

Only the horses were gay, sniffing the morning. More than an hour's morose silence ended when they reached a creek.

Refreshed, they went on, and now the Indian trail appeared. The bare rut was worn deep. Every year from time immemorial the redskins had assembled at Pipestone to mine the red stone for their pipes and ornaments. White men had made the dim wagon track beside the savages' trail.

The road ran on through Pipestone. The low bluffs along the creek were rough with stone ledges, red, brown, and striped, which the Indians had exposed and dug away. Grass was creeping into bald spots of earth, where teepees had stood or fires burned. There were the ashes of dead fires, long rained on, and paths.

They could hardly believe they had reached Pipestone so soon. The team must have covered seventy miles the

18

day before. Aroused, Dr. Thorne exclaimed, "By gravy, Dave, you've got a team that can't be beat !"

The horses were fresh as daisies. To himself, David thought that they might reach Yankton that night ; a hundred and fifty miles in two days.

Before noon they came through river bluffs to Big Sioux river and the town. There were some log houses in Sioux Falls, and a grassy sod fort. David called to a man on the sidewalk, "Which way to Yankton, sir ?"

"Straight ahead, stranger, can't miss it !" The man called after them, "What'll you take for that team ?"

David shouted back, "A hundred miles since yesterday morning, and look at 'em !"

Beyond Big Sioux river the prairie stretched endless. The sun blazed and a hot wind came scorching from the northwest. They drove on, hour after hour, hoping to find water and trees. The wind parched their lips, and Eliza wanted to know if there was any water this side of the Missouri river. "I'm perishing," she declared. "Positively perishing."

An hour past noon, David pulled up. Nothing was to be seen but tall grass blowing under the hot wind. He unhitched the horses, and held the halter ropes while they lay down and rolled, then tied them to the wheels and put on their nose-bags.

Eliza uncovered the lunch-basket, but they were too thirsty to eat. Sucking a pickle, Eliza said that a woman would have found out where she was going, before she started.

"Why didn't you ?" David inquired. While Eliza replied, he hitched up. The road climbed gently on a long prairie swell. Whitefoot and Star took it at an easy trot, and pricked their ears forward. Not a mile ahead, a windmill's blades revolved above a shanty.

19

The shanty appeared deserted, but the mill dripped and a spout gushed into an overflowing trough. The horses plunged their noses into the water while David hastily pounded on the shanty door.

"Don't let them drink like that !" Eliza ordered.

"Whose horses are they ?" he asked her. He ran his hand under their manes ; they were not too hot to drink, so soon after the noon rest. A yawning young woman, barefooted, opened the shanty door. Unable to stop yawning, she said they were welcome to all the water they wanted. Her cheeks were swollen and creased from sleep.

Nothing had ever been so good as that water. They drank from the spout, paused for breath, and drank again. It was sweet water, and cold. The young woman brought out two glasses and a tin cup. Sleepily smiling, she said that she had nothing to do but sleep. "I sleep all the time. The wind'd drive me crazy if I didn't."

She was holding down the claim for her husband, a brakeman on the railroad. This was the third summer ; only two more, and they would get the patent and never have to see the place again. It would be worth something some day ; she didn't suppose you could earn money any easier.

"You got a good wheat crop there," David said, looking at a patch of stubble. Vaguely she said she didn't know. You had to cultivate ten acres ; that was the law. Her husband hired it done.

They drove on, talking about the country. Only rich soil would raise such grass, and David had never seen thicker wheat stubble. There was exhilaration, too, a sense of unlimited freedom, in so much space beneath the large sky. They had traveled six miles or so when Whitefoot stopped, uneasily lifting a hind foot toward her belly. David saw her slightly swollen side.

He knew then, before his feet struck the ground. She put her head against him, sure that he would take care of her, but her knees were bending, she was lying down in harness. She had gone on as long as she could. He got the straps off her quickly, saying, "Doctor, can you be any help here?"

Eliza exclaimed, "I must say! Now you have got us in a pretty pickle! 'Way out here, you would kill a horse."

She did not mean that. She was silent when she saw that it was true. David could do nothing. They had no medicine, there was no help. He could only watch Whitefoot rolling in agony, up on her feet, down again, frenzied, rolling from side to side. It was a relief when the panting and thumping ceased and her eyes stopped pleading for help and glazed.

"Father refused three hundred for her," David said. It seemed a tribute to the dead mare. He had been thirteen when she was foaled; he had gentled the little colt, fed and taught and groomed her. He had broken the trusting four-year-old to harness and plow and buggy.

"She wasn't too hot to drink," he said to Eliza. "It was the oats. Eating oats, thirsty, and then drinking."

"Don't blame yourself, Davy," Eliza said. "There's no use crying over spilled milk. How are we going to get to Yankton?"

5

Yankton was about thirty miles ahead. They could only go on with the one horse.

Star was full brother to Whitefoot; they had not been separated before, and no horse has any heart for work after seeing another horse dead. Star plodded along drooping. The road was level and the load not too heavy, but it was clumsy for one horse hitched beside the tongue. David walked in the empty place, keeping Star in the wheel-track with his hand on the bridle reins under the bits.

The wheels turned slowly, the hot wind blew and a mournful sound came from the restless grasses. After a long time, Eliza called, "What's that, up there ahead?"

"Been watching it. I can't make it out," the doctor said. David got into the buggy. Some distance ahead, a dark mass lay or crouched in the grass by the wheel-tracks. Beyond it a slough crossed the road, its tall grass almost hiding a camp of some kind. The doctor asked if David had a gun. Neither of them had thought of bringing a gun.

The dark object was a horse, some days dead. Star balked. He reared and backed, snorting. The gentle obedient gelding had become almost unmanageable. David had to lead him in a wide circle around the rotting carcass and fight shoulder-deep in coarse slough grass to get him back to the wheel-tracks. Rearing and lunging, shying at empty air, he all but lifted David off his feet. The doctor called, low, "It's a prairie schooner we're coming to."

David drove through the slough and stopped. The covered wagon stood in a grassy swale. A dog rose growling under it. Beyond it a picketed sorrel raised his head and whickered. No one was in sight; the dog went on growling.

"I don't like the looks of it," Eliza said.

Behind them a voice said sharply, "Then don't look at it!"

22

A girl had come out of the slough grass. She was perhaps sixteen years old, and carried a rifle. Her hair, redder than a buckeye, hung in braids beside her cheeks, like an Indian woman's hair, and her thin face was as brown as an Indian's. Her eyes were bright blue.

"You folks in any trouble?" David asked.

"No." Her eyes did not miss anything. She looked at David again and added, "Pa's sick, and we lost a horse, is all. But we're all right."

The doctor asked what was wrong with her father and she said it was fever 'n' ague. With a shyly formal air she said, "Our name is Peters. I am Nettie Peters."

Children were stirring in the slough grass, peering out. She explained that they were shy of strangers. "They got scared of Indians, down on the Verdigris river. There's my mother."

Mrs. Peters came from the wagon, gentle and composed. The doctor and David swiftly took off their hats, and getting out of the buggy David respectfully introduced himself and asked if the sorrel were for sale.

"I'm afraid not." Mrs. Peters gently smiled. There were gray streaks in her smooth brown hair and fine wrinkles across her patient forehead. "My husband would not sell the horse."

"I raised him on a bottle, and money will not buy him," Nettie stated. "We have to get to Yankton." She looked at Star. "Is he your horse?"

"Yes. I raised him. I just lost his full sister, back the road a ways. Colic."

She knew how he felt. She said, "I'll lend you my horse, if you're only going as far as Yankton and coming back this way."

Half in joke, David asked, "What makes you think I'd bring him back?" Her eyes were the deepest he had ever

23

smiled down into, and they filled with blue laughter. She was too thin, she was young, with a wildness in her, playful and awkward, like a colt's. Her mouth was fine and clear, with a quirk at the corners. A man could not be blamed for knowing that some other man, some day, would kiss that mouth.

The young ones came out of the slough; Flora and Lucy and the youngest, Charley. Barefooted, sun-browned, shy, in clean clothes faded gray, they made David think of quails. He walked slowly along with them, behind her mother and the doctor, to the wagon where her father lay in bed, having a chill. His tousled red hair and beard flamed over the edge of the quilt. His long body shook and his teeth chattered. David spoke to him about hiring the horse and he managed to answer, "If Mrs. Peters says so."

Mrs. Peters said that five dollars a day would be more than ample, and Nettie went with him to get the sorrel. She said that she had been born in Illinois. Her father had sold his farm there, because a man wrote to him from Washington that the Government was going to open up Indian Territory. "He knew Senators," she said. "He wrote Pa, first come, first served. We got down there a whole year before anybody else came."

David asked her about the Indian country. She said it was beautiful and rich and wild. There were herds of deer and packs of wolves, thousands of birds, every kind of game and fish. They took a beautiful place on the high prairie, and Pa hunted and fished, built a log house and a barn, and broke the sod.

"It was a beautiful house, so snug," she said. "With a solid puncheon floor, and glass windows." She clapped a hand to her mouth and after a guilty pause she said

24

bravely, "Only one window, and we didn't have it long. Pa hardly got it in before the soldiers came."

"What soldiers ?" David had heard nothing about any trouble in Indian Territory.

They were government soldiers. That was the second year, but the sod had rotted, so that they had a garden that spring. Pa had gone to Independence to trade his furs and get the seeds, and he had brought back the window glass, forty miles without cracking it. But first he planted the garden and the crops, so he had barely put the glass in the window when the soldiers drove them out.

David could not understand why the Government did that. She said it was because thousands of Indians were powwowing in the creek bottoms.

"They yowl worse than wolves, but wild Indians couldn't scare us out. Some more settlers had come in and Pa and the other men were going to build a stockade. But we couldn't fight government soldiers. We had to leave the garden and that nice house and barn and everything. What hurt Pa most, the soldiers rode right along beside the wagons. They said we were making trouble with the Indians, when we never would have gone there at all, only Pa had the word straight from Washington."

David supposed that someone in Washington had an ax to grind ; it was hard on those settlers but could not be helped now. He pulled up the picket pin and coiled the rope. The sorrel was a rangy gelding, with a good eye and good action. His dam had died when he was foaled, and Mr. Peters had traded a swan's skin for him. "I was going to have a swan's-down coat, but I wanted the colt instead. He's not blooded stock like yours, but he's willing and his wind's good. He's soft, off grass. He hasn't had corn since we left Iowa."

The banker had taken the Iowa farm. Her father had to buy it mortgaged, because he had nothing left when they came back from the Indian country. And nobody could live and pay interest, raising corn at fifteen cents a bushel.

From the buggy Eliza stated that they had no time for dawdling. Nettie helped harness the sorrel, her thin hands expertly letting out the bits and check rein. The wind whipped her skirts, showing glimpses of bare brown feet. She said, "When we get our homestead in crops, he's going to have oats."

"He'll get his fill of 'em on this trip," David remarked, and wished that he had bitten his tongue. A flush darkened the girl's cheek. David raised his hat as the buggy started, and she flung up her hand in a gesture he remembered, gay, independent and friendly.

Eliza leaned and screeched against the wind, "Pity's sake! Could you do anything, doctor?"

The doctor replied that you had to wear out fever 'n' ague. They had quinine and now they knew enough to stay away from rivers and to shut out the night air, as well as they could, living in a wagon.

"It's a mercy if we don't all catch our deaths, on this trip!" Eliza cried.

6

At ten o'clock that night David pulled up at the Smithsonian Hotel in Yankton. A hundred and fifty miles in two days would have been something to brag about, if he had brought Whitefoot through alive. The sorrel was in a lather but breathing easily. At the livery stable to which the clerk in the imposing hotel directed him, a hostler would have taken charge of the team. With his own hands David rubbed them down, and gave strict instructions to let them cool for an hour before watering and feeding them.

He was surprised to find that horses were higher-priced here than at home. His impression of the west was that herds of wild horses roamed the plains. Wild horses were farther west, the hostler told him. Gentlemen in Yankton owned a carriage and pair, farmers and the new settlers had their workteams, but there was no surplus of horses for sale. You had to figure that freight charges by railroad or river steamer were clapped on top of the eastern price, and that the demand for good horses here was larger than the supply. David looked over several fine animals ; the asking-price was so high that he did not discuss it. Even if he had the money with him, it would be foolish to buy a horse here. He went out to stroll around and look at the capital city.

Even at that hour, Yankton was a wide-awake town. Kerosene lamps on poles shed disks of light over wheel-rutted dust, board sidewalks, and brick fronts, all along the wide main street. David glimpsed several residences perhaps even more impressive than Banker Holcomb's. There was a street of smaller houses behind the main street, and on higher ground beyond them, a small cluster of lighted windows sketched in the dark some large residence illuminated for a party. Yankton was, of course, an old town, founded long before the war.

Down on the river levee, the third street blazed and blared. In a hubbub of voices, boots, song and jangling piano music, wide-hatted men with pistols on their hips, and men bowlegged in cowboy pants and rattling spurs, roistered in and out of dance halls and saloons. Beyond the railroad tracks was a boat, its funnel dark against pale water lapping away into the night.

David did not drink, but he went into the saloons and threw dice for cigars. The Far West was Captain Grant Marsh's river steamer, in from the Black Hills diggings. David saw gold dust, poured and weighed on little scales ; he saw blanket Indians ; he heard the screaming laughter of girls and drunken shouts, a maudlin uproar.

Along the decorous street where the hotel stood, a few gentlemen strolled in tall silk hats and tailed coats, carrying in gloved hands the elegant absurdity of useless canes. Two carriages passed, ladies and gentlemen drawn by high-checked, high-stepping horses, raising a smother of dust. The lights on the hill were out, the party over. By David's gold locomotive-case watch, the hour was midnight. The street lamps burned with a passive acceptance of loneliness till dawn ; apparently no one put them out. It was a waste of kerosene appalling to think of. David went sleepily to bed.

In the morning Eliza appeared as if she came from a bandbox, in fine French calico, lace mitts, chip-straw bonnet. Her hoopskirts swayed elegantly and her chin was imperious as she swept into the dining room. There was plenty of food, dozens of dishes immaculately protected by individual bee-hive fly screens, but she took only the smallest morsels on the tip of her knife, barely opening her pursed lips to receive it.

By daylight the town seemed bare without trees. There was only one tree in Yankton ; the streets were lined by whipstock saplings, recently set out. The roistering street of the night before was shut and silent now ; the green banks of Nebraska appeared beyond the wide and sullen yellow river. A steam flourmill racketed at the end of the street of little houses, puffing white steam into the sunshine.

A young clerk was opening the Land Office. He spread

a map of the Territory on the counter and with his pencil
pointed out the new railroad survey. The townsites were
marked by quarter sections crossed off, pre-empted land,
bought by the railroad or by rich men in cahoots with the
railroad, at a dollar and a half an acre. Dr. Thorne made
a strangling sound; the veins stood out on his temples.
With a shaking finger he pointed out a cluster of crosses
on the map.

"Looks like something's leaked about that townsite,"
the clerk agreed. "End of the division, mm?"

That dirty crook of a railroad clerk in St. Paul must
have sold his information to others beside the doctor's
brother. All the sections around that townsite were
gone, homesteaded or pre-empted. The nearest open
land was two miles northwest of it.

They could only do the best they could. Politely the
doctor and David yielded the best location to Eliza. The
clerk began to fill out the papers.

"My name's Thorne, Gaylord Thorne. Age over
twenty-one." The clerk smiled wisely, but said nothing.
According to law, a man must file on his claim in person.
Dr. Thorne was so excessively honest that he was helpless
in a horse-trade, but dealing with the Government is another thing.

David planked down his own fourteen dollars and a
half, and stated that he was twenty-one. He pushed back
his hat and felt fine. Beating a legality was a satisfaction,
like paying something on an old grudge. A man knew
instinctively that Government was his natural enemy.

The friendly clerk asked why they did not take tree-
claims. They could have a second quarter section apiece,
by setting out ten acres of trees and cultivating them for
five years. David put his papers in an inside pocket,
saying, "I've done some farming, brother, back in York

29

State and in Minnesota. Where God don't raise trees, I'm not betting I can."

The clerk asserted that the whole plains country was going to be a Garden of Eden when the tree-claims were groves and the orchards in bearing. He argued, "Anyway, who says you got to raise trees? Plant 'em and cultivate 'em, 's what the law says, and Uncle Sam's giving you the land."

They took tree-claims. David chose the quarter adjoining his homestead on the west. Two strokes of the clerk's pencil doubled his acreage; he had three hundred and twenty acres. His father, after a life-time's work, owned only two hundred.

Leaning on the map, he looked at it while the clerk filled in the tree-claim papers. One vacant quarter was left in the section south of his. A man came in, then another. A covered wagon stopped, two men got out of it and came in. A second clerk passed behind the counter, hung up his hat and rolled his shirt sleeves. There was a small crowd behind David, the vacant quarter and the pencil were under his hand. In an instant he made the small cross-mark.

He reasoned that it was only fair to hold a good claim for the Peters family. They had got a raw deal on their first claim, in the Indian territory, and they would have reached Yankton before now, if their horse had not died. He paused in the livery stable to make a rough sketch, with the section number, on the back of an envelope.

The sorrel was in fine shape. Five minutes in harness worked off his slight stiffness. Both horses traveled with homeward zest, and before noon they reached the covered wagon. Mrs. Peters was spreading a washing on the grass. Her husband came weakly toward the buggy, saying, "You folks made a quick trip!"

Leaning on the wheel, he asked about the road to Yankton. His red hair and beard flamed in the sunshine, his blue eyes were hot with fever and his legs quivered. He hardly had strength to stand up. His boots had been mended till new stitches cut the old leather and his bare toes stuck out. He wanted to know if he could get his wagon to Yankton by pushing it to help the sorrel on the upgrades. He was acquainted with a contractor on the new railroad, and if he could reach the camps before they closed he expected to get shelter for the winter and be first on hand for a job next spring.

David told him about the road to Yankton, and handed him ten dollars for the hire of the sorrel, saying he was much obliged besides. Mr. Peters looked at the bill and returned it. "Sorry I can't make change." He said, "You owe me five. Five dollars a day was the agreement, and two half days make a day."

"I don't look at it that way," David began.

"I do," said Mr. Peters. His tone did not permit any argument. A man who does not have shoes to cover his feet can not take one penny more than he considers his just due; it would be accepting charity.

David unhitched the sorrel slowly. He liked to finish anything he started, and he did not know how to speak to Mr. Peters about the claim he had marked off the map. A prosperous man would take the act as a neighborly favor. David doubted, now, that Mr. Peters could take it in that way. He was certain, too, that Mr. Peters did not have fourteen dollars and a half to spare. He saw Nettie coming from the wagon.

She wore a dark woolen dress so tight that her arms and breasts strained the seams. The sleeves pulled above her white wrists and the skirt did not hide bare, brown ankles. She carried a halter, and said decisively to Eliza, "I must

31

ask you to excuse my looks. Ma washed my summer dress. It's not dry yet, and I have to picket my horse."

David slid the harness off the sorrel and buckled the halter. "You fetch the rope and pin, and I'll picket him."

The young ones handed them from the wagon, where they were waiting half-dressed for their clothes to dry. Mrs. Peters thrust buffalo chips under a pot of rabbit stew and said, "I hope you will stay and take potluck with us. It's almost noon."

"Oh, do please stay !" Nettie waded through the grass beside him. "I shot the rabbit myself, straight through the eye, and Ma is a wonderful cook."

The grass was blowing all around them with a constant sound while he drove the picket pin into the hard sod. Still squatting and lightly tapping the pin with the back of the ax, he told her about the rush for land near that town-site, which would be division headquarters. "The town's bound to grow fast, and land prices 'll sky rocket." He handed her the sketch and showed her the claim marked off for her father. "Make the clerk look up the records and he'll find it's vacant."

Excitement popped a button off the back of her dress. She searched for it carefully in the grass while he knotted the picket line to the halter rope. He said, "It costs fourteen dollars and a half to file on a claim."

She got to her feet. "Fourteen dollars and a half ?"

"That's what it costs."

Limpness went down from her shoulders, all through her. She looked as patient as her mother. "Then we can't take a claim till Pa earns the money. We did get twenty dollars from the corn-crop, over the mortgage, but we've spent some since. We have to buy salt and powder, and soap."

"That land's going like hot cakes, fifty to seventy miles

ahead of the rails.   If you folks don't get a claim this fall, you won't get one anywheres near the railroad.   See here, I'll lend you the money."

She refused vigorously.   Both of them talked at once, clashing.   She had a horror of debt, debt had taken the farm.   Angrily David said that he couldn't stand there arguing all day.   He jabbed her closed hand open and thrust bills into it.

"I won't !" she cried.   "I can't.   Pa wouldn't — "

He strode away.   Over his shoulder he shouted, "Pick up the ax, or he'll step on it !"

At the buggy, Mrs. Peters was repeating her invitation to dinner and Eliza was saying that they must push on. David swung up into the seat and held his hat lifted while he drove out of a chorus of goodbys.   The girl stood where he had left her.   The sorrel, too, was watching them go, and sent a whinny after them.

7

In Sioux Falls the next afternoon David bargained till dark for a spavined roan.   He could not beat the owner down to a fair price.   They went on with Star.   A hundred miles was a long way to walk.

On the second day Star loosened a shoe and began to limp.   David had no blacksmith tools.   He led the limping horse into the barnyard late on the fifth day.   Alice and Perley clamored questions till his mother rushed out and Eliza's scolding diminished toward the house.   His silent father paused a moment and went on to the barns. It was chore time.

While David was husking corn for the hogs, his father came with his own stool and husking peg.   In a dry rat-

33

tling of fodder and ripping of husks, they kept alternate ears flying into the basket.

"When you going out to your claim, son ?" James Beaton asked.

"I got to put a claim shanty on it before snow flies."

They filled the basket. James Beaton swung it to his shoulder and paused. "I'd price Dobbin to you at a hundred-forty-five."

"Cash ?"

"It's a cash price."

David looked at his shoes among the husks. The price was low for a Morgan gelding turned seven, sound in wind and limb. David was still worth well over a thousand dollars, but he was sobered. With less than seven hundred in cash, and figuring costs of lumber and living two years before he could make a crop, he did not see how he could pay for a horse.

"Take him and pay me when you can," his father said, and trudged into the barn.

Gay Thorne strolled across the meadow while David was filling the steers' hay-rack. They leaned on the gate and talked. That was a fact about Gay ; men stopped work when he came around. Farmers did not like him for that reason, but there was a quality in him which held you, so that work undone never nagged sharply enough to end a talk with him.

He did not want to go west with David to build the claim shanties. David knew he could not budge any careless mood of Gay's, but he argued, wanting company on the trip. Gay was good company, always amusing. An inch taller than David, slim and light, he was so quick that he could give a good account of himself against heavier men. There was an indefinable air about him ; something in the tilt of his hat, the angle of his cigar, the

34

light brown sparkle of his eyes. The waxed ends of his black mustache turned upward and gave him always the look of a smile. When he did smile, white teeth shone under the black and his eyes became half-moons brimming with fun. Nobody could help liking him.

He would not come in to supper, and David left it half understood that they might meet at the pool room later.

When he was crossing the dark front porch after supper, his mother stopped him with a hand on his arm. "My, you smell nice. Sit down and talk awhile with your father and me, why don't you? What did Gaylord Thorne want?"

"He wants me to build his claim shanty." David did not sit down. "If he'll pay me forty dollars for an eight by ten sod, without a floor, I figure I can make about fifteen dollars on it. I ought to be seeing him." Suddenly he thought that this was as good a time to tell them as any, and an uncontrollable grin stiffened his face. "But I'm stepping up the road. Mary says she'll go west with me."

They were not surprised. His mother did a strange thing; she pulled him down and kissed his cheek. He did not remember that she had ever kissed him before. She sighed, letting his sleeve go with a pat, and all she said was, "Mary's a real good girl. Run along then, Davy."

In the Lathrop's kitchen Mary turned from the dishpan to smile at him, then went on working quickly, the back of her neck pink. He knew she had told her folks. Her mother welcomed him warmly and her father got up to shake his hand. Jay punched him, and they pummeled each other while the young ones scurried and Mrs. Lathrop cried, "Careful of the lamp!" She edged Mary from the dishpan, telling her to go entertain her company.

35

"David's not company." Mary blushed hotly. She washed her hands, hung up her apron and went out to the hammock with him.

Before he went west to build the claim shanties, everything was settled. Her father gave her the bedroom furniture, their mothers were giving them quilts, pillows, blankets, dishes. They would be married on Thanksgiving day and go to their claim.

8

He set out at two o'clock in the morning; only his mother got up to give him a hot breakfast. The Lathrop house was dark when he passed it. He turned the plodding team into the straight road beside the railroad track and dozed until dawn. In mid-morning the train passed him, fireman, brakeman and passengers waving. The train was running as far west as Tracy, but he would need the team beyond the end of the rails and driving all the way was cheaper than paying freight.

The first wagons full of men were coming east from closed railroad camps. The men were morose, surly as a bear with a sore head. They complained of the little they had to show for the summer's work; they did not know how they were going to live until spring, when they could get work again. Many of them had taken homesteads; they told David about the land, the hunting, and the railroad. They hoped next summer to work in Gebbert's camps. Gebbert, they said, was the only square contractor out there.

At night they camped by the road, but David stayed in the towns. He was not a hired man; he was a farmer's son, used to the best of everything. Cheerfully he shelled out quarters for his meals, and half dollars for the team's feed and comfortable bedding in livery stables.

All day he looked at low-rolling prairie, proclaiming the soil's richness by luxuriant grass. The enormous sky was soft and the distances hazy in Indian summer. Beyond Tracy he drove all day and saw no human being. Myriads of geese and ducks were flying south, ceaselessly calling to each other. The large buffalo wallows were now grassed over. In the afternoon a distant rider appeared small against the sky and soon vanished; an Indian on an Indian pony.

Sunset spread in rainbow colors around the level rim of the earth and purple shadows rose. The low stars were huge and quivering. A solitary prickle of yellow lights ahead promised shelter in a railroad camp.

Next day he reached the townsite. No buildings were there, only wooden markers in the grass. Small shanties scattered on the prairie, deserted, made the place seem more lonely. David drove through high untrodden grass, searching for his claim.

Late that afternon he found the corner of his homestead in a wide slough which ran diagonally between his land and the townsite. The slough grass was shoulder high. He broke a way through it, leading the team, and stopped on his own soil.

The homestead rose from the slough in a low swell, from which he could see ten miles in every direction. To the south, the railroad embankment cut raw through the blowing grasses. Beyond it to the southeast, two horses were picketed and a man was shingling the roof of a shanty. They were tiny in the distance. To the west, a smoke of dust showed that men were working on the railroad.

David was thoroughly pleased by the lay of his land.

37

It could not have been better. His homestead sloped toward the townsite, and from the swell it ran level with his almost level tree-claim. He had three kinds of grass ; tall slough grass running three tons of wild hay to the acre, thick bluestem three feet tall, and large patches of curly, matted buffalo grass curing on the stem. The horses fell eagerly to cropping it, the best of fall pasture.

He owned three hundred and twenty acres of the best land on earth.

The setting sun gave him no time to waste. Before walking his boundaries, he must get to work. He dug a hole in the slough and reached water. While the mud settled he mowed the grass from his house-site and set up his cookstove there. He watered the horses, picketed them, gathered dried buffalo chips and set tea to boil while he fried ham and eggs. The land darkened. Thousands of ducks and geese were settling into the slough. Around him there was a silence not touched by the sound of the wind or the wild birds' clamor.

With the darkness, coyotes came slinking. Their eyes winked out and shone again beyond the edge of lantern-light. Their distant yapping was an evil sound on the black wind.

At dawn he was hitching up, eager to put the plow into his land. Whistling as tunelessly as the innumerable small birds, he put his shoulders into the lines and chir-ruped to the willing horses. The sod shocked him. The earth he knew was friendly, but here was an enemy. Some grass-roots were as thick as his wrist. The plow-point, driven into them, stopped.

His stomach was battered by the jerked plowhandles and the horses struggled, lathering before the sun was up. The plow was too light for such work.

He picketed the team, and attacked the earth with ax

and pick. A kind of hate possessed him. The land's rebellion against a man was monstrous, a spirit to be broken
by brutal strength, like the spirit of a vicious horse. He
worked till sparks danced through darkness in his eyes,
and stopping to mop his face where dust made mud of the
sweat, he admitted that he was in for a long, hard, grueling
job. He must tackle it with dogged steadiness.

Wild land had never been easy to tame. He reflected
that this grass was nothing to the forest that his grandfather had cleared in York State. And once uprooted,
grass would die. There would be no endless years of
labor with a sprouting hoe. Ninety acres of huge trees,
so close together that a wagon could not be driven between them, his grandfather had brought down with an
ax, and because there was no market for lumber then, he
had left them lodged in heaped confusion to dry for a
year before he burned them. It had taken his grandfather three years to put the plow to land which it would
merely scratch because of the great roots, still alive and
sending up a young forest every spring.

David himself, at ten years old, had worked one end of
a crosscut saw from dawn to dark, and helped to load and
haul the logs away, pile and burn the brush, when his father cleared the south forty in Minnesota. For six years
he had sprouted that field, spring and fall, before his
father was able to buy dynamite and spend the time to
blow out the stumps, and even yet the green oak sprouts
with rosy-red crumpled leaves unfolding would spring up
between the corn rows, from jagged root-ends left under
the soil.

He could count himself lucky, having nothing but grass
to contend with. But the days were not long enough.
He ate by lantern-light, stopping at noon only to wolf
cold scraps from the frying pan and drink dregs from the

39

teapot. In ten days he had cut barely enough sods for one small shanty. By lantern-light he set up the studding and nailed the low-sloping rafters. All day he cut sod, and at night laid it up like bricks against the studding.

Eliza's quarter, southeast of his homestead, was cut across from corner to corner by the wide slough. She had only herself to thank ; politeness had given her first choice. He set her shanty on the low corner of her land, south of his house-site and not far from the tall slough grass. A quarter of a mile west of it, he built Gay's.

The wind grew colder, piercing through his heavy clothes. In the cold, the blowing dust stung like sand. He tried to work quickly, but time went faster. There was snow in the gray air and the last teams were going east from the railroad camps.

He put up a hovel to shelter the horses, and moved his stove and bedding inside roofless sod walls. One night he flattened out a brown-paper nail-sack and wrote on it with his carpenter's pencil :

On our claim, Nov. 1, 1879
Dear Mary, i take my pen in hand to let you kno that i am well and hope you are the same. i can not make it as quick as i sed but will make it by Thanksgiving or Bust a Hame Strap. This Sod is tough but i am tougher. Weather is fair. This country is Fine. Our land lays Perfect. Will get thair as soon as i can. Yours truely, D. Beaton. P.S. please Excuse paper.

Next morning he went down to the wheel-tracks and stopped a wagon. The muffled men spoke the first words he had heard since he reached his claim. They said this wagon was the last one out. The teamster charged nothing for mailing the letter in Tracy, taking only a nickel for envelop and stamp. He asked, "Digging in for the winter out here ?"

David kept his foot on the hub, regardless of the teamster's tightening the lines. A man in the wagon told him that a family was wintering in the surveyors' house, twelve miles southeast. The teamster tightened the lines again, saying, "Well, so long." David said, grinning, "Neighbors of mine. Who are they?"

Again the teamster said, "Well, so long." Nobody in the wagon knew anything about the family. Under David's foot the hub turned. "Got to keep moving if we make Tracy tomorrow," the teamster said. "So long."

David stood looking after the wagon a moment, on his way back to work.

Next morning he woke in snow drifted over the blankets. A sharp wind soon drove the snow from the prairie swells into the hollows and sloughs. Frost whitened the ground till noon. The last wall went up with frozen sods. The sun shone brightly without warmth, then snow fell again, a spume blowing from every drift, and only the sloughs were brown streaks on the white land.

David battened down the tar-paper roof of his house. His jaw and his stomach ached, clenched against the cold, and his breath froze in ice-drops on his mustache.

On the fifteenth of November he finished Eliza's shanty and Gay's. He built rude bunks against the walls and nailed the windows in. He hung an old dress and sun-bonnet in Eliza's shanty, and threw worn-out overalls and a boot into Gay's.

"Eliza's notion of fooling the government men," he said while he fed the horses. He laughed. "Shows they're living here, say a neighbor drops in. Well, I agreed to it and I did it. That's fourteen-sixty profit. Stop talking to yourself, you'll go crazy. Hud up, Dobbin! I always talk to horses, it gentles 'em."

His house was twelve by twelve, with two doors, two

41

windows, a floor and a wooden ceiling. It cost him a hundred and nineteen dollars. He stretched unbleached muslin neatly over the studding; it hid the sod walls and brought a clean light into the room as plaster would have done. He built a big stack of slough hay by the back door, and when a hay fire was burning in the stove the house was warm.

On the last morning with the lantern he looked the place over. He had worked late into the night before, chinking the windows and the back door with strips of muslin. He had put up shelves in the corner behind the stove. With a grain sack he brushed sawdust and hay from the smooth floor, and rubbed the stove clean. Mary would be with him when he came back.

The stars were fading. An ice-green streak, level in the western sky, was the only color in the world. Wind had scoured the snow again from the prairie swells, where the dead grass was gray, and the sloughs held white drifts among dark ridges of grass. David climbed into the wagon seat and tucked in the lap robe.

"Skedaddle, you scalawags!" he yelled. "Hit out for home!" The iron-rimmed wheels bounced ringing on the frozen ground. "Hi! Yipee! Yi! Yi!"

9

At home the big barns and the granaries were crammed with provender. The cackling, feathery henhouses, the smoke houses, the cellars, butteries, pantries, attics, were full of an abundance which he had always taken for granted. Until now he had never really seen the town's lighted windows, heard the school bell, the church bell, sleigh bells, the shouts of skaters on the pond, the bustle and talking in the kitchen when Alice opened the door for him with brimming pails of milk.

Roofs were snow-covered now, icicles fringed the eaves, and the big base-burners heated the sitting rooms. Hickory chunks were put into them before supper, to make beds of coals for popping corn. David doubted that a hay fire would pop corn. The big lamps were lighted; there were books, newspapers, magazines, pitchers of cider, pans of pippins. At the Lathrops the parlor base-burner was fired up to warm the parlor for him and Mary.

"Take some along with you," her father said, scooping a panful of buttery popcorn from the heaped dishpan. Little Emmy and Bob hung around them for awhile, listening to the sea in the curled seashell and sliding off the horsehair chairs until their mother called them out and shut the door. There was still a sense of the family near, talk muted by the wooden panels, and a rattle of coal and the stove-top sliding. Across the pan of popcorn David tried to tell Mary about the west. She did not mind starting out with little; their parents had done that, and look at them now.

He wished he had Gay Thorne's gift of gab. "It's lonesome," was all he could say. "It's big and — lonesome. I didn't see a soul. Coyotes come around in the night."

"I never saw a coyote. What do they look like?"

"I didn't to say see one. Only their eyes in the dark. They're some kind of wild dog, I guess, but they sound lonesome and queer, barking. It's a lonesome country. There's no trees, only grass. If we go out there now, there isn't a neighbor nearer than twelve miles — "

Mary got up quietly and set the pan on the center table. She looked straight at him, without a smile. "If you don't want us to get married, David, say so. Right out."

43

"Mary !"

Her hands on his shoulders held him off. "You don't seem like yourself."

"Don't get notions in your head. I only — "

"Well, what ?"

"Maybe if we — I'm afraid you'll get lonesome out there. Maybe I ought to go out by myself till the country's more settled."

All at once she was soft in his arms, and laughing. "Goose ! When we're all by ourselves, is that what you'll do ? Be lonesome ?"

They were married in her mother's parlor at eleven o'clock on Thanksgiving morning. The house was jammed ; everyone they knew was there. Eliza softly played the parlor organ while David waited with the preacher. The whole end of the parlor was a bank of flowering house plants. Eliza suddenly pressed the loud lever, and the bride appeared with Mr. Lathrop. She was strange in rosy-shining stuff, with white roses in her dark hair and a big bouquet of roses in her hands. David was so shaken that he hardly knew what was happening, until the solemn moment came and he knew that God heard him and knew his heart. "I take this woman — to have and to hold, to love, honor and protect — forsaking all others, so long as we both shall live. So help me God."

It seemed that after all nothing had happened but a confusion of shaking hands with neighbors while tearful women kissed the shimmering girl. David always remembered the crowding, and the long white tables, the perfume of roses and of the row of glistening brown turkeys dotted down the damask cloth crowded with dishes, and the sounds of fun in the parlor where the young folks waited for second table. Gay was cutting monkeyshines there and some girl played the organ the whole time. Mary told him that her roses had come from St. Paul. Eliza had sent for them, June roses in the dead of winter. The stuff of the shimmering dress had come from St. Paul, too; it was changeable taffeta. A rosy sheen ran over the pearl gray, and down the front was a panel of pure rosy silk with tiny white cords in it. The roses drooped in her hair. More and more food was brought from the kitchen and women warned their men to leave room for the pies and fruit cake.

There was a time when Mary was gone, and David kept on answering everything that was said to him. Many women said that it was a beautiful wedding. Then she came down the stairs in a new black cloak, with fur somehow around her face and her hands in a muff.

He drove his wife to the station in his father's small cutter. A jingling line of sleighs followed them. He left her only long enough to make sure that Star and Dobbin were safely tied in the immigrant car. They stood in the crowd on the platform till the clanging train roared and stopped.

"Take good care of her, David," Mrs. Lathrop said through the confusion. His mother said, "Write often, Davy." His father shook his hand. "Let us know how you get along." "Good luck, you old skeezicks!" That was Gay. "I'll be out in the spring." Perley begged, "Can't I come, too, sometime?" "If he does, I am!" Alice declared. He helped Mary up the steps while she kept answering, "Goodby, goodby! I will, you write!" The train jerked, the bell was ringing. Eliza called, " — as soon as school closes!"

They were inside a train. The seats were luxuries of plush. The whistle screamed, outside the windows the

45

whole mass of faces jolted and began to slide.   David kept his balance and put his hat on the rack as he noticed that other men had done.   The car's woodwork was red, inlaid with some yellow wood.   Under the floor the wheels were grinding.   David sat down.   "Well, we're off."

Mary gave his arm a quick squeeze of delight.   Her gray eyes shone and her lips were parted in excitement.   They looked at the flying country and she exclaimed, "Goodness, I had no idea !   How fast are we going ?"

David supposed their speed was all of thirty miles an hour.   He mentioned that some fifty years ago scientists had proved that people could not live at half that speed. "And look at us now !" Cinders sleeted against the windows, telegraph poles ticked past with swooping wire, smoke from the engine billowed over the snowy fields.

"We'll be in Tracy tonight, Mrs. Beaton."   He held her hugged close, but the train's speed rocked her head in its little fur cap against his shoulder.   "Like being married, uh ?"

"I do," she declared.   "I'm not scared a bit, but I would be if you'd stayed in the immigrant car."

He could have traveled free in the immigrant car, but it was worth the price of a ticket to be with Mary today. And this was their first ride on a train.   "We'll make a long trip some day," he said.   "We'll go to Chicago, and Niagara Falls."

Before sunset the ride ended.   David and the conductor assisted Mary down the car steps.   He took their satchels in one hand and offered her his arm.   They stepped across the frozen slush of the street to the hotel.

The landlord was in the barroom, but his wife came hurrying from the kitchen.   Mrs. Mincy was a young woman with a round face and straggling fair hair ; she

46

carried the baby on her arm. She said in welcome, "Back again, Mr. Beaton !"

"Always on hand like a sore thumb ! Mrs. Mincy, I'll make you acquainted with my wife."

"Pleased, I'm sure," Mrs. Mincy said with reserve, shifting the baby.

"We want supper, and the best room you got." He set down the satchels. "I'll be back, soon as I see to my immigrant car."

He soothed the frightened horses while the engine shunted the car onto the siding. Then he watered and fed them. He could hold the car for three days without extra charge, so he locked them into it. The sun was setting in red and the wind was rising.

Mary was in the kitchen. She had put on an apron and was feeding the baby while Mrs. Mincy dished up supper. All three were talking when David went in.

"Oh, Mr. Beaton !" Mary said radiantly. "There's nobody else for supper and I told Mrs. Mincy why bother to build up a fire in the dining room, we'd just as soon eat in the kitchen like home folks. Is that all right ?"

"Suits me." He hung up his overcoat and hat, while Mary held the baby under one arm and poured hot water from the teakettle into the washbasin for him.

He had not realized how hungry he was. He had eaten hardly a bite of that enormous dinner. The supper was good and there was plenty of it ; chicken with brown dressing and gravy, mashed potatoes, turnips, cranberry sauce and pumpkin pie. The Mincys had not had turkey or mince pie. In winter there was little hotel business and it was hard to make both ends meet with only the barroom. Mrs. Mincy thought business would be better when the country was more settled, but Mr. Mincy said that trade would move west with the end of the rails. He was holding down a homestead and a tree-claim, though, and they would be worth something in time.

"You folks been married long?" he suddenly asked. David choked on a gulp of tea, but Mary was quick as a flash.

"Thanksgiving's our anniversary," she said. "And if anybody'd told me two years ago, Mr. Beaton, that you'd forget our wedding anniversary, I wouldn't have believed them. He hasn't mentioned it once all day," she said to Mrs. Mincy.

"I mentioned it every whit as much as you did," David retorted.

"That's right, don't let her bamboozle you," said Mr. Mincy.

Mrs. Mincy said, "Don't let me forget after supper to put more covers on your bed. That wind sounds like zero before morning."

Their room was the warmest in the house, over the kitchen, with the stovepipe running through it. The walls were well battened and the window caulked, and all night Mr. Mincy was getting up to keep the kitchen fire burning. But when they woke next morning, there was fine powdery snow over the quilts, and Mary often told later that before they got out of their wedding bed her husband tried to wash her face with snow.

"I did, too," David would say.

"Not till I was worn out from laughing. And I gave you as good as I got, a good big handful down your neck."

David had never seen a finer winter morning. Sunshine struck up from the snow like slivers of ice in the air. There was not a breath of wind ; nothing moved but sparkles of light. The snow crust was so solid that the station agent offered to bet a quarter that it would hold up a team

48

and wagon. David did not believe this, and lost a shin-plaster.

He unloaded the car that day and then taking the wagon box off the running gear he put runners on it. Mrs. Mincy agreed to store most of the carload for fifty cents a week. David packed into the wagon sled only enough feed and supplies for a couple of weeks. Traveling light over the hard snow, he could take Mary to the claim in one long day's journey, and haul the rest of their goods later as weather permitted.

At supper Mrs. Mincy worried. "I declare, it worries me to see you two start out like this. If you get lost in a blizzard out there, it'll be spring before anybody finds your bones."

Mary laughed. "Oh, we're neither sugar nor salt, and we want to get settled on the claim before spring planting time."

"Shucks," David said. "We can't get lost, following the right of way. If a storm comes up, we'll stay at the empty railroad camp."

"Blizzards come up mighty sudden sometimes, from what I hear." Mr. Mincy went on to tell some tall stories of blizzards, but none of them were first hand.

10

They started before sunup, with Mary's flatiron and hot bags of salt in the straw at their feet, and quilts tucked in snugly. David had put strings of sleigh bells on the horses. The bells rang to their trotting, the rising sun sent their blue shadows far before them, and the sled's motion was as smooth as flying. Every instant the colors changed on the glistening snow.

A black woolen veil swathed Mary's head, and through its blackness David could see only sparkles from her eyes. She was excited and gay. She had never imagined a sky so vast nor a country so large.

"Not a tree, not one solitary tree," she marveled.

"That's what I told you."

"I know. But I didn't know it would be like this." She leaned back across his arm to see the whole sky. "So clear, like glass. And so thin and far."

She cuddled against him in her thick wraps, and he tucked the covers in. There was plenty to talk about. In midmorning they saw a herd of antelopes moving as if swiftly blown low over the white land. Two timber wolves, big gaunt beasts, came out of the prairie and stood gazing with ears pricked at the horses and sled. David had brought his Uncle David's old army musket, but the wolves were too far away for a shot. For some time they trotted side by side, keeping pace with the uneasy team, then easily loping ahead they crossed the railroad embankment and vanished to the southwest, where the antelope had gone.

At noon David stopped the team, and walked around the sled to get their nose-bags out of it. Mary was groping for them behind the seat. She had turned her frosty veil back over her hood, and looking up at David she asked, "Where did you — "

He pulled down his muffler and snatched a kiss. Her lips were chilly. He said, "That's a cold kiss to give your — " and yelped. She had pressed her icy nose into his neck.

He clawed up her hoops, smartly spanked red flannel, and rolled her out of his way. The startled team was moving fast. In the second it took him to grab the lines they had made so much headway that it was some little

50

time before he stopped them.   It gave him a shock to see Mary, a lone little figure on the vast snows, trudging toward him and carrying the quilts that had spilled out with her.

Her whole face was red, whether from cold or anger he did not know.   She was not smiling.   When she reached the sled she laid the quilts on it and walked up to him, where he stood holding the lines.

"Let that be a lesson to you," she said.   Her cheek almost dimpled and her arms slid around his neck. "From now on, mister, you kiss me like this."

He told her that every time was different.   "Every time, it's more so !"

In the afternoon they lost the railroad embankment. They had been skimming along beside it, talking, and suddenly Mary asked where it was.   The snow, imperceptibly growing deeper, must have buried it.   Nothing was to be seen around them but the glitter of snow swells from which thin shadows were beginning to lie northeastward.

David urged the horses on.   The railroad camp was not far ahead and the sun was a full three hours above the horizon.   Its glitter made black shapes dance before his eyes.   There was no movement of the still air, but a level gray cloud was rising in the northwest.

Rubbing his eyes, David was almost sure that he saw real shadows ahead.   From the top of the next swell he pointed out the railroad camp to Mary.   Motionless shadows lay beneath pale vertical walls which cracked open the sides of snowdrifts.   The long cookshanty was there, and the bunkhouse and stable beyond it.   The horses went faster without urging, and David wrapped the lines around his mittened hands.   His fingers were growing too numb to feel the leather.

The camp was not more than half a mile away, but he

51

had never seen a cloud rise so swiftly. It was a strange cloud, fleecy white beneath a level gray top. A strong wind suddenly blew toward it, yet the cloud came on, as fast as a train or faster.

David shouted to the horses. Their swift trot broke into a run, and excited by the race he said, "What'll you bet we don't beat it ?"

She shook her head, laughing. "Bet you we do !" She enjoyed a race as much as he did.

Beyond each swell they expected to pull up at the camp, but another empty curve appeared. He saw that he would not have time to stable the team before the storm came, but he would get Mary under shelter and he had often done the chores in a snowstorm. The wind, whirling, lifted up particles from the frozen crust and the sky went gray ; the storm struck as a blindness.

David could not see the horses. Even Mary was dim. He exclaimed, "By golly ! This is something to write home about !"

Icy particles stung his eyes. He heard Mary's voice thinly saying something about getting there all right. The horses were trudging on. His hands were so cold that the lines were dead leather, but he thought the team was bewildered. The thing was to keep them walking straight ahead. The camp was less than a quarter of a mile away, at most.

There was no direction in this storm. Winds came violently from all sides, even upward and down. The horses had seen shelter ahead. Horses would stop when they reached shelter in a storm. They would turn tails to a storm and drift, but in this storm there was no direction.

Tears ran from his tormented eyes, narrowed to slits

between cap and muffler, and straining to see through pale blindness. It was impossible to keep them open at all without exposing the eyeballs to agony. The noise of the winds was astounding. He could guess with fair accuracy when the plodding team had covered somewhat less than the distance to the camp. He pulled up and listened.

He heard the whine of driven air splitting against an edge. His eyes were useless ; his ears saw, not far away to the right, the corner of a shanty standing out of a snow-drift, standing firm against the storm, holding behind thin boards a space of quiet air, a rusty stove, benches and a table, shelter, safety.

Mary heard it, too. She started up, glad, and as suddenly they were both still. They heard the shanty swing around the sled in a rising spiral and pass overhead while they stared blindly upward. They heard it break into scores of corners against the winds.

David pulled down his muffler. He was startled to feel its whole length, the folds of it around his neck, frozen and crackling. The woolen stuff was stiff with icy particles driven into it.

He pushed aside an earmuff and curved his hand behind his ear. With eyes shut, holding his breath, he turned his head slowly. The winds screeched, whistled, howled, and from every side came that unmistakable whine. It rose and fell in pitch ; he could detect no difference in intensity.

The pain of cold was leaving his ear and cheek. He rubbed them briskly, slapped them, fastened the earmuff and tightened the stiff muffler again. His mittens, too, were stiff with ice and the outer quilt was rigid. He put that from his mind, and sat carefully placing cookshanty, bunkhouse, stable and store as he remembered them.

53

"Hold the lines," he said to Mary. She took them. He tucked the icy quilt around her, and got out of the sled.

At this moment he first realized what the storm was. He stood in chaos. The sled was the one solidity, it was his identity. To leave it was to be lost in space and time. He could not leave the sled. He stood holding to it, blinded, deafened, buffeted by whirling blankness.

What can a man trust when he can not trust his own senses? He plainly heard wind rushing against walls, squealing when eaves cut into it, splitting with a continuous whine against corners. Long lines of shanties were on all sides of the sled, shanties were piled high above it. He believed his own ears though he knew they were lying, and this made a kind of sickness in him.

He took the picket lines out of the sled, knotted them together, tied one end to the sled and the other round his wrist. He leaned over Mary. "I'm tied to the sled with a rope. Going to find the camp. Keep yourself warm."

"I'm all right," she told him.

Two paces from the sled he could not see it. He could see nothing. The winds struck him solid blows; he could hardly keep his footing. He paid out the rope, loop by loop. It jerked and tugged behind him. He counted thirty paces; he was near the end of the rope. He counted ten more. The rope was still slack. He knew that he had tied it firmly to the sled, but its whole leaping length told him that it was flying loose in the winds. The jerking was not directly behind him, but to the left.

With all his strength he shouted, "Mary!" The sound was plucked from his mouth and gone. He heard no human answer. Fear got him. He did not have the courage to pull in the rope.

54

He turned and followed it, gathering it in. Suddenly he knew that it was leading him away from the sled. He was possessed by an overwhelming desire to turn back, to turn back and reach Mary, alone and helpless in the sled, in the sled behind him. He stood still.

His thoughts were clear enough now; he could map the whole thing. Starting from the sled, he had gone forty paces south; then he had made a half turn to the left, and gone six paces. The loose rope, therefore, was leading him eastward. He concluded that there must be an eastward direction to the storm, though it seemed to beat him with equal violence from all sides.

The thing was to use his head. Pay no attention to anything but reason. Forty paces north and six paces west; there was the sled.

He made another half-turn to the left, and miraculously his sense of direction came back. The north was a strong sensation, directly before him. He stepped forward with confidence and saw a darkening in the opaque air. A second step, and the thing was solid, dark, breast-high to him and long, with whiteness beneath it and above it.

"Thank God," he said. His eyelids were scoured raw and his eyes weeping in the whirl of powdered ice, but he saw the shanty wall holding a snow-laden roof up from the snowbank. He was sure he saw it; he had found the camp. Suddenly he felt warm. He groped against the wall and felt it start alive. It was a horse, a harnessed horse. It was Dobbin.

The pain in his middle, knotted from the cold, melted and turned over. He broke away the muffler, but the spasm passed without forcing him to vomit. Dobbin, he saw, was headed the wrong way.

In a fury, he got to the sled and shouted raging, "How the hell can I do anything when you move the sled?"

"I didn't," Mary answered. "The team hasn't budged."

He pulled himself together, resting a moment.

In walking forty paces, straight forward, he had somehow circled the sled. He must have gone no more than a few feet from it.

"You warm enough?" he asked Mary.

"Making out. Get in and warm."

"Nope, I'm exercising. Keeps me warm."

This time, he told himself, he had the hang of it. He made sure that the knot would hold, and at each step he paused and jerked the rope taut against the force of the winds. It was necessary to believe what the tightened rope told him, even when he knew it was lying. At the end of the rope, keeping it taut, he circled. He made a complete circuit of the sled and came back to it.

To reach the sled, to make sure of it under his hands, was a return to certainty. The sled was the one solid thing. He held onto it for a moment, resting. Then he led the horses a little way, and went out again.

He continued to do this. There was always the sound of wind against shanties. The cold increased. The stuff of his clothes was driven full of sharp particles of ice. The swirling paleness became darker, then black. In a sanity remote from this nightmare, the calm sun had gone down.

The solid black was no more blinding than the white had been. All these hours he had kept his eyes not quite closed. When he let them wince shut, he could not force himself to go forward; then he knew that he was on the edge of an abyss.

Going from side to side, to the limit of the rope's length, he had covered nearly a quarter of a mile. Whether the camp was to the north or south of them, they had passed it. The violence of the winds was wearing him out. He staggered against the sled.

"We've missed the camp," he told Mary. "I'm going to turn around." Fumbling over the load, he found the lantern and gave it to her. "Get down under the quilts and light it if you can."

He blamed himself for not thinking of the lantern before. It might make a guiding glow. And once lighted, the heavy glass closed down around the flame, it would give a little heat. His hands were stiff claws, numb ; he beat them together while he waited.

"David, I can't." Mary groped for his shoulder and called at his ear. "Only eight matches left."

"Give them to me." Crouched in the sled, under the quilts, he warmed a hand in his armpit. He sheltered the lantern inside his coat, laid the sulphur head of the match to the wick, and contrived to ignite it with his thumb nail. The flame sprang from the wood and was gone before he fairly saw it. He used another match, and another. There was no refuge from the winds. Only four matches were left ; he dared not risk them.

The hopelessness of the horses, hunched together and enduring the storm, came to him while he groped along Dobbin's side. The horse's hair was matted full of ice. He took the reins at the bits and turned the team carefully, pivoting the sled, a half-turn. Mary, too, was sure they were now headed north. When the sled, the only solid point, was moving, there was no certainty. But he led the team a hundred paces, turned them eastward, and went out again with the rope.

While he was struggling in the lightless chaos, he knew he would find nothing. But when the sled was under his hands, he knew that one more try might find shelter.

He could see so clearly that the camp must be there, hidden only by the howling dark. He led the horses a little way and set out again. Every muscle was drawn tight against the cold; he could not relax that aching hardness; yet he felt soft and trembling from weariness.

At last, holding to the sled with numb hands which could hardly feel it, he knew that he must have passed the camp again. He was too cold to keep on going much longer. He edged onto the seat, clumsily tucking the quilts over him and warning Mary away. "Wait till I warm up."

She pressed herself fiercely against him and shook with the cold. He pulled the quilts over her head and she tucked them behind him. They drove on.

A thin warmth grew between their bodies. The cold pressed against it, through flesh and bone. His feet were numb and his hands could not feel the lines. He had at times an illusion that the team was standing still, the sled shaken only by the winds.

It might be possible to drive out of the storm. If he could be sure of anything, they were headed back toward Tracy. But he could be sure of nothing; he could hear the winds against buildings which actually might be there.

Suddenly he heard voices. He stopped the team; Mary burst up from the covers. Through the noises of the storm, both of them heard human voices talking. They could almost distinguish the words. These sounds of men talking, at ease, relaxed, idly speaking and answering each other, were so near that their clenched eyes strained against the scouring darkness to see a lighted window. The voices were not more than a dozen feet away.

David tucked Mary in and gave her the lines. He took the coiled rope. The voices continued to speak as he approached them, till a wild halloo circled overhead and

58

pounced down. The voices broke into jabbering clamor and fled shrieking. David went out to the full length of the rope and circled the sled. He heard chuckles, and such screams as come from rabbits when the dog's teeth close. He found nothing solid.

Under the quilts again, Mary pressed against him and he held her close. They went on, growing rigid with cold. The ache centered in a sharp increasing pain below the breastbone and under the locked jaws. As long as they were suffering, they were not dying ; death would be comfortable.

He could not guess how far they had come, when he felt Mary relaxing against him. The horses were stumbling. He stopped them and seized Mary's shoulders. In the whirling darkness full of sharp ice-dust he felt her whimpering, her head rolling limp ; he shook her with all his strength, in a terror like hate, shouting at her, slapping her, swearing. She answered him.

"Get out," he told her. "Hang onto the quilts. You hear me ? Get out and hang onto the quilts. I'm going to unload."

11

He groped over the horses, clumsily stripping off their harness. Their icy sides labored, their knees were giving way, their heads hung to their knees. Pulling off the bridles, he discovered that their noses were covered with ice. Their frozen breath was smothering them.

He smashed the ice off and held their nostrils closed for a moment while the warmth from their lungs melted the frost. They gulped air and laid their heads against him. He struck them away brutally, he drove them with blows away from him, in the storm. They must take their

chances. He knew they could hardly live till morning;
his horses.

Unloading took a long time. Fearful of losing Mary,
he tied her to the sled. She stayed on her feet, awake,
and helped to empty the sled, but he continually groped
for her to make sure. He could not see the things he
handled, often he could not make out what they were, and
in the fury of winds he could not judge directions or distances. His hands and his legs were wooden.

They turned the wagon over. Afterward, they did
not know how they had done it. The seat raised one end.
Mary got out of her hoops and crawled under the shelter.
Somehow he found and pushed in to her the quilts, the
lantern, a sack of sugar. He piled other things against the
opening. He inched backward through it at last, dragging a sack of oats to close the space.

Violence howled around the sled and shook it, but it
held a kind of quietness. They lay in some relief from
the winds. There was not room enough to let them sit
up, but they rubbed their numb ears and noses with snow.
They contrived to take off their shoes and rub snow on
their feet till burning pain replaced the numbness.

The air around them became more quiet. David risked
a match; he was able to light the lantern. They looked
at each other and saw faces smeared with blood from
raw and swollen eyelids. Against the inside of their barricade a tapering mound of snow had grown nearly to the
top of every crack. Soon they would be under a snowbank.

Snow is warm, and there is air in it. David remembered that in York State snow was called "the poor man's
fertilizer," and farmers plowed their snowcovered fields
to give air to the soil. He said, "We can make out to
live for quite awhile."

60

"Better wind your watch," Mary reminded him. The gold watch that his parents had given him last Christmas reassured him, somehow. Few young men owned a watch, or ever hoped to own one in a gold locomotive-case. The time was eleven o'clock.

They lay huddled together, wrapped in the quilts. David blew out the lantern. To cease all effort was bliss.

Mary stirred first. "What time is it, David?" She asked again, "David, how long have we been asleep?"

They could hardly force open their swollen lids. His whole body was stiff and sore. The air was still, the lighted lantern burned with a steady flame. "Four o'clock."

"In the morning?"

"I don't know." He pressed the watch against an ear-muff. "It's run down. Must be day after tomorrow."

They could hear the storm, an unabated fury diminished to the tiny. Snow must be deep above them. They lay drowsy, yawning. They spoke of bears. Bears live denned up, all winter. It was an effort to lift a hand. They ate some sugar and snow, and slept.

They woke in an absolute silence. They could hear the light rasp of their breathing, the blood in their ears. The storm had ended, or the snow was so deep above them that they could no longer hear the winds.

Dry snow poured down like sand when David tugged at a barricading sack. The cold air burned his nostrils. Clawing and wriggling his way through the snow, he heard wind rushing overhead, and he thrust up through a snowcrust into a driving snowstorm.

For a moment he crouched, retreating, but a desire to stand on his feet made him stagger upright. His sore eyelids clenched against sharp pain. The sun was shining. He leaned against the wind, waiting till he could see.

The low winter sun, nearing or past its zenith, hung in

61

the northwest. This was not possible, but there it was. The impossible northern sun was the only thing in color- less space. Beneath it a white scud was flying level, ceaseless, endless, as if the whole earth had become foam.

Pain shut his eyes again. He stood leaning against the wind, telling himself that the sun must be in the south- east. But directions refused to adjust themselves. He must have been driving west when he stopped. It was impossible to guess where he was. The question of what to do, without horses, with no means of guessing where he was, how far or in what direction from Tracy or from the railroad camp, had no answer. Two weeks' supplies were under the snow. To stay with them, without shel- ter, without fire, was not possible. Mary's strength would not take her far, if he knew where to go. Spring was three months away.

He thought he heard a shout. A furry body, legless, some distance away, seemed to be rocking on the glitter- ing snow scud. He made out a man, hidden to the hips by the driving snow. The man came angling down the wind, calling out, "Need some help?"

David did not answer. The man was shapeless in fur coat and cap, his face muffled. His eyes were bright blue. David recognized Mr. Peters.

They shook hands, and David asked, "Where'd you drop from?"

"Living three miles south. Thought maybe I'd find you. So you weathered it."

"Come through in fine shape." It was difficult to talk in the wind.

"Your team drifted in, three nights back. I got 'em stabled."

"Much obliged."

"Better come to my place. Your shanty's nine miles northwest."

David tried to take this in. "Where's the railroad camp?"

"You passed it, eleven miles back."

Invisibly, space shifted; the sun was in its place and the snow scud flying south. He could never know where he had been when he thought he turned eastward in the blizzard. It was necessary now to believe that his invisible feet, lifted, would find solidity under them again.

"Got supplies with you?" Mr. Peters asked.

"My wife's with me. First thing's to get her to shelter."

12

Mary made the three miles without help. When she missed her footing, she was scrambling up before they could get a grip on the quilts in which David had wrapped her.

For some time they saw the house, its shingled roof blown clean of snow and the smoke from its stovepipe lying flat on the wind. They did not see that it was a two-story house until they reached it. Snow was banked to the attic window. They went down through a trench and a tunnel, and Nettie flung open the door, crying out, "Pa! You found him!"

In the warm place Mrs. Peters was swiftly lighting the lamp. She took charge of Mary, saying, "We'll look after her, Mr. Beaton. You tend to yourself." The youngsters brought in a pan of snow. Mary's bare toes curled in Nettie's lap. David rubbed her white ears and his own with snow. Mrs. Peters filled bowls with bean soup and

63

cut thick slices of bread. The good soup roused a wolf-
ish hunger. It seemed to run warm and tingling through
every vein, and their faces grew blazing red.

"Golly, that hits the spot !" David said.

Mr. Peters urged second helpings. The young ones,
well-behaved, quietly waited their turn. Mr. Peters said
they had plenty of beans ; they were out of fresh meat only
because the blizzard stopped his hunting. If this clear
weather held, he would get some venison. He was well
fixed for the winter. The railroad company gave him
the house till spring, rent-free, for taking care of the tools.
He had earned enough, before the camps closed, to buy
beans, salt and molasses, and some flour.

There was only one slice of bread apiece, but Mr. Peters
filled the bowls a third time, saying jovially to David,
"Don't be bashful, there's plenty more down cellar in a
teacup."

The house was not finished inside, but the cracks were
battened. It had been well built, for the surveyors to live
in. They had left the cookstove, the lamp, the table and
three chairs. Mr. Peters had made benches, a cupboard
and shelves from packing cases. Everything was clean.
The stove was polished, the clear lamp chimney guarded
a trimmed flame, and white patches were set neatly into
the red-checked tablecloth. A slate and some schoolbooks were stacked on a shelf.

Mr. Peters said they'd better start out for David's supplies ; this clear weather might not hold. They went
through a lean-to full of hay, and through a snow-tunnel
to the barn. Star and Dobbin, with the sorrel, were eating
hay. They whinnied in welcome to David.

"Obligation's the other way. I owe you fifteen dollars. I filed on that claim, when we come through Yankton." Mr. Peters said that but for David's mark, he

64

could not have got a claim within six miles of the railroad, unless he went forty miles farther from the settlements. That far west, and six to eight miles on both sides of the right of way, all the land was filed on. By law, homesteaders were supposed to be living on their claims now, but his nearest neighbors were in Tracy.

They dug a new tunnel from the barn, in order not to break through the one that went to the house. As long as that tunnel kept out the wind, a man could do his chores in comfort.

"And I thought we had winters, back in Minnesota!" The wind took the snow from David's shovel.

"Things balance up," Mr. Peters remarked. "Out here we don't have trees to contend with. So nothing breaks the wind. It brings the Polar regions straight down from the North Pole."

They led the cringing horses three miles against the polar wind. They dug out the buried sled, buckled the frozen harness on the horses and hauled the sled onto the snow crust. They excavated the supplies, and the scattered pots and pans, ropes, nose-bags, Mary's little frozen muff, David's satchel, the lunch-basket. David dug out Mary's hoops, but he forgot the iron spider. The wind lifted while they worked and the snow scud settled. At sunset the cold was tightening in deadly stillness.

A twinkle through the dark guided them toward the house. With difficulty the horses dragged the load through the soft drifts. David and Mr. Peters trotted by the sled, sometimes pushing it, sometimes kicking away snow clogged before the runners. David's laboring heart could not drive any feeling of life below his knees.

They left the load at the attic window, stabled, watered and fed the team, and went through the tunnel to the house. Mary, giving David a look like a kiss, took his

65

snowy wraps. "I had a bath," she announced. "We melted a tubful of snow for you, so you can have one after supper."

She was fresh and pretty in a thin woolen dress, cream-colored, printed all over in tiny flowers. David had not seen that dress before; no doubt it was part of her wedding outfit. They had been married only six days.

She said, "I hope to goodness, Mr. Beaton, you've fetched my hoops." The slim-hanging dress was basted up at the bottom.

"You're all right without 'em," David teased her. Mrs. Peters remarked that she had not worn hoops since she left settled country; she was saving hers for Nettie, in the hope that when she was a young lady there'd be occasion to dress up again. Gently she said that this house was not large enough for hoops, and they were all more comfortable without them. Mary's face was so stricken that David told her the hoops were in the sled. He sat down quietly and took off his shoes.

Nettie was hugging herself in delight. "Indian pudding for supper!" she told him. "Baked beans, and Indian pudding, both! Because you're here. You and Mrs. Beaton."

The heat tortured his hands, but his feet did not feel it. Reluctantly he pulled off a sock. His foot was dead white and the flesh was cracked.

Mary was talking to the young ones who pressed against her, watching molasses fall sluggish from a jug. Flora explained that Charley got first lick because he was youngest. Mary cut off the molasses and held out the knife. The others urged, "Lick fair, Charley!"

Nettie stuffed twisted hay into the stove. Firelight shone on her thin face, rapt in anticipation of the Indian pudding. She turned quickly, as if David had spoken, and glanced at the bare foot. The change in her face confirmed his fear. She brought the lamp from the table and knelt down with it, then set it on the floor.

Mary exclaimed, "What's the matter? David! What's — " Mrs. Peters sent back the crowding young ones. David did not like so much fuss. He told Mary not to worry, and said to Mr. Peters, "There's feeling in the calves."

"Put 'em into this," said Mr. Peters. Nettie came dragging a tub, and with her fist broke the ice in it. David set his feet into the water. A man does not think of himself with no feet. Other men may be maimed, but not he. David looked up at Mr. Peters, then down at his own flesh unconscious of ice against the skin, and knew what it would be to live with legs ending at the ankle bones.

He kept saying to Mary that he was all right. "Don't bother about me. They'll thaw all right. Go eat your supper." She brought him a plate of beans, then a portion of Indian pudding laced with molasses. Mr. Peters told several jokes at table. After supper he put on his wraps and sent his wife and Mary upstairs with the lamp, to help him unload the sled through the window.

David was squeezing the blood down through his leg from knee to ankle. Nettie rolled up her sleeves, knelt by the tub, and flinging back her braids she began to work capably at the other leg. There was firelight through the cracked stove lid and the drafts.

"Any feeling in them?" she asked.

"Some. Not much." Tinglings of agony made a sickness in his stomach. "What do you think?"

"They look bad."

He felt eased, like a man who ceases to huddle himself against cold and takes a deep breath of it. He looked at

67

her thin cheek and clear, sober mouth. She was not much older than Alice, but he could not imagine her crying. Whatever happened, her face would only become more still. His mother slapped at trouble, saying briskly that what can't be cured must be endured, and so would Mary. This girl would say nothing; endurance was in the marrow of her bones.

Some bond was between them, some deep, quiet thing, a kind of sureness, there, in their silence.

At nine o'clock that night his feet were blazing torture. Sweat burst through his pores; he had to collect his thoughts and unclench his jaws to speak. The water was pink with ooze from the broken flesh. Mary made their bed there on the floor, so that he would not have to walk.

"David, do the covers hurt your feet?" she asked anxiously.

"No, I don't know. I guess not."

"You've got a fever. I brought some snakeroot. I'll brew you up some in the morning, there's nothing like snakeroot to bring a fever down. They are going to be all right, aren't they, David? I thought Mr. Peters was real encouraging."

"Yes. Good night."

"Good night, David. I do hope you get some sleep."

13

His feet were swollen and purple, as if the flesh had been bruised to the bone. The blistered skin sloughed off in running sores. His fever grew hotter, though he drank quantities of the bitter snakeroot. There was not enough turpentine. Mary used it sparingly, and when next day she moistened the bandages and eased them off, bringing bits of flesh, the pain was less than the fear of what they might see. David would have given a great deal to be able to call a doctor.

For two weeks he lay in the bed on the floor. Figures tormented him in his fever; besides the homestead and the tree-claim, he was still worth around a thousand dollars and that was big money; he had four hundred dollars in cash, more than a man could earn in a year; on the other hand, he owed his father $145, leaving $255, he could call his own, and even the four hundred was two hundred dollars a year to live on till he could make a crop and he must buy tools, he must pay Mr. Peters something for board, the two weeks' supplies were gone, and fifty cents a week for storage was piling up in Tracy. There was the sickness from his feet and the fear of losing them.

He joked, while the bandages came off, "I'm a tenderfoot, all right."

Flora laughed. She was a sharp little thing, bright-eyed and quick. Lucy was shy and grave, always quiet at her lessons or patchwork; all her strength was going into a heavy growth of long, fair hair. Charley was a sturdy little chap, like a New Foundland pup.

Through all the movement and talk in the crowded room, and the confusion of his fever, he always knew where Nettie was. She washed the dishes and swept; she put on wraps and went into the lean-to to twist hay, came in now and then to warm her hands, at last took off her wraps and hung them up. She sat looking over beans, he heard them fall trickling between her thin fingers, then the cup in the water-pail and her hands in the water washing the beans. When she threw back her braids, he knew it. Her being there was something to hang onto.

Another blizzard, in one howling night, swept the

ground bare around the house. The cold came in then. All day Nettie and Mary, or Nettie and Flora, twisted hay in the freezing shed, and at night the beds were brought from the other room and someone kept the fire burning. Thick frost covered the windows, pale yellow in sunshine; the children scraped peepholes through which to watch for their father. Mr. Peters brought in an antelope; it hung frozen in the shed and Mrs. Peters cut meat from it with a hatchet. Wolves scented it and howled in the night. David heard Star scream, and asked, "Any danger to the horses?"

Mr. Peters had got up to feed the fire. He answered, "Not a bit, they're only scared. It's a good, stout barn, solid doors barred and padlocked."

"Padlocked?" David said. Mary was awake, listening beside him.

"There's gangs of outlaws, horse thieves and cutthroats, out in the Black Hills. Summers, they thieve from the railroad camps. Take a spell of clear weather like this, no telling what they'll do. That's why I get the use of this house, to take care of railroad property."

The clear weather continued for several days. Then snow fell steadily day after day and night after night. Drifts against the house warmed it again, the drive of twisting hay relaxed, the woman left off their wraps, the children again did their lessons regularly, played quiet games, drew pictures on their slate and in the frost-fur on the windows. One morning David felt that he was getting well, as one feels in winter that the earth has turned toward spring.

"You're pulling through, aren't you?" Nettie said to him that morning.

By Christmas he was walking, painfully, but walking. On Christmas Eve, bathed and dressed and shaved, he sat at table and ate a hearty supper. The young ones could think of nothing but Santa Claus. They hung stockings on the back of a chair, and Nettie hustled them off to bed. "The sooner you're asleep, the sooner Santa Claus will come."

Breathless with excitement, she helped her father fill the stockings. Their blue eyes sparkled joyously. Mr. Peters had whittled a wooden gun for Charley and wooden rabbits for the little girls. Nettie and her mother had knitted three small pairs of red mittens, and Mary had made two rag dolls. When these were in the stockings, David limped up and dropped a penny into each one.

Now that he could walk, the bed was in the attic. When he went crippling up the stairs, Mary was sitting on it, wrapped in her shawl and ripping a ribbon collar off a bodice.

"Trying to freeze yourself to death?" he asked.

"I'm bound and determined Nettie shall have something!" Her breath puffed white on the air. She smoothed out the short, brown-striped ribbon. "David, do you care if I give her my silver thimble? I've got a steel one."

"Do you like her that much?"

"I do. I admire her spunk. Don't you?"

He uttered a shivering sound as he slid into bed. The cold sheets made his teeth rattle. He had no idea what he thought of Nettie. He said, "A man gets him a wife to warm his bed. What kind of a woman I got?" She leaned over him, laughing, and the shawl buried their heads while they kissed. "Don't stay up all night."

"I won't be a minute," she assured him.

Squeals from the children woke them. Nettie was transfigured. She flung her arms around Mary's neck and hugged her, silent. She gloated over the ribbon, and

71

cuddled her silver-thimbled hand to her cheek. On the chair hung a stocking and a sock, labeled. Mary drew out a picture of a lady, cut from a fashion plate and framed in pink tissue paper. David had a booklet of tissue paper leaves, tied together with a bit of red yarn; shaving papers, on which to wipe the razor.

"From now on, we're David and Mary, we aren't going to have you folks calling us Mr. and Mrs. Beaton any longer," Mary declared.

There was a Christmas breakfast of pancakes and molasses. Then Mary went outdoors to play in the snow with Nettie and the young ones. Their laughing shouts made it seem, in the house, as if there were neighbors.

For dinner there was plenty of venison and baked beans, and afterward Mrs. Peters boiled down some molasses. They all brought in plates or pans of snow and dribbled the thick syrup on it, to make a waxy candy. Nettie's thin elbows hugged her sides and she gave a shiver of delight. "Oh, isn't this the best Christmas!"

David was able now to do his share of chores and to help haul hay. He did not go hunting with Mr. Peters because the cold became intolerable to his feet. It did seem that during some spell of clear weather he should be able to travel the twelve miles to his claim, but Mr. Peters shook his head.

"Use your own judgment, but you don't know where the sloughs are. There's holes under the snow where the slough grass is lodged. Your team and your load'll go down and no telling how long it'll take you to dig out. I wouldn't risk it myself. Blizzards strike sudden."

Unexpectedly, late in February, a thaw came. Listening to the drip from the eaves at night, Mary said, "I declare, I'll miss being with Nettie. I feel as if she was my sister."

72

That was the answer. That was the way David felt about the girl. He said, "Well, we better be moving on to our claim. If this keeps us, we can't get there on sled runners."

The next morning was as warm as May, but Mr. Peters advised against setting out. "You can't see the sloughs yet, and this weather's not settled."

At three o'clock that afternoon a blizzard struck, and did not let up for three days. In the mornings Mr. Peters did the chores. Holding to a rope stretched between house and stable, David went out to do them at night. He said savagely to Star, "What the hell kind of a country is this, anyway?"

14

Spring came abruptly with a downpour of sleety rain ending in sunshine and blustering winds. Hardly any snow remained ; the earth was spongy wet and the sloughs brimmed full of water reflecting the blue sky. Mr. Peters lent David his wagon to make the trip to Tracy for his own running gear.

The time had come to settle up. Figuring board at two dollars a week for himself and Mary, reckoning the horses' hay at three dollars a ton, and deducting his own supplies and the fifteen dollar loan, David owed Mr. Peters thirty-nine dollars. He handed it over cheerfully.

"It goes against the grain to take it," Mr. Peters said. But only a few messes of beans were left of his supplies, and it would be weeks before the railroad camps opened.

"We et your supplies, and you've stinted yourselves. It's only fair to replace them," said David. He refused absolutely to take any pay for hauling new supplies from Tracy.

Mrs. Peters made out the list; beans, salt, molasses, kerosene, fifty pounds of flour. In the barn Mr. Peters handed David another dollar and asked him to say nothing to Mrs. Peters, but to bring half a pound of tea and two pounds of fat salt pork. His eyelids crinkled with pleasure in the surprise for his wife. He would have a job when the camps opened, and he said, "There's such a thing as being too saving, but you can't tell a woman so. That's one of the things you'll find out, Dave."

It took five days to make the round trip, because of the mud. Every pound that the team could pull must be supplies, so David went alone. Men from the east were already tramping into Tracy, eager for railroad jobs. The train was bringing contractors' supplies, and David saw carloads of steel rails on the siding. He ate Mrs. Mincy's filling meals with a kind of shame, thinking of Mary, and he bought dried peaches, butter, farina, crackers and cheese, as well as the tea and salt pork.

At early lamplight on the third day from Tracy, he stamped into the surveyors' house, covered with mud, and dumping all those packages on the table he stood back with Mr. Peters to enjoy the excitement.

That night in bed, Mary said to him, "Seems to me I never ate such a good meal in my life. That tasty salt pork, and those peaches. When you think how we're used to living at home."

"We're going to be living that way again, soon as we get going out here," David said.

At dawn he was putting his wagon box on the running gear, and in the windy morning they set out to their claim. Mr. Peters would build his sod shanty before the surveyors came back, and they would be neighbors. The whole land was alive with birds, and a ceaseless clamor came down from myriads of wild geese and ducks flying

74

north.   Enormous piles of white cloud sailed in the deep
blue sky.   Mary tucked her hand under David's arm and
gave it a little squeeze.   It was good to be by themselves
again.

"By golly, we're beating Moses !" he said.   "Took him
forty years, and we're making it in under four months."

"Where was it, we stayed under the sled ?"

"Over that way, couple of miles."

"You're going by there, aren't you ?"

"What for ?"

"Why, to get the iron spider," Mary said, surprised.

"I'll be darned !"   He had completely forgotten the
iron spider.   He looked at the rolling brown land, streaked
with blue water, extending to the limits of vision where
it met the sky.   Somewhere in that immensity was a
rusted iron spider, and this little woman expected to find
it.   He felt an expanding emotion, and putting his arm
around her he said, "I'll get you another spider."

"But David, that's plain silly.   We've got a perfectly
good spider.   I can scour it."

To humor her, he drove that way.   Not a trace was left
of the days and nights they had spent under a vanished
snowbank.   He could not say precisely where the place
was.   To the northwest, scattered claim shanties indi-
cated the townsite, and there were glimpses of the railroad embankment.   Ahead was a claim shanty with a
shingled roof ; David remembered seeing, far away and
small, the man at work on it.   He said, "It was around
here somewheres."

"Stop and let me out."

"You'll only get your skirts wet and ruin your shoes."
He pulled up the team and sat looking at the shanty, wondering if they might have found it in the blizzard.   Probably it had been buried under snow.   He noticed that the

shingled roof was dry, then that the sod walls were dry at the top. There was no smoke from the stovepipe, but something moved behind the windowglass.

Mary came to the wagon and put the spider in it. She climbed up beside him. He said, "Somebody's living there. They've been looking out at us."

"Are we on their land? Whatever will they think we're doing?"

"We'll drive up and tell 'em." Beyond the shanty a calico mare came into view, grazing on buffalo grass. The horses whinnied and the mare replied. David got down from the wagon. Still the door did not open, and he went to it and knocked. He heard no sound inside. Puzzled, he raised his hand to knock again, and the door suddenly opened.

It struck him that he should have hailed the shanty from the wagon, where the musket was. The man wore a revolver. He was a short, solidly built fellow, with a mat of beard, a thick nose and cold eyes.

"Good morning, sir. My name's Beaton," David said. "We're on the way to our claim, north of here. Don't want to take up your time, my wife thought we'd better explain —"

The man did not open the door wider. His cold glance sized up Mary, the wagon and the team, and did not lose sight of David. He laughed, a short laugh but a real one. "You're welcome to your spider."

When they were out of earshot, David said, "Looks like a tough customer. He didn't have much to say for himself. I wonder if he's been baching it there alone all winter."

"He was horrid," Mary declared. Afterward she always said that her blood ran cold the minute she laid eyes on that man.

76

David began to point out the townsite to her, and after they had got the wagon over the railroad embankment they could see their own shanty. But they could not cross the slough. It had become a long, narrow lake, noisy with ducks, geese, swans, cranes and many kinds of birds they did not know. David had to drive three miles around it to reach their homestead.

But they drove up to their shanty in the light of a marvelous sunset. Great sweeps of flaming color washed across the sky. The sod walls were pinkish brown under a silvery-shining tar-paper roof.

Everything was as David had left it. The prairie-chimney, solidly anchored with wires, had resisted the storms and kept the stove dry. The chinking still held around the windows and only a little wet had been driven in under the tight front door. The muslin walls were not stained ; they gave the room a clean light.

"It's sweet, it's positively sweet." Mary stopped to give David a kiss. "As soon as we get our things in and settled, it's going to be homelike as can be. You must bring the bedstead, your next trip. Now the first thing I want's the broom, and the table, and the barrel of dishes."

While he unloaded the wagon and led the horses to their hovel, David observed fresh prints of hoofs and boots about the place. One man with a horse had been there recently. He went into the house and took his musket. Everything was tidy, the bed was made on the floor, the table was set with a white cloth and the wedding-present knives and forks, silver plated. The lamp stood ready to light.

"Whatever are you doing?" Mary cried. "I thought you were going to dig some dry hay out of the stack, so I can heat up supper."

"I'm going to. How about a kiss, first? And how'd you like a fat goose for tomorrow?"

He followed the hoofprints along the edge of the slough, past Eliza's shanty. The rider had not dismounted there, and the tracks changed to those made by a gallop. David shot twice, and went back to the house with a brace of geese.

15

Two weeks later the geese and ducks were flying above musket range. Their leaders' calls, repeated down the long lines, had a warning sound. The point of the V blurred as tired birds fell back and others took the lead. They saw below them their old resting places, the sloughs offering food and sleep, and they saw covered wagons, campfires, yellow skeletons of buildings at the townsite. They heard saws, hammers, shouts and clattering boards. Brassy commands echoed along the flying ranks, the beat of wings quickened and the birds rose and went onward to the north. Wild ducks and geese never again darkened the slough with their numbers at twilight.

It was a marvel to see the endless line of teamsters, outfits and prairie schooners advancing all day along the road. David called Mary from the house to look.

"Bet you that's something the way it looked in pioneer times," he said. "Take away the railroad, the building, and the shanties and all. Just imagine back."

"I can't imagine away what's plain before my eyes, and I don't want to," Mary stated. She was glad that pioneer times were over and done with; some of her mother's folks had died on the Oregon Trail. "Listen. You can hear the hammers." Even against the wind, they could faintly hear the noise of building.

Six months ago the townsite had been a pre-emption claim. The Government had sold it for a dollar and a half an acre. Now town lots were selling for fifty dollars and up, as fast as an agent could make out the papers. Without telling Mary, David risked a hundred dollars on a corner lot and sold it a week later for $125., better wages than any man could make working. Mary put her foot down then ; she did not believe in gambling. Neither did David, for that matter, but with sixty dollars in an unfinished building on that lot, it sold for $200., and again for $225. And prices would go up with a boom when the railroad began building the roundhouses.

"No," Mary repeated firmly. "We're going to need what money we've got, we can't tie it up in more property."

They were going to have a baby ; their first child would be born about next Thanksgiving. Mary hoped he would be born on their wedding anniversary. In Tracy for his last trip, David bought fine, soft flannel, and some embroidery silk which clung to his fingers when he touched it.

On that trip he paid thirty dollars for a sod-breaking plow, twenty for a bargain in a secondhand saddle, and $52.50 for a grade heifer that would be fresh in June. She was a cheap buy, and the calf would be clear profit. They must have a cow ; farmers always had milk and butter. He also bought oats ; his horses must have oats, they could not do hard work on grass. Oats were sixty-nine cents a bushel, because of the freight charges.

Driving homeward at the slow pace of the heifer tied behind the wagon, David had less than two hundred dollars left of his saved six hundred. He owed his father for Dobbin, and not an acre of his sod was broken yet. He could not make a crop until next year and before he could

79

harvest wheat he must buy a mowing machine and feed threshers. Meanwhile, he and Mary must live; they must live for sixteen months on land which gave them nothing but grass.

He had known that he could not make a crop this first year, but he was used to land that gave a man a living. He had not realized what it meant to pay for every mouthful of food. Even the calf would be a starveling unless he bought feed to winter it through. He might as well be living on city pavements, like his brothers in St. Paul. He must get a job.

David could stomach that better than his father would. At least, he did not have to come down to a dollar a day, under a foreman. He owned a good team and wagon, and there was some independence in being a teamster. And he was in the country early, so that his chances of getting a job were not bad.

He rode on cheerfully enough through the windy day. Over the drying prairies a dancing mist of wild onion blossoms was splashed with the satiny colors of crocus. A teamster's loaded wagon pulled through the mud ahead, and a prairie schooner crowded with youngsters came lurching along behind.

Toward sunset, a team of glossy bays forged alongside. Mud-splashed to the bellies, they were stepping out briskly, their proud heads holding loose the ivory-ringed check reins. A piano-finish buggy flashed by, with a glitter of sunshine on nickel-plated lamps. David glimpsed the driver, and an older man who shouted a greeting to the teamster ahead. The fast buggy soon appeared against the sky and went down with the dip of the road.

The teamster could not contain his pleasure. He leaned and shouted back along the side of his canvas-covered load. "That was Gebbert! The old man himself!"

There were songs about Gebbert. He had been a pioneer, an Indian fighter, a sheriff; he was a square shooter. Gebbert's men bragged about the work they did for him; others said that he was the only honest contractor on the line.

When David pulled into the camp at sunset, he found a kind of hush because Gebbert was there. He would spend the night there, on his way to build his own camps farther west. David looked at his horses, and joined the men around his buggy. Gebbert himself was washing up in the superintendent's shanty.

He came out, and stood solidly on his feet, looking the camp over. Age had settled his body down, but he still looked able to stop a fight before it started. His combed gray hair and beard had a mild air which would not deceive anybody. He put his hand to his inside breast pocket, and took it out empty, glancing toward the store. There was a brown stain edging his mustache.

David stepped up to him quickly, and respectfully said, "Can I offer you a cigar, Mr. Gebbert?"

It was a good ten-cent cigar. Gebbert glanced under bushy eyebrows, took the cigar and looked at it. "Thanks. Quick on the uptake, uh? What can I do for you?"

"I want a job, sir."

"You won't get it for a cigar," Gebbert remarked, pleasantly enough. He bit off the end of the cigar and David lighted it. "Good cigar. What kind of job?"

"Teaming, sir."

"You look pretty young. Team and wagon here?"

"Yes sir."

"Let's have a look at 'em." The other men stood back to let them pass. Star and Dobbin, curried and rubbed down, were tied to the wagon and eating their oats. "Mm, Morgans. Light for heavy hauling."

81

"Let me handle 'em, and they'll move as much as any team of Percherons, I'll put up money on it," said David.

Mr. Gebbert rolled the cigar to the other side of his mouth and said, "I don't know your name."

David started. "I forgot, sir ; Beaton. David Beaton."

"I'd take you for a farmer, Mr. Beaton."

"I'm homesteading, Mr. Gebbert."

"Any relation to the Minnesota Beaton that raises Morgans ?"

"He's my father, sir."

"Well, your father raises damn good horses, son. So you're baching it out here ?"

"No sir, I'm married."

"That's sensible. Always like to see a couple starting out young. This country's hard on women and oxen, as they say, but it's a great country. You young folks'll make something of it. Where's your claim ?"

The superintendent came up while they were talking, and Gebbert said, "Well, Beaton, look me up at my camp Number One, sixty miles west, the tenth of May, and I'll put you on the payroll. Three dollars a day, you feed yourself and team, suit you ?"

"You bet, sir ! I'll be there !"

David did not eat in the cookshanty. He bought ten cents' worth of crackers and cheese, and slept on his load. He figured that, with economy, if he made his job last five full months, he could clear around two hundred dollars for the summer's work. He did not quite know how to tell Mary that he was going to be a hired man.

She was pleased when she saw the heifer, but he knew the figures were adding up in her mind. After supper she put them on paper, and looked at him aghast. "Why — David ! We're practically down to borrowed money."

He looked cheerful. "What of it ? Father won't

press me for it. Anyway, maybe we won't have to use it. I've got a job teaming on the railroad."

She put her hands flat to her cheeks. Her eyes widened, then looked down at the tablecloth. She asked, "When ?"

"Tenth of May. I'll be hauling for Gebbert." He saw that the name meant nothing to her.

"Then — will you be gone, all summer ?"

"I'll be back and forth, till after the train runs west of the townsite. I ought to make it back here every fourth night or so, for quite a while."

"Oh." As if she were angry, she asked, "What's he paying you ?"

"Top wages. Three dollars a day, feed myself and team. If I don't save two hundred dollars this summer, I'll eat my hat."

She laughed a little. "I guess you would, I don't know what else we'd eat next winter." She got up and began to clear the table briskly, turning her back to him to put the dishes in the dishpan. "Well, if you must, you must, and there's no more to be said."

16

The wild onion blossoms vanished. A green shimmer was over the land, and the diminishing water in the sloughs was no bluer than hollows paved with violets. Buttercups, pale windflowers and pinkish sheep-sorrel blossoms faintly colored all the slopes. Then the grass came up with a rush.

At dawn when David went to the field, meadow larks were flying straight up into the sky, letting their three clear notes fall like rain in the sunshine. Dotted over

83

the prairie, hired men with ox teams were setting to work at breaking the ten-acres patches required by law. Most of the homesteaders were working on the railroad. Already at the townsite the saloons and lumber-yard and blacksmith shop were doing business, and storekeepers were unloading goods which they often sold before they got them into the unfinished buildings.

An ox team was better than horses for breaking sod, but the Beatons had always owned horses. There was something lower, something foreign, in driving oxen. David argued with himself that his team, well fed with oats, could hold out to break ten acres. The heavy breaking-plow would go through the matted roots if they could stand pulling it. Sweat darkened their straining flanks and their shoulders quivered.

When he let them rest, Mary always came to bring him a drink. She was restless, with nothing to do but sit in the house and hear the wind. The water was brackish from the shallow slough well; he must dig a deeper well when he could get to it.

"How you making out?" he asked.

"All right. David, you'll kill those horses."

"What were you doing, out on the prairie?"

"Looking for greens." She added quickly, to save him from disappointment, "Don't expect any. I'm not sure what things are, out here. There's not a single sprig of dandelion or mustard, I believe I'll send for some seeds."

"Those pests? You do, and I'll wring your neck." He smiled at her. "Why don't you go over and see how the Peterses are getting along?"

"Well, I was over there most of yesterday. Maybe I will, and help Nettie."

Down along the slough to the southwest, less than a mile away, Nettie was battening down a tar-paper roof on

84

the sod shanty. They could see the sunshine on her red hair. Mr. Peters had not gone to work on the railroad; he was making more money doing carpenter work in town.

"She's put up her hair," Mary said. "It got in her way, on the roof, and she put it up yesterday, so now she's a young lady."

David gulped the last swallows from the pail. Mary took it and he settled the lines around his shoulders. He told himself that he was driving his horses no harder than he drove himself. The heavy plow was a punishment to arms and shoulders. He fought the rebellious land from dawn to dark, pausing only to let the horses rest. It seemed to him that all night long he drove the steel into that vicious obstinacy and felt the slow, painful ripping and turning of the sod. But he was killing the horses, and making almost no progress.

One night when Mary brought the lantern to him at the stable, she was wearing her hoops and the cream-colored gown. She had walked to town that afternoon. David did not like the idea of her walking in the town-site without an escort. He had tried plowing a hollow on the tree-claim that day, thinking that damper ground might be easier, and he had not seen her go.

At supper she told him about it. She was still excited, and nothing had happened, no one had spoken to her. She had seen the new buildings, the railroad ties already nearing the skeleton depot. There was a postoffice in Townsend's store; she had inquired there for letters. Eliza had written asking him to break fifteen acres for her.

"Write and tell her I can't spare the time. I'll hire it done if she says so. It'll cost three dollars an acre."

Eliza's reply came promptly. Mary unfolded the letter at the supper table, saying that Mr. Peters had brought it from town and Flora had run over with it. David was

85

too tired to sit up while he ate ravenously, his elbows on the table. He had given up, in his own mind; horses could not break that sod. He had to hire a man with oxen to break enough to hold the claims, fifteen acres; forty-five dollars.

"What a beautiful hand Eliza writes, like copper plate. I do admire it so. And such an admirable gift of expression. David, are you listening? This is what she says:

"Dear sister Mary and brother David,
I confess I am somewhat at a loss for a reply to your esteemed communication this day received. Such wages are ridiculous. Prices of goods are no doubt exorbitant there, as you state, because of the excessive costs of transportation by wagon, but such wages for common labor are preposterous. My own honorarium, in a position of grave trust and responsibility, is, as you know, but twenty-five dollars a month, and this after obtaining a diploma from the Seminary at the cost of no small sum, as well as diligent burning of the midnight oil. I can but feel that David has not sufficiently considered this matter, and, thanking him, I shall attend to it myself. I arrive on the train of May eleventh. Everyone here is enjoying the best of health. Trusting that this finds you both well, I am your affectionate sister Eliza. Post scriptum. I open this to add that if David does not find it entirely convenient to meet me in Tracy, pray let him give himself no concern, as I am fully capable of taking care of myself. E.B."

"But of course you will meet her."

"Eliza? Not on your tintype." David drank his cup of tea, thrust his rolled napkin into its ring, and pushing back his chair he began to take off his boots.

"David, but how can you? You can't let a lady, your own sister — "

"You watch my dust. Let her fend for herself, if she's so brash about it." Letting down his suspenders, he pulled the sweat-stiffened shirt over his head. Mary's voice came to him dimly. He said, "Eliza's no spring chicken." The sods began to resist the plow as soon as his head hit the pillow.

Mary stood looking at him for a moment. Then she laid Eliza's letter in her writing case. She washed the dishes with care to make no noise. Her darning basket was empty. She opened the Bible under the lamp, but insects dashed against the glass chimney and fell squirming on the page, and early flies buzzed in the circle of light on the ceiling. She turned down the wick, blew out the flicker, and went to the doorway.

The land was a level darkness under the stars. She could not see the claim shanties on it. There was not one friendly tree to hold its branches against awful space. There was nothing but darkness, the sound of wind in grasses, and the stars that seemed near but were so far away.

For a long time she sat on the doorstep, her chin on her fists. Men are tired in planting time. But women are tired, too, where there are gardens to plant and weed, radishes to pull and curly lettuce leaves to pick and wash, where there are attics and parlors and cellars to clean, where ash hoppers are dripping and the big soap kettles must be skimmed over fires in the yards, and the brown soap poured out to cool. Where there are leaves to rake from lawns, hens to set and chicks to take from the nests, henhouses to whitewash and fresh straw to be put in the nest boxes, where there are butter buyers to bargain with and the emptied butter tubs to scrub and scald and sun, carpets to be beaten and tacked down again, greens to be gathered and washed and boiled, steaming deliciously, and the yellow dandelion blossoms brought in crammed bushel baskets for the making of dandelion wine, there spring comes with a rush for women, too.

A sudden shiver ran up Mary's spine and tingled over her scalp. Something was watching her. Something she could not see, low against the house in the dark, was near her, stealthily creeping nearer. Her breath tightened in her chest, her eyes stared ; she could not move nor think. In the dark two eyes glimmered and blinked out. A coyote. Mary sprang up, slammed the door, and tremblingly held it shut, until around her the dark shapes of things told her how silly she was and she heard David breathing undisturbed.

17

The next morning was gay. David was rested ; if he must pay for breaking sod he must pay for it, and he put the matter from his mind. Enough of the obstinate stuff had been torn up to make a potato patch, and while Mary quickly did the housework after breakfast he opened the last sack of potatoes. On the back step, they picked out together a mess for baking and a mess for boiling. Mary promised mashed potatoes, with gravy if he would buy a bit of meat, for it was the mating season for wild things and he could not hunt. He put the sack on his shoulder and they went out together to plant the sod-potatoes.

Kneeling in the grass, Mary cut the potatoes. There was no bushel basket or peck measure, so she used the wash basin and the iron spider. She filled one with the cut potatoes, carried it to David and brought back the other. With the hatchet, David slashed into the rooty underside of upturned sods, pushed in a bit of potato, and pressed the cut together with his foot. They talked

88

while they worked. They were both full of fun that morning.

About ten o'clock, they saw Mr. Peters on the sorrel galloping out from town. David said, "Wonder what's the matter with Peters?"

They saw him pull up at his shanty. Nettie ran out to him, and back. Mrs. Peters came out, and the children. "It can't be anything wrong there," Mary said. "It must be — Listen. Something's happened in town." There was not a sound from the townsite, not a man on a roof; building had stopped. Nettie handed her father's rifle up to him. "Oh, what is it? David, what — No, David! No, don't!"

"You better go back to the house," he said over his shoulder. She had almost to run to keep up with him. Mr. Peters came toward them rapidly on the sorrel. They met on the high ground above the slough, beyond Eliza's shanty.

"We're making up a posse, Dave," Mr. Peters said. "That fellow in the shingle-roofed shanty south of town, he was a claim jumper. That was young Jack Allen's claim he was on. He shot Jack Allen before his wife's eyes yesterday when they went out there, she with a young baby. We just heard of it. She couldn't lift him into the wagon nor get any help, all day yesterday. Halfbreed Jack come by there this morning and brought them in. Allen just died in the depot."

"Where's the man that did it?"

"Lit out, right after the shooting. He's got a day's head start. Coming along?"

"Quick as I can saddle up," David said.

"See you in town." Mr. Peters turned the sorrel and David started back to his stable. Neither of them had paid any attention to Mary. She walked along by the

89

edge of the potato patch and past the sack of potatoes spilling out in the grass. The butcher knife was still in her hand. She picked up the hatchet and went into the house and laid them down, went outdoors toward the stable, then came back and made up a package of baked bean sandwiches. David rode to the back door on Star.

"I put you up a lunch," she said.

"Good idea. Get me some piece of cloth, to tie it onto the saddle with." He was thinking about the tracks he had seen, here, around his own place. His house was larger than the other and his land was better, nearer town. Suddenly he understood why a claim jumper had not taken it. Eliza's shanty and Gay's were too near; a murderer did not want witnesses.

"The musket," he said. Mary gave him the musket and the box of cartridges. "Don't know when I'll be back. Take care of yourself. Stay at Peterses or have some of the young ones stay with you nights."

"I'm all right," she said, not meaning anything, just saying the words. The look in his eyes made her feel that she did not know him. She went into the house and wrapped the loaf in a cloth, washed the bean pan and the butcher knife carefully. Then she put on her sunbonnet and set out across the wide prairie toward the Peters' shanty.

Nineteen riders were at the depot in town. No more horses were able to make a long trip. The men from town and from the nearest railroad gangs milled through the waiting room where Jack Allen's body lay covered with a sheet, only his stiff, unshaven face revealed. Mrs. Allen with her baby were upstairs with the station agent's wife. Mr. Peters took the lead, riding south.

"Take it easy, men," he said. "It's a long ride ahead

of us and we'll take it easy and keep our horses going. We won't quit till we get him."

At the claim shanty it was easy to see what had been done. Everything was plain in the wheel-tracks, the trodden grass, and the brown smears.

The trail of the calico mare went to the southeast, easy enough to follow on the spring grass. Mr. Peters followed it and the others spread out a little behind him, trotting, galloping, pulling down to a trot again. David rode with the pack. There was an unholy fervor in hunting a man. The little that was said was commonplace, but underneath it there was a loathing eagerness.

Mary escaped from the prairie and the sky at last, running. She stood trembling in the doorway, without breath to speak. Mrs. Peters said, "There, sit down and rest and don't take it so much to heart. They have to go after him, or no telling what would happen to all of us, out here with no law. It will be different when the county's organized."

"Killing's too good for him," Mary said. "I don't know why I feel the way I do. I'm just upset, I guess." She fanned her face with the sunbonnet. "You know, we saw him. We drove right up to that shanty and David went to the door. My blood ran cold the minute I laid eyes on him. He had on a gun, and the way he looked at David — It's only the mercy of Providence we're alive to tell it, and David happened to say first thing we were only passing by on our way to our claim. 'Our claim's two miles northwest of the townsite,' he said, almost the first words out of his mouth. My goodness, it gives me goose flesh to think what if he hadn't.'"

Mr. Peters had known the Allens while they were camping at the townsite, a real nice young couple from Wisconsin. Jack Allen had teamed from Tracy for awhile, taking his pay in supplies till he had enough to start out with. "Poor Mrs. Allen, poor thing, what a thing to go through and she with a nursing baby, what will she do ?"

"She'll go back home to her own folks," Mary said.

Since Mr. Peters was not there, they ate a pick-up dinner of cold corn-bread and molasses, without setting the table. "You'll soon be having milk," Mrs. Peters said. "Yes," said Mary, "I'll be glad when the heifer freshens. I like working with milk, we had a stone springhouse at home. I suppose they can't catch him today. David said at the time, 'We'll have trouble with that fellow,' he said. 'That's an ugly customer,' those were his very words." She started up. "Why am I sitting here ! I can be planting our sod-potatoes !"

Nettie asked eagerly if she might help. Her father had not yet bought their seed potatoes, though he had paid for breaking five acres, and meant to pay for five more. Mrs. Peters agreed to let Nettie stay all night with Mary, saying, "She can take supper and breakfast with you, if you'll eat dinner with us tomorrow."

They walked along together in the young bluestem grass above the slough. Already there was almost a path between the two places. Nettie let her sunbonnet hang down her back so that she could see the whole land and the sky.

"You like it out here, don't you," Mary said.

"Oh yes ! I like it where there aren't any people, where it's big and new and — fresh. Don't you ?"

"I hate it !" The words burst out with an angry sob. Mary had not known how much she hated this country, the bareness, the emptiness, the winds. She hated the grass swishing at her skirts. She walked along weeping furiously in the shelter of her sunbonnet. "I hate it, every bit of it. If it wasn't for David — but I hate it so, I can't hardly stand it!"

"You'll get used to it. Don't cry, Mary. People get used to things they can't stand."

18

After they had planted the sod-potatoes, so that again there was nothing to do but the bit of housework that could hardly be made to last an hour, Nettie was still company. They kept on talking, so that Mary hardly heard the wind. Nettie enjoyed the larger house, with its muslin walls, the varnished furniture, the board floor and ceiling. Mary opened her trunk and they talked over her things, and the photographs of people back home.

Every day before noon they strolled to the Peters' shanty and stayed there until it was time to bring the heifer and Dobbin from their picket lines for the night. The shanty had only one window, and no floor yet. The stove, bunks, table and benches and cupboard left hardly room to move between them, and overhead the rafters were bare under the tar paper. But everything was as clean as could be, and Mary liked to be in the midst of the family. She tried all the time to keep from thinking that perhaps David was hurt, and from suddenly imagining what, at that very moment, the posse might be doing.

"They'll have to shoot him," she said one afternoon. "There aren't any trees."

They had been talking about patchwork quilt patterns, but Nettie answered, "They can find a tree. We saw some, coming up from Yankton."

93

The wind was blowing against the sod walls and the grass was so tall now that they could hear its rustling like an endless sigh.   Mary and Nettie were sitting at the bare table because the benches were there.   The children were playing outdoors and by the window Mrs. Peters mended a shirt.   Without looking up she said, "It's best to put it out of our minds.   Maybe we'll never know.   To this day Mr. Peters won't say, about the Bordens."

Mary had not heard about the Bordens.   Nettie remembered Kate Borden well, a big, heartily joking woman in men's boots under her skirts, who had invited them all in and had offered Nettie a piece of white bread and sugar when they camped by her house on their way to the Indian country.   The Bordens had the only house on that route south of Independence, and the only well.   Kate Borden was a good cook and set a fine table ; she fed all the settlers coming by, who could pay twenty-five cents for a meal.

Mr. Peters had camped there again, two nights, coming and going on the trip to Independence when he traded his furs and brought back a year's supplies and the window glass.   He had not eaten Kate Borden's cooking because he could not afford to pay for it.   She had urged him to come in anyway, but he had thanked her and eaten by his campfire.

The Bordens had hung their wagon cover across their house ; women did that who had houses so large that they could hide their beds behind a curtain.   Nettie had not gone in, but she had lingered around the doorway looking in until her mother called her away.   She remembered the curtain, the bench against it behind the table, and the fine stove, the numbers of cooking pots and dishes, and the good smell of Kate Borden's cooking.   Kate Borden fed people at that table, and while they were eating and

94

talking to her, leaning back against the curtain perhaps in laughter at her jokes, from behind it her husband or her brother smashed in their heads with the blunt end of an ax.

That was why so many settlers coming into that country with teams and wagonloads of supplies never wrote home to their folks in the east and never were heard of again. So many settlers left Independence and were not seen beyond the Borden place that men began to wonder why their garden was always plowed and never planted. At last a posse rode to the house to ask questions. The Bordens had left in a hurry ; someone must have warned them. But clothes of all sexes were stacked behind the curtain, and there were stains on the floor, and two muddy shovels. The men started to dig in the garden patch. When they found plain proof that children had been buried alive with murdered men and women, they went after the Bordens.

"They'd gone off in a hurry, in a wagon, making for the southwest, likely for Mexico or California," Mrs. Peters said. "Nobody will ever know what was the end of them."

"I know very well what was the end of them," Nettie remarked.

"All you know is what your father said to me when he came back."

"Yes, that's all I know. What he said, Mary, was 'We agreed not to talk about it, but Kate Borden will never bury any more young ones alive.' "

"He didn't realize you were big enough to take notice, Nettie. To this day," Mrs. Peters told Mary, "Mr. Peters won't speak about it. They agreed not to talk, likely before they did it, and not a man in that posse would tell his own wife more than, 'Kate Borden will never be heard of again.' It's best not to think of it, but she was the brains of that family, Kate Borden was."

"She deserved killing!" Mary was defending Mr. Peters; he had done right, but she felt differently about him. She could not say why her feeling had changed, nor precisely what the difference was, but there was a difference. You can not feel the same toward a man who has killed a human being. "They did exactly right," she declared. "I'd have done it myself, like I'd kill a snake."

"So would I," Nettie said quietly. With a kind of chill, Mary thought that might be true.

"I couldn't say so, myself." Mrs. Peters bit off the thread and smoothed the patch. She knitted the thread, turned a raw edge under with a stroke of the needle, and went on setting even stitches. "No, I can't say I could bring myself to it. But it must be done, so we'd best be thankful there's men that can, and turn our thoughts elsewhere. I don't know why I ever brought this up, in the first place."

Mary looked at the graying hair and the fine wrinkles across the forehead, the gentle face. "You brought it up because it's on your mind till you have to come out with it," she thought. She determined never to repeat whatever David told her when he came back. She thought of a thing like that between man and wife; it would come into her mind when his arms were around her, but a rope or a gun does not make hands bloody.

"There's so many, I don't suppose any of them are hurt," she said. The words were out before she could stop them.

Mrs. Peters folded the shirt, leaving the needle in the seam. "You start the fire and put the kettle on, Nettie. I'm going to call in the young ones and we'll have a cup of tea. Of course they won't get hurt! They're doing the right thing, we must put our trust in Providence and keep on praying."

David came home the next day, in the late afternoon. The sun was so low that half the prairie was shadowed, but when he rode out from town he saw his house standing on level golden-green. The sunlight on the land that belonged to him was like a welcome home.

Nettie and Mary were at the well in the slough with the heifer and Dobbin. The pond had shrunk since he left, it was barely a sheen of water over mud now. Mary was letting down the pail on the rope, he heard their voices and the splash of water pouring. Then Dobbin whinnied to Star.

He reined up by the well, and looked down at Mary. Through the tunnel of the sunbonnet she looked up at him intently, her lips parted a little, not speaking. He said, "Well, here I am! Everything all right?" His hand was jerked by Star's reaching to meet Dobbin's outstretched nose.

"Are you?" Mary was breathless. "Are you all right?"

"Hungry as a bear," he said, dismounting. "Guess I look like one, too. I never once thought of my razor till the second day out." He took the pail from Mary's hand, and saw only the side of her gray sunbonnet. "I'll water 'em, while you get supper on the table, uh?"

"Did you get him?" Nettie asked.

He let the pail down rapidly into the well. He wanted to forget the whole thing. How he felt about it he did not know, and did not want to know; he wanted to forget it. "Nope," he said shortly. "He got into Iowa. Sheriff over the line had the word by telegraph and jailed him, before we got there. They're going to try him."

He emptied the water into the scrub pail set in the grass. "You wash that out good?" he asked Mary. "Star won't drink if it tastes of soap."

"I guess it's all right," she said. "Dobbin does."

"Your father'll be out in a few minutes, I left him in town," he told Nettie.

"Well," she said, "I'll be going along home." Mary went with her up the path.

When he went into the house, a rich smell of food made him ravenous. Strips of salt pork sizzled in the spider, and in the hot fat Mary was frying raw potatoes, carefully turning each browned slice with the case-knife. There was bread on the table and the teapot was singing. He declared, "I could eat a wolf!"

"It'll be on the table by the time you wash up," she said, holding her face averted from the sputtering fat. He washed with abandon, sputtering and puffing, plunging luxuriously into the roller towel, and grinning at his bearded face in the looking glass while he ran the comb through wet hair and mustache. He let Mary set down the emptied spider and pulled her against him.

"Don't, David," she said faintly.

He was dumbfounded. "What the dickens! Aren't you glad I'm home?"

"Of course, but eat your supper first."

He shook her a little in his arms, between playfulness and irritation. "Gosh, not one kiss? One little one?"

He could not make out what was in her eyes searching his, while her hands on his chest held him away by no more than their weight. Her eyes were not afraid, but something like fear was in them. "Something happened, David. Tell me."

"What's the matter with you?"

"I want to know what happened."

98

He was indignant. "I told you what happened. What's the idea, think I'm a liar?"

"David — please."

He let his arms drop. "We made a hell of a trip for nothing and I don't want to talk about it." Anger rose. "What's more, I'm not going to. You can put that in your pipe and smoke it." He pulled his chair to the table and made an effort to say pleasantly, "Come on, let's eat."

She sat down, and cutting a slice of bread laid it on his plate. "Help yourself," she said when he offered her the fried potatoes. She poured the tea, and then, beginning to eat, she remarked, "Nettie and I got all the sod-potatoes in, did you notice?"

It always touched him to see her eating with her fork, in the new fangled way. She was so gravely absurd, changing the fork from hand to hand and overcoming the difficulty of balancing food on the curved prongs ; he felt tenderly toward her. Eliza, if she took that idea into her head, would nag him every time he lifted a knife to his mouth. He was a little ashamed of speaking crossly, and when Mary got up to clear away the dishes he pulled her onto his lap and would have told her so. But it was not necessary to say anything.

He must leave early next morning to reach Gebbert's camp on time. She wished he did not have to go. So did he, but if he had no trouble on the road, he would be at home every fourth night.

"I know," she said. "But I feel — I don't know how to say it."

Something was taking him away from her. He was somehow changed, as if he were older, or in some way like someone she did not know. She wished they were farming. She wished they were renting a farm, or if he must be a hired man, that he were a hired man on a farm in set-

99

tled country, where everything they did would be done together, and when he went away he would not be away from her really, but only driving cattle to market or trading horses with someone they knew.

Telegraph poles already marched through the townsite and linemen were stringing a wire on green glass knobs. The steel rails were coming. Driving to Tracy in the hearty spring weather, David passed the pick and shovel gangs, the teams and scrapers. Then he hailed teamsters unloading ties, then men laying them, at last the gang working in a clangor of sledges on steel.

Behind them crawled a chuffing engine. The engineer leaned out, his hand on the throttle, cautiously inching forward that marvel of steam and iron. Along the tracks the men stood cheering and on his wagon David waved his hat and yelled. Those were great times to be living in. It was a great thing to see the railroad opening up a new country.

Some day the whole of that wild green country would be broken and tamed. David could expect to see all the miles of it in fields and pastures, meadows, groves, and orchards.

In the distance he saw a parasol above a teamster's load, and grinned to himself. Eliza sat erect above billowing skirts, her face bare to the wind and her narrow eyes snapping with excitement. She was very well, she said ; everyone at home was well and sent regards ; she was having a most instructive journey and she found this new country enchanting, positively enchanting. The hunched teamster glanced at her warily.

The next night David pulled into the townsite again. The train came west of Tracy now, unloading at the end of the rails and shortening his haul. He unhitched in the lumber yard and rode one of the harnessed horses out to his claim, leading the other. Now that the slough was dry, he took a short cut across the unfenced sections and through the coarse slough grass. He heard voices in the dark at his house.

Mary and Eliza were sitting on the front doorstep. Dr. Thorne in a chair, Gay and Nettie on the grass. If there had been a porch, and trees, a picket fence and the scent of lilacs, this would have been like a summer evening at his father's house with neighbors dropping in. It was a deeper ownership in the place, to be welcoming visitors.

"Come out west to grow up with the country, uh?" He clapped Gay's shoulder.

"Plenty of room to grow in."

"You bet! One thing we've got plenty of out here, is room!"

He had to picket out the doctor's team, to feed and bed his own hard working horses in the stable. Rubbing them down, he thought of the big barns he would have some day, and it struck him that Gay's words could be taken two ways.

While he ate the supper that Mary set for him at one end of the table, he sized Gay up. Mary was wearing her hoops and French calico, her hair was done in a new way and she was merrier than she had been for a long time. Eliza had hired her breaking done, at three dollars an acre. Gay had hired his done, too.

"How are you going to put in your time?" David asked in surprise. Gay laughed. He was going to make a trip around the country with his father, before he settled down. Dr. Thorne had always wanted to see the west.

It was cheaper to hire breaking done than it was to buy oxen and breaking-plow. Gay was willing to bet that he'd make more from his land than David would from his, in the long run.

At last David agreed with his father's opinion of Gay. He could not say that Gay had changed, but now he seemed too good-looking, his black hair and waxed mustache too sleek, his hands too slim and soft, tossing and catching a pearlhandled penknife.

Nettie murmured good night and would have slipped away quickly, but Gay interposed. "Allow me to escort you, Miss Peters. We can't have charming young ladies walking across these prairies alone." His smile lifted his mustache from white teeth.

It was a shock to hear her called Miss Peters. In a slim dark dress without hoops, her hair piled on her head, she was a young lady. Her eyes widened and a flush came up under her tan.

Eliza spoke up. "We'll all enjoy a stroll, won't we, Mary?"

Mary did not go, and Dr. Thorne left with the others. The quiet gave back the house to them and Mary leaned against him. He kissed her. "How are you, Molly girl?"

"I'm all right."

"You tell Eliza about the baby?"

"Not yet. Mrs. Peters knows. David, she's going to have one."

He whistled silently. That was tough for Mr. Peters, with five mouths to feed already. While he took off his boots, Dr. Thorne's light shone in Gay's shanty; a quarter of a mile away, it was small on the dark prairie.

"They're only camping, David. I don't believe Gay'll settle down to stay. Eliza's is real nice, considering.

She's put down a strip of rag carpet on the grass and she has her trunk and a chair and some books."

He was glad that Mary had company to talk to while he was gone. He reached and hugged her against him. "Miss me?"

"Yes." She smoothed his hair.

"Don't let Eliza boss you. We're boss of this she-bang."

"She don't try to. I can't think how you ever got that idea, just because she's capable. David, did you ever think she's smitten on Gay?"

"Great Caesar's ghost, no! Eliza's got better sense."

He rode away in morning starlight and was on the road again at dawn. A teamster saw the landscape always changing as he drove along and the whole life of the country was on the road. Prairie schooners were thronging westward, homesteaders going to their claims farther on. Their campfires sparkled along the road in dusks and dawns; they stopped David to ask questions and told him about weather, crops and politics in the east. Every day the railroad gangs advanced westward. David knew a hundred men in the big and little camps; nearly eight hundred were scattered along his sixty-mile haul. Teamsters carried the gossip, news, jokes and songs from end to end of the line; a teamster was always welcome among the evening crowds in the company stores.

One day on the road David met Dr. Thorne. The doctor turned his buggy out of the road and stopped, and David pulled up his wagon alongside. When the wheels were still, you could hear a silence under the sound of the wind. The birds' chirping was weak against it and a voice seemed too loud.

The doctor was excited. "I'm on my way home. Get

down here, Dave. I'll give you a look at something, the like of which you never saw !"

He unwrapped a bundle done up in grainsacks. His hands were shaking. "Look at that !"

The thing looked like some kind of idol. It was in a narrow basket, its head bound to an extension of the reed-work. The closed eyelids and the cheeks were slightly withered. It had a flat nose and a drooping, shrunken mouth. It was all a dark brown, and seemed to be made of some kind of wood, but its coarse black hair and its eyelashes were real hair. David drew back a little, exclaiming "Good gosh, doc, what is that ?"

"It's a discovery, Dave, it's a big scientific discovery. I'm going to send it to the Smithsonian in Washington, D.C. It's an Indian mummy, Dave, a genuine mummy, a papoose, and they've mummified it somehow. There's a whole grove of trees hanging full of them."

"Where ?" David asked eagerly. He would have liked to have such a thing himself.

"Out about sixty miles west of Turtle Creek. I didn't have a map but I can take anybody to it. By gravy, this'll be a sensation ! You'll see those big scientists piling out here from the east, so fast you can't see 'em for dust. I haven't unwrapped it, I'm leaving that for them to do in Washington, but feel — it's all there, solid."

David poked at the thing. It had a queer smell. "By gosh, doc. Barnum'd pay you a young fortune for that. Say, don't show it to Mary."

The doctor had not thought of Barnum. He almost turned back to get another. But this was the only papoose he had found in the grove. At a venture, he'd say it died at about a year old. David agreed to say nothing about the find until the doctor decided what to do and perhaps got an offer from Barnum. The grove was safe enough, since nobody but Dr. Thorne and Gay knew where it was. David said again, "Don't let Mary see that thing."

"What? What's this about Mary?"

David could not help grinning. "Don't let on I told you, doc, she won't let anybody know till she has to, but she's bound it'll be a boy about next Thanksgiving."

Dr. Thorne shook hands with him, saying that was fine news. David thought so. He rode on whistling. It was a fine, large day, with a strong wind and the whole country rippling green.

When he pulled into Gebbert's camp that evening, he found the granary empty again. He heaved his load into it, puzzled. Four teamsters were hauling oats to that granary. He examined the door hinges and tried the padlock twice after he snapped it.

The scraper-men were driving their teams to the stable. The pick and shovel gangs were tramping in, singing some new verses of *Working for Old Gebbert on the Northwestern Line*. Gebbert stepped out of the cookshanty. He saw to it that there was not a fly under the crusts of the pies his cooks turned out, nor a bug in his bunkhouses. David walked up to him, smelling the clean smell of bread and meat and pies. David was feeding himself on forty cents a day, less than half the cost of board in the cookshanties. Of course he had no pie.

He handed over the granary key. "There you are, sir. It's locked, and I tried the padlock."

"Thanks, Dave. Something on your mind?"

"Well, yes, Mr. Gebbert. We can't seem to get ahead on the hauling. The granary was empty again when I come in just now."

The old man's mustache quivered and his crowsfeet deepened. "Don't worry, son. Keep right on hauling, you're doing fine."

David could not figure it out. Gebbert was working forty teams, and drawing from the railroad company enough feed for sixty. He was running far into debt; it seemed to David that if this leakage from his supplies went on, the old man would be bankrupt when he settled with the company at the end of the summer.

He picked up the answer one night from the talk in the store. One man after another told how Gebbert was selling supplies. Storekeepers, settlers, sub-contractors, were hauling supplies from Gebbert's camps at night, so fast that Gebbert had hired two more teamsters to haul them in. He was underselling the eastern wholesalers and the railroad.

"Be jaybers and he can, the stuff don't cost him anything!" A pick and shovel man let out a roar of laughter, and the others joined in. When he could, David asked what the joke was.

He was talking to old Gebbert men, who had worked two years for Gebbert. They said that the old man had cleared a fair profit the first year, though his cookshanties served pie seven days a week and fresh beef on Sundays, and he kept his teams sleek. But last fall, when the job was finished and approved and he went in to settle up with the company and collect what was due him, the company handed him a bill. It had run up the price of supplies, and according to the books he owed the company money for the summer's work he had done.

Contractors had to feed their men and teams, they had to draw their supplies from the company, and the company set the prices. You might think there was no way to beat that. Some contractors, when they found they

106

were in debt to the company, tried to pay their way out by taking another contract, skimping their men's meals and working their horses gaunt. Others blew up, quit broke, and told the company to sue and be damned.

But Gebbert was made of different stuff. Gebbert had been raised on the frontier. He had gone up against Indians and wolves and the Rocky Mountains, and no sleek easterner could back him down. He took it cool and easy, and signed up for a bigger contract this year.

The foreman slapped his thigh. "Jiminy crickets! I'd give an eyetooth to be there when he settles up this fall!" Gebbert would be flat busted. He would owe the railroad more than ten outfits like his were worth. He would say, Gentlemen, you can not get blood from a turnip. "And him with enough salted away in the east to keep him in clover the rest of his days!"

"Takes a crook to beat a crooked game!" the new teamster thought he was chiming in. He saw his mistake at once, and added that he meant no offense.

"You ain't acquainted yet with Gebbert," the storekeeper told him. "The old man's straight as a string. Hell, a man that won't steal from a railroad ain't honest."

David had never before known a man admired for stealing. It was not a thing he could explain to Mary. He said nothing to her about it, and went on hauling oats to the always emptied granary.

The first train reached the townsite when he was at the western end of his haul. Driving back, he came at night into Dixon's big camp, and saw teamsters unloading heavy timbers.

"What you hauling?" he asked while he unhitched.

"Timbers for the roundhouse."

David could not believe it. But it was true. The railroad was building its roundhouse there. The railroad had put the end of the division thirty-five miles west of his homestead.

Before he reached home, David began to see that this was a joke on him. He thought of Dr. Thorne, when he heard the news, and that made him chuckle. The men at the townsite were cheerful enough. They were saying now that nothing could keep a good town from growing. The arrival of the roundhouse timbers on flat-cars had sent their spirits up, and when they saw those timbers loaded on wagons and hauled away, they had mobbed an empty freight car.

"Too bad you missed it, Dave," Mr. Peters said. "That freight car made the finest wood you ever saw. We didn't twist hay at our house for two days. Don't tell Mrs. Peters, she don't know how I got it."

"Hell," David said, "a man that won't steal from a railroad ain't honest."

The talk in town was that a big speculator named Fickert was responsible. He had hired men to pre-empt claims for him, all around the townsite, but for some reason he had fallen out with the railroad company, and the division headquarters had been moved to leave him holding the bag.

At home, Mary did not see that it made any difference to them. The land was as good as ever, and would raise the same crops, when David could get it broken. She said, "It's Eliza it's hard on. She was holding her claim for the profit."

"Don't waste sympathy on me," said Eliza. "When I think of that Fickert, I feel like the man that wouldn't get up when he sat on a wasp. It's hurting him as much as it's hurting me."

20

There were no more rains ; the wheelruts smoothed out and powdered to dust.   A bit of pink in the green caught David's eye and he got down from the wagon to cut the thorny stem of a wild rose for Mary.   It was pleasant now to sleep on a horseblanket by the ashes of his supper fire.

He woke up one morning on the ground by his wagon in the Turtle Creek camp.   Moisture frosted the iron rim of the wagon wheel and its spokes fanned upward into a ground mist.   The light was false dawn ; it was not time to get up, but his eyes did not close again.   He sat up, stretching, and saw Indians.

He had not seen wild Indians before.   At first he could not believe that he saw them now.   Hundreds of naked, painted Indians on ponies surrounded the camp.   He saw the tufted scalplocks on their skulls, and rifles in their hands.   The mist seemed full of free, unbridled ponies and brown bodies, paint-streaked chests and faces, goblin-like, impossible.

A sharp, brassy tang hit the back of his tongue, he swallowed.   Men were snoring in the bunkhouse.   There was the sound of a loud yawn ; the fat cook stood on the kitchen step, petrified.   David got to his feet then and started toward the bunkhouse.   He walked.   It was an endless walk, a hundred feet or so, perhaps forty steps ; he tried not to hurry and did not realize that he had left off his boots.   A sharp report shattered him ; the cook had shut the kitchen door.   David stepped into the bunkhouse and said, "Mr. Gebbert."

He was profoundly glad that Gebbert had spent the night in this camp.   One thing about Gebbert was that he slept in the bunkhouses.   A stir went along the rows of double bunks; it was dark there and the breathed air was heavy. Gebbert answered, quick enough, "What's up, Dave?"

"Look here," David said urgently.

Gebbert stepped out past him and looked. The men were yawning and stretching, scratching, fumbling half awake for their clothes. Gebbert came in. "Wake up, boys," he said. "Hand along my boots." The boots came along to him and he stamped into them. "There's four to five hundred Indians out here, in war paint. They've got us surrounded. Get this straight, every man jack of you: if anything starts, not one of us will live to tell it."

When this sank in, the men rolled out, swearing. Gebbert shut them up. He said this was not an attack, yet. "If it was, they'd have hit us an hour ago. What they want's a pow-wow. Pete."

"Yes sir."

"Got that baby revolver of yours with you?"

"Yes sir."

"Put it on you where they can't see it. Make sure of that. I want you and Brown to come along with me. Got a gun, Brown?"

"Not here, no."

"Neither have I. Now boys, we're going out there to find out what they want. You stay inside here. Don't start any funny business. Anybody that wants to kill the three of us, here's your chance. One move out of one of you'll do it."

Passing David, Gebbert said to him too low for anyone else to hear, "Forget your boots, son?" Nobody but Gebbert could have said that as he did, not making fun of David, but sharing a joke they could both appreciate.

The men pulled on their pants and boots and in low

110

voices reckoned up a hundred and forty-eight men in camp. Most of them had a gun, some had two, but there were only a few cartridges. Gebbert had gone out of sight beyond the granary. David, by the door, could see eighty-six Indians. The man opposite counted in the other direction more than ninety. Gebbert stamped in, swearing like a trooper, calling the dumbfounded men a dozen fighting names, demanding to know what man had stolen a baby's body from the Indians' burial grove. "Speak up! Step out here and own it like a man, or by the living eternal!"

"Dr. Thorne did, sir," David said.

"Who the blazes is Dr. Thorne?"

David told him. Pete had noticed the bundle when the doctor drove through. David could not say whether Dr. Thorne had reached home yet, nor whether he had sent the mummy to Washington, D.C. or to Barnum's Museum in New York City.

"Come along, Dave," Gebbert said. "We'll tell it to the chief."

Pete and Brown followed them. At his wagon, David put on his boots. The Indians were galloping in a ring around the camp, galloping at full speed on free ponies without saddle or bridle. Bare-skinned, painted, with tufted heads, the Indians brandished their rifles in free hands and let out yowls that made the scalp prickle. In the stables the frightened horses squealed and kicked.

David stood beside Gebbert while a number of blanketed Indians rode toward them. Four dismounted and came forward, while David advanced with Gebbert.

Gebbert spoke their lingo; it did not sound like words to David. He had no idea what they said. They looked at him with black eyes, snake eyes. The streaks of paint on their faces kept him from seeing them clearly, as if they

111

were behind a picket fence.   Their stiff blankets were not clean and some of their feathers were broken.   David was never able to describe their smell ; he could only say that it was a wild-animal smell.

He told about meeting Dr. Thorne ; he described the mummy.   From their questions he understood that they had traced the doctor's buggy as far as this Turtle Creek camp.   The numbers of redskins on those unbridled ponies distracted him.   Colors began to show in the dawn.   Then it was over ; he walked back with Gebbert. Except for the uproar in the stables, the camp seemed asleep.

Gebbert said, "Take my bay mare, Dave.   Ride back to the telegraph and get hold of the damn fool by telegram if you can.   We've got three days to hand over that body."

"There's eight hundred men between here and Brook-ins, Gebbert," Pete said.   "And any white man can handle six Indians."

"Maybe.   Custer's men didn't.   And don't think there's only five hundred Indians in this.   That old chief out there can bring ten thousand down on us.   If this thing starts, it won't be stopped west of Big Sioux river. It'll be another Minnesota massacre, boys ; they stopped that one, too."   He went on toward the bunkhouse.

David saddled and bridled the excited mare and led her out.   He was in the saddle when Gebbert came up. "Use your head, Dave.   I don't want men piling in here. Tell 'em I'm handling this.   Come back day after to-morrow.   If you can't get the body that quick, bring me a telegram, something to show 'em."

"Yes sir.   Mr. Gebbert, you think they'll stay here?"

"I think so.   Got a wife, haven't you ?   On a claim. Do no harm to move her to town for a few days."

David had a close view of redskins swerving and circling on their free ponies, rifles swinging as he went through. He was four miles from camp before the mare showed any signs of slowing.

About nine o'clock he met two teamsters, and told them to stay at Miller's camp till the shindig was over. He figured that it would do no good to haul supplies among those savages. Now that he could remember them, he remembered the hunger showing in their ribs. At the camps he stopped to breathe the mare and say that Indians were threatening trouble at Turtle Creek.

"Gebbert's handling it," he said. "He don't want help."

The men said that if anything started they would go swarming in there like bees and not leave a redskin alive east of the Missouri river.

21

It was sixty miles to the townsite. David rode in that afternoon. When it came to wording the telegram, he wanted help. Clint Insull, the station agent, wrote it out for him and read it : Five hundred Indians on warpath threaten massacre settlers must have papoose back quick ship to me by express today without fail important hurry answer by telegraph at once. Clint said, "Gosh."

"How long'll it take to get that telegram delivered ?"

Clint said that he had a direct wire. He began to click the instrument and David leaned on the window ledge, waiting. Clint's narrow shoulders humped under his shirt, his bony hand worked agilely with a bucking movement. Gus Roberts would be at the other end of the wire ; David had played hookey with Gus when they were youngsters. Every settler had some kind of gun for hunting and there were guns for sale in the stores but not many cartridges; David did not see how the town could be defended, anyway. The buildings were scattered. He felt faint, and with relief he remembered that he had not eaten that day.

Fatty Hardin stepped out of his hotel across the street and raised a racket between a spike and a stove shovel; it was suppertime. The Boles young ones guiltily stopped playing with sawed-off bits from rafters and gathered them up for the wood-box. With a few final licks for good measure, shingling stopped on the roof behind the new saloon's false front. In all, six men hustled into the hotel for supper.

The clicking stopped. Clint said he could not raise Gus, who had probably shut up the depot and gone home. "I'll keep trying, on the chance he'll come by and hear me. Gosh, Dave, everything I've got in the world is out here."

The door at the top of the waiting-room stairs opened and Mrs. Insull called down. "Mr. Insull! Supper!"

Clint got hold of himself and called back that he was busy. The door shut exasperated, and he said, "The missus sets a lot of store by her furniture. How many redskins you say? Hell, if they start, the men in the camps'll handle them, won't they?"

There was a big territory to cover, and the Indians knew the country. Dave went across to Boles' store. Jeremiah Boles came in from the back room, wiping his mustache, and David asked for ten cents' worth of cheese and crackers. Mrs. Boles and the young ones were at supper beyond the kitchen doorway.

"Indians are threatening trouble at Turtle Creek," David said.

"They start anything, I guess we can handle 'em," Jeremiah Boles replied. He handed over the crackers and cheese, but David's mind changed and he asked him to wrap them up. Mary might fancy them ; she had not tasted any delicacies for a long time.

At the hitching posts Mr. Peters was looking over the bay mare. He said in surprise, "She yours, Dave ? Trade for her ?" Then ; "What's up ?"

He got on the sorrel in a hurry. The bay sighed under David's weight but started willingly. They rode along the path by the railroad embankment where it crossed the slough. Darkness was rising from the land and the rustle of coarse slough grass in the wind gave a man the impression of an ambush.

"You think Gebbert can hold them three days ?" Mr. Peters asked. David said they were on a hair-trigger when he left, but Gebbert would hold them if anybody could. What they wanted was the body of that papoose ; they raised a row about that, as if they had human feelings.

Mr. Peters said that nobody could depend on the treacherous devils. They gave no warning, and a prairie like this might be full of them. In Indian Territory ten thousand of them were in the creek bottoms before a settler knew it, and he had known fifty to appear on an empty prairie in the time it took a man to turn the plow at the end of a furrow. He intended to move his family to the townsite that night.

There were lights in the shanties beyond the slough, one in Eliza's window. Three lights within a mile, eight more scattered to the east, and the houselights in town, looked like settled country. But there was loneliness from the large pale sky and the unbroken sound of the wind.

The horses pricked up their ears, halting a little ; something was in the darkness ahead. Mr. Peters reined sharply, the sorrel's shoulder struck the bay's. A last creak of saddle leather stopped. There was a solid shape in the dark. Rustles crawled in the slough.

David's idea was to ride on quietly, taking the chance. The lights still burning in the shanties made it impossible to turn back. The brassy tang was on his tongue again. Mr. Peters let out his breath in a roar. "Who's there?"

Nettie answered gaily. She and Gay stepped from the narrow path when the horses came up. There was something white at her throat; she held her head proudly, one hand was tucked in Gay's arm.

"We're moving in town tonight," her father told her. "There's an Indian scare."

"A what!" Startled, Gay laughed.

David was suddenly furious. "Indians, you fool! You and your blithering idiot of a father! Coming out here, robbing their graveyards, of all the dum foolishness, bringing those screeching redskins down on us, women and children, you —"

"Say!" Gay cried out.

"None of that. Settle it later." Mr. Peters took Nettie's hand and she went up behind him. "You moving to town, Dave?"

David said he was. Mr. Peters had his wagon and the harness of the dead horse for the bay. David said the bay must have feed and rest; he would bring her over in an hour or so. That gave the Peters family time to pack. At their shanty he dismounted and walked on with Gay. Gay was astounded by what David had told him; he asked who could have imagined that redskins gave a darn for bodies they left hanging around in trees. Dr. Thorne had spoken of traveling through Iowa; Gay did not think he had reached home yet.

116

Eliza was writing in her journal. The window framed her, stylishly dressed and inclined with elegance above the writing case on her knee, David spoke to her through the window.

"Indians? Mercy!" she exclaimed.

"Get your things together, both of you." David went on to his own house. From the doorway Mary peered into the dark, then came rushing.

"David! My goodness, I couldn't think who. I thought you weren't coming till day after tomorrow." She kissed him.

"How've you been, Molly girl?"

"David, I'm sorry, there isn't a thing to eat in the house, I didn't expect you and we've just been picnicking, Eliza and I, Gay's hardly here at all. If I'd only known."

"It don't matter. Molly." He stopped. "It don't amount to anything, but Peters has got a notion. There's some talk of Indians — " He could feel the word make her rigid. "Nothing to be scared of, they're a long ways from here. Only to be far over on the safe side, Peters thinks we might as well move to town for a few — "

"Move? You mean now?"

"Well, he's loading up now. There's no hurry — "

She saw the mare then. She looked at the tired mare, and again at David. "Some day I hope and pray you'll have sense enough to stop lying to me as if I was a child. How much have we got time to take?"

He told her they had all the time in the world, but only one wagon. "Likely there's no real use in going. I don't have any idea there's — "

"Then we can't take the stove or bedstead." She cried out, "All our furniture! Well," she said, "I'll put what I can in the trunk."

117

He watered and fed the mare and rubbed her down. In the house the bedding was rolled up and Gay forced the trunk lid down. Mary and Eliza were in their best bonnets and old dresses without hoops. Scraps of food were on the bare table. David heard a crunch when he sat down, and ruefully pulled out the smashed parcel of cheese and crackers. "Here's something I got for you."

They ate up the scraps to save them. There were dabs of cold mush and oatmeal, heels of loaves, and jam in the bottoms of jars that Eliza had brought out.

"I told you we had plenty of time, why didn't you make tea ?" David asked.

"We're out of it, and anyway I packed the teapot and cups," Mary said. Tea cost a dollar a pound, but David would have liked a heartening cup. Licking a fingertip, Mary picked up the last crumbs of cracker. For David's benefit she said, "I don't know when I've tasted anything so good."

It was ten o'clock before they could get everything settled, the old harness adjusted to the bay, the wagon loaded, and the heifer tied behind it. They all walked, Nettie holding Flora and Lily by the hand, her mother and Mary bringing Charley between them. David led the team and Mr. Peters and Gay brought up the rear.

"To my mind, it's pure nonsense !" Eliza stated. "Traipsing across country this time of night. If there's no Indians, it's downright folly, and if there's Indians what's to prevent them scalping us this minute, I'd like to know !"

David said there was no danger. He was tired, and he could not get those racing savages out of his mind. There was starlight, but it was misty and the rustling prairie was dark. He led the team along the wagon tracks be-

118

tween tall grass. It was less than two miles to town, but they could go no faster than the slow heifer, heavy with calf.

Outside the town they were hailed cautiously. Two thirteen-year-olds came up, Young Jack Kelsey and Dick Hardin, with rifles. They were on guard. They said that Jeremiah Boles had put out guards, and sent word to the settlers. The town was still awake. The campers' wagons were pulled into the street between the stores and the depot, and homesteaders' wives and children were settling their bedding for the night on the floors of Boles' store and Townsend's. Clint Insull had not been able to raise Gus Roberts, and had given up till morning. David buttonholed Fatty Hardin and told him it was highway robbery to charge twenty-five cents apiece for four ladies and three young ones. Hardin said that the ladies' room was crowded, but if they had their own bedding and could squeeze in, he would call it square for a dollar. Mr. Peters stayed with the loaded wagon. Gay helped David lug the bedding upstairs to the ladies' room, and offered to shake dice with him for cigars.

"Nope, got to take care of the mare," David said. He saw her comfortably bedded in the livery stable, and pulling off his boots for a pillow he slept on the depot platform.

The sun was up when he woke, and half a dozen men were in the depot. Clint had got an answer on the wire. You could see the little brass contraption clicking, not a hand touching it. Gus Roberts, a hundred and ten miles away, was clicking the thing here. It beat all, what men could do nowadays.

David asked, "What does he say?"

"Says he ain't sold. Wants to know what's the joke on Doc."

"Is he there? Has Doc Thorne got there yet, ask him."

"Says he don't think so."

"You tell him I say it's no joke. Tell him Doc vamoosed with an Indian baby's body, for a curiosity. It was petrified, tell him. If he don't get it back here to-day, nothing under God Almighty'll hold those redskins. I saw them with their war paint on, tell him. Tell him I say they mean business. It's another Minnesota massacre, tell him."

The clicking replied that Gus would shut up office and go look for Doc Thorne.

"Hold on!" David shouted. "Doc's driving back through Iowa. Tell him to get men out, down the roads on horseback. We got to get that body, tell him."

Campers' wagons were pulling out, headed back east. Mr. Peters put on his carpenter's apron and climbed back to his job on the saloon roof. In the livery stable David found the mare rested and well fed; that cost him forty cents. He heaved a few empty barrels on to Jake Mostar's wagon for him; the town well was not yet dug and Jake hauled water from Gooseneck Pond and peddled it in town for six cents a gallon.

"Keep your scalp on, Jake!" somebody yelled when Jake started out. Jake lifted his rifle in reply.

The stores were sold out of cartridges, and the store-keepers were telegraphing orders for more to be sent by express. David washed at the hotel's wash-bench and combed his hair and mustache. In the griddle-smoky lean-to, Mary was frying pancakes. He told her not to wear herself out, and she gave him a saucy nudge with her shoulder. "Shoo fly, don't bother me! I love to cook when I've got things to do with."

Gay showed up for breakfast, with forty cigars. He

had been shaking dice all night. Sitting at the end of the long table, he shoved back his hat, put his thumbs in the armholes of his vest, displaying seried cigars in the pockets, and gave an imitation of a city drummer. He wedged a dollar in his eyesocket and talked like a dude Englishman. Breakfast was one long roar. Hilarious, the eaters pushed back their plates reluctantly, and only because ladies were waiting for the table. Gay handed out cigars and they were lighting up when a woman screamed.

It was a terrible, deathly scream, in the street. There was a distant shout, and boots pounding by. Men jammed in the dining room doorway, David could not get through. He ran from the lean-to and up the alley, making for his musket in the wagon. He got hold of it; it was loaded. The street was a confusion of men pouring into it with guns, asking, "What direction? Where are they?" Women were screaming for their children and nobody could hear Mr. Peters' shouts from the roof. Mary ran across the street, dodging among the men, and picked up the Insulls' baby.

Little Jackie Insull had fallen off the bed and out of the depot's upstairs window. Mrs. Insull had screamed that scream when she saw him falling.

Not a bone in him was broken. The yell he let out as soon as he got his breath showed that he was not even hurt. Mary jiggled him, crooning, "There, there, poor lamb, was he scared?"

Mrs. Insull sobbed, taking him, "I just turned my back a second. I wasn't quick enough to catch him." She wept proudly, "It never entered my mind he could climb onto the bed, he's only twenty months old."

"There, there, then. Well, your troubles are only beginning," Mrs. Boles consoled her.

David walked with Jeremiah Boles out past the lumber-yard and the banker's house. The western prairie looked level but it might conceal anything. A faint smudge against the sky was probably dust from a dump where men were working. There was no wind and the day was intensely hot for the time of year.

They went back to the depot. The women were tending store, and Townsend, Cliff Wyatt, Max Stine, Luke Fagarty from the livery stable, were in the depot office. The instrument was clicking, but Clint said that messages were going between stations in the east. The train schedule had been changed since David came west; the train would leave at noon, with or without that papoose on it. That left two hours.

"Maybe all these modern inventions don't amount to so much, after all," David finally said.

"You're dead right," Jeremiah Boles agreed. "They don't amount to any more than the caliber of the men behind 'em. Till every living soul's in a state of saving grace, and with brains to boot, all this speed don't do much but spread cussedness faster."

Clint Insull was up in arms to defend his job, the railroad and the telegraph. "If we do get hold of that doctor and he ships that thing today, that's covering two hundred and twenty miles between sunup and sundown. Two hundred and twenty miles, and that's going on all over this country! Why man alive! We're living in the greatest age this planet ever knew or ever will! And what makes it? The locomotive, and this thing right here. The whole future of this country's part and parcel of railroads, railroads and telegraph. If it wasn't for them, not one of us'd be sitting here today. And look at California. Would America be the greatest nation on earth today if it wasn't for the transcontinental — "

He jumped to answer the instrument. Gus clicked

back that Dr. Thorne had not come home. Boys were riding down toward Iowa looking for him.

Flies buzzed in the sultry air. The heat would probably breed a thunderstorm. The long hand of the clock moved with the ticking. At a quarter to twelve Mr. Peters left his job. He stood jingling the nails in an apron pocket, and with his hammer absently clenched a few sticking out of the depot wall. The hands of the clock finally stood at twelve, then the minute hand jerked past. It jerked twice more, and David said, "Guess she's pulled out."

"Hear the report in a minute," Clint admitted.

Fatty Hardin anxiously asked if this meant certain trouble. Jeremiah Boles said, "Well, boys, got plenty of cartridges coming." They spoke about sending women and children out on the train, and stood around silent. The train fare would be considerable and nobody knew for certain. You couldn't tell, maybe the whole thing would blow over.

"If there's anything short of a cyclone will take Mrs. Insull away from her furniture — " Clint broke off, and taking his pencil from his left ear, he leaned to tap a click or two. He listened, and jumped up, snapping the pencil in two. "He's got it! He held the train! He's got it on the train!"

He went on listening and telling them. Dr. Thorne had not gone through Iowa. Gus had happened to catch a glimpse of him coming down North Elm Street just as the train pulled in between them. Gus had held the train, boxed the papoose, and given it to the conductor, no express charges. "Says Doc's in a lather about it, there now."

"The darn skeezicks, the son of a gun!" David pounded Clint's bony shoulder as if he were Gus. "You

123

tell him I say he's a son of a gun, blast his darned old blasted hide !"

Going jubilant across the street, most of the crowd dropped into the saloon for a drink. Others went on to dinner. In the lean-to kitchen Mary was helping Mrs. Hardin dish up fried beefsteaks and gravy, mashed potatoes, corn-bread. A row of pies was under mosquito bar on a shelf ; so much food reminded David of his mother's kitchen.

He leaned against the doorjamb, taking off his hat. "Well, it's coming. Gus put it on the train. So if the train don't go off the rails, I guess we're all set."

Mary lifted the knife from the corn-bread. "Who's going to take it out there ?"

"I am," David said in surprise.

"Seems to me you've done enough for one while. Somebody else might do something for a change. I'd like to know what that Gebbert thinks he's paying you for."

"Gosh." David straightened up. "Gebbert's all wool and a yard wide. I don't know what you're talking about."

"I'm talking about you staying where you belong. I don't know why somebody else can't go out there. I think you've done enough and that's flat !"

She was trembling. David said quietly, "See here, you're all tired out. Why don't you go upstairs and rest ?"

"Because I don't want to, that's why !" Mrs. Hardin tactfully stepped into the dining room. Mary slashed furiously through the corn-bread. "He isn't paying you for anything of the kind !"

"What, Gebbert ? That don't have anything to do with it. Anyway, I've got his mare."

"What does have anything to do with it, I'd like to know? There's men enough that aren't married. All you think of's that old Gebbert and his old horse!"

"She's turning six-year-old." He could not believe that Mary was ranting at him so. She turned away from him and he pleaded, "Mary."

He grew slowly angry, standing there behind her rigid back while she piled slabs of corn-bread on plates. Suddenly she faced him, pale. She leaned on her hands gripping the edge of the table behind her and her eyes, not meeting his, looked blind. "All right, David. I'm all right now. Do you have to go tonight?"

"Soon as the train gets in. I ought to make Miller's camp by dark."

"Well, go wash up so you can get to the first table. There's dried-apple pies but they won't hold out and I made one with cinnamon and nutmeg like you like it."

22

At work on the saloon roof, Mr. Peters was first to sight the train smoke. The train was coming, it had not gone off the rails. David led the saddled bay to the hitching posts and strapped his musket on her. He wore Luke Fagarty's pistol and cartridge belt.

On the platform Clint Insull came up to him and said, "About that telegram, Dave. It's a dollar-forty-three." David paid him.

They could see the bell-mouthed smokestack now, and the shine of sun on the headlight. Sparks flew upward in billowing black smoke. At the mile post the whistle shrieked, a white geyser rose against the black, and the rails began to vibrate. Nerve flinched before the monster looming up at inhuman speed. At the last instant it rushed by with a deafening roar, clanging, grinding, snorting steam, bringing a blast of oily heat, the sooty fireman jerking the bell cord. Coal-tender, baggage car, box cars, immigrant car, coach and caboose banged to a stop.

Gus had packed the mummy in a wooden cracker box. It was difficult to rope on the mare ; David decided to carry it. In a fight or a run from Indian ponies, its weight would be something to get rid of in a hurry. Luke said a last word about the pistol and others called out, "So long, Dave !" "Good luck !" Mary was among the women on the street corner, her hands twisted in her apron and a sunbonnet shading her face. Eliza looked anxiously excited, Nettie lifted her hand. He put the mare into a long easy gallop which lifted the dust behind him.

The level country kept coming in low swells. Nothing ominous appeared on the horizon but there was no reassurance in a land which concealed itself, and no knowing what else, in its folds.

Every few miles a smudge of dust appeared, then men and horses working. They stopped to answer his shout. They had no news from Turtle Creek. David rode on, watchful till he saw the next smudge. The road was empty, not a prairie schooner nor a teamster on it. Beyond Miller's camp there would be a stretch of eighteen miles without a gang working ; Gebbert's sub-contractors there had finished their jobs and pulled up stakes.

The slender moon followed the sun below the skyline. He rode on through the long twilight and on in starlight. On a grassy land rolling so shadowy, a man can see anything and eyes are worse than useless. Miller's camp was there, undisturbed, asleep when he rode in. Sleepily from his blankets the stableman said that they had no news from Turtle Creek.

At three o'clock David saddled up. Eighteen miles would not have been a long ride if the country had not been deserted. The mare's hoofbeats were a lonely sound. A slinking thing on the crest of a swell was no doubt a coyote. The air brightened, thin sunshine lay on eastern slopes, meadow larks sprang upward singing. A wide column of smoke stood against the sky ahead. It rose from Turtle Creek camp, or near it.

David looked at it while the mare loped on. It was not thick enough to come from burning buildings. It might be rising from a smolder of buildings burned the night before. If a man wanted to turn back, he could not tell himself that he went to report that smoke ; it was certainly visible to the awakening camp behind him. Fear was not quite as strong as the necessity to act like a brave man.

There were nine miles to go before he could see the camp-site. Nine miles ahead, a long, gentle slope went up a swell through which the railroad cut. From the top, when driving in with his teamster's load, he first saw the long, low shanties, the stable, granary and store at Turtle Creek, a mile farther on.

Only the vigilance of God could have watched those miles of prairie. Beyond the corner of the eye things moved, gone before David could look at them. Birds took to wing suddenly, as if startled. A small herd of antelope leaped out of the level mid-distance and fled. The small of the back knew that something was there. But each dip of the road went through a shallow hollow where David could see nothing but grass and wild flowers in sunshine.

At the bottom of the last one he dismounted, tethered the mare to the box, and took his musket. The sun was two hours high, the birds had stopped their morning clamor and the country was still. He and the mare cast the only shadows. The slope lifted the horizon, near and green.

He went up it cautiously, stooping. Near its top he took to hands and knees, then stretched out and hitched forward between bluestem clumps.

It shocked him to see the tar-paper roofs. The camp was there. He saw its long, raw-lumber walls and then he saw against them the Indians on their ponies. Their rifles glinted. Mounted Indians swarmed through the camp like ants. He saw a line of them wind past the store and out between granary and stable. In the murmurous silence of the prairie there was not a yell nor a shot. Then he made out blue shirts bent and moving, a shovel flashed minutely. A team climbed the dump and a scraper glittered belly-up from a puff of dust. Another team followed. Work was going on as usual.

David scrambled up and waved his hat, swearing aloud in admiration. He galloped into camp past smoldering fires and through the swarm of Indians as if they were gnats. Pete hailed him from the embankment. "Hi yuh, Dave?" Casting an eye over the dump, he gave an order, "Fill 'er in over here, boys," and hitching up his suspenders he sauntered down. "Got it, uh?"

"You bet you! Where's Gebbert?"

"Pow-wowing out there with the chiefs. He saw you coming, don't worry." Pete spat tobacco juice and grinned across the mare's rump; turning, David saw the Indian coming. The painted redskin and the free pony came

128

like one animal in fluid motion, and swifter than the mind could follow the rifle flicked this way and that, at Pete, at the cook. David's breath stopped. The round black muzzle held steady, a black eye squinted behind the accurate aim, the brown finger curled on the trigger. The blackness of the muzzle swelled enormous. This passed before David could think. It passed at a gallop, and on the store porch the lounging storekeeper yawned at it.

"Whew!" David let his breath out.

"Gets you the first time. Gives a fellow the willies," said Pete.

"How long has this been going on?"

"Off and on, since you left. They quit awhile when they see they can't scare us. You ought to heard the jamboree last night around their fires. Say, this place was lit up as bright as day, and talk about yowling. Seems the chief's had quite a time to hold 'em. We ain't slept since Hector was a pup. Well, I better get back on the job. Old man'll be along in a minute."

Nobody but Gebbert could have held so many men peaceably working through that. He came along among them, speaking a word here and there, and asked David to take the box out of sight of the Indians and open it up. "Make sure it's all right, like it was when you saw it before. We don't want a slip-up now. You made good time, son. Take dinner in the cookshanty before you start back, there's pumpkin pies."

While the team drew his wagon over the swell that afternoon, David looked back. On the prairie beyond Turtle Creek hundreds of Indians were massed. Around them their scattered ponies grazed, and in the midst of the mass a thread of smoke rose from a small open space. Because he knew what to look for, David made out six blue shirts in a circle of blanketed chiefs.

129

Toward sunset Halfbreed Jack overtook him and rode a little way beside the wagon. He said that the Indians had left Turtle Creek, and David asked him to take the word to the townsite. The halfbreed galloped on. His pony was gaudily bridled but he rode without a saddle, he rode in the Indian way. David would never forget that fluid motion of free redskin and free animal together, nor the shock of facing small, black death in the muzzle of a gun.

23

A terrific thunderstorm broke the heat that night. It drenched David in his blanket and turned the road to mud. He stopped twice next day to unhitch and help haul out bogged teamsters, and he made less than ten miles. Two days later he saw locomotive smoke and came to the end of the rails.

The train had advanced twelve miles west of the townsite. Another town was growing there, its saloon already doing business, and Gebbert's goods were there in box cars. David's haul would not take him home again that summer.

He borrowed a saddle and rode Star on, taking a day and a half off without pay to see that Mary was settled at home again. In town Mr. Peters told him that the women had moved back to the claims. He had not been able to help them, since the building boom was ended and he would lose his last carpentering job if he left it. Nettie and Mary had led the sorrel back and forth through the slough-mud after the rain, hauling back the load little by little. "You can't stop a woman when she's got her dander up," Mr. Peters said.

"Where was Gay?" David demanded.

"Didn't he run across you?" Gay had lit out to the camps.

"Well — " David let that go. "If you're going to be out of a job, how about a deal to cut my hay?" He owned a scythe and pitchfork, and undertook to buy the lumber for a light hay-rack if Mr. Peters would make it. Using one of the doubletrees as a singletree, even without shafts, the sorrel could pull a light load. Slough hay was so much better than any other for burning that Mr. Peters agreed to put up David's for half, and to stack his bluestem for two dollars an acre.

It was good to come home. Grass was green on the sod walls of the house, white curtains were looped behind its clean windows. Mary came running out. The sod-potatoes were pushing up crinkled leaves, and beyond the sod stable, knee-deep in blowing grasses, the cow was grazing with the wobbly-kneed calf beside her. The calf was a heifer.

There was time before supper to walk over the land. Mary held onto his arm while they leaned into the wind that flapped her skirts and her sunbonnet. He showed her where the pastures would be, and the meadow, the wheat field, the cornfield and the oats. That wild-goose chase with the posse had not left him time to set out a windbreak or the tree-claim, but next year they would have a garden, and almost fifteen acres of wheat.

"And next spring, by the eternal, I'll break fifty acres of this sod if it kills me. By year after next, we'll really begin to get going!"

After supper, when Eliza had gone to her shanty, he took Mary on his lap. She turned down the lamp-wick and he blew out the light. Windows and doors were open, but the wind struck the north end of the house and blew past, so that only eddies flapped the curtains. There

131

was a faint shine on the prairie, from the setting moon and the stars. Far out on the grasslands paler than the sky, coyotes yapped laughing.

They talked a long time, and David said, "When the little shaver's big enough to ride, we'll get him a pony."

He found that Mary's cheeks were wet with tears. She tried to stop them and could not. She kept saying that she was all right. "It isn't anything, don't pay any attention." Suddenly she was crying like a child. "I want to go home. Oh, please, please let's go home! Can't we go home?"

Immediately she was saying that she did not mean it, she did not know what had got into her. Everything they had was here, and there was no real danger from Indians. "Don't pay any attention to it, David; I wasn't myself for a minute, that's all, I guess it's my condition. I didn't mean it, honestly. I don't. I wouldn't give up and go home now, if we could."

He had thought that this was their home. But there was no use in saying so, if she did not feel that it was.

24

Eliza and Gay were going home in October. In September Gebbert's camp was thirty miles west of Turtle Creek. David took three days off to spend one day at home. The prairie was tawny, the nights were cool, and the wild ducks and geese were flying south.

He found Mary in good spirits. There was butter now; in the cooler weather the milk no longer soured before the cream rose, and though she did not have a churn, Mary made shift to beat the sour cream with a spoon until the butter came. She had always liked to work with milk; proudly she showed the half-pound pat with the clover leaves turned from her butter-mold. It was pale because the cow was on wild grass and she had no carrot-juice to color it, but it was good, firm butter. She and Eliza had dug the sod-potatoes, and they had helped in the haying. Long stacks of slough hay were on either side of the back door, and well-cured bluestem was stacked by the stable for the stock.

Eliza asked why David did not let Mary come home for the winter, to have the baby at her mother's house, and quickly Mary said, "I wouldn't think of it. I wouldn't dream of leaving David to bach it all by himself out here, and we can't both leave the stock." It was plain that she had been thinking about it.

Eliza said smartly that she and Gay had served their time for that year, though Gay had been let off for bad behavior. Gay laughed. He had bought a fine saddle horse, he was smoking ten-cent cigars, and he carried himself with a jauntiness which David could not have shown in his place. David wondered that such women as Mary and Eliza seemed to admire it. Gay had raked in so much money from card games that Gebbert had ordered him out of his camps.

"You're popular around here, Thorne," Gebbert said. "And I don't say you're crooked. But you're too damn lucky. When work shuts down, my men go out with enough in their jeans to live on till work opens up next spring. I see to it they do, savvy? Be glad to see you around here again, any time you're looking for trouble."

Now in late September, other contractors saw forfeits coming down on them for not winding up the work on time and they were driving their men to hurry, while the men were slowing down to prolong their jobs. They worked sullenly in the cold and the sharp, blowing dust;

133

they lost tools and broke them, tangled harness, even lamed horses, and they moved slower than molasses in January. The company had taken back most of their wages through the company stores and the cookshanties, and on riotous pay days they had wasted the balance. Now the long winter was ahead, when they could not get work. Fights broke out in the camps. At Miller's there was a big riot. All along the line the men dropped tools, jumped on horses and went piling into Miller's. They strung up the paymaster and wrecked the company store.

Only Gebbert's men worked with a Hurrah, boys ! from sunup to sundown, and came tramping back to the cookshanty singing a new verse of the old song.

> Finish up the contract for the day comes around,
> Can we do the job, boys, we'll do it up brown,
> And hit the high places for a high old time,
> Working for old Gebbert on the Northwestern Line !

They said and swore to it that Gebbert owed the railroad forty thousand dollars ; the company would never see a red cent of it ; Gebbert had it salted away in the east. He was a rich man. Every mother's son of them was going out with cash for the winter. They cheered old Gebbert and Gebbert's clean bunks and Gebbert's cook and the cook's pies, and the cheering wagon loads pulled out to go singing along the road to the east.

David drove home. There would be no more work for wages ; next year the railroad camps would be far to the west. The country was settling down to homesteaders. David said, "Well, Molly girl, here I am, home to stay. Here we are, you and me, on our farm."

They figured up what they had : $204.63, after paying for the breaking and the haying. They had fifteen acres to be sowed next spring, the house, the stable, team and wagon and two plows, the cow and calf. The calf was clear gain for that year. "And we've lived, don't forget that, Mary."

They had fuel for the winter, the stock could get through on hay ; they could manage to live and buy seed with the money he had earned that summer. It would last longer if Mary spent the winter with her folks ; they both thought of that, but neither of them spoke about it. He would not ask her if she wanted to go.

He took the plow out next morning. The dry sods were tough mats of grass-roots not yet rotted, rough to stumble over and clogging the plow, but the weather was fine for fall plowing. He worked the fifteen acres over, both ways. Toward the end he was plowing under a light fall of snow, and he finished in a cold drizzle which became a pouring rain while he was doing the chores.

Steadily the rain fell all next day and another night, and when brisk winds cleared the sky about ten o'clock, David hitched up to the breaking-plow. Star and Dobbin were still strong and spirited from the oats he had fed them all summer, and the sod was as wet as it would be in the spring.

He set the heavy steel into it. Straining, with quivering knotted haunches, the horses tugged the share through the earth filled with interlaced roots. It lurched and lodged, stuck while they gathered their strength and jerked it. David stood and swore. He struck his fist on the plowhandle and ground his heel through the dead wet grass till the skin of the sod felt it. He jerked the plow loose and turned the sweating team toward the stable.

Even if he could afford to give Star and Dobbin two quarts of oats at a feeding, they could not break that sod. He must sell them or trade them for oxen ; let them go the way of horses among strangers, from hand to hand

135

till they ended old and sick, underfed, overloaded and beaten.

Mary came out to meet him. She was wrapped in her heavy shawl, though the day was not cold. Heavy and clumsy now, she hid herself as much as she could. Her face was fuller, softer than it had been, and the sheen was gone from the dark hair. She asked him anxiously, "What's wrong, David?"

"Just putting up the team. Thought I'd dig a pit for the potatoes."

"Oh." She hesitated. "Eliza's ready for you to rope her trunk when you have time."

"Mary," he began, but his mind changed. "Be kind of nice when we're to ourselves, won't it? It's a snug house, and the Peters for neighbors. You'll have Mrs. Peters with you when the time comes, and I've been thinking, there's the sled runners saved from last year and it won't break us to buy a couple of boards, I'll make us a pung. Along towards spring when we get a spell of fine weather we can wrap up the little shaver and go to church meetings in town."

"Yes," she said. "Let's. I'd enjoy going to church again." Her smile dimpled her cheeks now; he could not be sure what was in her eyes. She gazed across the graying prairie. There was no skyline, the distances were hazy, and high overhead the wild birds called to each other, flying south. "I'll go tell Eliza you'll rope her trunk for her, then," Mary said.

That evening the Peters family came over to tell Eliza goodby. She was going on the train next day. Gay had already gone, on his saddle horse. Many of the homesteaders had gone east, or moved to town for the winter; the only lights were the houselights in town, and one glimmer from a sod shanty across the slough where a man named Johnson was baching. The moon filled the sky so full of light that there was no stars. Above a shadowy flatness there was only the cool radiance, full of wild birds' calling.

They all sat outdoors, talking late in the moonlight. David spoke of the amazing change in the country since he built the claim shanties a year ago. Now there was the town, the railroad, the telegraph, and some sod broken on almost every quarter-section. He remarked, too, that the weather seemed to promise an open winter.

Mr. Peters pointed out that the geese and ducks were flying in multitudes through the night, and high. He said that the rabbits' fur was the thickest he had ever seen. All summer David had had no time for hunting, and they agreed to make a full day of it, with horses, as soon as the weather turned cold enough to keep meat. Mr. Peters believed they could get an antelope apiece.

Toward morning David started awake ; Mary was getting out of bed to put more covers on it. Winds were howling. He told Mary to lie still, and swung out into the biting cold. He spread quilts over Mary and she asked, "Is the water-pail freezing ?"

He lighted the lamp and saw the solid white swirl against the windows. It was three o'clock ; the thermometer stood at thirty degrees. He got into his clothes and lighted a fire. Only a few sticks of hay were in the box, but he could not get lost between the haystacks at the back door.

"This time we're fixed for a blizzard !" he said, glad to see Mary lying disheveled and cozy, and the lamplit walls around them. The blizzard did not even shake those solid walls. It seized him when he opened the door, but blindly he got in again with all the hay he could carry. The house was full of smoke.

137

He got his breath, wiped away the bloody tears, and saw smoke puffing through every crevice of the stove. The fire was blazing in gusts. The mercury had gone down to zero.

He would not let Mary get up. He set back the table with its leaves down, pulled the bed close to the stove, and sat twisting hay and feeding the fire. Powdered snow, driven through the cracks around doors and windows, drifted on the floor.

Unexpectedly Mary laughed. "This time," she declared gaily, "I'm going to wash your face with snow."

"Don't you stir out of that bed."

"Hand me my clothes. Don't be a goose, one person can't do everything." She coughed, strangling in the smoke. "I saved those muslin strips, I'm going to caulk the windows."

"Where are they? I'll do that, you stay by the stove and twist hay."

With the case-knife he forced the cloth against the sharp cold. Ice-powder still gritted underfoot but the mercury stopped falling. He hung a quilt over the back door, weighting it down with hammer and flatiron, and laying chairs on the bed he hung quilts over them to the floor. The cold lessened in that corner. Mary was cheerful.

He must bring Eliza from her unheated shanty, and there was no rope in the house. He thought that he could make his way along the slough and, with a short line of some kind, reach the shanty.

"You don't set foot out of this house, David Beaton, without a rope the whole way," said Mary. That was not possible; the distance was nearly a quarter of a mile. "You don't do it," she told him. He had never suspected such force in her.

138

"Look here, Mary. I've got to — "

"Wait." She opened her trunk and took out her sheets. He knew how proud she was of them, made and laid away through her girlhood, every one of the best quality bleached muslin with wide knitted lace across the top, and pillow cases to match.

"How about tablecloths? and the curtains?"

"They'd ravel easier. I don't trust them."

With quick jerks at the thread, she ripped off the lace. She slashed the shears through the hems. He helped her tear the strips and knotted them together.

"David. Take care of yourself."

"Don't you worry," he told her. "I can't get lost now. I'll be back."

It took a long time to find his way. When at last he groped around the shanty and burst in, a deadly quiet voice said through the dark, "Stand still or I'll shoot."

They might have known that Eliza would have sense enough to stay in bed. She dressed and lighted the lamp, and he was amazed to see an actual pistol lying on the tumbled bunk. He looked at her dumbfounded; he believed she would have used it. They made a roll of her bedding. He tied it on his back, she took the kerosene can, and he warned her on no account to let go of him.

She gasped when the blizzard struck them. The cold seemed to be increasing, but that might be only the icy particles penetrating their clothes. Eliza's weight leaned heavy or sagged away, as the winds flung it. He groped along the edge of the slough, in terror lest the whips of coarse grass break the fragile line. The stinging blackness was gray before they blundered against the house.

Mary weighed the quilt against the door again and helped them take off their stiff wraps. She had set the table on end; it held up a quilt pinned to those over the chairs on the bed, and to the window curtain. The heat penned around the stove made that corner comfortable. Tea was boiling and Mary had stirred up pancake batter. She cut chunks of molasses from the jug into the cups and said, "We'll have breakfast in a jiffy."

The smoke made them all cough. Eliza declared, "Well, I wouldn't have missed it. So this is a blizzard. Land! Listen to that!"

"Sounds like it might blow up a storm," David remarked.

Mary put pancakes on their plates. David sat on the hay-box; it was almost empty again. She said, "Eat your breakfast first, David."

Their hair crackled. Eliza put out the lamp to see more clearly the queer light flickering down the stovepipe and over the stove. Flashes leaped when Mary touched the case-knife to the iron spider. Globules of fire dripped from the stove and rolled harmlessly on the floor. They would follow David's jackknife blade. Eliza tried to lift one on a darning needle, but it vanished.

Outside the barricade of quilts, the mercury had climbed almost to freezing. It fell again when David twice opened the door to bring in a supply of hay. The storm was gray, the sun must have risen. The time was a quarter to eight, and the milking not done. David took the pail and set out to the stable.

The level ground gave him no help, but he was so sure that he could go to his stable that he did not stop until he had to admit that he must have passed it. To circle, there, might snag and cut the muslin line on the plow. He went back, gathering it in carefully, and advanced again in short arcs. Every sound that winds can make was fierce around him; he could not trust his ears, but he thought he heard a strange thrumming note. Some unknown thing tripped his legs, a blow of the wind caught him off balance and flung him headlong, and the line parted. He felt its tautness jerk and cease in his grip.

The breath had gone out of him. He waited a moment, trying to think. Gingerly he moved his hand; it was true, the line was gone.

He could not think why he must not stir, why he must lie prone where he had fallen. Then he knew. Something had tripped him; he had fallen over something solid. It was there, somewhere, in the storm, and with care he might reach it.

He rolled onto his back, and sat up. Certainly, now, he was facing in the direction from which he had fallen. He leaned and stretched to grope about his feet and beyond. Nothing. He hitched forward, doubling his knees to set his feet down, then he stretched out his legs and bent forward again. His stiff hand struck something. It was the wagon tongue.

The wagon seemed to him to be turned around, but he knew that it stood by the stable. Between the wagon box and the wall, the space was so narrow that his outstretched hands could touch them both. He found the wall, and reached the stable door. The thrumming sound was distinct now; he recognized the cow's moo vibrating inside the walls. Until then he had forgotten the milk pail, dropped when he fell.

He pulled the door open to step into the familiar place, and a weight struck his legs and was snatched away by the winds. The stable floor impossibly rose, sliding under his feet. He clung to the violent door till it slammed and he latched it. There was relief from the winds. The cow bawled above him; her dim head hung against the roof, with weird light flickering on her horns. He was wallowing in a snowbank.

141

Everything was unreal. He managed to take a match from his pocket and light it. The brief light cupped in his hands flared and was gone. He saw the stable half filled with snow, the cow and the horses on it, their rumps against the sloping low roof, their heads held down by halter ropes. The calf, tied shorter, was buried to the ridge of its back. The cow bawled, the calf blatted, the horses shrilly whinnied. In the dark he heard them scrambling and plunging.

Mechanically he said, "Whoa, Whoa-oa, Star, steady. Whoa-oa, Dobbin." The racket of horseflesh against wood ended in a ripping crash and the wind's yell. The blizzard was in. Flapping tar-paper tore and nails squeaked, boards clattered. The whole flimsy roof was going. Star's whinnying scream was lost in turmoil.

David reached for a wall which might not have been there. The picket ropes were leaping on their spike. Often enough his father had thrashed him for not putting things in their places. The ropes were there. He knotted them together, made fast to the wagon wheel, and in time reached a house.

He could not quite account for this unknown house, but after knocking for a time, he fastened the rope to the door handle and went in. He saw two women by a stove, inside a curtain of quilts. They had been twisting hay, neatly, over a spread cloth. Smoke eddied in the air. On a bench a milk pan was set by a lamp. The younger woman, staring at him, let the hay fall from her hands. \

She was pretty, with dark hair curling in bangs above a broad forehead and dark-lashed gray eyes. She had the look of a merry and capable woman, now desperately anxious. Under the prettiness you could see how she would look when she was old.

"I don't mean any harm, ma'am, don't be scared," he said.

"David!" she cried out. "What's the matter?"

"That's my name," he said. "David Beaton. Must be we're neighbors. I'm living on a claim somewheres near here. I got lost in the storm."

She took him by the shoulders, shaking him so violently that his solid weight rocked a little. "David, wake up! David, you know me! I'm your wife, I'm Mary, your wife, you know me. You know me, David!"

It seemed to him that she must be crazy. The other woman stood there, frightened, not offering to help him. He looked at the crazy face clamoring close to his and was sure that he had never set eyes on it before. Firmly, but not roughly because of her condition, he put her away from him. And he knew her. She was Mary. She was his wife, and this was their home, the muslin walls, the quilts, the lamp, Eliza, the stove, the hay-box, everything lost its strangeness and was familiar.

He sat down. Nothing had been like this terror, this knowing that his own mind was not sure, not safe. It shook his body. Mary held a slopping cup of tea to his mouth and urged him to drink. He took it from her steadily enough and said, "I'm all right."

"Mercy on us! What a turn you gave us," Eliza gasped. He gulped the scalding hot tea rank with the taste of sorghum. There was safety if he could trust it; he knew what he was tasting. Sorghum molasses, made in Nebraska. New Orleans blackstrap was a smoother sweetness; it cost twenty cents a gallon more. He ventured farther, with increasing safety: twenty cents a gallon more, at Boles' store in the townsite. The prices at Townsend's were the same. "That hits the spot," he

143

said. "Got another cup of it?" Suddenly he remembered. "The stock! The stable roof's gone. I've got to get the stock in here or they'll freeze! They're freezing now."

It was past nine o'clock. He did not know how long ago he had left the stable. Mary begged him not to go out again, but a man can not let his stock freeze. He told her that he had the picket ropes, and he tightened the icy muffler around his face.

Eliza said that he could not get the stock in. "You can't possibly. There isn't room."

"Make room. Take down the quilts, pile things up. Throw 'em out! There's got to be room for the stock. Drive some spikes into the studding, to tie 'em to."

Star and Dobbin came docilely. They crowded together between the bed and the wall. Trunks, table, cupboard, chairs, piled to the ceiling would not make room for the cow and calf until he took down the bedstead. "Pile that stuff up again against the wall and put the bedding on it."

He knew that it would be a hard job to lead the cow and calf through the storm, and untied the rope from the door to give him leeway for the struggle. The calf was not broken to lead, the cow was frantic and brainless; neither would stir without the other, and though David tied them together it was all but impossible to make them both move in the same direction at once. They wore out his strength jerking him about, blind in the storm. Many times, at the end of the rope, he was near giving up and letting them go, but he took a fresh grip on himself and held on.

He blundered at last against a haystack and the headlong brutes almost knocked him down. If these were the haystacks by the stable he would give up, licked. But

144

he found the back door. The cow would not go in. He tightened the rope behind her haunches, cornering her and the calf against the haystack, and kicked and belabored her while she hooked the hay, till the calf lunged over the threshold and she lumbered after it.

He sat down, too tired to struggle with his wraps. Mary took off his shoes. Pain blazed through his scarred feet in the oven, so they were all right.

"Nothing like exercise to keep a fellow warm," he said, easing the solid ice from his mustache. "What's the temperature in here?"

It was below zero again, the door had been open so long. "Well, there's no great loss without some gain," Eliza continued. "The stock will help keep us warm. How long will this last?"

"God Almighty knows," David replied. Snow had come in while the door was open; Mary was sweeping it up. The stove puffed out more smoke. Star and Dobbin whinnied hungrily and pawed the floor, the cow did not stop bawling. Her swollen udder dripped. It was past eleven o'clock and she had not been milked yet. David jammed the shoes onto his feet.

Mary protested, "Rest and warm a minute first." But the hay-box was emptied again, and he must lug in hay and snow to water and feed the stock. He knew that this settled it; Mary must go back to her folks in the east for the winter.

"Good Godfrey, milk that cow!" he roared at Eliza.

25

The blizzard lasted five days. Three more days passed before they saw the smoke of a train advancing above the low-blowing snow. The next day was clear, and he drove Mary and Eliza to the train.

Mary did not want to go without him. He did not want to see his father until he could pay for Dobbin. A year ago he had left the east with nearly seven hundred dollars in cash ; he would not go back now, in debt, to live all winter on his folks.

"You go along," he kept saying to Mary, until she flatly refused. Then he agreed to follow her, for a short visit. The baby would be born about Thanksgiving time.

The snow was melting and under a bright blue sky the wind was mild. The sod was moist ; this was weather in which a man with oxen could get a little fall breaking done.

He helped Mary carefully up the steps and carried the satchels behind her hoop skirts squeezing along the aisle. The plush seats, the rich woodwork, were the same as they had been a year ago. He put the satchels on the rack and said, "Well, settled all right for the trip ?"

"Where is the lunch ? Eliza, have you got our lunch ?" Eliza had it. He took off his hat and leaned on the back of Eliza's seat, looking at Mary. Her gloved hand took his and clung to it. The train would stand there five minutes.

He said, "Well, remember me to the folks."

"I will. David — " Tears brightened her eyes. She bent her head and he saw her little fur cap. She was wearing the shawl over her coat because she could not button the coat now.

"Take good care of yourself," he said. He could not kiss her, there in public.

"You'll be coming. It's only five weeks. David, write to me. Let me know what day to expect you."

"Sure I will. I'll be there, sure. Let me know how you are."

"I will, I promise. I'll write you a card tonight as soon as we get in."

"Well," he said, "give my regards to your folks. Tell Jay hello."

"I will. You will write, David?"

"You bet. You be sure and let me know how you're getting along."

At last the train jerked. "Goodby," he said hurriedly. "Goodby, Eliza." He stood outside the window, stiffly smiling at their faces looking out. Bareheaded men were loading eight pine boxes into the baggage car. Mary could not see them; she nodded and waved, a smile set on her face. David walked along beside the window till the noisy wheels took it away.

Mr. Peters told him that the pine boxes contained a whole family, father, mother, and six children. Their folks had telegraphed to ship their bodies home. They had been found frozen to death in their claim shanty two miles east. The blizzard had torn out their stovepipe and ripped off most of the tar-paper roof.

"That's a risk I'm not taking again," said Mr. Peters. He could not pay rent, but he was determined to shelter his family near neighbors in town. The telegraph reported more than two hundred western settlers killed by that one blizzard.

David suggested that they might make some kind of a three-cornered deal. They inquired around town, and ended by renting an unfinished store building with a roofless sod shanty behind it. Jake Hewitt, the banker, had taken the property on the mortgage when the boom collapsed; he had no use for it until spring. It needed carpenter work, and the heifer he had bought would not be fresh till April, so he rented them the building for carpentering and two quarts of milk a day. Mr. Peters agreed to take care of the stock while David was in the east, for the balance of the milk, if David with his team would haul in the hay from their claims.

The mild weather continued while David hauled the hay and roofed his own stable with sods, tied down till the grass-roots would take hold in the spring. A sod roof was dirty, but he figured that it would stay on. When the stock were out of the house he scrubbed the scarred, manure-stained floor as well as he could. It needed scrubbing with lye, but there were no wood ashes to make lye. Nothing would clean the smoke-grimed muslin walls, every attempt only streaked them. He tightened the wires that braced the prairie-chimney, locked up, and drove to town with the bedding and sod-potatoes, the cow and calf tied behind the wagon.

Mr. Peters was putting up partitions to make a kitchen and bedroom in the rear of the store-building. David unrolled his bedding in a front corner, and Nettie came with a dishpan to help him carry in the potatoes.

"I bet I carry more dishpansful than you carry pails !" she teased him merrily.

"All right, what'll you bet ?" He saw the long, fine curve of her mouth. "Bet you a kiss !"

"You can't win ! I'm three ahead already !"

"See here !" he called after her. "Whichever way, I can't lose !"

They raced in and out of the windy sunshine and the big room smelling of new lumber, where Mr. Peters was sawing boards. Flora squealed in excitement, carrying her apron full to help David. Charley clambered into the wagon and jumped out to clamber up again, counting wildly, "Seven, six, nine, ten !" Mr. Peters enjoyed the fun. Breathless, they scrambled for the last potatoes and dumped them hilariously on the pile.

"Pay up, you win !"

She made a little face at him. "Come wash, it's dinnertime."

Snow began falling that afternoon while he thatched the stable, and Mr. Peters came out to help. The large flakes fell pleasantly, with little wind, but so thickly that they could hardly see each other. Wind rose with the early dusk and they worked on by flaring lantern-light to get the stock under shelter. Nettie did the chores. It was ten o'clock when they blew through the snowstorm into the lamplit kitchen where she was keeping supper warm for them.

Next morning the snow was eight inches deep and still falling. The children went out to play in it. Clint Insull's little boy had a sled, which he kept to himself while Charley and Flora and Lucy looked at it wistfully.

"If I had a few boards, I'd make a sled," David said. He and Mr. Peters were working, wrapped up, in the unheated store. They were putting up shelves.

Mr. Peters set his knee on a board and started the saw, then he paused and gave David a quick glance. "Here's the boards. All is, I'd have to think up what to tell Mrs. Peters." David grinned under his muffler. If Jake Hewitt ever missed a few feet of lumber, he would have hard work to prove anything. The banker and his sister lived in a fine house, four rooms, shingled, weather-boarded, even painted. They burned hard coal, at seventeen dollars a ton, in their parlor base-burner and in their kitchen stove.

Next morning when the young ones found the sled in the lean-to and dragged it in, big-eyed and stammering with ecstasy and doubt that it could be theirs, Mrs. Peters told them to thank David. Flora climbed onto his knee and hugged him. Her thin little body in his arms and her

149

kiss smacking under his eye were strangely upsetting. He knew then that his son, or daughter, must not grow up to be a thief.

The snowfall continued, with shouts of children building a snowman in the street. Every man in town turned out to watch the train come roaring in spray from a snowplow. On the sixth day it did not come. The storekeepers, expecting goods, were anxious, and almost everyone was at the depot next morning to hear news of the wreck.

"Great guns, boys, listen to this!" Clint Insull sang out. There was no wreck. The snowplow had stuck in the drifts. The train had backed to Brookings, and the division superintendent offered two dollars a day for men with shovels to clear the tracks.

"Hurrah!" Cliff Wyatt yelled. They slogged pellmell across the street behind him; he was sold out of shovels as fast as he could hand them over. In the excitement he would have sold the last one and had none himself, if Mrs. Wyatt had not stopped him. David burst into the store, shouting, "Come on with your shovel, Peters!"

Jake Hewitt and Clint Insull were the only men who did not go. Twenty-two men and six boys went tramping down the tracks through the snowstorm, eight miles to the cut that had buffaloed the steam engine's snowplow. Shovelfuls of snow were already flying when they got there. The train was puffing on the track; it had brought fourteen men from Brookings.

There were too many men. They cleared out that cut almost before they were warmed up to the job. They came roaring down the track on the train, stuck in another cut, shoveled that one out, came on again. They shoveled through five cuts and brought the train in at six o'clock that night. In nine hours they had shoveled themselves out of that job. Even at the double wages, they had earned only $1.48 apiece.

Before noon next day, Clint Insull was pounding on the door. The train was stuck again, this time between Brookings and Tracy. That day it dawned on everyone that this snowstorm was a bonanza.

It kept on, it did not stop. When snow ceased falling in a temperature below zero, the wind blew. It filled the cuts with packed snow. Every man in the country had work at two dollars a day, though scores and hundreds came out from the east to get those wages.

With lanterns and shouldered shovels, in the black mornings, all the men but Clint and Mr. Hewitt set out. "Don't worry," they told their women folks left at home. If a blizzard came, they had shovels, they could shovel their way back along the steel rails. Every day they cleared a way for the snowplow through the cuts, piling the snow higher on either side. Every night the wind filled the cuts to the top of the banks.

A threatened thaw ended in a brief rain which cased the snowbanks in solid ice. With ten feet more of snow piled on that, a sleet storm coated it two inches thick. Now they had only a three mile walk to the first cut east of town. It had been a five-foot cut, but they had built its sides forty feet up. It took three rows of men to move snow to the top. The job promised to last all winter.

Those were good times. Any man feels good when he is piling up double wages. The train left wood and coal for them ; they had fires around which to eat their lunches. They cut up high jinks at noontime and kept on joking while they worked. The train arrived full of men picked up at the other cuts ; it plowed cheering through between the high snowbanks and roared on down the track with red cinders flying back and the rocked crowd singing, "I've been working on the railroad, to pass the time away," and "Nelly was a lady, last night she died."

David wrote Mary that he had earned forty dollars and did not feel he ought to quit such wages, but he would come anyway on the twenty-third. He mailed the letter November nineteenth. The next day was clear, with a wind so cold that a man could not long endure working at the top of the bank. The lines changed places continually, the top men coming down and others moving up. At the bottom they shoveled in a snowstorm blown by the wind over the rim above. The snow came back almost as fast as they shoveled it up, so that they had to hustle to gain on the drifts.

The train did not come on time. At sunset there was no sign of its smoke in the east. They had shoveled down to the rails and they stood about the fire, stamping their feet and turning about to the little heat it gave. The sun sank red and cold. Jeremiah Boles sent a boy to the top for a last look. He slid down too chilled to speak, shaking his head. Jeremiah Boles shouldered his shovel. "Well, men, we better walk in."

From the cut, the embankment stretched clear enough, the driven snow-scud rising over it and blowing. There was no relief from the wind during those three miles. At the end, they kept on going toward a green switchlight in the dark. They got to the station and clumped in. Clint was apologetic.

"I'd 've sent out for you this morning if there'd been anybody to send. The trains 've quit running."

It took a minute to get that. "Quit?" Jeremiah Boles repeated.

"Hell, no, not *quit*. I mean they can't get through." An engine with two miles' flying start under full steam had been driven head-on into the snow in a cut east of Tracy. Engine and snowplow were stuck there, imbedded in solid ice. The superintendent had ordered all work stopped west of Tracy until further notice.

They were all too nearly frozen to say much. They thawed till the ice came off their beards and mustaches and then went home to do their chores. Mr. Peters remarked to David, "We're short on flour. This will run prices up."

David said that if there were no better news tomorrow, he would walk out. There were settlements not more than fifteen miles apart, the tracks were practically clear between cuts, and there were telegraph poles all the way. A man ought to be able to make it.

After supper they went to Boles' store. Nearly everyone else had had the same forethought, but Jeremiah Boles had already raised his prices a little, and so had Townsend. They had only small stocks of groceries because they depended on selling to get the cash to buy more in the east. Everyone said that the trains would be running again soon. While they were talking around the stove, the building shook suddenly. The insane winds had hit it. Fortunately no one was out that night who could not reach home by feeling along the walls of buildings.

26

That was the beginning of the Hard Winter. No such weather has been known since then. At the time, men spoke as if that country intended to drive out or kill the settlers who had come into it. They never felt that that blizzard quit ; it paused only to gather strength for greater violence.

When the telegraph wire went dead, Jake Hewitt started the run on the stores. He bought more than half of Townsend's small stock ; he bought the last tons of coal at the lumber-yard and every foot of lumber. The banker had the cash to lay on the counter ; he planked down good money for everything he got, so he was entitled to it. He kept two fires burning from first to last, feeding them shingles, siding and good matched flooring. But in January he sat in the dark like everyone else, because there was no kerosene.

David paid fifteen dollars for the last sack of flour in town. He paid forty cents a pound for beans. There was no molasses left ; he paid a dollar for a pound of sugar. For seed wheat he paid three dollars a bushel ; ground in the coffee-mill, it made a palatable kind of heavy bread. That was at first ; later, it was found to last longer in the form of a thin gruel.

In February, most families ran short of hay. They doubled up then, twelve to fifteen persons crowding around one stove, and men risked their lives and teams to haul hay from near-by claims during the blizzard's short and uncertain breathing spells.

For the most part, it was a cheerful winter. Hunger dulls itself soon, and it was not as if there had been work to do. After the morning chores, the men gathered in Boles' store. Even through blizzards they groped their way to it along stretched ropes, and in easier times went through snow-tunnels, for after the families crowded together the women and children needed all the warmth of the stoves. Only Boles' store was open ; the other stores, the saloons, pool hall, barber shop, closed.

Boles' store was the most tightly built ; there were bolts of goods on the shelves besides, and a hay fire in the heater. So many men together helped to take the edge off the cold, too. They kept their caps and mittens on, and wrestled, played practical jokes, told stories, and sang. At suppertime they went home cheerfully enough. Only death can lick a man who doesn't know when he's licked ; and death can't, because he won't know it.

The temperature ranged around forty below zero. The potatoes froze in the corner of the kitchen. All day and all night someone in the lean-to twisted hay to keep the fire going, and someone all day long was grinding wheat in the coffee-mill. The stove warmed the air around it. At night the beds were spread on the kitchen floor ; there was barely room for them all to sleep there. Limbering his hands over the stove in the middle of the night, when it was his turn to keep the fire going, David looked at Nettie under the covers. Often she woke, uncovered her face, and they talked.

"You get some sleep, I'll spell you awhile," she'd say, a pale blur of face in the dark.

"No, you stay under the covers."

"David, remember how hot it was that day by the slough ?"

"The day I met you coming over to Eliza's."

"Yes, then, too. But I meant when I was a little girl and rented you the sorrel. That day by the slough east of Yankton."

When one of the youngsters stirred and hungrily whimpered or Mrs. Peters sighed, they were silent a moment. Threads of light flickered around the stove's closed drafts and smoke puffed out ; the blizzard raged around the building and shook it.

"David," she asked him once, "were you engaged then to Mary, that day ?"

"Yes," he said. All those days seemed long ago, sweet to remember and sad because they were memories. He

155

did not know how to say what he felt, or whether to try to say it, he did not know what the truth was. If he wanted her, he must not let himself know it ; he did not want to want her, to spoil what there was between them now, he did not want to hurt her, or himself.

She put out her hand and sitting there on the edge of the pallet he took it, and held it, held it tightly, trembling and shaken by her bony little hand, the palm cut across in ridges and calloused from twisting hay, and the fingers so alive to his. "Nettie, we — "

"I know. Only I was thinking, if things had been different, then maybe — "

"Yes. If things had been different." Yet this was not what he meant, he would not have anything different between him and Mary, his wife. "It's not the same thing," he blundered on. "It's different, with you. Nettie, I — it's — You're so — "

"I know," she said again, turning her cheek to the pillow. "It's one of the things that don't happen."

Through the worst of the dark days without lights, when the young ones huddled silent in the little heat from the oven, and one of them incessantly ground the coffee-mill, while the cold was so cruel that he and Nettie by turns could endure only a few minutes of twisting hay in the lean-to, they were precious to each other. There was a bond, a loveliness, a special feeling between them.

In February Mrs. Peters' time came. The town was buried under snow then, and there was no kerosene. David herded the little girls and Charley through black-dark tunnels under the snow to Boles' store where he left them with the Boles children and brought back Mrs. Boles to help Nettie. He spent the afternoon helping to dig a tunnel to the Henderson's shanty on the edge of town ;

no one had seen the Hendersons for two weeks, but they were found to be all right.

That night the blizzard swept away the snow to the bare ground, and though David and Mr. Peters twisted hay and stuffed the stove all night, they could not bring the teakettle to a boil. The blizzard shook the walls as if it would tear them down. Now and then in the bedroom the twisted rag set in a saucer of axle grease flared its hoarded dim light. David did not know how Mary could have lived through what Mrs. Peters was suffering.

At dawn there was quiet outdoors; the blizzard had paused. The sun shone. A little lightheaded from sleeplessness and hunger, David and Mr. Peters moved the last haystack; they piled the frozen snowy hay against the north wall of the building. The kitchen seemed warm when they came in. The teakettle was bubbling, and Nettie had put four frozen potatoes to boil in their jackets. David ate his, skin and all; he could hardly believe that he had ever left creamy mashed potatoes with gravy uneaten on a plate. He set to twisting hay in the lean-to.

When he went in again, the baby was there. The wonder of it was in Nettie's tired eyes. Birth was a thing he had never got used to, himself; there was a strangeness in the thought of a living creature who had not been in the world and now was. Nettie opened the cocoon of blanket to show him a small red face, with eyes screwed shut and incredibly tiny hands under the chin. This was the first time he had seen a new baby. He would have given a great deal to know whether his own was a boy or a girl, and how Mary was getting along.

"Well, you're elected, Dave!" Mr. Peters told him jovially, but hushed because Mrs. Peters was asleep on the pallet by the wall. She had named the baby William

David, for her brother William and for David. "If your young one's a boy, we'll have to call him Bill. What do you think of him ? Some pumpkins, uh ?"

"You bet your life, he is !" said David.

The hardest time began then, in March when everyone was tired and it seemed that milder weather must come. As if the blizzard knew its failure and the short time left, it increased its ferocity. Mr. Peters said, "I'll be darned if the tarnation thing'll let go any more to spit on its hands." There was no rest from its noise and the cold stayed around forty below zero.

Many families had burned the last of their hay. They began sparingly to burn shelves, cupboards, lean-tos, chairs, bedsteads, tables, at last board by board to tear up their floors.

David had to stint the animals. The famished cow gave less than a quart at a milking, and one day David fought along the ropes to the banker's house and told Mr. Hewitt and his sister flatly that they would get no more milk. They agreed at once that the Peters young ones should have it. They knew nothing about the hunger in town ; being well provisioned and having no chores to do, Jake Hewitt hardly stirred out of his house. He was entirely willing to wait until spring for the balance of the milk due him. He made no objection to delay in the carpenter work, either, when David told him that the store was so cold that no man could handle tools there.

"You'll find me agreeable to what suits you folks," he told David in parting. "I'm always ready to be accommodating." He meant well, he was good hearted ; he was in fact a prince of a fellow.

Late in March Clint Insull offered to split fifty-fifty with any man who would haul hay from his claim a mile and a quarter east of town. Clint was hard-pressed for fuel; he had burned the office shelves and chairs, the waiting-room benches, and nothing remained to burn but his wife's fine furniture. The blizzard had let up that morning. The temperature was thirty-six below zero, with freezing sunshine on almost bare prairie. Clint's haystacks were plain to be seen from the porch of Boles' store.

"I'm making a fair offer," Clint urged. "Fifty-fifty to any man with a team, that's got the nerve to try it."

"You ask me," said Jeremiah Boles, "none of you'll take any such damn fool chance."

"Hell, Clint," Wyatt said, "it's your hay, and your furniture."

"Say, you got another think coming, that's my wife's parlor set," Clint replied, dropping the matter.

There was hay in the lean-to and some stacked against the building, but the stock were hungry. David and Mr. Peters stepped out behind the store and inspected the weather. The wind held steady from the northeast and in the northwest there was no sign of a cloud. The rim of the snow-streaked land was hard and clear against the paler blue.

"What the dickens, I'll try anything once," said David.

Mr. Peters agreed, "Nothing ventured, nothing gained."

They went out at a trot, loaded the rack, and headed back to town. They had made less than a quarter of a mile when the northwest skyline blurred gray and began to rise.

"Let's unhitch and ride for it," said Mr. Peters.

"Hell, we're hauling hay," David answered. He braced himself upright against the load and tightened his hold on the team. "Light out, you scalawags! Hi! Yi! Yipee!" Star and Dobbin took the wheels off the ground; he was there, firm and light, straightening them out, set-

159

tling them down to a dead run. They went down that straight prairie road so fast that it would have taken three men to see them.

The blizzard came at a speed beyond reckoning, swallowing the earth like a rush of flood water, and now the swiftly closing strip of sunlit prairie showed itself as the trap it was. "Yi ! yi ! Yip !" David talked to the flying team.

Hanging on for dear life in the jouncing hay, Mr. Peters shouted, "We got to ride for it, don't be a dum pighead !"

"They'll beat it !" David yelled. Upright in the bouncing jolting, braced on his legs, he stood shouting his lungs outs. He could not be licked ; he knew it. The blizzard was taking the town. Hewitt's house was gone, the church, the lumber-yard, the depot. Ten yards yet to go to Henderson's shanty, the belly-down horses against the blizzard roaring head-on down the street. "Whoopee !"

He met the blizzard in slam-bang collision, straight at it, yelling. It took the breath out of his mouth and his lungs. But he went out of the wagon, feetfirst over the wheel, holding the lines and setting a shoulder against Henderson's shanty. He had beat the blizzard. With his team on the loaded hay-rack he beat that blizzard by a matter of seconds, and seconds were enough. From Henderson's, there were ropes on in.

They said that day in Boles' store, "By Jinks, Dave, a fellow'll have to get up in the morning to beat you driving horses."

"Well, we went after hay," he said. "We kind of figured we'd haul it in."

Three days later the blizzard lifted from snowdrifts eleven feet deep. It took them away that night. It struck again on the twenty-seventh, again on the twenty-ninth. April came in with a six days' onslaught.

The winter that had not been able to kill them with violence had settled to wearing them down. No one was able any longer to expect an end of it. Men stayed with their families. The fire went out in Boles' store. Tunnels were dug no more through deep snow, the drifts came and went as the blizzard pleased.

David's head was clear as a bell, there was even a faint, pleasant ringing in it. He felt fine, and said nothing only because there was nothing to say. It was fortunate that he was not hungry because the potatoes were gone and less than a peck of seed wheat remained. He ate a little gruel reluctantly, having no taste for it, and left most of his cupful for the children.

There was a beauty in the bones of Nettie's face. Her chapped mouth held its long curve. They took turns in the lean-to, twisting hay. Silently he went into the deeper cold and silently she got to her feet, leaving the gray horse-blanket almost holding the shape of her body, a shelter to back into and draw over his shoulders.

The days were alike, there was only one endless day. There was the blizzard, the baby's ceaseless thin squalling, the ceaseless grinding of the coffee-mill, the hay-twisting and the recurrent chores. The horses' ribs ridged their hairy rough sides, the cow's hip bones were sharp. The ceaselessly blatting calf, the bawling cow, even the horses, could be eaten at last.

The milk froze in the pail. It was a clear evening, sometime in April. The sunset was red and gold and the sides of the pale blue snowbanks were rosy. In the kitchen the baby was crying, the coffee-mill grinding. Mrs. Peters was stirring the gruel. Lucy stood in the warm corner behind the stovepipe. In the quilt-draped chair before the oven, Mr. Peters held the baby in his arms and Charley and Flora on his knees. Flora unconsciously sighed, doggedly turning the coffee-mill's handle.

David set the milk to thaw and took the box from her, careful not to jar the little drawer and perhaps spill grains of the wheat-meal. Holding the mill against his chest, he ground away. He said, "We can kill the calf."

After a time Mr. Peters answered. "A pity, to kill a heifer calf. I'll pay for my share of it when I can."

Next day they killed the thin calf. It dressed out light. David sold half of it, meat and bone, for a dollar a pound. He gave some to men who had children and could not pay. The hide was left, that was something; a good piece of leather always comes handy about a place.

The boiled meat made them hilarious, it made them drowsy, it caused sharp pains in the stomach. The children vomited it up. After that first meal of beef, they were hungry. The young ones cried in their sleep from hunger. It clawed at them all and they could not satisfy it.

One day a shout came from the street. Clint Insull shouted, "A train! Train's coming!" He had seen it from his upstairs window, the smoke on the sky. It might not come beyond Brookings. Perhaps it could not get through the cuts. Shouldering a shovel was not easy; the men collecting in the street set the blades into the softened snow and leaned on the handles, looking at each other, wondering how long a walk the others were good for.

Jeremiah Boles tallied them as they came staggering out of the stores and shanties. Every man in town was still on his feet. They had weathered that winter and pulled their families through, every one alive. They stood in the slushy snow, in thin sunshine, the wind on their faces warmer than freezing, and they saw train smoke rising from the eastern skyline. They repeated to each other, "Well, we weathered it, by gosh and by golly." "Yep, we pulled through." Twenty-seven men and six boys. No one thought to take the news to the banker.

They saw the train coming. It had left Brookings, it had got through the cuts, it was coming. Down the last mile it came shrieking, steaming an unbroken whistle-blast up through the smoke rolling above the blur from the snowplow. With all his strength, every man set up a feeble cheer.

The engine passed them, and the snowy tender, the baggage car. They hurried along by the walls of sealed box-cars. There was an immigrant car, which surely contained food. They beat on the door. It did not open, no one was in the car. Some clawed at the door, some said to get Clint, or the conductor. David thought that the immigrant might be in the caboose by the stove. At the steps of the passenger coach he ran into Jay Lathrop.

"Dave?" Jay said. "Good God Almighty."

David could think of no reason why Mary's brother could be here, unless it was bad news. News so bad that Jay had come to break it to him, instead of writing it. "Well, what? What? Speak up, what is it, for — "

Then he saw Mary, standing at the top of the steps. Clean, buxom and rosy, in her little fur cap, she stood holding a soft bundle trailing fluffy white stuffs down the length of her cloak. David took a firm grip on her arm, to help her down.

"Well," he said, "How are you?"

Though she held the bundle clasped in both arms, she had eyes only for him. "Oh, David! David!"

"She's been worried sick about you," Jay said. "Noth-

163

ing would suit her but I had to bring her out here on the first train." Mary was saying that they had brought hams, turkeys, bread, butter, eggs, everything. Jay said, "We couldn't believe it was as bad as all this. Don't you raise anything at all to eat, out here?"

"What do you expect, it's a new country —" Neither of them told him anything about the baby. The men were smashing into the immigrant car. Mary was mourning, "How you ever stood it all these months, I couldn't sleep for thinking —"

"Shucks," David said. "Not a soul died in the whole town." Both of them were incredibly sleek with fat, and clean. He could wait no longer; looking at the bundle, he blurted, "Well, which is it?"

Mary paid attention at last. "He's a boy, and David! he weighed ten pounds, Dr. Thorne said he never saw a more bouncing baby, he was born the twenty-sixth of November at half past five in the morning, and we call him Davy for short, I wouldn't name him till you could have a say-so. Stand against the wind a minute, just a peep won't hurt him — He's the best baby, he hardly ever cries — There, muzzer's precious blessed was it!"

David looked at the face of his son. It had a freshness, a newness that one would not dare to touch. The lids had dark lashes, the mouth pouted round and pink, the cheeks were fat against a fuzzy snug pink bonnet. The whole face puckered alarmingly; then the blob of the nose emitted a tiny perfect sneeze. "By golly! you see that?" David exclaimed.

His son looked at him with round blue eyes. For a long moment he stared, doubtful. Then he grinned a wide grin. The whole bundle of him bucked against his mother's arm and his mouth sputtered pleased sounds.

"Here, give him to me." More politely, David added,

"I'll carry him for you." Mary tucked veils and flannel over the boy's face. David held the live bundle firmly and said that anyone would squall with all that stuff smothering him. Raising his voice he said, "He wants to see what's going on. Shows he's got good lungs."

"Everybody says up and down he's the living image of you," Mary told him.

27

That spring was glorious. There had never been a spring so swiftly coming. March winds, April skies, May warmth, all came together over the prairies where flowers lost their seasons in a jostling rush of blossoms.

The moist sod was springy under the tread, but winds hastened to dry the lumpy fields. Rotten sods crumbled under the harrow and the reluctance that clogged its teeth with dead roots was no more than futilely annoying. Whistling, David pitched the windrows into the wagon. He had an idea that those big tangled stacks of grass-roots, dried, would be fuel.

The soil was beautiful. When Mary came out to plan the garden he squeezed a handful of that earth to show her how it broke apart dark and rich on his palm. There was no bottom to that soil, so different from the thin, rocky fields of York State, and here were no forests to be ceaselessly fought.

"Great country, huh, little shaver?" He circled a finger at his son's middle, careful not to touch the clean blanket. The tiny sunbonnet, blown crooked, let only one round eye stare out. With flapping arms and an effort to kick up the weight of long skirts, the gurgling boy applauded. "You bet you!" David agreed. "By golly, the little scamp acts like he knows me."

"Of course he does. Muzzer's precious knows him papa, don't him? Say papa, blessed: pa pa. Say it, angel. Pa pa."

Oh well, there was no time to spend idly. The little rogue would be talking plainly enough, one of these days. David slapped the lines on the horses' gaunt flanks and started them again.

The harrow had cost sixteen dollars; in this country, the lumber and teeth and irons to make one would cost as much. Seed wheat out here was $2.50 a bushel because of the freight charges; for fourteen and a half acres, that was $57.37. A man needed a seeder; David considered an end-gate seeder, but that cost $12.60, and in these rough winds it would serve little better than careful hand sowing. A real seeder cost sixty dollars. One afternoon while the horses rested he listened to a glib salesman.

"Only fifteen dollars down, and we take your chattel mortgage for the balance at only ten per cent. Yes siree sir! Two cents under the legal rate. That's what this company's willing to do to help you people out here build up this western country. You want to know why, well sir, I'll tell you. A seeder's an investment, you'll more than pay for it from what you'll make in bigger yields, and then you'll be coming right back and buying more machinery from us. Now there's a lot of old stick-in-the-muds that don't know they're living in these progressive modern times, but you're a young fellow right up on your toes, you know what's going on, you're the kind that keeps abreast with the times, you are. Yes sir, you're the man'll jump at the chance to get this very latest fine modern improved machinery straight from the biggest factories in the east with no middleman's profit, and a saving of two per cent in interest rates. A seeder guaranteed to last you a lifetime, that'll more than pay for itself inside the first five years, you know that, I don't have to tell a farmer like you what a seeder's worth to him in dollars and cents. Just put your John Henry here, and — "

"I guess I better think it over," David said.

He knew that the salesman drove away swearing in his livery-stable buggy, with three empty miles to go around the slough pond. That night he cut strips from the calf's hide and made an old-fashioned shoulder harness sewed to a grain sack. He sowed his fourteen and a half acres by hand, trudging back and forth with the load, sifting out the costly grains with the motion of arm and wrist that he had learned as a boy, and anxiously watching where the wind carried them.

Hand sowing should be done on a still day. No day was windless here, and best he could do, the fields were sown too thickly in spots, too thinly in others. But he was determined not to mire down in the quicksand of debt. He would have a seeder when he could pay for it.

"Done?" Mary asked brightly when he came into the stable with the empty sacks.

"All over but the shouting!" He hung up the shoulder harness and stood looking down at her. She was slipping eggs under a broody hen, snatching her hand quickly from the slashes of the angry biddy's beak. "Where's the little shaver?"

"He's all right, I put him on the floor where he can't fall off. There, that's fifteen." She stood up, shaking down her apron. "Now if only they all hatch — David, we've got to have some kind of chicken coop. The horses'll step on them, in here."

He could hardly get used to having no wood on the place. A chicken house big enough to shelter pullets next winter, with a roost and nest-boxes, would cost twelve or fifteen dollars for lumber and roofing. A small coop now for the chicks would cost two dollars, best he could do. "All right. Let's take a look at the garden."

The filmed earth was already cracking minutely along the rows of radishes and lettuce. Mary had planted peas and beans, carrots, beets, onions and ground cherries. Tufts of grass were pushing up here and there, but hardly a weed was to be seen. The harrowed wheat field was a faintly purplish gray under the rosy sunset.

"Well, we're coming along, mama!" It was fine growing weather. They could count on a first mess of new potatoes and peas by mid-June, and after that they would have garden stuff till frost. He asked, "What's this row here?"

Mary's face was a study. She blushed, stammered, and finally got out, "M-mustard, and David I — planted some dandelion, not very much. You needn't scold, I'm so hungry for greens I dream about 'em. Not a bite of green stuff since year before last, I simply can't wait. Please don't be mad."

He could not scold her. "You little dickens! You see to it they don't go to seed, that's all I say."

"Oh, I will! I promise." She was relieved. "The way I feel now, I can eat 'em all myself faster'n they'll come up. Just think of a big mess of boiled greens with hard-boiled — No, we won't have eggs to spare, but anyway with buttermilk and corn-bread."

"Sounds good," he admitted.

He plowed and finely harrowed the balance of the large garden plot, and with the light plow checked it off. Most of their potatoes would be sod-potatoes again this year, but they treated themselves to one garden row. Mary dropped the cut pieces in a furrow, while with the hoe he covered them. Then she brought out the sacks of seeds

168

which their folks had saved for them from last year's gardens ; sweet corn, popcorn, beans in small cloth sacks, and cucumber, squash, pumpkin and melon seeds stuck in their drying to sheets of newspaper. They planted the corn with climbing beans, between the corn-rows they made small hills for the crawling-vine seeds.

The little shaver yelled in the house and David said, "Bring him out here, why don't you ?"

Mary said that he only needed changing and that there was no shade outdoors. He dropped the hoe and followed her into the house. He scooped the little fellow up from his blanket on the floor and held him up laughing between his hands. "There, see ? He's lonesome in here by himself. Want to be out with your folks, don't you, skeezicks ? Look at that ! What'd I tell you ?"

"Give him to me." Mary was expert with clothes and pins. "Well, if you'll fix some shade. I won't have the sun making him squint-eyed."

David took the boy against his shoulder, a chair and quilt in his hand. They made a shelter on the wild grass, against the westering sun. The little rascal lay there, turning his head from side to side, flapping his arms and trying to move his legs under the weight of skirts. They could see him while they came along the rows, Mary dropping seeds and David covering them, heaping and patting the hill with the hoe. Their shoes sank a little into the mellow earth, dust blew away, the sun and wind were hearty, the hoe went pleasantly into earth light with tiny dead grass-roots and without one jarring stone in it.

"Golly !" David said. And again, "Golly !" He tickled the little fellow's middle. "Having a good time, son ? That's the ticket !"

All over the prairie, folks were working at their little patches of broken sod. Hardly a dozen claim shanties within sight were vacant. Ox teams crawled small, back and forth, wearing away the grasslands. The train came smoking and steaming, its whistle clear. The whole Peters family was working on their ten-acre patch. Mr. Peters had been working there nightly by lantern-light. At sundown he came over, driving the sorrel and carrying the harrow on edge bumping over grass tufts.

"Much obliged, Dave. Where you want it put?" he asked. The last row was planted; Mary gathered up the youngster and David told her he would bring in the chair. He helped Mr. Peters lift the harrow into the wagon by the stable; some day he would have a tool shed.

They talked a little about crops and prospects, and Mr. Peters said, "Well, Dave, I can't make it. I got to go east and hunt me a job."

David could see that there was no other way, for a man with a family and no capital. Mr. Peters could not even break his sod. He had paid out three dollars an acre for breaking last year, but this year there were no jobs in town.

Mr. Peters broke a spear of hay into bits between thumb and forefinger. His red-bearded cheeks had not filled out since the Hard Winter. "Where I made my mistake was coming west in the first place, but that's water gone over the dam. I've got pretty near ten acres of wheat in. If I can make out to feed my family till harvest, and if we got a crop, I figure I can hang on. A quarter section will make us a living some day, if I can hang onto it and get it broken."

"Now you're talking," David said.

"So if you'd kind of keep an eye on the folks, if they need anything while I'm gone."

David assured him that he would be glad to do that.

"I'll be obliged to you, Dave." Mr. Peters shook hands

and said goodby. He was leaving next day. The conductor would likely let him ride in the caboose as far as Tracy and from there on he would try beating his way on the brakerods.

David did the chores soberly, currying and rubbing the winter hair from the horses' gaunt sides. It hurt him to see his horses so poor, and he hated to think of letting them go into strangers' hands. Spring plowing was done; now for breaking sod he must have oxen. It was a long time since he had whistled while currying Star and Dobbin.

They seemed to know what was in his mind; his hand following the comb along their backs and over their flanks felt their uneasiness. He knocked the matted hairs out of the comb and as he hung it on its nail he heard himself sigh like his father.

At least the cow's yield of milk was coming back on spring grass. Mary need not disturb the night's cream now to fill out the two quarts that Flora carried every morning to the Hewitts in town. That debt would soon be paid and Mary would be making butter again.

He carried in the milk and said to her, "Tell you what let's do. I got to get cuttings from Gooseneck for the tree-claim and a windbreak. What say we make a day of it, take the Peters family along, and have a picnic!"

28

There was no perfume like the smell of prairie air before dawn, and the weather could not have been finer. At the Peters' shanty the excited young ones climbed into the wagon box and Mary crowded closer to make room for

Nettie on the seat. Mrs. Peters handed up a package of picnic lunch ; she would not go because little Billy was ailing, but she was pleased to see her children setting out for a good time.

They all helped push the wagon up the railroad embankment. Crossing the slough on the tracks saved the long trip around it. They walked ahead of the racketing jolting wagon, David leading the team, until the scene became so strange and beautiful that they stopped. They stood silent in the stillness, looking.

The whole world was black and gray. Almost level with the narrow track, the silvery gray water stretched far on both sides. Thin black stalks of grass, curved or sharply broken, thrust up through its edges. The land was a black rim beyond, and over it hung the morning star, bright silver.

Silently the water became pure silver, the land a darker gray than the sky. The great star lost its brightness and melted into growing light. A spark of fire twinkled and spread on the edge of the world, suddenly the whole air twittered with bird calls, gilt wind-ripples ran across the silver water. The round sun sprang up.

As long as they lived, none of them ever forgot that sunrise on the slough. They never forgot that whole day, but when they spoke of it, one or another always said, "Remember the sunrise on the slough ?"

Gooseneck Pond, at this season, began less than seven miles southwest of town. It curved in a long gooseneck between the prairie swells, to its head some three miles farther south, where water stood all summer and there were three huge cottonwood trees. David drove along the tracks that Jake Mostra had made when hauling water ; grass was springing up in them now because the town well was dug. The wheels went softly, the sun

172

grew warm. Star and Dobbin kept on going with zest, sniffing the prairie scents and pricking their ears this way and that with interest in the new scenes. The youngsters chattered, holding onto the back of the spring seat, shouting and bouncing it in their excitement at jack-rabbits leaping up and away, and road runners racing ahead of the team.

"Oh Uncle David, why didn't you bring your musket?" Flora cried, thinking of all that meat. David explained that the rabbits and birds had young ones; spring was not the time to shoot any wild thing. "I know," she said. "I forgot."

Gooseneck lay blue beyond the green, and seeing brushwood among the coarse grass, David turned the team toward it. The nigh front wheel crunched over something and the rim came up dripping yellow. Before they fairly saw it, the off wheel crunched and dripped.

"Mercy on us, what is it?" Mary exclaimed.

They were running over prairie-chickens' nests. David thought he must have driven into a collection of them; he turned aside, but every few feet a wheel went crushing through eggs. He stopped the wagon. They all got down into grass full of scurrying prairie-hens, and everywhere they found the low nests full of eggs. In every direction the prairie-hens fled before the children's dashes.

"It seems a pity," Mary said. It was a pity to break so many eggs, and suddenly she exclaimed, "I do believe they'd be good to eat!"

"Of course they are," Nettie answered. "We eat them. We used to hunt for them and suck them out of the shells, didn't we, Flora? Down on the Verdigris river."

"It never came into my mind, such a thing as eating birds' eggs! Would you, David?"

"Why not? I'll try anything once," he said. "Prairie-

173

chickens are good to eat. Only they're setting on these eggs, won't they be addled?"

"As to that, we'll soon find out." Mary laid the little shaver in the grass, set her sunbonnet over his face, and knelt down by a nest with Nettie. The children were already running wild. David unhitched and picketed Star and Dobbin. It was only a little way to the brushwood along Gooseneck.

Hundreds of little cottonwoods and willows were thrusting up through a tangled mat of many years' dead grass pierced with lusty new blades. Rooted in damp earth, the small saplings were easy to pull. A musty smell came up with the dangling roots, and dust rose from the dry top layers of grasses.

The land belonged to somebody, but it must have been pre-empted, for there was no trace of improvement on it. A man must swear that he had put a habitable dwelling on his claim, when he pre-empted it, but he could buy the land from the Government thirty days after he drove his claim-stake, and habitable dwellings set on wheels were movable. Men made good wages pre-empting land for big speculators. It might be that some cattle-baron had bought up the permanent water of Gooseneck Pond.

David went on drawing the saplings from the moist earth. He bunched them in twenties and bound their roots with mud and grasses. This was a treasure-trove. Not being able to buy costly nursery-stock from the east, he had supposed he would have to layer cuttings from the old cottonwoods. In fact he had not thought much about it, or he would have conjectured that there must be seedlings, but he had never before seen Gooseneck.

He worked his way around a curve of it, and saw in the distance another man digging, who at sight of him dropped into the grass to hide. David turned back and

174

worked toward the head of the slough, taking pains to get every seedling sprout.

At noon the sunshine was scorching, and the young ones helped to stack the saplings in the narrow shade under the wagon. Charley struggled manfully through the tall grass, tugging a load almost as big as himself. David did not say anything, but he had a new feeling for the panting little boy, as if his own son guzzling at Mary's breast were old enough to be making these efforts to help him. He took Charley to help him water the horses, loosened the picket pins for him to pull up proudly, and let him lead Dobbin, who walked with care not to step on him.

In the blowing clean grass, under a cloudless sky, they sat around the picnic lunch. Hunger is the best sauce. The cold bean sandwiches were filling, the limp molasses sandwiches were sweet, and there was a bottle of tea. Mary and Nettie had found more than half of the prairie-hens' eggs fresh, and they had gathered dozens. They had been picking the little clover-like leaves of sheep sorrel, too ; the stems had an acid taste, almost like lemon, and enough of them would make a pie.

That was a perfect hour. No more troubles than shadows were under that blaze of sun. The heat distilled a warm green scent from the endless waves of grasses, and already a faint shrilling of insects was tuning up for the full chorus of summer. The little shaver slept in a hollow of grass-stems, his head under the tent of Mary's sunbonnet and his little hands relaxed. Nobody wanted more to eat. Mary tore the last molasses sandwich into three parts for the replete youngsters, who savored it slowly. The lunch basket was empty for the prairie-hens' eggs, but she sat still, nibbling a sheep sorrel stem. Bit by bit its furled lavender blossoms crept nearer her lips, till her teeth bit through the petals. Her dark hair was wind-tousled and her skin, flushed by the sun, was already wind-dried and parching in tiny wrinkles. She blinked sleepily, and yawned. The youngsters licked their fingers and sighed from fullness. Nettie lay flat to the heat of the sky, an arm across her eyes and a fold of gray-faded calico skirt fluttering a little down the long line of her legs.

They were so still that a jack-rabbit stood up quite near, his long ears erect above the grass tops and his eyes peering, his nose sniffing the human scent.

"Shoo !" Flora yelled, and clapped both hands over her mouth in agony lest she had waked the baby. None of them saw the rabbit go. The little shaver's fist clenched, his mouth opened wide, but it closed in a yawn and his eyelids smoothed again.

David lay back and pulled his hat over his face. The hot, strong light soaked through him, the earth sent up a vibration. An infinity of green stems quivered below rustling blades, narrow green banners fluttering against blue, high above the insects' saw-tooth shrilling. A small red-pepper ant toiled up a stem, gripping some morsel with his jaws and foothold by foothold climbing, shaken to a desperate clutch when the stem quivered, lifting himself again step by tiny step. The morsel was as large as half of his wee bisected body. It slipped, he could not hold it, it fell. The ant hastened down the stem and hurried clambering under and over dead stems lodged in heaps like the trees that David had helped his father fell in Minnesota. Out of a pile, backward, the darned insect tugged that morsel. It pushed and pulled the load through the chaos of logs, dropped it, found it, clutched and dragged it, encountered another rooted grass-stem and again began to climb. There was no sense in it ; nothing for ants is at the top of grass. When it got to the top, if it ever did, it could only lose its burden or more painfully lug it down. The sun's heat quivered through muscles and bones, the whole earth was alive in heat, the grasses and the insects were in tune with the sun.

"Have a good sleep?" Mary asked smiling when he sat up and yawned. He did not say that he would not have lost in sleep an instant of that bliss.

"Mm," he answered. "Have to get back to work now, though."

They drove home through slanting rays from the low sun. The wagon was loaded with saplings enough to plant the tree-claim, with hundreds of eggs and with heaps of wilted sheep sorrel. There was hardly room to crowd the children in. They all rode bareheaded, singing, the little shaver wide awake and lively in his mother's arms.

"Oh, I wish a day like this didn't ever have to end," Nettie said, when the wagon jolted across the railroad tracks in town. It had been a day long to be remembered.

David pulled up at the hitching posts, and Mary told him, "Cornmeal, salt, saleratus and matches, and maybe half a pound of salt pork. Now don't stay all night. I know how you men are when you get talking. If we're not here when you come out, we're tired of waiting and we'll be visiting Mrs. Hardin at the hotel."

"I won't be a jiffy, so don't you keep me standing around waiting, it's almost milking time."

29

At this supper hour, the store was almost deserted. Only two strangers lounged against the counter, thinking over some problem with Jeremiah Boles. They looked up, and Jeremiah Boles took his foot from the nail keg.

"Meet the Garner boys, Dave. Lafe, Duane. They're from Missouri."

David stepped up and shook their hands. Of course he had always heard of Missourians ; these were the first he had met. They topped his height by a couple of inches, but they were beanpoles. They handled themselves in an easy-going, loose-jointed way inside their butternut jeans, still he judged that they could be as quick as greased lightning. Their leathery faces, lax on bones, were an old yellow from fever 'n' ague. There was a humorous look around their eyes and their flexible mouths.

"You know anybody'd part with some cash for two good yoke of work oxen, mortgaged, and going at a bargain, Dave ?" Jeremiah Boles asked. He said the brothers had weathered through the Hard Winter on their claim nine miles northeast, though nobody in town had known they were there. After the October blizzard they had stayed through the fine weather to break more sod, intending to go back to wood-cutting in Missouri after the winter set in, to earn money for seed. They had fifty acres broken. The Hard Winter had caught them, and that spring Jake Hewitt could not see his way clear to lend them more than forty dollars on their oxen.

Seed for fifty acres would have cost $182.50. They had sowed five acres, and eaten up the balance of the forty dollar loan. Now they had to live till harvest, they owed Jake Hewitt $42.50 with the interest, and he would not let them take the mortgaged oxen out of the county. They would sell the oxen cheap. The oxen were strong and well-broken, though gaunted from living all winter on frozen turnips.

"Turnips?" David was interested. "You raise turnips last year on sod land?"

The Garners said they had raised, on broken sod, the biggest crop of turnips ever a man saw in his born days. Duane stated that they had not been able to sleep of nights, for them turnips quarreling and fighting among theirselves, hollering to each other to move over and leave them room. Expecting no such crop, and having no market for it, they had left it in the ground, and they hoped never to see another turnip as long as they lived. When the Hard Winter caught them, the one solitary thing they had had to live on, and to feed the oxen, was those frozen turnips.

Between blizzards they had dug those turnips with picks, out from under the snow. What time they had not been working up an appetite at mining turnips, they had been putting an edge on it, wrestling uncut slough hay out of the drifts to build up a fire. They slept with the oxen for warmth, but if given their preference in eating frozen turnips, they'd take them thawed.

Now they had to let their oxen go on the mortgage, and leave the country on foot, or make out to live on credit until harvest and figure on living another twelve months on whatever they might get from five acres of wheat.

"It's put our shoulders to the ground, that's the sorry fact," said Lafe. "We're plumb discouraged."

"You've struck a stretch of hard sledding, all right," Jeremiah Boles admitted.

David said he would like to see the oxen. They were grazing by the Garners' wagon-camp, on the prairie beyond the blacksmith shop ; four big-boned, horned beasts with muscle enough on them, and indifferent ox-eyes. They chewed cuds while he prodded their flanks and shook their heads by the horns. There was no mark of ill-use on them. The rope harness was in fair shape and the yokes were ash.

David put his hands in his pockets and stood looking at them. "If I was you fellows, tell you what I'd do. I'd make a trade for a good team of horses and hit out for the railroad camps. You put in a summer hauling, you can come back here next fall with enough of the needful to get by on and put your fifty acres into wheat next spring."

The talk wandered around that idea. Eventually the Garners sauntered along with David to the hitching posts. No one was in the wagon. Star and Dobbin were skittish when strangers took hold of their mouths to look at their teeth. Star jerked loose, snorting, and showed the whites of his eyes. "Gentle as kittens, a lady can drive 'em," said David. It was true of his horses, they had always been gentle with him.

He offered to trade them and the harness for the two yoke of mortgaged oxen with yokes, harness and goad, and the five acre wheat crop.

Jake Hewitt was closing up the bank, but he stepped back inside. He was agreeable to the trade. He made out a legal transfer of the wheat crop, charging only a quarter for it, and both the Garners signed it. David put his name on their note for the forty dollars.

He had broken and driven a yoke of calves when he was nine years old, he could not now remember why. It had been the kind of thing a boy will do, for no reason. Even then, and back in York State, only the French drove oxen. But now that he had to do it, he knew how. No one need tell him how to adjust the yokes, put in the hickory thole pins, fasten the ropes and handle the goad.

"Glad to met you fellows," he said to the Garners.

"Any time you're around my way, be glad to have you drop in. You take a notion to part with the team any time, let me know and we might make another dicker. In fact I'd be obliged if you would keep it in mind. My wife's partial to the team, we raised 'em from colts."

The Garners led Star and Dobbin away, down the side street toward their wagon. Star looked back, whinnying. The sun had set, supper smokes were rising from the stovepipes. David gee-hawed the oxen around and walked them up in front of the hotel. He said to Fatty Hardin, "Mind saying to Mrs. Beaton we're ready to go home ?"

The oxen stood like lumps, chewing their cuds and letting strings of saliva hang from their rubbery lips. Mary stopped short when she saw them. David pushed back his hat and spoke cheerfully. "Well, what you think of my trade ? Good husky brutes, just what I need for breaking sod."

"That's no lie," Hardin agreed. "The amount a double yoke of oxen'll turn over in a day is surprising. It'll be a long day in January when we see a team around here that'll equal those matched Morgans you had, though."

"One thing about oxen, they'll stand without hitching !" David spoke as if that were a joke. He took the little shaver, and with his other arm gave Mary some help in climbing into the wagon.

In a low voice she said to him, "I wouldn't mind so much, if you'd told me."

It was an accusing cry. He answered quickly, "I didn't have time."

Why that lie came out of his mouth he did not know. He had not thought of telling her. Talk would do no good ; the sod must be broken and his horses could not break it.

181

He did not risk taking the clumsy oxen on the railroad track across the slough. He headed them north, the long way around the water. Nothing will hurry oxen ; they keep a load moving but their deliberation is slower than a man's walk. At the flank of the nigh lead ox, David shortened his steps and kept himself from using the goad. Now and then he said, "Hup, Buck ! Hup, Bright !"

In the wagon even the young ones, tired by the long day, were for the most part silent. Color faded from the sky and from the blowing grasses, the whole land became a sighing darkness. Stars pricked through the gray and descended to hang large and trembling.

The wagon came along like a piece of black pasteboard cut out. Mary's sunbonnet looked down at the little shaver in her arms. Nettie was bareheaded, facing the wind. She began to sing, and when the sunbonnet-shape slid back from Mary's head and she was singing, David came in with the bass. He could not follow a tune, but he would do his part.

> In the starli–ight, in the starlight,
> We will wander, (we will wander)
> In the starli—ight, in the starlight,
> We will wander, gay and free.

It was nine o'clock and past when the oxen lumbered up to the stable that was not large enough for the four. Unexpected light was shining from the house windows. Gay Thorne opened the door and quickly shut it on a glimpse of Eliza behind him. He called out, "Whoever you are, you've missed your road. No thoroughfare here !"

Their laughter answered him. He could see them now, and came politely to help assist the ladies from the wagon.

To David he said, astonished, "I'll be darned. You folks come down to oxen."

30

That night David told Mary that this would be their hardest year. As soon as the land was broken, everything would be clear sailing.

Mary agreed that it had been wise to trade for the oxen. They would have horses again in a year or two. David spoke cheerfully, but he was disgruntled. The look of Gay and Eliza, sleek from their soft winter in the east, rankled in his mind. They had not changed, they were as they had always been, what he was accustomed to, but while they were telling news and gossip in a bustle of unwrapping presents, they seemed out of place. They were cramped in the small, crowded room. Eliza was too elegant against the smoke-grimed walls. Once she could not have held a candle to Mary, and now Mary was blowsy, roughened and tanned already by the sun and wind, and too thin in a common calico dress.

Gay had come out with a load of supplies, lumber, some furniture, and a team and buggy, in an immigrant car. He was going to put a frame shanty on his place. David supposed that Dr. Thorne had given him the money. Well, his own father had started him out with as good as fifteen hundred dollars, and lent him the price of Dobbin to boot.

In the morning he yoked the oxen and broke sod for the windbreak around the house. Mary came out, with the little shaver, to help him set the trees. It was a brisk and hearty morning; the sunshine was warm and the wind blew vigorously. Flora and Lucy were helping Eliza get settled in her shanty. Gay was hauling his supplies from

183

town in David's wagon, and between trips he hauled
water from the well for the planting. So much coming
and going made a merry day, the day they set out the
windbreak.

David dug the holes wide and deep, pulverized the soil
thoroughly, and choosing sturdy, well-shaped saplings he
spread out their roots and crumbled earth over them, lifting the tree a little. Then Mary watered it down, and
held it while he filled in around it and firmed the soil.
They planted fifty-six trees that day, for their windbreak,
and twenty-six more northwest of the place where some
day the big barn would be.

The remainder of the saplings he heeled in, a long
garden-row of them. He would transplant them next
spring. There was plenty of time ; the Government gave
him seven and a half years to prove up on the tree-claim,
and the trees had to be on it only five years.

The sun was setting when he covered the last roots and
trod the soil firm. He looked across his land and turned
and shouted. "Mary ! Come out here !"

Over her shoulder she asked Eliza to mind the baby,
and came hurrying from the house, expectant. "What ?
Where ? The beans ?"

"Look, look at the field. No, across it, level. See ?"
For a moment she could not, then she did. "It's up !"

After they had waited through the long barren year, at
last seed had sprouted. At their feet the field seemed
bare, but looking across it they could see the green mist
of threadling wheat on the little ridges of harrowed earth.

They looked up at the sky. Great smears of thin yellow cloud streaked the clear hemisphere. On the circle
of the far horizon, one above another lay bands of rose
and yellow and green and darker blue. The wind was
mild.

"Well, nobody knows, but anyway so far it's good growing weather," David said.

Next day he settled to the job of breaking sod. He loathed the oxen. There was no pleasure in working with them. Their clumsy, awkward rears, the splay hoofs dividing and sprawling at every step, the heavy necks and heads without pride or spirit, and most of all their blank placidity, infuriated him. They were hunks of muscle, power without feelings or brains. The empty stare of their eyes affronted a man.

Smouldering, ill-treated, resentful and lacking anyone to blame, he went to dinner. He saw that on Wednesday, of all days, Mary was doing a washing. The wash-boiler steamed on the smoky sod-pit, the tub of soaking cloth stood on the bald ground near by, the clothesline was flapping full of white. He supposed that a hard-working man was expecting too much if he wanted a decent noon meal in his own house on Wednesday. He walked in.

The muslin walls were gone. Naked studding, streaked with mildew, stood against earth from which blanched grass curled sickly. The place was like a cellar. The bed was in the middle of it. The table was set for two, and at the stove Mary was busy, the little shaver held in one arm burbling over her shoulder. Everything else from the house was piled outside the front door.

"What the dickens," he said.

Mary racketed at the stove, stuffing hay into it. "I'm sorry I'm behindhand but I'll have it on the table in a minute. Eliza went with Gay to get her trunk, they're eating at the hotel in town and I'm as well satisfied, I want to have room to take hold when I'm house cleaning."

"So that's what this is."

"Yes, and David, the walls are coming out beautifully, they're going to be almost pure white, this one washing and bleaching. Well, I did put in one pinch of sal soda but I don't believe it's hurt the muslin a mite, I rinsed it thoroughly in two waters, and I'm going to starch and iron them. I saved every tack and there's hardly a dozen I can't use over." She pushed back a straggle of hair with one parboiled hand. "If there's one thing I can't abide it's dirt, and there's more than one way to skin a cat. All's needed is some gumption."

Her bib-apron was draggled with suds, her hair was slipping from the pins and soot smeared her cheek. No kiss could have begun to express what David felt. He said, "Well, you've got gumption, all right."

At dinner he told her to call him, next time she wanted heavy things moved. "What you got a husky husband for, anyhow?" When she asked him how he was suited with the ox-team, he said that oxen beat horses all hollow for breaking sod.

Everything continued to be promising. The chickens hatched, and Mary raised the first brood by hand, keeping the hen on the nest to hatch a second. The house was freshly white-walled; Gay's frame shanty going up showed that the country was progressing. A letter came from Mr. Peters; he had got work in the east and sent five dollars. Nettie was radiant. Her father was safe, he had a job, and she had a pair of shoes.

"I don't know, we need so many things, Ma shouldn't have done it," she worried a little, but joy burst up again, irrepressible. Her elbows hugged against her, to contain it. Now that she had shoes, she was going to school. There was a schoolhouse in town now, and a teacher, but Nettie had not thought she could go; she was ashamed to go to school barefoot, at her age. Now that she had

186

shoes, she went every day with the barefooted young
ones, and often in the evenings she came over to do lessons with Eliza. Her mother had taught her so well
that she was well advanced, and she wanted to graduate
quickly and be a school teacher. Eliza said that she was
smart as a whip.

The corn sent up young blades, the beans popped up
on leaves that soon dropped them, and the peas began to
curl their tendrils. One Sunday there were radishes for
dinner. Milk soured quickly now; David had no time
to dig a deep well in which to hang the milk and butter.
He was breaking sod from dawn to dark, trying to break
all that he could before the land became too dry to break.
There was cottage cheese every day, and for a treat they
ate the clabbered milk with brown sugar sprinkled over it.

David loathed the oxen, but they did break sod, and
they fed themselves, filling their first stomachs with grass
during the nights, and chewing it and drooling while they
pulled the plow. And where they grazed, the sun dried
their droppings to cow chips.

One Saturday afternoon David saw Flora and Charley
dragging a bushel basket and searching over the bitten
grass where the cattle had grazed. They came lugging
the heavy basket over the upheaved sods, and showed him
their load of cow chips. Cow chips made a better fuel
than hay, and they cost no labor but the picking up. A
little anxiously Flora told him, "Aunt Mary said we could
have them."

He told her that she was welcome to them. She was
shooting up, tall for an eight-year-old, but she was scrawny,
and Charley could hardly lift his side of the basket.
When they got it off the rough sods, Flora took both
handles and carried it as a woman carries a washtub. It
seemed heavy to lug more than a mile, but hay was al-

187

most gone and there would be no more till after haying.

That evening Mary came out toward the picket lines to meet him. She said that she had told Flora to help herself to the cow chips.

"I will not burn cow chips !" she said passionately. "I know it's only the idea, but I will not do it ! I'll wear my hands to the bone, I'll do anything, first !"

"Keep your shirt on," he said good-naturedly. "Come look at the wheat. You can't sometimes most always tell, maybe we'll be burning coal !"

A look at the rippling silkiness of the young wheat-field rested a man after a day's work. Something had been gained, one more day of the wheat's safely growing. Lusty as the wild grass, the millions of stems pushed higher every day their lighter, more golden green. All over the prairie, amid the coarse wild grasses, squares and oblongs of that pale smoothness began to tame the land. Now one saw that the shanties had come to stay.

Twice in one week, crashing black thunderheads rolled up so swiftly that rain was pouring down before David could unyoke the oxen and reach shelter. Mary gazed from the window while in the doorway he stood dripping, watching the gray onrush on veiled garden rows and bending wheat. The icy air made them fear hail. But none fell. Every blade sprang up next day rejoicing, and Mary hoed the garden.

Then peas, beans, potatoes blossomed, and the wheat put up its tasseled heads. Only the mercy of God could guard it now. Barefoot before dawn, David stepped outdoors to feel the air. All day he watched the sky. The last thing at night he looked at it, and Mary asked anxiously when he came in, "Everything all right ?"

"Sure," he said, but no one could be sure. In this country the stars quivered always in wind, and one never knew when the wind would change.   Rain on the pollen would be disaster.

Clouds drew their shadows across the prairies, lingered and darkened and lowered, then passed away harmless. One night silver-fleeced sheep covered the moonlit sky, the feeling of rain was in the air, and Mary said stanchly that anyway they would make part of a crop, and they had the garden now.   Rain did not fall that night, and dawn came clear and hot.   Too hot, it threatened scorching heat too soon.

Nothing hurt the pollen.   The kernels began to form. There was a little rust in the field, but not a great deal, and the weather settled hot and dry.   Steady dry heat would curb the rust.   Every day the wind was hotter.   The fields, no longer silky, were covered with the young green heads.

A swift hailstorm came down, bringing night at noon. In twenty minutes the temperature dropped thirty degrees ; it rebounded in sunshine.   The hail had stopped a mile north, like a weapon fallen short of the mark.   Most of the storm had passed over wild grass.   Only three homesteaders' crops were damaged.

After church on Sundays, all the talk was about the wheat.   No man in the country had seen such a yield as the fields were promising.   David's wheat stood as high as his chest, a table-flat mass of heads so thick that the wind-ripples passed over it like light changing on a solid surface. Some heads were as long as his forefinger, and the grain was in the milk.   One scorching day would wither the kernels.

This was too much to stand.   David decided that he was not a gambler ; he was no wheat farmer.   This was not farming as he had known it in settled country, where seasons brought varying fortunes but a farmer was always safe. There were not enough people here; there was no market here for anything a man could raise from land. The market was in the settled east where the people were, and his market there was only for wheat.

When he could afford to build fences and barns and sheds, and when the country was more thickly settled, then he would raise pork and mutton and beef and horses, and no longer have all his eggs in one basket. But for that, to begin with buildings and stock, he must have money, a thousand dollars at least, and money must come from wheat. Every thought circled back to the wheat, the wheat and the weather. The dawn wind blew hot on his face in the dark, the sun rose pitiless in a cloudless sky.

At noon he walked to the tree-claim field. He husked pale grains on his palm. Smooth yet, they were standing the burning weather. He crushed them milky between thumb and forefinger. How long could they stand it? The mercury climbed while he ate dinner; the worst heat of the day was yet to come.

At sunset he could not say that the wind was cooler. All around the edges of the fields the sampled kernels held their soft roundness. The mercury did not fall when night was there, and the hot wind did not stop blowing. Mary was too cheerful, she and Eliza talked about everything but wheat, and the little shaver fretted. David dreamed that the wheatfield burned, and through the nightmare despair there was a relief because the wheat was gone, the dread of losing it was ended.

The wheat survived. The kernels hardened, large kernels filling out every husk to the blunted tip of long heads. Such a crop was incredible, it was not possible. It was real, there before their eyes, there on his palm, the large solid kernels, the solid heads, the solid-crowded field, thirty-six, thirty-seven bushels to the acre, safe and sure, actual, true.

David sang out, "There's spots it'll run forty bushels, or I'm a liar!" He hugged the breath out of Mary. This was the greatest country on God's footstool. Let the wind blow, let the sun blaze! The wheat was safe. The hotter the better now. Heat and dryness would ripen the wheat.

31

Breaking the drier sod was tougher work but it did not tire a man who was sure of making his crop. At her work around the house Mary sang, "Every day'll be Sunday bye and bye!" Saturday night's bath and Sunday morning's dressing-up, the whole bland day of church and rest, suited the way they felt.

Wheat fields crossed the old diagonal way to town, so in Gay's buggy Eliza drove Mary and Mrs. Peters the two miles in the sectionline roads. They set out eagerly, dressed in Sunday best, the starched and bonneted babies sitting on the dust-robe tucked carefully over their laps. David and Gay went on foot by the short cut along the slough and the railroad track.

Gay's frame shanty and the wire fence he was putting up had a prosperous look but David did not know what it depended on. Gay and Eliza had hired nursery trees set on their tree-claims and the broken sod on their homesteads satisfied the law. Eliza, of course, depended on her school in the east. David remarked that it was a pity they had not sowed wheat.

"That takes the wherewithal," Gay replied negligently. "How much cash you put into that crop of yours already? Better than a hundred dollars, and a binder and twine and sacks and threshing'll cost you around another three hundred. Not to mention killing yourself working in the dirt. Well, everybody to his taste, as the old woman said when she kissed the cow."

A binder was an investment which lasted a good many years, but David did not argue. The special Sunday feeling was on the prairie, the fields, the masses of wild roses in bloom. Gay's distant buggy was followed by a small haze of dust, for the wheel-tracks cut through the dust now. Wagons full of families crawled toward the town. Heat waves rippled from the track's steel rails and the oil-blackened ties were hot to the soles of shoes.

Down the track, Nettie was shepherding the bare-legged young ones. The brown ribbon that Mary had given her encircled her yellowed straw hat. Her hair glowed under the brim. The wind held her skirts against her and whipped them, fluttering glimpses of petticoats under the brown calico. She walked with a light, springy action, free as a young thoroughbred.

"What you bet I don't take her spooning this afternoon?" Gay said.

"I'm not betting." Her father had left the family in David's care. He thought of having Mary speak to her mother, still he could say nothing definite against Gay. He dismissed the thought of speaking to her himself without allowing himself to think why.

She was sitting beside Eliza and Mary. David and Gay took places on the bench behind them. It was remarkable how much she had changed since she had shoes and was going to school. There was a kind of light about her, like dawn which passes so quickly. She lifted her head as a fine yearling colt does, fearless and gay and shyly proud, before it is broken to harness. The congregation rose and sang, "Work, for the night is coming when man

192

works no more." Jeremiah Boles asked the guidance and blessing of God, and the Rev. Brown began to preach from the text, "Out of the fullness of the heart, the mouth speaketh."

Tall in black behind the unpainted pulpit and the large Bible, he preached earnestly. Pitch fried from the board walls and trickled in clear drops. Dry heat came through the windows into the steamy church, where fans rustled and men furtively wiped their necks and tucked handkerchiefs into collars. Now and then a child sighed or fidgeted. Babies whimpered. The little shaver complained in spite of everything that Mary could do. Crawling over her, he disheveled her wilting dress and tugged her hair. Suddenly he struck her hat awry and let out a roar.

David took him hastily. Mary gave him a glance of anguish and shame ; the Rev. Brown was pausing until he could again be heard. David fled through rising squalls feebler than his son's full-lunged bawling. Outdoors, the rascal laughed with tears still bulging from his eyes and rolling on his cheeks.

"This what you want, uh ?" David asked him. The little chap jiggled contentedly on his shoulder. They walked awhile through the grass, then got into the shade of Gay's buggy top. Young Davy sat up, clutched David's fingers and bounced on his knee. His grip was so strong that he could almost be lifted by it. He glanced roguishly, crowed, and swiftly flung himself backward. David barely caught him. His back was sturdy and his padded buttocks firm, his knees tried to climb David's chest. He slapped a fist at David's eye, then mauled his hat. He yawned hugely, went limp, and slept.

David sat holding the little fellow. The town was baking under an intensely blue sky. Piles of white cloud-puff sailed above shadows drifting across grasslands and wheat fields and tiny shanties. The tied horses stamped, switching at flies. From the windows the Rev. Brown's voice urged each to contribute according to his means toward paying for the church building. Young Davy slept relaxed and wholly trusting, in sweltering twisted yards of cloth and crooked bonnet. He did not wake when the choir sang nor when the congregation poured out.

Mary took him apologetically, sorry that David had missed the sermon. Eliza was keeping Nettie under her wing, among the women who held onto their parasols in the wind and discussed means of paying for the church. David drifted into masculine talk. Jake Hewitt stated that a good binder properly used would pay for itself in grain and labor saved. His four-square, painted house across the street was proof of his good judgment, if a banker needed proof. He mentioned that he might be driving west of town that afternoon, and David said hospitably, "Be glad to have you stop and pay us a visit."

The homeward procession stretched along the path and wagons began to pull out. Impulsively across the trodden grass Eliza came hurrying. "Oh, Gaylord, just a moment if you please?" She touched Gay's sleeve with the tips of fingers daintily protruding from lace mitts, and boldly dashing she said, "I'm cheeky as the camel in the black-smith shop, but may I ask you a favor?"

David stopped short. This was a strange glimpse of Eliza. With earrings swinging and the circle of parasol behind imperious head and sloping shoulders, this was the same handsome, elegant female, the same thin face, thin nose, frizzed bangs under the tilted hat, narrowed eyes smiling, but a softer woman, charming, alluring, and to David's perceptions somehow more dangerous.

"It's for Nettie, poor girl, nobody takes her buggy-riding,

you dashing young men are positively horrid snobs, thinking only of your own pleasures. If you haven't a rendezvous this afternoon, do let me have the rig for a little and take her for a short spin ?"

David could not believe that she knew what she was doing, not even Eliza could mean to do this. She must mean a simple kindness to Nettie, she was always kind to younger girls. This must be a glorious accident. It was a huge joke on Gay. The whole Sunday became mirthful. Whistling, David went on to the buggy, helped Mrs. Peters and Mary into it and untied the team. Gay handed Eliza in and they stood bareheaded while she swung the team about expertly; Eliza was a capable driver. Nettie was far down the railroad track, hurrying home to start Sunday dinner.

That afternoon was the first time that Eliza took Nettie buggy-riding with her and Gay. They drove away merrily, soon after dinner. Outdoors in the shady shelter of the house, Mary and Mrs. Peters settled down in their chairs on the grass to visit away the idle afternoon, watching the babies crawl on a quilt and the children playing through the slough grass. Sure enough, the Hewitts drove up. The one thing lacking had been visitors. David stepped to the buggy to welcome them heartily, and after a sufficiently long chat he took his guest away from the women to show him the place.

They strolled between the garden's weedless rows. David displayed the tasseled corn, the blossoming vines and the small melons and squashes under their leaves. He showed the wheat. They walked along the edge of his acres of broken sod, pausing to stand and talk when they felt like it. There was no hurry. They had time to waste. Pondering before they spoke, they discussed the different kinds of grasses, the soil, the lay of the land for various

195

crops. They exchanged news, and expressed considered opinions about prices, politics, railroad charges, middlemen, and the new wheat elevator in town, all this in the special smooth leisure of a Sunday afternoon.

From a distance they saw the women folks walking about the stable and the hencoop and through the garden. When the sun was low and the Hewitts were leaving, David put behind their buggy seat a sack of green peas and a large bunch of new beets. He was pleased that Mary had gathered them for the visitors. The Hewitts had a garden of their own, but farmers should give of their abundance to town folks.

The day had been a perfect Sunday. The little cottonwoods of the windbreak were thriving. Some day they would shade a large house and a white clover lawn, and there would be a barnyard fence, a board fence on which a man could lean his arms while he looked at the country and considered tomorrow's weather. Good barns, and shade, granaries and a paddock, a cow lot, a sheep-fold, and behind him a wide front porch and a cellar, pies along the buttery shelf. Still these were not needed for contentment. It had been a good Sunday, and David decided to buy a binder. He would have to have a binder next year and he might as well have the good of one now.

On Saturday he walked into the bank and said, "How about it, Jake? My credit good for a binder?"

"It certainly is, Dave," Mr. Hewitt replied. "And if you want some money to see you through harvest, that's what we're in business for." David took only fifty dollars in cash for twine, oil, sacks, and extra groceries to feed the threshers, a short-time loan at three per cent a month. He had twenty dollars to pay down on the binder, and covered the $180. balance by a long-time note and chattel mortgage, at ten per cent a year.

196

He drew the bright machine home behind the ox-wagon. Mary and Eliza and Gay came out and the whole Peters family arrived to stand around it, looking at the steel parts and the new paint. David had thought that Gay might like to use his team in the harvest, but Gay spoke vaguely of making a western trip. Owning a binder, David would have no trouble in trading work with some homesteader who owned horses. The machine was a beautiful thing, standing there in the grass by the green-gold field that would pay for it and for a shed to cover it.

32

Johnson, baching in a soddy on his claim beyond the slough, was glad enough to trade work for the use of a binder. He had a good scrub team, strong and willing, and he took good care of them. He was a husky young fellow, not afraid of work himself. David saw him pitching into it before sunup and staying with it till dark. Wind and sun had burned his skin dark red, and bleached tow-white his hair, his eyebrows and the hair on his muscular arms and chest. He was always ready for a joke or a song, and he kept up his end of a talk without stopping work.

He had twelve acres in wheat, all the land he could afford to pay for breaking. David, with the Garner field and the Peters field, had nearly thirty acres to harvest. They would have to work fast when the wheat ripened.

They drove first to the Garner claim, making a holiday of the eleven-mile trip. Neither of them had seen that part of the country before. Inquiring of women in scattered shanties, they passed a number which had been abandoned since the Hard Winter, and found the claim marked by the five acres of wheat. The crop was a marvel. It was a pity to see the unseeded acres of broken sod.

The stable and the shanty were melting down into the wild-grasses ; their sod roofs had fallen in, no doubt over-weighted by rain during the spring thunderstorms. In the shanty a rusted stove and some molding clothes protruded from masses of grassy earth. But the weather was fine for sleeping in the open.

The binder worked like magic. With a jiggling clickety-clatter, it advanced beside the thick-standing stems, slashing them down, rattling them along, catching them into bundles, girding them with twine and dropping bound sheaves onto the stubble. A man who remembered cutting grain with a cradle, whose very arms knew all the motions of gathering, holding, binding with a withe of the wheat-straw knotted and tucked in, could hardly get used to a machine so uncannily human. Riding at ease, with nothing to do but drive the horses, handle levers and listen to the complicated parts, David did as much work as a hired man with a mowing machine and he and his father hustling on stations had been able to do.

The wheat was ripening quickly in the burning heat. A threshing crew would not haul their machine so far and set it up, to thresh only five acres. David and Johnson hauled the sheaves four miles and stacked them beside the nearest neighbors' crop. By that time the full harvest rush was on.

There was no relief from the heat. The sun's first blaze came through air already beginning to quiver. The dry earth cracked wide and the hay was needing cutting too soon. Before the full heat of the day, all a man could see was a dizzy shimmer with black spots dancing through it. Johnson's horses wore old felt hats with slits for their

198

ears, and David carried a small pail of water on the binder and kept a wet cloth in the crown of his hat to prevent sunstroke.

Time could not be spared to stack the last of his cutting or the Peters'. Mary and Eliza knew how to set up cocks; they showed the young ones how to lean the sheaves and cap the pyramid. Only the absence of dew saved Johnson's crop; with a lantern on the binder, David was able to work all night, twenty-six hours in the last stretch. A few grains fell from the shaken bundles, but not many.

They finished the stacking more easily, all by daylight, with a full hour off at noon. When they drank from the water jug, they took time to wipe faces and necks, soak the cloths in their hats, look around the country and drink once more before starting the bundles moving again.

Every distant sight was distorted by heat waves. Wheat stacks cracked apart, wagons crawled along separated from teams trudging on air, in town the buildings split and slid, the wheat elevator swayed and the railroad track crawled in humps. Dust devils appeared whirling along the road, spun twisting the wild grass, and with a flutter vanished. A colorless shimmer lay in the low places and filled the slough to the grasstops; it was called a mirage, but no man in his senses could mistake it for water.

About two o'clock Johnson remarked, "Looks like it might blow up a storm."

"Don't feel like it," David answered. The unsettled heat was nothing like the pressure before a storm. Little gusts came up like invisible flames from the cracked stubble field. Without stopping the rhythm of his pitchfork, he glanced along the western curve of sky. Three thin and distant thunderheads were low upon it, as if peering over the edge of the earth. He let a number of sheaves fly from the tines to Johnson on the stack, and looked again. The clouds were not advancing. A few more clouds were forming in the higher air.

"Maybe settle in to rain before night," he decided. "Be good for the gardens. They certainly need rain." A good downpour on the wilting garden stuff, rain on the roof all night perhaps, would be fine. The stacking was almost done and the wheat would be safe.

They went on loading the rack and emptying it again, building up the golden stacks. Numbers of clouds hung darkening in the northwestern quarter of the sky. Around the whole horizon thunderheads appeared and remained almost motionless. The gusts of wind ceased, no more dust-devils whirled, and the shimmering air was so light that the lungs felt empty.

A loud growl of thunder, followed by a clap, made both men look up. Most of the sky was burning blue, the lazy thunderheads no more than silver-edged piles of gray upon it, but a mass of clouds high in the northwest was angry. Lightning flicked along its black edge and cracked again.

"We better get a hustle on," David said. There were still five or six loads to put up.

"Maybe miss us, at that." Johnson was right, you could never tell where one of those small thundershowers would pass. Both wanted the rain on their land, but not before the wheat was safely stacked to shed it. Saying no more, they quickened the rhythm.

"We'll get it, all right," Johnson shouted while they filled the rack again. David did not divert attention from bundles and fork to reply. The black anger was nearly overhead and the noise terrific. They would better cap that stack quickly, and make another smaller one if they had time. There were enough bundles on the rack ; David caught hold of it and ran while Johnson drove across the stubble at a gallop. There was still sunshine on the yellow glitter of sheaves rapidly diminishing underfoot, but the crashing thunder said that at any moment the deluge would fall. David put on all the speed that any stacker could handle.

A shout from Johnson stopped him. Johnson on the stack and David in the almost emptied rack held pitchforks suspended and stared. The deafening noise was made visible in the sky. The black clouds were in turmoil, boiling in flashes of red light and green light. Black, streaked with livid green, the mass of them turned, twisted, coiled in upon itself and thrust out, flaring incredible colored lightning, red, green, roaring and crashing. Mary was out in the yard. Hands to her ears, she stared upward. Her sunbonneted figure, the house, the stable, the binder and the wheat stacks, were small and peculiarly clear. The writhing clouds stretched down a black tentacle groping for them.

David ran. He heard some shouted curse or prayer from Johnson. The thing in the sky was moving swiftly, there was no time to unhitch, cut loose, a horse for half a mile. He was running the lungs out of his body, trying to think what to do. There was no cellar, no cyclone cellar ; he had dug no cyclone cellar. The potato pit had fallen in. The well in the slough had no cover. The air was full of screaming, of birds' screaming, and rabbits passed him, coyotes, snakes. But a cyclone is a picture in a geography.

Mary met him outside the house. She was clutching the little shaver in a mass of bedding. Through the young one's squalling she asked him what to do.

There should have been a cyclone cellar. The cloud had not touched earth. Beyond the tree-claim, impossi-

201

ble to say how far beyond the tree-claim, it was still groping downward. Blind but knowing what it wanted, it
reached down and reached again. The oxen were going
high-tailed across the country, dragging the loose picket
ropes.

"The well," he shouted.

"We can't all of us, it's too small, it's no good, open.
Oh, all our wheat? Where can we go? There's somewhere. Think! There must be somewhere, somewhere
to put Davy in. If we can only put Davy —"

There must be, there had to be, some refuge. Somehow there must be a way to crawl into the earth, some
place, some safety. He should have dug a cyclone cellar.

"Come away from the building. Maybe if we lie flat —
Where's Eliza?"

"She went to town. There's got to be somewhere.
For Davy."

Antelope came pouring across the garden, the corn.
Mrs. Peters ran along the railroad track toward town, the
baby in her arms. Little figures scattered out from the
schoolhouse and the town.

"The potato pit. If I could wedge timber over — But
how could we mark it? No way to mark it so anybody'd
find him —"

The blind tentacle touched earth and roared. A terrific wind rushed toward it, blowing the squawking chickens like leaves. It was coming.

They saw it coming toward them, an expanding column
of roaring blackness, till the daylight went out and they
could no longer stay on their feet against the wind.

It sucked up a quarter-mile of railroad track, cut a
swath three miles wide through the homesteads south of
town, killed ninety-four men, women and children, wiped
out three towns, and carried a baby in its cradle seven-

teen miles without a scratch. The eastern papers mentioned it ; David always kept the clipping his mother sent him.

A deluge followed the roaring blackness. When the wind steadied they got to their feet under an icy downpour and dimly saw the house still there. David ventured into it with caution. He found the lamp smashed and lighted the lantern. Many things were blown about, the stovepipe was down and roof leaking, but the house was solid. He brought Mary in. Both of them were shaking uncontrollably and in the dripping quilts the young one, near exhaustion, shrieked furious terror. They untangled dry clothes and got into them. The little fellow, quieter, enjoyed his rubbing and slept.

The rain slackened, daylight came under scudding clouds, and David saw the wheat stacks flattened and scattered. Every sheaf was sopping wet on muddy ground.

33

No time could be given to the joy of being alive. To exist, merely to exist and be conscious of existence, to breathe, to see light again, was an ecstasy, but there was no time to know it, barely time to thank God for life, safety, each other and the little one. The tornado had passed them, but the terrific avalanches of air displaced by its passing had left a wreck of things. The prairie chimney was smashed, the cattle were straying, the roof was gone from the Peters' shanty. The first, the important thing was the wheat.

Fortunately the sun sent down an intense heat between scurrying clouds and the wind blew dry. The brief violence of rain was ended. Mrs. Peters minded both babies while she pulled rain-soaked things from the ruin of her house. All the others went into the fields. Even Charley helped. They shook water from each sheaf, set it upright in the muddy stubble and parted the straws above the twine so that the wind could reach the heads. The straw would be somewhat musty, but there was a chance of saving the grain.

They were soon soaked to the skin and the wet and the mud were a drain on energy. The work went on doggedly, but everything helped it. The day was long and a waxing moon in the east picked up and brightened the twilight. The changing wind continued hot through the night and dawn broke clear and blazing. All over the country, men, women and children were moving their sheaves to dry them. Johnson, single-handed, turned over his scattered stacks with a pitchfork. This was an emergency; it was every man for himself.

When the bundles were dry, they traded work again. Two men, in stacking, can do more than twice the work of one. Johnson was willing to help David stack the greater amount of wheat, in return for Mary's cooking for his threshers. The problem of feeding threshers had bothered him, for in his eight-by-ten soddy he lived mostly on pancakes.

Word came across country that the Garner stacks had not been disturbed. The straying cattle, too, had been taken up and David could get them any time by paying the small fee. Watching the grayed sheaves on the pitchforks while they built up the stacks again, both David and Johnson were reasonably sure that his grain was not damaged.

Everything was ready when the threshers came. Two whole days' baking had been done, and before breakfast

Mary and Eliza were busy. Mrs. Peters came to help them, bringing extra plates and pans and cups.

Threshing is the best time of the year. A man has competition in work then, for threshers paid by the bushel are not laggards, and the huskiest farmer humps himself to keep up with the machine-driven work from dawn to dark in sweltering heat and noise and dirt. Then noons are horseplay and tall stories and huge meals for huge appetites. And then there are pies, for threshers must have pie.

The steam engine puffed sooty smoke, the long machine clattered and shook, the smothering chaff-exhaust drove into sweating necks the sharp prickles which there was no time to wipe off, and the grain poured into the sacks. The brown-golden kernels were a jostling rush like a liquid, rising in the sack and brimming it in that split-second when a man heaved away the weight and another burlap mouth was swung under the fall.

The threshers had seen no grain to beat this. Lift a handful from a sack left unsewed at noon by the man who folds the top together and whips along it quick stitches of coarse twine ; let the warm grains trickle between the fingers, clean wheat, every kernel heavy and plumped fat from its tiny side-seam. Taste it, chew the whitey-brown resilience between the grinders and taste the nutty flavor of good wheat, scent and flavor of the goodness of the earth. "A No. 1, if you're asking me, and running darn near forty bushels to the acre, by gosh and by golly ! A man'll go some to beat that !"

Noon ended. They felt the shadeless heat take a deeper grip. They sloshed sopping wet cloths into the crowns of their hats, tightened the rolls of shirt sleeves, hitched up their suspenders. The head feeder asked,

"All set ?" He yelled to the engine man, "All right, Mac. Let 'er go gallagher !"

Go gallagher she did, the steam-driven machine without mercy to nerve and muscle, the endless belt ceaselessly demanding speed with the slashing knife, speed in evenly spreading the loose stalks, and the steel teeth snapping to nip a finger and drag the whole man into a bloody shredding, the stream of grain relentlessly pouring, from dawn to noon, from one o'clock to seven. It was threshing time, the time of year that proves what a man is made of.

Every bushel of that wheat was top quality. Decker at the elevator had to pass it as A No. 1. It was clean, he could not dock the quantity for weed seed or dirt. He rated it at top price, eighty cents a bushel, and David lost no time in delivering it, afraid the price might fall. Now the two ox-teams were useful. He borrowed the Peters' wagon. By lantern-light after supper he loaded both wagons, and at dawn he was already afoot, prodding the two yokes of oxen along the road. He got the last load of the Garner wheat in, barely before the price fell. Eighty five bushels he reserved for next year's seed, ten to be ground at the mill for flour, and Decker handed him a check for four hundred and seventy-seven dollars, sixty cents.

The town was lively with men and teams, wheat coming in and cars loading, stores and saloons and pool hall doing a land-office business. Everything was high, wide and handsome in the flourishing country. David paid the boss thresher and stood him a drink, taking a ten-cent cigar for himself. It was a long time since he had had a cigar. He flung out a dime for another, and handed it to Jake Hewitt in the bank. He paid the two short-time notes, $124.80 including the interest. He paid

206

his taxes. In Boles' store he bought everything on Mary's list : salt, molasses, lard, saleratus, kerosene, soap, matches, and still he had nearly three hundred dollars. Coal for the winter would cost seventy, he owed $180. and interest on the binder, and he had not paid for Dobbin, but he felt fine, he felt prosperous.

He bought boots for himself, and an innocent small pair for Davy. He bought six sticks of peppermint candy, he bought dried peaches. The bolts of flowery goods on the counter enticed him, but he hesitated and decided to bring Mary to see them and choose. She had once spoken of having nothing to read ; he subscribed for the town weekly and for the Chicago Inter-Ocean. Then he walked the oxen along to the lumber-yard, and after figuring the bill and beating it down somewhat, he loaded up.

"David ! Oh, what have you done !" Mary wailed when he stopped the two wagons between the stable and garden. She had been hoeing.

One glance at her tense brown face changed his whole mind. He said, "I got to have a frame shed for the binder. It'd rust, in sod."

"Yes, but not —"

He interrupted, suddenly angry. "Goldarn it, we're going to live like white folks !"

"That's all very well for you to say but we can't, how can we ? We're bad enough in debt as it is, and a whole year to live and pay interest before we can get hold of another cent, out here where I can't do anything, there's no sale for garden truck or eggs or butter or anything on earth but wheat. And now you — Oh, whatever possessed you ? All that studding, and windows, and shingles — "

"We got to have a roof. That tar-paper's a sieve, it

won't last the summer out." That was true. He thought it would be enough, after all, to shingle the roof they had ; he could take back the extra studding he had bought, and the windows.

"Oh, will you stop beating about the bush ! I guess I've got eyes in my head. How much did you go in debt for that lumber ?" She was almost crying in anger. "I declare it's too much for a body's patience. I can worry along in a one-room soddy and if I can I guess you can. You can turn around and take that lumber straight back. I don't want it ! I won't have it. Loading us down with debt. Why don't you say something ? Don't stand there like a bump on a log."

He began to unyoke the oxen. She was right, he had acted without common sense. He did not know what had possessed him, but he did know that no power on earth could make him take that lumber back to the lumber-yard. He knotted ropes into the rings in the oxen's slob-bery noses and led them away to picket them.

Until milking time he walked about on the tree-claim. There was a good stand of bluestem hay. The soil would raise fine timothy-and-clover when he got it broken and the buffalo grass would be good fall pasture if it were fenced. Fence posts cost fifteen cents apiece. He had been a fool, but a woman might appreciate a man's want-ing to give her a decent house to live in.

He went to the house for the milk pail and saw that Mary was making a pie. The dried peaches were soaking in hot water and she was mixing the crust. His mouth watered. The heat in the room was overpowering and she had undressed Davy. In only a short flannel gar-ment and diaper he squalled from his quilt on the floor, threshing his arms and legs raw from heat rash.

"I didn't give him the candy," she said. "I don't know if it's good for him or not when he's so feverish ; what do you think ?" Her eyes were anxious and a little timid but still stubborn.

The candy was peppermint, good for an upset stomach. She knew that as well as he did, so he saw no use in telling her. He took the milk pail and went out. Though the sky was cloudless, the heat was as heavy as before a thunderstorm. It pressed down like the weight of all the work he had to do : digging a well, shoring up the cyclone cellar, digging a house-cellar and building the front room and the tool shed, and fall plowing. He decided that Davy should have that candy, no matter what she said. It was monstrous of her to deny the little fellow a stick of candy in his misery.

Mary was turning the pie in the oven. The fruity smell poured up around her while she touched her lips to hush David. The little chap had fallen into a whimpering doze. There was a kind of complacency about Mary, as if she thought the way to a man's heart was through his stomach. And when she told him to hush, he had to hush, he could not even give his son a stick of candy. He set down the milk and trudged out to the barn. The turnip seed was there, and the cobwebby sowing-harness on its nail.

Mary came from the house and crossed the garden to intercept him on his way to the field. "What is it, David ? Whatever are you doing at this time of day ?"

"It's the twenty-seventh of July," he said.

"But — my gracious goodness, not now ! Supper's all but on the table. Why, I've heard you say a dozen times with my own ears it's nothing but an old-fogy notion, a day more or less don't make any difference."

He trudged on. "You go ahead and eat."

"Well !" She let the word out on an explosive breath. "If that's the way you're going to act !"

It was. He intended to do what he set out to do. By the old rhyme, the twenty-seventh of July wet or dry was the time to sow turnips. He was going to sow them.

"After I made a pie !" Mary cried, but the tears in her voice were angry. "All you're doing's cutting off your nose to spite your face !" He started across the broken sod, flinging out the first scattering arc of round seeds.

His father must have run bushels of the dried pods through the fanning mill. Thinking of the Garners' turnips, David had merely written on a postcard, "Can use turnup seed if you have sum to spare," and his father had sent him by the train conductor enough seed, it seemed, to cover the Territory with turnips. They were good stock feed and David had intended, in some breathing spell of work, to sow perhaps four or five acres.

Walking was pleasant on the springy bellies of the long sods. There was an easy expertness in spreading the light seeds with a swinging arm and dexterous fingers and wrist. The air was so still that without seeing the seed fall he knew that he was doing perfect sowing. He pushed back his hat, then at the end of a row he took it off and flung it on the grass. Between streaks of shadow, the gray earth held all the light there was. It was paler than the pale sky. Fifty acres broken that year, nearly sixty five ready for crop next year, showed that he was getting ahead. Few homesteaders had been able to do as much. Only the big bonanza farmers, rich men able to buy thousands of acres from the Government and to pay for machines and hire scores of men, were doing more. Ten thousand acres in one field must be a sight to see. David thought that some day when he owned a team and

210

buggy, he would take Mary and the little chap on a trip to see those big bonanza farms.

Insensibly the air brightened and the shadow of his arm swept across the sods. The stars burned large and steady, hung low from the high darkness. One by one the yellow lights on the land went out. The Peters' shanty went dark, then Eliza's, and the town became only a green spark of switchlight. The house waited for him with lighted window and doorway as he approached it and turned back.

Mary came out again. "Aren't you coming in?"

"Sure, when I get done. It's a fine night for sowing, not a breath of wind."

She looked around at the sky. "Yes, it's a fine night. David, are you mad at me?"

"No," he said.

"Then do for pity's sake come in and eat your supper! You're only throwing away good seed, there's no earthly use for so many turnips. You've sowed a good five acres already."

He said pleasantly, "I figure I'll sow fifteen."

"Fifteen acres — of turnips? My goodness, why, whatever — fifteen — What for?"

The words had come out of his mouth, fifteen acres. He could think of some reason, later. "Don't you worry, there's no flies on me. Run along in, I'll come when I'm ready."

"Yes, well, I — I'm saving supper for you. Whenever you want it, David."

"All right." His hunger had ceased some time ago. "How's Davy?"

"He's asleep, poor little mite. I greased him over with lard, it seemed to ease him some."

"Well, don't wait up for me."

211

He wondered if he had committed himself to sowing turnips all night. There was no sale for turnips in town, no sale nor even any trade value at the stores for anything the land produced. Four oxen could not possibly eat fifteen acres of turnips. If the cow ate too many the milk would taste so strongly of them that it could not be used. Maybe turnips, plowed in, would fertilize the soil, but the soil did not need fertilizer. He felt fine, however. The houselights shone welcomingly, and he went on sowing the round, light seeds in the warm night, pretty well satisfied with everything.

He was at the end of the long field when he heard hoofs. Somewhere on the arc of the west a number of horses were trotting. Though the starlight seemed so clear and the horizon was a clean line, he could see only a little way into the dark. From the sounds he made out forty to fifty horses, riderless and coming in a drove. He thought of the droves of wild horses farther west. There was no kind of pen on his place and he could not use a lariat if he had one ; he gave up the impulse to try to capture one of those horses before he realized that they were driven. Loose horses would not travel so long at that untroubled speed without pausing to graze.

The hoofbeats grew louder. The thin darkness solidified in the shape of a herd of horses. He could see their free heads and a moving mass of bodies. One of them broke away from the mass and loped toward him, where he stood plain in the starlight on the gray field, and then he saw the rifle and the rider moving with the free animal in the Indian way.

He glanced toward the house and saw dark shapes risen between him and the lighted doorway. They were shapes of the corn rows in the garden. It was too far to run. He could not outrun an Indian pony and no one

212

can outrun a bullet. His breath swelled for a shout and he held it, trying to think, knowing that a shout would bring Mary running out, helpless, away from the baby, the musket.

The galloping thudded louder and abruptly ceased. In full gallop, the unbridled pony braced back on its haunches and the Indian said, "Hullo, Beaton."

It was Halfbreed Jack. David let his breath out carefully, and swallowed. He felt sick. "Hullo. Where'd you drop from?"

"Traveling east to sell horses. Wild horses we rounded up on the range. What you doing out here this time of night?"

"Sowing turnips. Twenty-seventh of July, wet or dry, 's the day to sow turnips. I got started late. Traveling pretty far into the night yourself, aren't you?"

"We come on, to make Thorne's place."

The drove was passing across a corner of the broken sod toward Gay's fenced house and shed. David saw two more riders now, but neither of them looked like Gay. "He with you?"

"Not this trip. Maybe next time, if we have luck selling these horses. Well, so long."

As if it understood the words, the pony raced to overtake the drove. David stood watching the horses pour eagerly into the fenced enclosure. Two riders unsaddled and unbridled their horses. Boots tramped in Gay's house and the window gave a silent shout of lamplight. David rubbed his jaw for a moment of some doubt, then went to his house.

"What is it? What's happened? Has Gay come?" Mary wanted to know. "What are all those horses doing at his place?"

"Seems as though he's gone into the horse business."

Without much appetite he ate some cold supper and a piece of pie. Mary was uneasy. "Ought you to let them stay there? Did he send you word to? Who are they, do you know them?"

He blew out the lamp. Starlight was enough to undress by. The garden, the straw stacks, the fields and the fenced horses came into view. Men moved about in the lighted shanty but they were too far away to recognize. "The place is Gay's lookout. He didn't ask me to take care of it. Come here, Molly girl. Kind of like me sometimes, mm?"

Toward dawn he heard the hoofs on the road through the slough. That morning Eliza took Mary with her to go through Gay's shanty. They found bedding on the floor and dishes unwashed. The men had used some supplies, and left an empty whiskey bottle.

All through dinner David listened to a flurry of indignant surmises. No one knew where Gay was. Mary thought that they should write to his father, and Eliza declared that if such men tried to use the shanty again and David did not stop it, she would. When he pushed back his plate, David told them that they would do nothing of the kind. "It's Gay's business. You'll keep your noses out of it and your mouths shut."

Looking up at him, Eliza changed her mind and did not speak. She seemed tired, she was thinner and more high-strung, as if some strain was wearing her out. David realized suddenly how hard it was on a woman to stay month after month in a claim shanty with nothing to do, hearing the wind and the wild grasses. He wondered why she did not give up her claim and go back to the crowded, busy summers in the east.

He did not think until later that he had won the old battle against Eliza, now that it meant nothing to him to win it. When they heard horses in the night and men's voices at the shanty, he went to sleep again. Mary said that Eliza did not even talk about it any more.

34

Work piled up on him so that he bought a mowing machine. Johnson was glad to trade work with his team for the use of a mower in putting up his winter fuel.

One afternoon when David was flinging earth out of the excavation for his house-cellar, Johnson loomed up on the rim of it. David was startled. "Hullo, what's wrong? Machine break down?"

"No." Johnson mopped his red face and the back of his neck. "Got any objection if I use it to cut hay for that family lives south of here, the Peters?"

David set a foot on the shoulder of the shovel and leaned on its handle. "Can't say I have, but what's the idea?"

"Well, seems only a neighborly thing to do. I come on the young lady in the slough grass with a scythe. Fact is, I already mowed down some for her. She was mowing on your sister's claim, seems Miss Beaton gave her leave, but I didn't know that till I got there. It's no work for a young lady, swinging a scythe out in this sun."

"You're dead right. Gosh!" Sweat trickled in the mud it had made of the dust on his neck. He mopped at it with his earth-colored, soggy bandana. "I can't keep up with the work. I had no idea — Cut what they need for fuel and feed this winter, I'll help put it up."

He pitched into the shoveling again and heard his muscles tear the wet back of his shirt, sweat-glued to the skin.

At the time he paid no attention to Johnson's remark that pitching hay was a light job if you took it easy. It came back to him when Nettie and the young ones helped Johnson stack their hay, and then he remembered the sheepish way in which Johnson had said it. In the cool of the afternoons, David heard their voices from the slough and saw them riding on the load of hay. Johnson let Charley hold the lines. Often on the stack Johnson loafed, leaning on his pitchfork and talking to Nettie who idled with her pitchfork on the wagon, and faintly David heard their laughter.

Johnson began coming to church, painfully clean in a starchy new shirt, stiff collar and brand-new suspenders. On several Sunday afternoons Nettie went walking with him along the railroad track. David could make no objection.

He spoke to her about it once, in a joking way, and her straight, clear look made him ashamed of himself.

"I like him, David. He's like you. But all I want is to be a school teacher so I can help out at home."

It was a Saturday morning in fall plowing time. David was using the heavy plow with the oxen and she had come to ask if she might borrow his light plow. With it and the sorrel, she could work the stubble field so that they could make a crop next year.

David was behind with his own plowing. The shortening days were catching up with him, and one job that is almost impossible to do well by lantern-light is plowing. He let her have the light plow. From the field he saw her lifting it over the grass clumps while the sorrel dragged it. The land must be plowed. Her father could not leave a job paying him thirty dollars a month in the east. From their wheat crop they had got next year's seed for ten acres, flour, and $209.10 in cash. It was not much,

216

to feed six and buy soap, matches, and the kerosene that Nettie must have to study by.   David had refused to take any pay for binding, sacking and hauling the wheat.   They had paid taxes on the sorrel, the stove and the clock, and they must have a new roof for the winter.   The thatch was poor protection against rain and they did not have a wooden floor.

When he turned the oxen he saw her struggling along the furrow.   The share came up in spite of her and she had to back and drive it in again.   She was too light, too thin ; her eye was accurate and she would not give up, but she did not have the weight to hold the plow.   It took all her strength to lift it at the end of the furrow.   She tugged the line to turn the sorrel and the share skipped twice before she dug it into the soil again.   She took off her sunbonnet and wiped her sleeve across her face.

David's own furrow was wobbling.   He steadied it, plowed across the end of his field and up the side to Gay's fence.   He tied the oxen and started cross-lots.   He was half way across Gay's claim when he saw Johnson coming across the stubble patch in the slough.   He stood stock-still.

Neither of them saw him.   He saw Johnson walk up to her and tenderly take the lines from her shoulders.   He saw her protest.   What Johnson meant by the few words he said was plain enough.   The way she gave up the plow was sweet.   They looked at each other for a moment, and it seemed to David that he could hear Johnson saying with love, "Go in the house, and rest."   She walked toward the house, and briskly Johnson slapped a line on the sorrel's flank and strode out behind the plow.

David went back to his field.   He had to admit that Johnson was a good man.   No one could wish any woman a better one.   If David was not pleased by what he had

217

seen, he knew he ought to be. After a time he was surprised by the absence of sunshine. A scud of clouds had come over the grayed sky without his noticing it. It thickened, and a sleety rain began to come in gusts, freezing on.

He put the oxen and the plow under shelter, and went to work in cellar and barn, sorting potatoes, cleaning mangers and stalls, mending and oiling his tools. He was coming pretty well to the conclusion that he was not a dog in the manger, and for the first time he felt the ache in knowing that time changes everything.

Toward sundown he thought of the light plow, which Johnson might have left in the field. It had been in his mind to go over and see how the family was getting along; now he started at once. He had no respect for a farmer who did not take care of tools, whether his own or borrowed.

Nettie was in shelter under a haystack, twisting hay. They did not even have a lean-to, because of the cost of the roof. Her beautiful mouth was musing till she saw him and smiled, blue eyes lighting up her thin brown face framed in the patched shawl. The plow was in the stable, and the sorrel, curried and rubbed down, was eating hay. He took the picket lines and stretched them from stable to shanty. "This time of year, it don't pay to take chances," he said to Nettie.

She asked him to go into the house and get warm. In the hollow under the stack she was out of the sleety rain but her bare hands were withered and stiff with chill. Her mother probably had no yarn to knit mittens. He gathered up the sticks of hay. "Come warm yourself; haven't you got enough for awhile?"

"Pretty soon. I want to use all the daylight."

The soddy was dark. Even with a good roof it would

be dismal in winter without kerosene to burn for cheer-fulness. The warmth from the stove did not let the freezing sleet stop the leaks through the thatch. Mrs. Peters had set pans under them. Everything was as neat as possible and she had been telling a story to the young ones huddled in the gloom, watching the chinks of light around the stove drafts, amid the irregular wet tinkle and splash of the drip from the roof.

They were all cheerful because Mr. Peters had written that his job would last only two weeks more, then he would start walking home. He had sent them some money before harvest and he had bought boots and a jumper for himself, but he was ending the work-season with one hundred dollars saved.

The freezing sleety rain seemed to have settled in for the night. David tramped home through crackling grass, every blade enclosed in ice. A cold light will bring out every little ugliness about a place, show up the untidy dead garden, the sag of a clothesline from a slanting pole, every small job not yet done, and in the same way dismal weather will make debts large in the mind. Even the rankling thought that Dobbin was not paid for would come up.

It was not as if he had nothing to show for all the money. Nor as if he had gone so far as to shingle the stable roof. The sod stable was now large enough to shelter the oxen and the cow and calf, and its costly rafters supported a sod roof, which would soon rot them but cost nothing but labor. Only the binder and the mowing machine were in a clean, dry shed.

The ten-by-twelve addition to the house had been folly, but at least part of the shingled roof and one of the prairie-chimneys had been necessary. From stable to house the haystacks were an almost unbroken row, and along their south side a rope was stretched. No blizzard would catch him napping.

The well by the back door had cost six dollars for rope and lumber to make the windlass. Eight days hard, fast digging, with Mary pulling up the pails of earth, had struck plenty of water. Lest Davy fall in, he had put a solid cover over the well ; no money could be better spent. The necessary windlass was now a luxury, making it easy to draw water. The raw earth, cleared away and heaped in a low swell over the cyclone cellar, was an added protection to the buried cave with its heavy, costly wooden door.

There was room to eat and work in the kitchen now, without knocking funny bones or skinning shins. Beyond it was the front room, with the bed, the trunks, the table and short strip of rag carpet from Eliza's shanty, and a new, unlighted heating stove in it.

"Well, we've got a lot to be thankful for," David said, getting out of his coat. The kitchen was clean and warm. Strings of onions hung by their braided tops, seed-corn ears by their husks, and on the shelves were dried sweet corn, beans, a small sack of popcorn and a few hoarded glasses of ground cherry preserves, costly because of the sugar. Potatoes and coal were down cellar, pumpkins and squash were outdoors under a haystack. He knocked the sleet from his cap. "I've been to Peters'."

"Yes, we ought to be thankful." Mary tasted the bean soup and peppered it. "Have they any news ?"

"His job runs out in a couple of weeks. Take him another couple to walk back, better than three hundred miles." Mr. Peters would not try again to steal a ride. The railroads were shutting down on tramps and some brakemen were vicious. Bodies of tramps were often found on the right of way. David said, "He's got a hundred dollars saved."

"My, that's good !" Mary checked herself at that. The Peters did not owe a cent. A look between her eyebrows showed that she was thinking of the debts. A hundred and eighty for the binder, at ten per cent ; almost three hundred and fifty at the lumber-yard and more than a hundred at the hardware store, for nails, hinges, the mowing machine, the heater, stovepipe and chimneys, all at three per cent a month ; the debt was piling up, nearly fifteen dollars a month for interest alone. But she did not speak of it.

Not a word had been said about the fifteen green acres of turnips. That land must be plowed before it froze, and still David could not think how to explain those useless turnips.

He looked around. Davy was sound asleep, there was half an hour to spare before milking time, and seeing nothing else to do he picked up the Chicago Inter-Ocean and sat down by the window.

He was not much of a hand for reading, which seemed to him like eating hickory nuts, too much trouble for the good dug out of the small words. In winter evenings he liked to sit eating crisp, buttery popcorn, then slowly peeling an apple in one long, transparently thin curling strip, and cutting off juicy hunks to set his teeth into, or with his razor-sharp knife delicately cutting a translucent slice and holding it to the lamplight to see the apple blossom, while women folks read aloud the editorials and the news. This gave him something to keep and turn over in his mind. The Chicago Inter-Ocean already made the evenings something to look forward to, though there were no apples and the small amount of popcorn was saved for Thanksgiving and Christmas. He handled the paper with respect and glanced down the columns in search of conundrums.

For some reason which baffled him, women always skipped conundrums. Mary hardly appreciated one when she heard it. In just such an idle moment he had discovered his favorite, which he would never tire of repeating : When is a bonnet not a bonnet? The answer was, When it becomes a pretty woman. His eyes were stopped by a small item.

Rutabagas, turnips, potatoes.
We offer top market prices for carload lots rutabagas, prime white turnips, or first quality potatoes, no sod wanted. Ship COD, we pay and deduct freight charges. Nineteen years in business, bank references. Smith & Robinson, Commission Merchants, Chicago.

He read it slowly through, paused, and read it again. Then quietly expanding, he remarked, "Well, here it is."

"What?" Mary turned from lighting the lamp. He handed her the paper and watched her face while she read. "You don't mean to say — David ! We can sell turnips ? Why, we've got — how many bushels is fifteen acres, how many carloads, what is top price ? So that's the reason why — Oh, why didn't you tell me ? Oh David, if we can sell turnips ! How many have we got ?"

"Well, fifteen acres, say around two thousand bushels," he said calmly. Mary's face was all he could ask for.

"If only this will let up," she breathed, listening to the ferocious sleet on roof and windows.

The storm continued through the night and the next day. They did not go to church. This was not winter weather, but Mary would not take Davy two miles through it in the slow, open ox-wagon, and the slippery ground made it risky to walk and carry him. Church would have shortened the long day of hearing the rattling sleet and knowing that it might be impossible to haul turnips without their freezing. The fury of the storm increased that night, but sometime before dawn they woke and heard silence. David got up to look at the thermometer. The mercury was rising.

Broadcast, the turnips could not be plowed out. Too many would be trampled, too many cut by the plowshare. They had grown firmly into the mass of grass-roots not yet rotted, but a steady pull brought them up between boots planted on the sod. They came up clean and smooth and firm, nearly all of a size, flattened round turnips with a faint purple stain on the ivory rind at the base of lush tops.

David sent an honest sample by express to Smith & Robinson, with a letter in Mary's most painstaking penmanship attached, and he received a telegram. "Can handle unlimited quantity up to sample. Ship carloads till further notice."

He let out a whoop, and Clint Insull asked, "What's this, you want a car? What you got up your sleeve, Dave?" David told him, and ordered a box-car. The news was all over town before he could hustle his packages from the store into the wagon and head for home. Men kept coming up to ask, "What's this I hear? You got a sale for turnips?"

"You bet you! And fifteen acres of 'em!"

"I'll be darned."

He went up the slope ahead of the oxen and swung Mary off her feet. "They want the turnips, all we got! They telegraphed!"

It was plain in her face, in her eyes, that there was no one like him. "To think, all this time, you didn't let out so much as a hint. You're getting to be as close-mouthed as your father. Honestly, David, why didn't you tell me?"

"You can't sometimes most always tell how a thing will turn out," he said.

35

Next day was Sunday. A sharp wind tore rags of cloud in the sky and sunshine raced with shadow over the graying prairie. The turnip field was emphatic where nothing else was green. When David took the morning's milk in he said hesitantly, "Being's it's Sunday, I don't suppose — "

"The better the day, the better the deed," Mary briskly replied. She hoped she was a good Christian woman, but to her mind that did not mean being strait-laced. "Christ Himself helped a donkey out of a ditch, and the minute you're through breakfast I'm coming right out with you, the dishes can wait."

They put Davy, well wrapped, into a hollow in the south side of a straw stack and barricaded him with the two wagons seats to keep him there. They gave him a turnip to play with. He was fairly quiet so long as he could see them. David pulled the turnips with a steady pull which did not break the taproots and Mary followed him, lopping off the tops with the butcher knife and filling the bushel basket. David carried the full basket to the wagon. They worked in a hurry for the clouds were settling and the wind growing colder.

Before dark they filled the two wagons and piled up another load. David covered the ivory heaps with straw. It was surprising that pulling turnips proved to be more tiring than hard work. Backs, necks, legs and hands were stiff and aching. After supper they could hardly stand up from their chairs and Mary laughed at their crippling around as if they were seventy.

Three o'clock in the morning was as black as a stack of black cats. David walked the oxen to town by lantern-light and got Clint Insull out of bed to unlock the box-car. "Say, you're a hustler from 'way back, Dave, and no mistake," Clint said. David replied that nowadays a fellow had to be. The railroad gave him only three days to load a car, and it held five hundred bushels; he would have to do most of the hauling at night. He loaded the car by basketsful, dumping the turnips gently, not to bruise them.

Next day he said that Mary could not stand the work. She jeered at the notion that topping turnips is work, but her hands were stiff and he guessed how her legs and neck ached. He said he would get Johnson to help him.

She would not hear of it. "He's got no work to trade, and we can't pay wages. Wait till we find out what we get for the turnips."

"Well. I'll tell Clint to hold off the second car till we hear."

"No, shipping don't cost us anything, and we've got a chance to make something, no matter how little. We better keep shipping the turnips as fast as we can, no telling when the price'll go down or the weather change."

There was no sunshine after the first day. Under low clouds the wind blew piercing cold, but before noon the frost melted wet on the leaves and made a slime of mud over unfrozen ground. Because of the wet, the sap and the mud, they could not wear their good wraps. They halved an old horse-blanket, cut holes for their heads, and belted the heavy stuff down with twine over their oldest clothes. To save their shoes they wrapped rags around their feet. Mary's skirts were dabbled wet to the knees, and their wrists chapped raw under sleeve cuffs wet from the turnip tops.

225

While David was piling the last basketful into the third car, little Nellie Townsend came blowing across the windy street in a shawl, to say that a letter had come for him, from Chicago. He opened it there in the store. A check was in it, a check for seventy dollars. Smith & Robinson wrote to speak well of the turnips and say that they wanted more of them. Deducting freight charges and commission on the first carload, they enclosed check. Seventy dollars figured out to fourteen cents a bushel.

Mary cried. She sank down on the rank-smelling leaves between small heaps of topped turnips and cried. Her skirts were wet and the horse-blanket stiff and gritty, so she wiped at her tears with the backs of her swollen, stiff hands. The wind blew teardrops off her cheeks.

"I can't help it," she sobbed. "To know it's really so. If we can only ship them all before it freezes. If only the price stays up. Oh, why are we wasting time like this !"

Frost thickened and David lined the wagons deep with straw and thickly covered the turnips. All one day the low clouds spit snow, but the ground did not freeze. They worked with bare hands because bare hands are quicker and the sap of the turnip tops would soon soak mittens. The strong-smelling sap corroded their hands. In the cold, the shriveled flesh cracked, and one day when he emptied a full basket David noticed smears of blood on the turnips. Mary's hands were bleeding.

"You go in the house and tend to those hands," he said. "I'm going to get Johnson."

She got stiffly to her feet. "Don't make me, David, please don't. I'm all right. It's the only chance I've had to be any help. Please let me, I'd rather. I want to."

Her teeth chattered. It was too cold to talk. The

wind cut to the bone and they were both trembling from cold and weariness. "Go in and warm up the house and take care of those hands."

"No! I won't!" she cried out. "I'm going to be some use! We don't get ahead, we're slipping behind all the time, and I can't do anything, I'm nothing but a drag on you. Please let me help with the turnips."

"You're not a drag on me. I won't have you killing yourself."

"What's killing me is being no use. I can't even trade-in my eggs and butter to help on the groceries. I'm nothing but an expense. It's not right. It's against nature. It makes me feel like we're not married."

A swear word was shocked out of him. "Don't say such things! You don't know what you're saying."

"I do! I know how I feel. I thought we were starting out like other folks do. I thought I'd do my part. For all the use I am out here, I'd better stayed home and saved you the cost of my keep."

"That's no way to talk. You're tired out." Unexpected fury rushed up in him and roared, "My Godfrey, this is your home! You'll like it or lump it. You're married to me, by all that's holy! And what the hades did you expect? I told you — "

She screamed at him, "I've got a right to be some use! You're not going to pay any hired man — "

A desolate, frightened bawling from the straw-stack silenced them. Ashamed, he muttered, "We can't have blood on the turnips."

"Cut me a slice for him to chew on. I'll wipe them, there's only a few. Careful, don't get it bloody, your own hands are just as bad."

That night she melted the pretty molded cake of

beeswax from her sewing basket, and mixed it with some lard and a few drops of turpentine. They filled the cracks in their hands with this salve and bandaged them. This protected the turnips somewhat, and Mary wiped the few that the bandages smeared. As she said, nobody would eat the peelings.

The cold hovered around freezing, but low clouds and mists held off the danger. Every minute was precious, for at any time the sky might clear. They worked as fast as they could, with no letup while daylight lasted. Mary did not stop to cook. They had cold beans and bread and milk, and she stumbled to bed in the cold house, asleep before she pulled quilts over her damp clothes. David slept on the loads of turnips, while the stupid oxen kept on going.

One morning he watched his car shunted onto the eastbound train. Gay Thorne swung down from the passenger coach and came along the platform. "Hi yuh, Dave? How's tricks?" he sang out, and added, "You look like the end of a misspent life."

David's bandaged and mittened hands were in his pockets and he left them there. "Can't complain. How's the world treating you, Thorne?"

Gay's tilted hat, the fine new overcoat and fur-backed gloves must have been ordered by mail from St. Paul or Chicago. He handed out a ten-cent cigar from a vest pocket full of them. He was on his way east for the winter, and inquired about all the folks.

David remarked, "Been some visitors on your claim, guess you'd call them visitors. Stopped two, three times. Driving horses east."

"You don't say! Oh, yes. Must be a bunch of fellows I run across couple of times out there. Rounding up wild horses on the range, pretty good horseflesh from what

I hear, when you get 'em broken." Gay laughed a little, showing white teeth under his waxed black mustache. "That's all right. Look 'em over sometime, Dave, you might get one cheap."

David looked at him and did not say anything. It suited him down to the ground that Gay's affairs were none of his business. He walked along to the wagons, headed the oxen toward home, and went to sleep in the straw.

The sky cleared while he loaded the last carload, but the weather had changed. A mild wind blew from the south and in misty moonlight the wild ducks and geese were flying lower than they had flown for a long time.

He and Mary had pulled and topped, loaded and hauled two thousand, five hundred bushels of turnips. Two hundred bushels were left over for winter stock-feed. They waited in apprehension for the last letter from Chicago. The price held up to the last, fourteen cents above freight charges and commission. He took the last check home, and laid them all on the table. "There we are. Three hundred and fifty dollars."

Mary spread them apart a little, to look at them. Her hands were still drawn stiff. The cracks were healing slowly because any use of their hands tore the raw edges apart. "What are you going to do with it?"

"Half of it's yours. I'll do anything you say."

She said passionately, "All I want on earth's to get rid of the debts so we can draw a free breath."

There was enough money to pay the greater part of the bills at the lumber-yard and the hardware store. Now they would owe, with accumulated interest, only a hundred and sixty three dollars at three per cent a month, besides what they owed for the binder, and for Dobbin.

36

In town on Saturday every settler was talking about turnips next year. David advised against them ; he did not intend to sow any. Such luck would hardly strike twice in a farmer's lifetime. Only a late, unpredictable failure in the eastern turnip crop could have sent the price soaring so high as to reach fourteen cents a bushel over and above commission and the freight charges on such a long haul.

"You got to figure you're a long way from market," he pointed out to the homesteaders in Wyatt's store. "Back east they've been raising all they need to live on for a long time and they'll go on doing it, barring some accident like must have happened to their turnips this fall. A man out here can't compete against 'em in their market and pay freight charges."

Johnson opined that that was the trouble ; all the money going east and little coming back. "Every man of us in here today to hand over cash to this bloodsucker here," he said, giving Wyatt a friendly grin. "How much you going to set me back for a lamp chimley, Cliff ?"

"It's them eastern trusts that's bleeding us to death," Dant Macray declared. He was the homesteader north-east of town, on whose claim David and Johnson had stacked the Garner wheat for threshing. "It's manu-facturers and railroads, grinding us down with their pro-tective tariff."

David was as much against the protective tariff as any man there. "It's un-constitutional," he stated. "The Constitution says, plain for any man to read, this govern-ment's got no right to favor anybody. 'Taxes for revenue only,' is what it says, plain black and white. We got to stop the protective tariff, next national election. But just the same, you can't get around the fact that every man's got to lift himself by his own boot-straps. It'll be hard pulling for every man out here till this country's settled up enough to make a home market."

He had said his say, and he listened to the argument going this way and that, till the slamming door let in the lanky Garner brothers. David greeted them heartily. "Hullo there!" He shook their hands and introduced them around. "Well, how you boys been making out this summer?"

They had been working on the railroad and all summer they had played in card-luck on paydays. Lounging on the counter to speak with David aside, they said that they were well heeled with cash money and if they could keep a hold on it and end up a winter's woodcutting in Missouri with maybe another five hundred dollars between them, they would tackle their claim again next spring.

"You reckon we could find witnesses to swear we been living on it enduring seven months this year, to comply with the law?" Lafe asked.

"Count on me," David told them. There was no danger of claim jumpers now; the land rush was over and a few settlers hit by wind or hail after the Hard Winter were already abandoning claims. The Garners could be sure the land would not be wanted until another boom. He asked how well satisfied they were with the team.

"I purely hate to tell you what that team happened to," Lafe said. Star had been stolen, and the Garners had just finished walking Dobbin more than a hundred miles, hitched single to their wagon.

"There's a right choicy gang of horse thieves operating out yonder," Duane told the crowd. "They taken none

231

but the best." In the night, without a flicker of light to waken the stableman, the finest horses had been quietly walked out of their stalls in the camp stable. It was plain that an accomplice, or more than one, was in the camps. Every man was under suspicion but guilt could be fixed on no one, and some thousands of dollars' worth of horses had been stolen. Tracks led toward the Black Hills but they were lost on the borders of that wild, arid and dangerous country.

"Winter coming on, we'll likely have some trouble with them outlaws working back this way," someone said. Forehanded settlers priced padlocks. David bought two stout ones and cartridges for his musket; more than four dollars gone in one wallop. Drifting with the Garners through the Saturday crowd in front of Boles' stores, he walked down the side street with them to look at Dobbin.

He could not reconcile himself to losing Star. In some sense, a man keeps a horse so long as he knows who owns him, that he is in good hands, taken care of, not underfed or abused. Now the brown colt with that marvel of a five-pointed white star swirled thin on the good width between blue-black wondering eyes, was gone.

On the prairie beyond the blacksmith shop Dobbin raised his head, pricked eager eyes and whickered joyfully. He was limping, but only because he had cast a shoe. He nuzzled at David's pockets, his old coltish trick of rummaging for an apple or a carrot. Shoulder and flank and round sturdy barrel were sleek, and nothing but dried mud broke the smoothness of knees and ankles.

"Tough," David sympathized. "You boys left stranded with only half a team, an old wore out — you might as well say, ten-year-old." By borrowing the Peters' sorrel, he could drive a team again. Dobbin alone was not worth a yoke of oxen, and David aimed at getting about thirty dollars to boot in the trade.

The Garners did not refuse to trade, nor seem interested. He had never before gone up against traders whom he could not get a direct word out of. The Missourians had all the time in the world, and gave no clue to their thoughts. That whole afternoon went while they stood around idly lounging against their wagon. When he was sure he had them pinned down, they wondered how tobacco would grow on their claim. In the end, milking time near and his Saturday buying not done, he offered an even trade, the yoke of oxen for Dobbin and the double harness, take it or leave it.

He had plenty of time to mull over a notion that they wanted cash to boot and to decide that it was no trade, before Lafe remarked that he didn't care if they did. Duane didn't care either. They had the better of the trade by about twenty dollars, but David had Dobbin.

It was an ill-matched team, but the plowing went more lightly. Though horses did no more work than oxen, the feel of the live lines around his shoulders, the feel and the sight of the team stepping out on decisive feet, made plowing a pleasure again. He finished turning over the Peters' ten-acre patch in return for the loan of the sorrel, and was well into his turnip field when Mr. Peters came across the fresh furrows one morning.

The drive of harvest work in the east had worn Mr. Peters down. He was thinner than ever, and footsore from his long walk home. But he was in high spirits, his eyes an intense blue fire.

"I tell you, a man don't know when he's lucky!" he said. In the east he had tramped with hobos. The little he told about them was enough to sicken any man.

David never told Mary about the young hobo who died of starvation, nor the old man's body found by the railroad tracks with every bone in his hands smashed by the brakeman's beating off his hold on the fast train. Mr. Peters was right; any man with a roof over his head was lucky.

He was going to put a shingled roof on his shanty, but first he wanted to borrow David's yoke of oxen and the breaking plow. "If I don't break this gol-darned land," he said, "it'll break me." He went singing to get the oxen, and the wind brought back some of the song to David.

> We don't live here, we only stay,
> 'Cause we're too poor to get away!

It was Mr. Peters who started that song, though others added scores of verses later. The tune was Beulah Land, but when people gave it words which came down to earth and everyday facts they sang it with a rollicking swing that it never had in church.

That was an open winter. Week after week the winds blew only a little snow over unfrozen ground. Alternately, as other work permitted, David and Mr. Peters broke sod till mid-November. There was still far too little snow, but the ground froze deeply and government experts said that deep freezing would hold moisture. Mary read aloud a piece from the Inter-Ocean, which stated that next spring the soil would thaw gradually, downward from the top, and little by little release moisture to the downward-growing roots of crops.

David did not know; he observed that on washdays Mary hung out the wet clothes to freeze dry. Still, this kind of farming was new to him, and in any case there was no market for anything but wheat.

234

37

The open winter let them go to church nearly every Sunday. Both families went gaily in David's wagon drawn by the clean-groomed team, with the two seats on it and the children down in the straw-lined box. They were all well bundled and cozy under quilts and laprobes ; they took extra covers and ropes, and David and Mr. Peters were confident that if a blizzard caught them they could reach safety by way of the railroad track and the slough.

A blizzard struck in January. It lasted only fifty hours and killed one homesteader south of town. A newcomer, he had been warned often enough, but he believed the open winter rather than what he was told. He was caught in the stable doing his chores, without a rope to the shanty. His wife kept the lamp burning in the window until the blizzard cleared and she saw him lying frozen solid, so near the shanty that he could have touched it.

He was the first man buried in the graveyard by the church. The other graves were small mounds over children. The weather was pleasant and everyone went to the funeral, the men with earlaps turned up so that they could take off their caps at the grave.

"Dust unto dust," the Rev. Brown said, standing black as a crow by the heap of frozen clods on the dun land. Davy uttered inquiring sounds ; he spoke a jargon now which Mary often understood. David hoisted him higher, whispering to him to hush. Apple-cheeked with cold, the boy stared at him wonderingly, then grabbed his neck in a laughing hug and breathed warm behind his ear. It was strange to know that some day new ropes would creak while men lowered another pine box into the earth, and David himself would be in it, under boards nailed down. It was even more strange to think that he would not be there, that his ears would not hear the clods thumping.

The widow was a thin woman, in a threadbare green shawl and red knitted hood. She did not know that the wind whipped a strand of hair across her face. Her twelve-year-old boy looked like her. There were four girls, younger. After it was over they climbed into their wagon while David and other homesteaders awkwardly told the boy to call on them if he needed help on the place. The storekeepers could not do this because the only help they could give would be credit, and the oxen were already mortgaged.

"Much obliged," the boy said. "I guess we'll make out. Pa got fourteen acres broken." He shut his mouth hard and headed the oxen toward their claim.

Mrs. Insull came rustling while David was handing Davy to Mary in the wagon. Mrs. Insull was a vivacious woman who must have been something of a flirt as a girl. Her yellow hair was frizzed under a velvet bonnet exactly matching her quick brown eyes. She wanted to be sure that they would all come to an oyster supper which the ladies were talking of giving to help pay for the church.

"We'll be there with bells on, Mrs. Insull!" David assured her.

"Yes, we shall be pleased to come, Mrs. Insull, weather permitting," said Mary.

Mrs. Insull sparkled. "And you, Mr. Peters? And Mrs. Peters. You must bring my little pupils, our whole class will be there." She smiled at the little girls and Charley, who were in her Sunday School class. When they heard that the oyster supper would cost ten cents, they knew they could not go. The look in Nettie's eyes hurt David. Mr. Peters said slowly that he and his wife

236

would come; they could not refuse to help the church, what they could.

It was on the tip of David's tongue to offer to take them all, but on second thought he waited to speak to Mary. He waited three weeks, thinking that the weather might settle the matter with nothing said. The temperature stayed around fifteen below zero, no more snow fell, and Sundays were clear. Around the church stove the ladies talked of nothing but the oyster supper, and at home Mary discussed every meaning of what they said. Mrs. Insull favored having the oyster supper in the Hewitt's large house, but Miss Hewitt's friends truthfully said that the depot was larger. The ladies decided for the depot. Many of them had never seen Mrs. Insull's fine furniture; Mary never had, and Mrs. Insull had pushed herself forward to head the committee; let the ladies of the committee help her do the extra cleaning.

At last David spoke of taking the whole Peters family and paying their way. Mary's smile thanked him, but she shook her head. "They can't go, they haven't anything to wear."

David thought that was nonsense. "They go to church."

"Yes, but they keep their coats on. It don't matter so much how a coat looks, it's only an outside wrap. But I know for a fact, Mrs. Peters told me, that Mr. Johnson asked Nettie to go and she wouldn't. Her best dress sleeves are patched on both elbows where they got so tight they burst through, and they couldn't match the goods in town. She'd have to take off her coat at an oyster supper and everybody there'll have good whole dresses."

"Seems like somebody ought to be able to do something," David said.

237

"I offered to take up my challis so she could wear it for the evening, but she wouldn't. She don't really want to go, David, she's never been out among folks, and she'd rather not. Mrs. Peters says herself she's scared she won't know how to act, it's been so long since she went anywhere."

David pushed back his empty plate with knife and fork crossed upon it. He drank his tea, wiped his mustache and rolled his napkin. "We might ask the young ones."

"We'd only cause heartburnings. Flora and Lucy's skirts are so short the little Insull boy made fun of them. Mrs. Peters cut up her good shawl and made new yokes and sleeves to their coats and lengthened their dresses, but it don't match and the seams show where she let them out. They look nice in church and it's all right for school but they couldn't take off their coats at a party. They don't expect to go, David. Their mother and I promised to bring them some oyster crackers, they're looking forward to that, and you might slip some in your pocket, too."

"Gosh, I'll buy them a nickel's worth tomorrow."

"That's not the same as something from a party, and my goodness, we'll be paying ten cents apiece, we might as well get our money's worth. There'll be plenty of folks grabbing for more than their share. Oh, if only this weather holds."

David would have given twenty oyster suppers for one good fall of snow to water the land. Still, he looked forward to a social evening again, and oyster soup. The Friday came, clearer and warmer. The temperature rose steadily above zero and snow began to fall in large flakes. There was little wind. No one could ask for better winter weather. After dinner David set bath water to heat on the stove and sat down to black their shoes while Mary

238

laid out their clean clothes. Her bangs were still in the curl-papers in which she had rolled them the night before.

They knew that in shanties for miles around other families were spending that week-day afternoon in slightly anxious preparation, and in town the excitement was even more intense. Davy toddled and sprawled underfoot, babbling and puzzled, unable to understand what was happening. In the gray light close to the window David sat with a towel over his shoulders while Mary cut his hair and shaved the back of his neck. Large flakes fell thickly beyond the glass but the kitchen was warm from the coal fire in the stove.

By early lamplight they were almost ready, clean from the skin out. David got into his Sunday trousers and settled his best suspenders over a starched shirt. He asked Mary when she was going to dress Davy.

"Nettie's going to keep him," she answered. She was wrought-up and nervous from worrying with her hair and corset laces, and he said no more. He had looked forward to showing off Davy at the party. As if he had accused her, Mary cried out, "He'll be perfectly all right ! Nettie's dependable as gold, and I don't know why I can't have one carefree evening !"

"Suits me," David said mildly. He buttoned his coat. Boiled shirt and collar and tie, and his shortened hair, made him feel sleek and setup. In her wedding dress, Mary rustled round to face him.

"How do I look ?"

Her eyes questioned him anxiously. The clear white-corded pink panel and the pearly waves of skirt flushing pink, made everything else look wrong. The walls needed paper and the floor needed carpet and the change in Mary's face was not only from the sun and wind that had dried her skin.

"You look great !" he said with emphasis.

"I declare, I haven't been anywhere in so long I'm nervous as a witch, it scares me to go out among folks again.   I guess it'll wear off, I used to be as up-and-coming as anybody.   You do think I look all right ?"

"Prettiest little filly ever came down the pike !   There won't be a woman there that comes anywheres near you for looks."

"Well, I don't know what's the matter with my hair, the more I fuss with it the worse it gets.   Go ahead, I'll have Davy bundled up by the time you're hitched."

Snow was still falling thickly and the outdoors thermometer registered two degrees above freezing.   Everything was snug at the barn.   When he had hitched up, David scraped the snow out of the wagon and brushed the damp seat.   He brushed it again after he had banked the fire and closed the drafts, and he spread quilts before helping Mary up.

The lantern hung on the wagon tongue showed the thickly falling snow dark in the air and white on the ground.   Davy could not understand why his mother would not let him clamber onto her lap.   She kept him from creasing her silk skirts and he was querulous all the way to the Peters' shanty.

There Mrs. Peters stood blushing while Nettie held the lamp to throw its light upon her and the excited young ones exclaimed in rapture.   David was amazed.   Mrs. Peters did not look like herself ; she was a pretty woman who must have been a saucy girl.

She had ripped and turned her brown alpaca Sunday dress ; every flounce and tiny ruffle, turned inside out, looked like new.   The small buttons down the front were beans, covered with bits of pink silk from Mary's scrapbag.   Nettie had done that, Nettie had made the flat bow at the throat, of the brown-striped ribbon that Mary had given her. A pink coral breastpin held it flat. Nettie had cut her mother's hair in bangs and curled them. They hid the patient lines in Mrs. Peters' forehead. Her eyes shone like a girl's, her mouth kept smiling irrepressibly, while Mr. Peters, sleekly combed and wearing his clean, almost new jumper, gazed at her with pride.

Everything was snug for the evening. The box was heaped with twisted hay and a pile filled the corner, ready to be twisted in the warmth. Nettie's schoolbooks and slate were by the lamp, and Mrs. Peters gave the little girls a piece of wrapping paper and the shears, to cut out paper dolls. She and Mary repeated their promise to bring oyster crackers. Billy was asleep and Davy yawned on Nettie's shoulder.

"Wish you were coming," David said.

Nettie smiled. "I'll have a nice long quiet time for studying, the sandman's coming for this little scamp already."

"Well, I — we're obliged to you, Nettie. Good night." Davy yowled at the closing door, "Papa!" He shut the door and told Mary to get into the wagon. "He'll calm down in a minute." Inside the shanty Nettie's lulling voice could hardly be heard. Davy shrieked as if he were being killed, "Mama! Mama, mama, mama! Mama!"

"Let me by!"

"See here, be sensible. You leave him alone, he'll — "

"He's making himself sick!"

"He'll calm down in a — " He could not hold Mary without hurting her. She burst into the shanty and he walked in, shutting the door. The boy sobbed wildly, clutching his mother's neck. David hardened himself. "A young one's got to learn he can't have things his way.

241

The sooner the better. You'll have him so rotten spoiled we'll have to lick the hide off him."

"There, there, poor baby, poor lamb, did he think his muvver'd leave him? Either he's going, David, or I'm not. There, see, Davy, see the pretty lamp. Mother's here. He don't mean anything against you, Nettie, he likes you, only I never left him before. There, there, bless him!" She fumbled a handkerchief from the pocket in her silk skirts. "Blow! Blow, Davy! There's a little man!" She mopped his face. "Now if you'll hand me his wraps."

"You going to take him looking like that?" David demanded.

"Yes."

He knew that argument was useless, even if he would have argued before Nettie. In the wagon he said, "Too bad you didn't dress him up." Mary tartly replied that if folks didn't like the way Davy looked, they could lump it. She was almost in tears of nervous apprehension.

The town was lively with lanterns bobbing through the dark. The depot's windows blazed and the waiting-room door, opening and shutting, flashed glimpses of ladies and children going in while men stamped their snowy boots and blew out lanterns. Mr. Peters helped out his wife and Mary, silent and breathing fast. David put the team in the livery stable, hang the expense! He could not enjoy an oyster supper while the horses stood blanketed in a storm.

The depot hummed like a beehive. Four of the waiting-room benches were set around the big stove and red spots glowed on its round sides. Lamps with tin reflectors hung on the walls. Wraps were piled on two benches and polite modulations of ladies' voices came down the stairs.

242

By the stove the men dried their boots and then went on enjoying themselves there. To loaf in an unhurried crowd, with time to talk, tell stories and jokes, was pleasure enough for anybody. On Saturdays they had errands to do, and talk after church was a temporary thing. Now the whole evening was before them, with its coming climax of oyster soup.

About eight o'clock David went upstairs with Cliff Wyatt. They stepped into a scene which stopped them, as if they had suddenly stepped all the way east. The walls were papered. Against gilt stripes and roses, all around the room the dressed-up ladies were sitting on horsehair chairs and sofa, their skirts spread on a carpet of huge flowers framed in brown and yellow scrolls. Big ribbon bows looped back the curtains from the window. A polished center-table held a china parlor lamp, a sea shell, and a vase of peacock feathers.

"By golly, Dave, you saved something when you hauled that load of hay!" Cliff muttered.

Mary came up smiling, a rustling silken wife to be proud of. Her eyes were shining and her breath came short. She said they must wait a little, the first table was for the older folks. Backs of chairs, shoulders, and heads bowing above the white table could be seen through the dining room doorway. There was silence while the Rev. Brown was heard saying grace. The milky sea-smell of the soup curled through the warm air.

David spoke politely to one lady and another, until he could take Mary to the table. Nine o'clock was approaching and he was ravenous. The Hardins sat down, and the Wyatts, and Dant Macray with a shy, dark-eyed little woman who must be Mrs. Macray. There were others at the table whom David did not know. In his ear aside, Mary murmured that the oyster crackers were giving out.

"Take plenty before you pass them." He scooped a good handful from the bowl for her, another for himself, and tucked corners of his napkin well into the armholes of his vest. In large white aprons over their wool dresses, the ladies of the committee set down the brimming soup plates, and the heady steam rose.

No doubt it was the shape of oyster crackers that made them more delicious than any other cracker. The small plump ovals were pleasant to the fingers. They swam half submerged amid tiny pools of golden melted cream and specks of pepper on the surface of the soup. They were half crisp, half soggy in the smooth tang poured from the spoon. Brimming from plate to mouth, the big spoon renewed that unique savor released by the black cove oysters sunk in the creamy hot milk. It poured down the gullet and spread through the whole body a soft but zestful ease.

"Are oysters a kind of fish?" Fatty Hardin wanted to know. Up and down the table, some said no and some said yes. Mary thought not, because they had shells. "They're molluscs," shy Mrs. Macray suddenly said, and blushed to her ears in the momentary silence. Not only fish lived in the sea; there were sea-weeds, vegetables. Oysters were more like snails. David saved his oysters until the last and slowly chewed the rubbery four of them. The last drop of soup from the tilted plate had more flavor.

He made up his mind and said, "I'll take a second helping. How about you, Mrs. Beaton?"

Mary had not yet finished her portion. Hardin and Wyatt took second helpings, too; another dime apiece, while the Macrays pushed back their chairs and a boy squiring his girl took their places. Fatty said he had once, in a contest at a county fair back east, eaten sixteen apple pies. "And I'm as fond of apple pie today as I ever was."

"My husband is a prodigious eater," Mrs. Hardin stated. "My land, no woman alive could fill him up."

David remarked that he was something of an eater, himself. He could not say as to pies ; he had never in his life had enough pie. But he had once eaten forty-nine fair-sized pancakes, stacked with brown sugar and butter. "Tell you what I'll do, Hardin. First county fair we have out here, if the women folk'll furnish the pies, I'll match you to see which — "

A solid blow struck the whole north side of the depot, jarring the building ; the blizzard shrieked and howled around it. Everyone was as still as if frozen, spoons empty or dripping stopped in the air, mouths half opened, all the faces bleak. Then Jeremiah Boles said loudly in the parlor, "Who's left teams out ?"

The men pelted downstairs. There were no ropes ; Clint Insull had no stock, no need to leave shelter in a blizzard. Two teams and three yokes of oxen were outside. Twelve of the forty men were homesteaders, come in from their claims to the oyster supper. All but three had left children at home, and four had cows.

There was room to shelter the teams and oxen in the barns across the street, behind the stores. It was a wide street, but forty men and six boys could cross it without a rope. They put on their wraps and linked themselves together with mufflers tied to wrists. Jeremiah Boles took the head of the line. They made it across the street without much difficulty and took ropes from the store. In an hour or so they stabled the teams and fought back to the depot, leaving a rope stretched behind them.

In the lighted, warm room where the women waited for them, suddenly they were all in hilarious spirits.

They laughed heartily at the tangle they got into, tied by the frozen mufflers. Warm tears of laughter stung their raw eyelids. Several turned their stamping into dance steps, and Luke Fagarty said, "Say, Clint, you got a fire in your office stove ?"

"Not yet, why ?"

"Come along with a lamp," Luke said. "Wait, folks, and you'll see something !"

No one could imagine what those two were up to, till the office door opened and they came in, with rumpled hair and vests turned inside out. They had blackened their hands and faces with soot, leaving wide darky-mouths and circles around their eyes.

"Yo, Sambo," Luke said, "is you got yo bones ?"

Gangling and thin as a rail, Clint gawped at him. "Is ah got ma what ?"

"Is yo got yo bones ?"

"Lawsa massa, ah is bones."

"Rattle dem bones, Sambo, rattle dem bones !" Luke urged him. They danced a hoe-down, singing :

> I'm Captain Jinks of the Horse Marines,
> I feed my horse on corn and beans
> I feed my horse on corn and beans,
> Although 'tis far beyond my means,
> For I'm Captain Jinks of the Horse Marines,
> I'm Captain Jinks of the Army !

The whole crowd was clapping and stamping, keeping time, and singing. "I'm Captain Jinks of the Horse Marines, I'm Captain Jinks of the Army !" Hands and feet and voices kept the dancers going till sweat was streaking their sooty faces. They gave up, collapsing comically. Then Mr. Peters sprang out and did a pigeon wing, changing the tune of the clapping and jigging to it. "Come on, you jiggers ! Let's see the man can jig me down !"

Dant Macray peeled off his coat and came out prancing.

David had seen good, fast jigging in his time, but nothing to beat those toes and heels. His own feet kept up the pounding, Davy bouncing and squealing against his shoulder. It was nip and tuck between the pairs of rattlety-tapping boots, when Mr. Peters doubled the time and no eye could follow them. You could see only jumping-jack bodies, quick elbows, wild flopping hair and glimpses of blood-dark faces pouring sweat. Neither would give up. Hurrahs came out of the fast-pounding rhythm that kept them going, hurrahs crashing into one shout when both gave up at once. In a hot smell of exhaustion, Mr. Peters flung himself down by David. When he could get the breath into his heaving chest he called out, "You're a jigger from 'way back, Macray! The fifth quarter's yours!"

"Not on your life!" Macray answered. "You're the pippin!"

The infernal noises of the blizzard came in and Cliff Wyatt struck up,

> Oh, drive dull care away
> And do the best you can,
> Put your shoulder to the wheel
> Is the motto for every man.
>
> Then drive dull care away
> For weeping is but sorrow,
> If things are wrong today
> There's another day tomorrow.

"I've got nothing to worry about," Mr. Peters said to David. "She'll tend to everything as good as I'd do myself, there's plenty of hay inside, and the rope's tied firm. I saw to that before I left."

247

"Not a thing to worry about, it may quit before morning," David answered. He said the same to other homesteaders and tried to be easy in his mind. When they were all singing they could hardly hear the blizzard. They sang, "Lord Lovell he stood at his castle gate combing his milk-white steed." They sang,

There was a little ship a-sailing on that sea,
And the name of that ship was the Merry Golden Tree,
As she sailed from the lowlands low.

They sang,

We'll rally round the flag, boys,
We'll rally once again,
Shouting the battle cry of Freedom !

They sang, Nelly was a lady, last night she died. And, if the wind and the tears don't blind me, I'll see again that pretty little girl, the girl I left behind me. And, I'm bound for Californy, with my wash-pan on my knee ! They sang,

Oh, when I left my eastern home so happy and so gay,
To try to win my way to wealth and fame,
I little thought that I'd come down to burning twisted hay,
In a little old sod shanty on a claim.

They sang,

Gee, there ! Whoa, there ! Back up, you fool !
I ain't got time to kiss you now,
I'm busy with this mule.

They sang, My darling Nelly Gray, they have taken you away, and I'll never see my darling any more. And, Whoopsy, Lizy Jane ! Lizy was a pretty little girl and she died on the train. And, It was from Aunt Dinah's quilting party I was seeing Nellie home. They sang Sweet Adeline. Jake Hewitt played the tunes on a paper-covered comb.

248

Nobody paid any attention to the hours going by and no one left. The Boles and the Hardins could have got across the street but no other ropes had been put up in town. The whole town was there, and no one need go home till morning chore-time. It was past midnight when the ladies heated what was left of the oyster soup and served it out, share and share alike and nothing to pay. There had never been such a mad night.

"Oh, I never had a better time in all my days!" Mary said. They were sitting on the horsehair sofa in the parlor, eating soup from one dish with one spoon; there were not enough dishes to go around. In spite of the stoves, the cold had come in so that they had put on some wraps. Over her black cloak Mary had tied a calico apron around her neck; she held Davy on it to eat his soup. Her hair was disheveled, her eyes sparkled and her cheek constantly threatened to dimple. She was calling Mrs. Insull, Nancy. All the ladies were using their first names.

"I had no idea!" she said. "I do believe we have the nicest people in the world, right here in our town. Dear me, I wish — They're surely all right, aren't they, David? With plenty of hay, and the rope was up."

He tipped the spoon between Davy's lips. "Sure, they're all right, bound to be."

"It may stop tomorrow. My, I'm thankful we didn't leave Davy — Goodness! It can't blow the depot down, can it?"

"Not a chance." The ice-dust coming through the cracks was to be expected in a blizzard.

"Well, you keep Davy awhile, I'll take these along and help Nancy with the dishes. It's past one o'clock and I don't feel one bit sleepy, do you?" Long after the men were settled for the night on the waiting-room floor they could hear murmuring talk and giggles among the women upstairs.

Next morning they took up a collection and David went with others across the street to buy groceries and kerosene. He could not get rid of the thought of his unmilked cow. He considered trying to reach home by way of the railroad track and the slough. From the depot the track ran level for a quarter of a mile, he could follow it there only with a shovel, but with ropes he could make his way through the town and perhaps strike the track west of the church.

He gave up the idea because this blizzard was the coldest in his experience. The man that Jake Hewitt hired to milk his cow was hardly able to get back to the depot and came in with his eyes frozen shut. The bloody tears were a solid rim of ice.

David's cow did let down her milk easily and the dripping would give some relief. At best, he would have a bad udder to deal with, and unless the blizzard let up in time he would lose the cow. The suffering that the beast was enduring gnawed in his mind, because a man is responsible for taking care of his stock.

The other homesteaders who owned cows had all left children at home who were ten years old or older. Any ten-year-old would do the chores and had sense enough to hang onto the rope. Dant Macray said that he did not have a qualm, his fourteen-year-old Sally was as level-headed as he was himself.

"This little shaver'll be big enough to take charge, next time Mrs. Beaton and I leave home in the wintertime," David said. Rumpled, chubby and lively, Davy was by far the smartest youngster on any man's knee around the stove.

The blizzard lasted fifty-two hours. It ended before dawn on the third day, leaving snow drifted four feet deep in places. The wind dropped quickly and the temperature rose to ten below zero. David had little hope left of saving the cow.

While he was winding his muffler, Jake Hewitt came up. "Dave, you want to hitch to my pung and take my sister and me home, I'll let you have it to drive you folks out."

"Say, you bet I'll take up that offer ! Thanks," David said. The livery stable bill was a dollar and a half. He led the team to Hewitts' and after some digging opened the carriage-house doors and dragged out the pung. It was a boughten pung, with a shining red body and steel runners.

Before he turned back to the depot he drove swiftly out past the church. Smoke was rising from the stove pipe of the Peters' shanty and the first ray of the sun brought out the yellow of the shingled roof while he looked. His relief was a greater happiness than happiness itself. He swung the team in a wide swoop of a circle and raced back down the street.

"They're all right, I saw the smoke," he told Mr. Peters.

After he had whisked the Hewitts up the street to their front porch, Jake Hewitt told him to keep the use of the big, softly fur-lined laprobe. It folded them all in luxury on the way home. The old team was frisky in the cold and the pung went over the drifts as slick as greased lightning. Dodging the bits of caked snow flung from the horses' hoofs, they were all laughing from joy in the speed.

"Oopfy-Davy !" Davy shouted. The little rascal thought he was repeating David's "Oopsy-daisy !" when swinging him high in air. The church was already behind them. They could all see the smoke and the yellow roof now. The road dipped and David shook the lines, urging the horses to a flying swoop.

"Oh, let's not stop so soon !" Mary bent her head to pluck the frosted veil loose from her lips. "Let's take just a little drive, I don't believe Mr. Hewitt'd care. Let's take Nettie and the young ones."

They swooped up from the slough, and there through the glistening drifts long tracks went away from the door. Nettie in a shawl nipped out. Everything was all right. The youngsters came floundering, shouting that they had had a party, too.

"Nate Johnson was here the whole time," Nettie said. He had brought a can of frozen oysters and some oyster crackers, to surprise them. He had chopped open the can and they were wondering how to cook oysters when the blizzard struck. The youngsters whooped around the pung, telling what a good time they had had, new stories and new songs, fried oysters, oyster crackers and hay dolls. Johnson had twisted hay dolls for the girls and a hay horse for Charley.

David told Mary to drop him at home and take Nettie and the young ones for a short drive in the pung. She was anxious about the cow, but he preferred to deal with that himself and to have her gone while he did it.

In the animal-warmed stable he stood dumbfounded, confronting the loose calf. This was the only time in his life that any animal got loose after he had tied it. Some special providence seemed to be favoring him. The weaned, half-grown calf had got to the cow, and the cow was suffering only from thirst and hunger.

When he had watered and fed the stock he came out of the stable and looked at the crisp winter day. The snow that covered his acres and made them beautiful would give them some moisture for next summer's crops. Faint sounds of laughter and sleigh bells came out from town. Everyone who had any kind of sleigh was out in the crystal cold, driving back and forth inside the safety of the town but circling out on the prairie at either end of the street.

38

Late that morning Luke Fagarty came to the livery shed where David was replacing the sled runners on his wagon box. Looking up, David exclaimed, "What's wrong ?"

Before words could come from Luke's mouth there was time to think of Davy left with Mary in Boles' store, of headlong falls from counters, of sharp plowshares, knives, the red-hot stove, all things that threaten children. Luke said, "Word just come in, Macray's young ones are lost. Everybody's going out that can, to help look for them."

Danton Macray and his wife had found the roof burned from their shanty. It seemed that the blizzard had shaken down the stovepipe and the piled hay had caught fire. There was no trace of the children ; Sally, two boys six and eight, and the baby.

Every man and boy went out from town and several homesteaders were searching when they arrived. The blackened walls of the shanty rose out of snow drifted in. The front door was open and the back door burned away. Fire had cut the rope to the stable. Under charred rafters the ransacked drifts revealed forlorn things. The bed had been stripped and some wraps were missing.

The snow had been thoroughly searched around the

stable and the straw-stacks. You could see traces of the frantic tracks that Dant Macray and his wife had made. Three men stood looking at the place. Several trudged about over the claim, poking into drifts which caught their attention. There was no means of even guessing in which direction the children had gone. Miles of drifts stretched on all sides, thousands of suave low mounds faintly reflecting the empty blue above them and faintly rosy in the light of the smiling sun.

"Still there'd be a chance," Jeremiah Boles said. "If it happened last night and we can find them in time."

He wanted to go at it with some system. They started out from the shanty, working back and forth through every drift big enough to cover anything. Dant Macray saw what they were doing and came in between David and Wyatt as the circle widened. Muffled as he was, only his eyes could be seen and not much could be said to him. "We'll do our damndest, Dant," David said. No one stopped to talk. They all worked as fast as they could, feeling the sun going down and the cold increasing.

What they were doing was sensible; it was reasonable to work with some system, but they were up against a thing that had no sense in it. No human effort could examine all those drifts soon enough. Time was going by; if the young ones still lived, their life was ebbing. System was no good unless a man was Joshua and could stop the sun. There were too many drifts, and no way of knowing. The young ones were under some drift, there before the eyes. It might not be too late to save them, and they were there, under some curve of those curves of snow which everybody plainly saw.

Mrs. Macray ran frantically stumbling, this way and that, as if she knew where they were if she could only reach the place. Two women floundered after her, trying to stop her; David recognized one of them as the neighbor from a shanty not far away. She came hurrying at Dant Macray's elbow, a large-faced woman with a small shawl tied around her head and a big patched one over a man's worn-out overcoat. "We can't do a thing with her, Mr. Macray; come speak to her and make her stop. We'll have her on our hands if she don't."

Dant Macray's eyes looked as if he had no mind of his own. He had been tramping through that empty snow since early morning. David said, "Go get her out of this, Dant." It was some relief when the women took Mrs. Macray into the shanty. Still, no one could tell; she might have found them.

Most of the men dropped out at sunset; they had their chores to do. One after another told Dant Macray that they would be back pretty soon. Everyone who spoke to David said that it was no use; nothing would be found till a thaw. Johnson came up and asked, "What about your chores, Dave?"

"You going back now?"

"Not if I don't have to. Boles thinks there's a chance yet."

The drifts for nearly a quarter of a mile around the shanty had been probed or scuffled through. They looked bloodstained in the red light of sunset. David stamped his feet and beat his hands together. The cold was settling down like iron. "Luke's going in. He ought to be able to find somebody'll take Mrs. Beaton home and do your chores."

They looked at the northwest. The sky was clear; not that anyone could say when a blizzard might strike. It made David uneasy to be so far from home, that burned shanty before his eyes. Still there was no way to be sure, to be safe ; any man that tried to be safe instead of going ahead and taking his chances was a fool.

About a dozen men continued the search with lanterns. Toward nine o'clock David tramped to the neighbor's shanty to warm his feet. The place was a confusion of women and children. Mrs. Macray sat quiet on a bench, only looking up quickly when the door opened. The women had not been able to get her to shed one tear to relieve her mind.

They were handing out sod-potatoes boiled in their jackets. Someone gave David a tin cup of tea sweetened with sorghum. Feeling soon came back to his feet and he crammed them again into his boots. The sky was overcast, the wind from the north. The few lanterns bobbing over the snow made no impression at all on the infinite dark.

The cold was so intense that before eleven o'clock there was no more hope. David went on from a kind of habit, his jaw clenched and the pain of cold in his middle. Several of the lanterns gathered together, two went off in separate directions through the dark. It was one of these home-going homesteaders who found them, stumbling by accident upon a quilt in the snow. His shout, and the lantern swinging high, brought all the others on the run. Running, Jeremiah Boles shouted with all his strength, "Stand still ! Be sure what you're stepping on !"

Dant Macray did not know that he was weeping and praying aloud while he clawed away the snow. All their hands quickly scraping revealed a frozen patchwork quilt. David thrust down his arm and felt the rigid coldness of the huddle under it. They broke back the stiff covers. The girl Sally lay covering the others with her body and holding a shawl around them. Two little caps showed beyond the edge of the shawl, and her forehead, bloodless as ice in the lantern-light. Her father called to her. Jeremiah Boles struck his hand away from her rigid arm.

"Don't do that! You'd break the flesh. Don't try to move a muscle of them. I've seen — We'll carry them as they are, on the quilts under them."

The man who had found them led the way to his frame shanty. It had two rooms. The bedroom was cold enough without opening the window. They tugged the bed around from the wall and lifted the load onto it. Under the shawl Jeremiah Boles found only Sally and the two boys, not the baby. There was some life in all three; their invisible breath dimmed his silver watch-case. Dant Macray said, "Get a doctor. Somebody go for the doctor."

A young fellow had put out his shingle in town, but no one had confidence in him. You could hardly rely on a doctor who would come out to a new settlement. There would be something shady about an old one, and if a young one was any good he would have plenty of chances to set up practice in the east, where there was more work for doctors and more money.

David helped to fill a tub with snow. The women folks had arrived from the other shanty and were cutting off the young ones' clothes and trying to force whiskey into their mouths. They found the baby under Sally's clothes, against the bare flesh over her heart. She had given him all the warmth she had, and he was warm and limber. He choked on spoonfuls of whiskey and his whimpers soon became a feeble squalling.

Before the doctor came the older ones were screaming

under the rubbing. It made sweat come through the pores to hear them. In the cold room, working with snow, Jeremiah Boles wiped his forehead and muttered, "We'd been more merciful to let them go."

The young doctor came in with a professional air too thin to deceive anyone. Underneath it he was quaking. He was lantern-jawed, clean shaven, and the lack of whiskers showed his nervous Adam's apple. It was plain that this was his first case of freezing; he could hardly conceal his shock at what he heard and saw.

Mr. Peters said what they all thought, while Johnson was driving the wagon load of them toward town through the false dawn. "Ordinary folks out here have had more experience with sickness than any doctor we'll see in these parts for some time to come."

Wyatt said, "Dant Macray's as square a man as you'd find in a month of Sundays. Sometimes I don't know if it pays, I don't know if there's any good in religion."

"I don't look at it that way," said Jeremiah Boles. "The way I look at it, a man's got to have his belief to hold onto. We got to have something to sustain us, something to steer by."

It was some time before the impression of that night wore dim in their minds. Next Saturday the talk in the stores was quiet and slow. Dant Macray's children would all live, but that young squirt of a doctor had cut off Sally's right leg and the younger boy's left hand.

He said gangrene was setting in, and he had to do it to save their lives. That might have been true. Dant Macray, not knowing, and not knowing what to do, with his young ones raving in torment and out of their minds, had finally consented to it. But there was always that doubt, and it made most of the change in him.

39

There were only those two blizzards that winter and no more snow fell. Spring was early, and so dry that David anxiously bought a seeder. It cost sixty dollars and he had to buy it on time at ten per cent, but it put the seed into the carefully mellowed soil where the chances of sprouting were better. He got a good stand, fifty acres evenly covered by thriving little lines of green. Now if only rain fell, two or three good rains, or even one long soaking downpour, he would make a crop.

Fifteen acres he put into oats, corn and garden, and then he set to breaking more sod.

Sometimes he remembered telling Mary that last year would be their hardest. This year was far harder. It was the hardest he had ever known, because nothing happened. It was a dry year, that was all. Day after day was clear, hot, monotonous with wind. The wind blew steadily, a flow of increasing heat over the suffering earth. The sun rose in a pale sky which at noon was brassy. It sank in a sky too pale to flush, and through the night the hot wind went on blowing. Lightning flickered around the skyline, but there was no rumble of thunder or smell of rain. It was heat lightning.

Even a sharp disaster, it seemed, would be a relief. There was nothing but thirst. The skin was thirsty; no amount of water swallowed would stop its craving. The wild grass wilted, hot to walk through, till it ripened early and filled the wind with a sandy dry rustling. Wide, straggling cracks broke the sod. A hoe digging into the garden came to solid earth before it reached a darker shade of dust. Next day again the sun rose clear and the sky became brass colored without a cloud.

The corn ceased growing and hastened to tassel. Radishes, carrots, beets and turnips toughened when small and threw all their strength upward quickly to make seed. Peas and beans stopped with a minimum of stem and leaf and hurriedly blossomed, while in the corn patch the vines halted and flung open their yellow or creamy flowers with stinted petals.

After sunset Mary and Eliza hoed trenches between the garden rows and David hurried his chores. Till dark they kept the windlass turning above the well and trudged to empty full pails on earth so dry that it held the water like flour. Stepping carefully over the vines, David filled the banked hollows around the roots of pumpkins, squashes and cucumbers. He turned the windlass while Mary and Eliza poured water along the garden trenches. To every tree in the windbreak they gave one full pailful, fifty six pails of water for the little trees alone. It was back-breaking work. By lantern-light David hoed dry soil over the damp, to shield it from the next morning's sun.

But the flat pods shriveled while the plants threw all their sap into filling in each pod one juiceless seed or two. The corn quickly made small nubbins. On the shadeless ground between the corn rows the vines killed their leaves and ripened small seedy globes scorched by the sun, keeping green only their crawling tips which with increasing effort made buds and pushed ahead of smaller and smaller blossoms opening. There is that toughness in life ; it will survive.

By mid-June David had broken thirty-five more acres of sod. Then the dry soil was as hard as wood ; the straining, gaunt oxen could no longer pull the plow through it, and he had to quit.

He had now a hundred acres broken, ninety in a long strip stretching from house and stable into the tree-claim, and the separate ten-acre patch set to trees, farther north on the tree-claim. The wheat was in head. On every little rise and northern slope of the undulating land it was too thin and short for cutting. Still, if hail or cyclone did not destroy it, he would make part of a crop.

He hitched the horses to the harrow and went over the tree-claim where the little trees, set deep, bent southward in the flowing heat of the wind and fought to hold their leaves. In dry May weather in York State and Minnesota he had trudged behind the big logging chains looped to the double-trees and dragging between corn rows. Breaking up the tiny cracks in the earth-film after too-little rain kept the moisture from evaporating. He reasoned that not letting this soil crack wide and deep would have something of the same effect.

"Well, we'll make it through!" he said to Johnson while they stacked the wheat. They cut and stacked the Peters' crop, too, while they were about it. Mr. Peters had walked east again ; he was tramping there and looking for work without much success for crops were poor in the east, too.

The grain was light in the husks and the heads were not filled out. There were some weeds in the sheaves. But if the market price held, they had a crop which would pay for threshing and meet interest and taxes.

"We might be worse off, and that's no lie !" Johnson said, thinking perhaps of Mr. Peters. He tipped up the water jug again. They kept it sheltered under a wheat stack but the water was flat and warm. The whole land was shaken again, dizzy in the heat. Clouds were forming, thin ghosts of thunderheads around the shimmering horizon and dark clouds in the northwest, but as yet they were not boiling, they were not green.

"Your head may be screwed on right, Dave, about

chances of selling turnips this year. But my stubble's going into 'em. They'll come handy to winter through on."

"Guess you're right at that." David had the team, the oxen, the cow and that year's calf to feed till spring. The potato crop was poor and scanty; the garden was practically a loss. "They'll be woody eating if we don't get some rain, but I can use a few acres of 'em, myself."

He had to compound the interest on the binder, and borrow seventy dollars on short-time loan to get through harvest. For the threshers, Mary made vinegar pies. A farmer must feed his threshers pie, it is a matter of pride. Some woman gave Mary the recipe after church; vinegar pie was a kind of imitation lemon pie, made of flour and water sweetened and flavored with vinegar. It was the only pie that David tasted that year, but he did not care for it. With a meringue, it might not have been bad, and the hens were laying. But sorghum sweetening turned the fluffy egg-whites into a nauseous, tough film, and Mary so angrily refused to buy sugar even for threshers that David did not do it.

The wheat field, allowing for the patches not worth cutting, ran under twelve bushels to the acre and it was second grade, and docked besides for weed-seed. David was certain that Decker docked it too much, but there was no other market. His taxes were forty dollars that year, because he was now taxed on the machinery. He paid for the threshing, he paid his bill at the blacksmith shop for shoeing horses and oxen and re-setting wagon tires, he paid the short-time loan with interest, he paid forty dollars apiece on his bills at Wyatt's and the lumber-yard, and he had less than a hundred dollars left. About twenty-five cents a day to live on until next year's harvest, and they would not burn coal that winter.

He drove up to the end of Boles' store porch to let the team stand in the shade of the building while he did his buying, and he sat there on the wagon seat. Dobbin was ten years old now, and hauling wheat on no feed but wild pasture had taken the spirit out of him. He and the borrowed sorrel let their aging, bony heads droop.

Dobbin was not paid for. Two hundred dollars now owing on the binder, sixty on the seeder, one hundred and twenty-two at Wyatt's and the lumber-yard, one hundred and forty-five for Dobbin. This was the end of the third year on the claim. The old, patched harness was no longer safe for driving. The tugs were now rope instead of leather, but if anything suddenly startled the team, the worn lines would not hold them.

He got down and tied them to the hitching post by the Boles' kitchen door. Standing there in the shade, he looked at the list that Mary had written : kerosene, molasses, salt, pepper, yeast, soda, soap, poison flypaper, 1 spool white thread size 40, ½ yard cheesecloth, 4 hanks gray yarn. The yarn was for knitting socks, the cheesecloth for a milk-strainer. There was not a scrap of waste fat nor any wood-ashes in this country to make soap. With rain next year he might raise cane, but to make molasses he would have to buy a mill and boiling pan and burn great quantities of fuel.

The earth was blistering through the thin soles of his boots. He lifted a foot and looked at a small hole worn through leather and sock to the skin. Taking off his hat he wiped his face and then the sweatband. Heat had curled the unpainted boards along the side of the store. A dust-devil suddenly whirled down the street and sprang upward, dropping an eddy of straws and bits of shingle.

It was harvest time, but no one was doing much business. Town boys sat on the thresholds of stores. The

Boston Racket Store and the Last Chance saloon had closed; they were boarded up. Henderson, the other saloon keeper, lounged in his doorway and so did the barber. Johnson's team was tied by the flourmill. Having less wheat than David, he was hauling the Peters' crop this year; if they had paid for hauling, they would hardly have got enough from their crop to pay taxes.

Johnson crossed the street whistling and when he struck the shady sidewalk he put the words to the tune.

> Come to this country and don't you feel alarm,
> For Uncle Sam is rich enough to give us all a farm !

"Hi yuh, Dave ? Finished hauling ? How's she pan out ?"

"By golly, if I was doing much better, I'd be making expenses !" They walked into the store. Little Jenny Boles gazed across the counter, chin on her hands and pigtails sticking either way from her shoulders. Her father was still hauling wheat from their claim. Lafe Garner, Dant Macray and three or four other homesteaders from their neighborhood were sitting around on kegs and boxes.

"That's a right pretty tune you was caroling," Lafe said to Johnson. "And if'n I could lay hands on the fellow that written it, the Lord 'd put mercy in my heart or his own ma'd never recognize her boy."

"Hold your horses !" Johnson replied. "It don't say Uncle Sam gives us anything. It only says he's rich enough to."

"I reckon then I'm a poor self-deceived half wit," said Lafe. "Saving present company, I reckon we all are."

"You don't look at it right, Lafe," one of the others said. "It's a bet. Uncle Sam bets you a quarter section against your fourteen dollars and a half that you can't

264

stay on the land five years without starving plumb to death."

"Say, and he's a tinhorn piker, betting on a sure thing," said another. "I'm pulling out, getting back east before snow flies. Anybody wants my claim is welcome to it."

"Well, my wife ain't got no folks. I ain't got no wife," Lafe remarked. "That sure was an oversight on my part. A man up and leaves his ma without getting him another woman to care for him, he's purely got to depend on his self. I was aiming to be free, and dog my soul, I'm independent."

"Where you from, Garner?" Johnson asked.

"Old Mizzoo. Duane and me, we're Missourians from 'way back. Our great grandpappy, he was one of the first Americans ever come into the Spanish lands, afore the time of Dan'l Boone. He come in search of a needle."

"You don't say so; how come?"

"It appears the redskins clumb down his cabin chimley in the night. He was a r'aring fighter, but the outcome was they finished off his first family and taken his scalp. He come to bare naked, the skin of his face hanging down off his skull and nary a needle to sew it up with. So he come across to the French settlements to sew his self up and he never did go back. Married him a French wife and lived to a hundred and two, hale and hearty and bald as a turkey egg. I remember him well. He cleared I reckon the first piece of farm land on the Gasconade river, and had Spanish title to it till Americans come in. Now Spain actually given away free land, but it taken cash money to get an American title up until my lifetime. So we ain't got that land on the Gasconade no more, a speculator whipped it right out in under grandpappy with boughten land certificates. Grand-

265

pappy never did lay eyes on him or there'd sure been a dead speculator. I've hearn him tell of it a many's the time."

He had stopped talking, so after a thoughtful moment Dant Macray said, "There was a Macray scalped in Michigan, my grandfather's uncle. But that was the end of him, and all I know about it. My grandfather come west into the Big Woods of Wisconsin when my father was a babe in arms, and pretty near the first thing he did, he was clawed to death by a bear. It was early spring, when it don't pay to fool with bears, and his flintlock missed fire. So my grandmother married again and my father never did know much about the Macrays. He run away from home when he was ten year old. To this day he maintains his stepfather worked him too hard, in among the sprouts and stumps, sprouting and plowing. I don't know, those were hard times. Anyway, when he got to be ten year old he run away as a cabin boy on the Mississippi. He worked up to be a Mississippi river pilot."

"You don't say so!" They were all impressed. David thought of the river steamer at Yankton, and asked, "Where is he now?"

"Well, of course he was in the war, and then he lost his savings in the panic, and the railroads come along and throwed the river men out of jobs. There's nothing like the river traffic there used to be before the railroads, and what's left of the old time Pilots' Union's not enough to shake a stick at. So he's back on a farm in northern Iowa, I guess he's making both ends meet."

For a moment they all heard the steady blowing of the hot wind. The shade in the store was no relief from the heat. Indeed it seemed hotter there because sweat

266

stood out on faces and necks and trickled down back-
bones under shirts clinging wetly to the skin.

David said, "Well, the Beatons started out in Plymouth colony two hundred and fifty years ago this summer. Some of my wife's folks died along the Oregon
trail, but so far's I know, nothing's ever happened to the
Beatons. We just keep on going along by main strength
and awkwardness."

He turned to little Jenny Boles behind the counter and
again unfolded Mary's list.

40

Driving home was no longer a pleasure. He felt no
eagerness to reach his shingle-roofed house, his land, beyond the slough. The monotony of day after day of
steady heat and ceaseless wind blowing always southeast
and always with the same pleasure, the same sound, made
him no more than a dull resistant core of himself.

He sat hunched on the wagon seat, the torn straw
brim of his old hat held down against his forehead by the
wind, the lines lax in his hands. The horses plodded
along the road blown almost bare of dust, and on the
seat beside him the packages rode slightly jolting. The
dry wagon rattled as if it would fall apart ; double-trees,
under-pinning, hubs and spokes needed a long soaking
and the wheels again needed new tires. At the square
corner two miles north of town the team turned without
guidance toward the west, going along as monotonously
as time did. Time takes a man along when nothing else
moves. Bare endurance becomes a kind of progress,
when not giving up is the most that can be done.

267

The wagon passed Johnson's soddy and his stubble field. Without looking up, he knew that the slough was not far ahead, when he heard singing. The light, thin voice brought the gay tune clearly. He let the wind blow up his hat brim and squinting against the westering sun he saw Nettie's red-brown hair and her skirts flapping around bare ankles. She was swinging along, her shoes in one hand and her head tilting against the wind her ribbonless straw hat. She was stepping in time to the words she sang.

> O Dakota land, sweet Dakota land!
> As on thy burning soil I stand
> And look away across the plains
> I wonder why it never rains.

Her voice rose to the rollicking chorus.

> O Dakota land! Sweet Dakota land!
> Thy skies are great, thy prairies grand —

The horses' interest flowed into the lines. David slapped the worn leathers encouragingly on their rumps and threw the full, tuneless roar of his bass into the familiar song.

> But we don't live here, we only stay
> 'Cause we're too poor to get away!

She turned, laughing, holding onto her hat brim, and stepped into the dusty brown grass. He pulled up. "Hullo. Like a lift?"

Nettie dropped her shoes into the wagon box and climbed over its side because the wheels were too hot. She gathered her skirts and swung around into the seat, taking some of the packages on her lap. "Oh David, guess what!"

"Well, what?"

268

"I've got, I'm almost certain I've got, next spring term of Number 4 school. If I can pass examinations this winter and get a second grade certificate." She was breathless. "Three months, David, at fifteen dollars a month. I can pass, I know I can. I'm *going* to !"

"Sure you can," he said.

She had seen all three of the school directors ; she had been walking since early morning and had found every one of them at home on his claim. A young man from the east had the fall term, but no one in the whole neighborhood thought he would be able to handle it. The young men who went to school after fall plowing was done would drive him out. Only little children went to school after farm work began in the spring ; there would be nine pupils, all under seven years old.

"They've got a nice schoolhouse, frame, with four windows, and a well right at the door. So light and airy and clean, I wish I could live in it. They don't board the teacher and it's seven miles, too far to walk twice a day and do justice to teaching."

"You could ride the sorrel," David said. Though he wanted the sorrel for spring plowing, the horse was hers.

"I thought of that, but I thought it made some difference if I'd board with the Lawsons', he's a director. They live less than a mile from the schoolhouse and they board the teachers. A dollar and a half a week, he said, and I'd help Mrs. Lawson some, they have seven children, four of them will be spring pupils. So I said I would. But that's twenty seven dollars clear at the end of the term !" Her arms squeezed her sides in her old childish hug of delight. Straightening herself, she said with a more proper primness, "I feel that the tide is turning for us. Maybe better times are really coming for the Peterses."

269

"Well, you deserve 'em," David said. In the east that summer her father had been able to get only odd jobs from farm to farm, at a dollar a day and board himself. David supposed that he had been working every day through harvest; that would be something. The cost of shoes was the great trouble; no amount of careful oiling would keep the uppers from cracking in the heat and dust. David needed new ones himself, so did Mary, and he knew that Nettie was barefoot now because she had outgrown hers so that they hurt her feet. She had worn them while she talked to the school directors and she would have to wear them in the schoolroom, or buy new ones.

She was scrawny from half starvation as she had been in the Hard Winter, and burned brown from working in the sun and wind, trying to save the garden that died. The bones of her face were beautiful and her blue eyes sang out of the brown like sudden band music. Without thinking, David said abruptly, "Johnson'll miss you."

Her mouth curved tremulously, her lids drooped. Under the tan she was blushing. She said firmly, admitting everything, "I can't help that, I have to do what I can to help out at home."

He slapped the jogging horses with the lines again, not meaning anything, and the team paid no attention.

The wind lifted her hat on pins pulling up her hair when she turned toward him; holding the packages on her lap with one arm, she pressed her other hand on the hat's crown. "David, you like him, don't you?"

The special feeling between them, whatever it was, something that neither of them would put a name to, was still there; deeper, maybe, because nothing would ever be done or said about it. He looked at his hand

270

gripping the lines, and said slowly, "Yes. He's a square fellow."

He did not see his hand, but perhaps it told him something, the leathery, dry skin, the engrained dirt in knuckles that no scrubbing could clean, the joint enlarged and stiff since it had been caught in the binder, and the nails broken as if by desperate clawing at some hard surface. He said gruffly, "I wish you didn't have such a hard time."

"Oh, I'm all right ! Everything will be better, if only I can get that school, if I can get started teaching and make good. I'll get it. I'm going to," she said again, fiercely.

The wagon lurched up out of the slough. He meant to grade that bit of his road but he had not yet had time. "Come in awhile ?"

"No, thanks, not now. I want to run home and tell Ma, she's waiting to hear. Will you tell Mary I won't come over this evening, I told her this morning maybe I would, but I'm going to be studying every spare minute." She went lightly down between the rickety wheels and took her shoes. "Goodby. Thanks for the ride."

Mary stepped back from the doorway to let him come in with the packages. Her fine steel knitting needles and a white thread-wad were in her hand. Lately she had been raveling the lace she knitted, and knitting it again. David knew from the feeling in the house that she and Eliza had been sitting through the afternoon in the front room, with not much to say. The steady sound of the wind was against the house and over the grass. A monotonous fretting from Davy broke off when David went in ; the young one in his short dress had been lying on his stomach on the floor, complaining drearily without rebellion.

"Thank goodness," Mary said. "Take him out with you, David. Nothing we could do would shut him up. I gave up finally and just let him squall. Did you get the yarn ?"

The monotonous dryness was in everything. A quarrel would be better than this arid emptiness of nothing to be said or done, no one to blame, neither patience nor impatience but only a waiting in the heat and the sound of the wind. Mary looked at the yarn, rolled the paper around it again, and put it in her workbasket. He supposed it suited her.

"I thought we'd have a cold supper." She spoke as if she did not care what they ate.

"All right. I gave Nettie a lift part way home. She's pretty sure of getting a spring term of school."

"That's nice." He did not know what had become of her habit of talking. Her upper lip was dewy with sweat. She put her hand to her forehead, under her bangs.

He asked, "Headache ?" She said, "No," setting packages on the shelves. The back of her bodice was soaked through between the shoulders. Eliza's chair rocked on the bare floor of the front room ; he saw her sitting there rocking, idle, her fingers tapping on the chair arms. The sound of the wind did not vary at all.

Davy came successfully walking, making it over the threshold between the rooms without a tumble. David picked him up, eager in the steamy-damp wad of clothes. The little chap's baby-blue eyes were heavy-lidded, there were tear stains on his cheeks and the creases of his neck were red. "Hullo, sonny. Want a ride on Dobbin ?"

There was nothing much to say at supper. David tried to think of some news from town, but there was only the small sum he had got for the wheat crop, and nothing to say about that. It was not even necessary to say that they would burn hay again that winter. As for trying to plan how to live until another harvest, there was nothing to do but not spend a penny they did not have to, as long as the money lasted. There was a kind of paralysis in being so poor. Thoughts got tired from going round and round and finding no way out, till they stopped, and talk stopped, and even muscles felt a sort of pressure, a necessity to be still, perhaps not to spend energy, so that merely to get up from a chair required a queer kind of effort.

At the same time, underneath the dullness an irritation grew into a frenzy. Taking off his boots that night to go to bed, David suddenly flung one across the room and swore at the wind. The loud oaths roared out of his mouth. Davy's sleepy fretting stopped ; he called out, frightened, and picking him up Mary said, "It don't do any good to swear. You only scare Davy."

He put on his boots again and went out. The wind was a steady force to walk against, and going between the dry-rustling garden and the stable he crossed a corner of the stubble field and tore through the crackling wild grass as far as the tree-claim field. There was no dew, but the layer of dust scratched up by his harrow had blown away and it seemed to him that the plow-land underfoot was settled and seamed by little cracks again. The lower leaves of the small trees were gone and some of those still hanging on crackled between his fingers. But there was a living limpness in the tips of stems, and some soft leaves remained. He would get into the field with the harrow again in the morning.

Hard times come to all farmers, they are to be expected. No one knows the weather. Good fall rains might come to make good fall pasture and even a late

273

garden, and a heavy snowfall that winter would mean another bumper crop next year.   One more big crop on a hundred acres would set him on his feet, pay off the debts, build sheds and fences, buy some breeding stock and even leave a nest egg in the bank.   The sky was clear, the moon setting, and nine o'clock stars rising in the east.   Another drove of horses was coming from the dark west, the third drove that summer, and he walked over the short, crisping buffalo grass, passing the horses and the oxen on the picket lines without stopping.   Both horses were listening with pricked ears, their manes and tails blown on the wind.   One after the other tentatively whinnied.

He was in the shadow of the stable when he heard the answering calls from the dark mass of horses flowing on the dark grass beyond his stubble field.   He stopped and saw the driver circling to head back the movement in the herd.   Dobbin whinnied again, full and clear and long. The answer came back again.   This time David knew that he was not mistaken ; he would know Star's whinny anywhere on earth.

41

He went into the house and took his musket, and fumbling along the shelf behind the stove he found the box of cartridges.   Mary came padding from bed and stood white in the doorway.   "David, what — It's those men again.   What are you doing ?   No, David !   No, *don't !*"

"They've got Star."   He did not hear her, he wrenched loose from her.   "If you think I'll — Shut up.   You want them to hear you ?"

The silent house behind him began to mean more

than anything she had said. He had to think of her and Davy; he must not run any fool risks. The hot wind pushed steadily against him from the immense loneliness of the dark land under the stars. He walked rapidly along the path by the stealthy rustle and movement of the slough grass, carrying the old army musket and looking at the yellow oblong window shining in the dark. The horses were inside the fence now; again and again Star whinnied and Dobbin replied.

There was no light in Eliza's shanty. He stopped by the open window and knew that Eliza was awake. She answered him in a low voice from the bunk. He asked, "You got that pistol?"

She sat up. "Yes."

"Loaded?"

"Yes."

"Let me have it."

"What for?" The sound in her voice was not joy, but something like joy, a kind of eagerness leaping up.

"That bunch of dirty horse thieves that Gay's harboring's got Star."

"I'll come with you," she said.

"You'll stay back here out of harm's way. Give me that pistol."

She said something about being as well able to shoot as he was, but she gave him the pistol. It would leave one of his hands free. He handed the musket in through the window. "There'll be no damn fool trouble if I can help it. You better dress and get over to the house, keep Mary quiet. Tell her I'm going to stampede 'em if I can, I'll be back all right."

He had forgotten Gay's well. The pail struck the water as he passed the corner of the shanty, and the brassy tang of fear hit his tongue. Before he could think he was behind the shanty's corner. He heard water dripping as the pail came up. The back door shut. On the other side of the thin board walls the careless talk was so loud that he heard every word. Stepping farther away, he looked from the edge of the lamplight and saw the men getting supper. One filled the teapot, another flipped strips of bacon in a frying pan over an open stove lid. He was the claim jumper who had killed Jack Allen.

David had heard that a jury had turned him loose, on a plea of self-defense.

The thought of rousing a posse was tempting. But there was law in the county now, and for some reason his mind shied away from a long, legal wrangle and a cold-blooded legal hanging. Telling about this, long afterward, he said, "I felt discouraged." He went quietly along the fence.

Star's whickering to him was so plainly welcoming his approach that every instant he expected the shanty door to open. The milling of the horses inside the fence was plainly to be heard, too. They were restless, excited by Star's excitement, some shying away from him and others crowding toward the gate in a confusion which Star could not get through. He lifted the chain that held the gate, and tried to release it silently, meaning to wait until he could get hold of Star's mane, but the iron links fell clattering, lamplight burst from the shanty's doorway with a yell, and he jerked the gate open wide. In the pellmell stream of horses he could not reach Star; he grabbed deep into the nearest mane and left that place with flying strides lengthened by the horse's speed.

The thing had been done with no fool trouble. Well out of sight in the dark, he let the horse go and circled running toward his picket lines. The whole prairie was alive with loose horses, shouts, calls and thudding boots. Dobbin's high excitement shrilled out through the dark. David had hardly pulled up the picket peg when Star came galloping. He looped the rope around neck and nose, and led both horses toward his stable.

A figure loomed in the dark. David halted. The man said, "I see you're taking up a couple of our strays."

"Sorry, stranger. You're mistaken." David held the pistol in his free hand; it was an old-fashioned pistol, too large to go into a pants' pocket. "I see you fellows' horses got loose over there, but this is my team. I raised 'em from colts in Minnesota. You got any doubts about it, be glad to prove it. Plenty of settlers around here'll tell you."

After a moment, the stranger muttered something and went on.

From the stable David called to the waiting house, then he put his horses in stalls and lighted the lantern. Star was badly saddle-galled but his wind was not broken. David felt down his legs and found no harm done to knees or ankles. There were whipmarks on belly and flank. His large eyes, blue under black in the lantern-light, could not tell where he had been, what had been done to him, but they rolled with a willingness to show the whites which they had not had before. He nibbled down David's sleeve and nudged his pocket, searching for an apple.

David filled the mangers with hay. He padlocked the stable door and went to the house. "Well, by golly! I've got Star back."

"Goodness! Getting you back is — " Jigging Davy on her knee, Mary spoke through his clamoring. "Gracious goodness, what will you do next? I don't have a peaceful minute. What happened? How did you

277

do it? Is Star all right? Be still, Davy. For gracious sakes, tell us!"

There was nothing to tell. He had simply turned the horses loose. Their ears could tell them that. Eliza was silent, more deeply excited than he had ever seen her. He admitted now that he had been sure from the first that Gay was in that gang of cutthroats and horse thieves, if indeed Gay was not the brains behind it. Nine o'clock struck and he advised them to go to bed.

He took his musket and sat on the back doorstep to keep an eye on the stable. Heat lightning played along the skyline and the hot wind blew, but his place looked good to him, the low dark stable and the straw stacks and the stubble field.

The crooks had caught their saddle horses and were mounted. Toward morning they had rounded up a number of the scattered horses and they drove them along the slough road and on toward the east.

Next Saturday afternoon in town, eight settlers reported that they had taken up unknown stray horses, all on Wednesday night or Thursday. They filed estray notices; the horses were theirs if no one claimed them. Lafe Garner wanted to know why anyone sang about lack of rain. He said, "I've heared of raining cats and dogs, and I've —" He sang,

> O Dakota land of fair renown
> I've heared of raining pitchforks down
> But on your cussed blistered plains
> It's raining horses — when it rains.

"I can cap the climax, Lafe," David said at last. "You know that old wore-out Star horse of mine, that you boys didn't keep a hold of when you had him? Well siree sir, last Wednesday night he come walking into my stable large as life."

Lafe thought it over for a moment. "Surely it appears to me we own that horse, Dave."

"Not on your life you don't! Possession's nine points of the law. I can use that old plug hitched up double, what use you got for one single horse? Tell you what, you boys might own a good yoke of work oxen provided I get enough cash to boot."

42

The satisfaction of having his own team kept him going through that fall. Star's saddle galls, healing, left a flaw of white hairs on his back; the old, patched harness was a trouble and an eyesore; there was no way to soak the wagon thoroughly enough to stop its rickety rattling, and the horses themselves were past their prime, but they were good horses, Morgans, a matched team. Aging as they were, still with proper care and food they had some years of work and beauty in them.

After a long day in the discouraging fields, he helped Mary carry water to the small trees. Eliza had given up and gone, abandoning her claim. Almost silently he and Mary plodded back and forth in the wind, careful not to splash and waste water, for the well was low. They gave each tree two pailfuls now. There was nothing to say at supper, nothing to do but endure the heat and wait. He pushed back his plate, drank his weak tea, remembering that tea cost a dollar a pound, wiped his mustache, put the napkin in its ring. He trudged to the barn. There were the horses.

With care he combed and brushed away the sweaty marks of the harness. He brushed the dust from the fine, short hairs, over the sturdy shoulder muscles and the round flanks, down the slenderness of tapering legs. He brushed and rubbed till the brown coats shone like satin. He combed the tangles out of black forelocks and manes and tails, and stroked the friendly noses. In each manger he put a small bundle of the unthreshed oats. It was a meager portion, but he could still feed his horses oats. He had no apples for them ; sometimes he broke in two a stunted, woody carrot from the garden and let the velvety lips nibble it daintily from his palm.

"There you are, Star, old fellow ! Tasty, uh ?"

Later there would be turnips. He sowed ten acres, hoping for half a crop. All over the prairie the green patches would appear if rain came in time. If rain fell, the whole country would be living on turnips that winter.

He did his fall plowing with the breaking plow, driving the heavy point more deeply than steel had gone before. The hard earth came up in clods through the lighter topsoil. He set himself to plow his hundred acres both ways, stirring a deep and mellow seed-bed to hold all the water that might come from the sky. He was holding the plow in blowing dust through every moment of the shortening days ; he cut down the noon hour and worked all day Saturday, walking to town after supper to do the week's buying and ask for the mail. It was midnight before he went out in his nightshirt to empty the Saturday bath-water at the roots of the small orchard trees.

One afternoon he saw Mary and Davy out on the prairie beyond the stable. He could not make out what they were doing, till he saw her dragging along the bushel basket. He jerked up the plow, and turned the team toward the stable. Star pulled back in alarm at the violence with which he tied the halter rope.

"What the devil are you doing!" he said to Mary. The basket was half full of cow chips.

"I thought I might as well — "

"If you think I can't tend to getting fuel, you've got another think coming. I'll put up the slough hay when I'm good and around to it. You don't have to burn cow chips."

"I don't know but I'd as soon, as twist hay," she said without anger or complaint. Davy was holding a cow chip in his two hands as if he might taste it. She took it from him and tossed it into the basket.

David kicked the basket over.

The shock of what he had done ended his anger. She looked at the overturned basket, the spilled-out heap of cow chips she had gathered. He could not see her face, hidden by the flapping gray sunbonnet. Her dress was faded gray, patched under the arms with scraps of the original bright calico. The dry, cracked basket was gray on the graying buffalo grass.

"What's the matter with us?" he asked. "We hadn't ought to be — like this."

She pulled Davy back from the gray heap, then lifted him on her arm. The side of the bonnet kept slapping across her face and her skirts snapped in the wind with small dull sounds. She took the empty basket by one handle.

"I won't if you don't want me to," she said wearily. "I just thought I could be some help. It's the wind, is all, I guess. I wish I was dead. We're going to have another baby."

It was a moment before the monstrous wrongness of their not being proud and glad shocked him into action. He overtook her in a couple of long strides and seized

Davy and the basket. "That's all right, that's fine! You go in the house and rest. You'll feel different when it rains. Everything'll be all right when it rains. Come on in the house where it's shady and I'll draw us up a pail of fresh water."

The baby would be born in January. She had been keeping the fact from him, letting it prey on her mind. She saw herself dragging him down with more and more babies, till they would be living like the Peters. Her very mind was sick from the heat and the wind. He joked clumsily, trying to get her to laugh at her foolish fancies. A big family was the best thing a farmer could have. "Another boy, uh? What we need's about six more husky chaps like Davy here, growing up to help in the farm work."

"I don't know what good we're getting out of all the work. We're going farther and farther behind all the time."

He brought in the fresh water and filled the wash-basin. "Cool off your hands and face and you'll feel better. What say we have a drink of vinegar and water? This calls for a celebration."

She mixed the vinegar, sorghum and a dusting of nutmeg in the glasses and he filled them with water. It was not a bad substitute for lemonade. They had to buy vinegar, having no cider or fruit-parings here to make it, and Mary used it sparingly. She let the few cucumbers grow large that year and put them down in brine instead of making pickles.

The refreshing drink made her feel better, however, and while they sat stirring and sipping it they heard thunder. Listening incredulous, they heard again the low rumble, and sprang to the door. Overhead in the hot blue the same dry piles of shining white cloud were floating, but to the northwest one of them was dark and flickering lightning. It was coming. The wind blew gustily with a wilder sound, a cool breath whisked past in more intense heat, and David exclaimed exultantly, "What did I tell you!"

They watched the looming cloud let down a gray curtain of rain. They watched it pass by and cease. The cool air blew moist on their faces and they smelled the rain, but not a drop fell through the sunshine in which they stood.

"Well, better luck next time," David said, putting on his hat to go back to the plowing. "It's proved it can rain, that's something."

He had to take the cow nine miles across country to breed her. He had intended to ride Star, but now he thought that he would take the wagon so that Mary and Davy could go with him. They could make a day of it. "Do you good," he told her that night. "You've never seen that part of the country, we'd have the ride there and back and you could visit with the women folks."

She said she did not like to drop in unexpected upon strangers. "It's just more prairie country, isn't it? I don't want to take Davy so far in the heat, he might get sunstroke. I'd rather stay in out of the wind myself, to tell the truth."

When he set out on Star, she gave him a packet of bread-and-butter sandwiches and hard boiled eggs to eat before he arrived. He could not get used to the idea that farmers counted the cost of feeding an extra person at table, but he knew she was right. It was like pulling teeth to hand over the dollar it cost to breed the cow.

On his way back in the late afternoon he paused to speak to Johnson at the end of a furrow. "How deep are you plowing?"

283

"Deep as I can hold 'er down. How your turnips coming?"

"Not coming. They won't till we get rain. Blamed if I know whether they will then, seems as though this sun must be cooking the seeds. They got some rain over north of Garners, though, that cloud went by yesterday."

"Well, it rains alike on the just and the unjust, if it rains. Guess it will sooner or later, it always has. Say, Dave, that fellow Thorne's some relation of your wife's, you know he's back?"

"He's no relation. You mean Gaylord Thorne?"

"Fellow has that frame shanty over beyond you. I thought he was." Johnson seemed a little embarrassed.

"Nope. So you say he's back?"

"Well, I was at the far side of the field, I wouldn't say for sure it was your folks with him. He come out from town in a livery rig and went back with somebody."

"How long ago?"

"Couple of hours." Johnson slid the lines on his shoulders and took hold of the plowhandles. "Wouldn't say for sure who it was with him, I wasn't paying much attention."

He had certainly paid enough attention to know that the woman was not Nettie. David said, "Thorne comes from our home town back east. Taking Mrs. Beaton for a little drive, I guess."

Johnson started to make some reply to this, but thought better of it. David was puzzled. After he had put the cow on the picket line he rode to the house and dropped the bridle reins over the handle of the windlass. Star whickered thirstily, but David stepped into the house. It felt empty; the wind gave it a hollow sound and his steps were loud on the floor.

284

There was a faint scent of cigar smoke and bay rum. The trunk was gone from the front room. The oblong where it had stood, fresher boards than the rest of the floor, was empty and the rocking chair stood where it had been pulled aside.

David pushed back his hat, tugged it down again. The clothes-curtain against the wall did not bulge at the bottom; he lifted it. She had taken her valise. Her comb and brush were gone. In a chair pushed under the kitchen table he found a wad of clothes; her patched gray-faded dress, petticoat made of flour-sacking, and the tumbled little flour-sacking dress that Davy had worn that morning.

The eastbound train went through town at sunset. He had about half an hour. Star lifted out of the slough at full gallop and lengthened out down the straight road. In town the hot board sidewalks were deserted, dust blew from the empty street. Only a few idlers lounged on the depot platform; a strange man and wife sat in the waiting-room. Store windows and doors went by rapidly, nothing behind them to stop for. Gay Thorne stepped out of the barber shop.

Sleek as a cat and as pleased with himself, he stood lightly twisting a point of his mustache. His eyes narrowed against the glare of the street brimmed with good-humored satisfactions. David held his fist down. "Where is she?"

What Gay began to say was not what David wanted. He repeated, "Where is she?"

With exaggerated politeness, Gay motioned him into the hotel. "Right this way, Dave, pleased to oblige. Follow me, and you'll wear diamonds!"

David did not bother now about what he would do when he could turn his fists loose. He tried to think what to

285

say to stop Mary's going home to her folks. He knew she was not going; not on that train, not with Gay's escort, not ever to stay. But his boiling thoughts moved too rapidly. At the top of the stairs he turned toward the ladies' room, but Gay was beating a tattoo with his knuckles on another door. David walked into the private bedroom.

There was the valise, the trunk, and Eliza standing by a chest of drawers in the act of lighting a cigar held in her pursed lips. Mary was not there. Eliza's eyes widened, startled, the flickering match-flame repeated small in them. The door closed and Gay Thorne leaned against it, amused.

"I always intended to taste for myself the pleasure of smoking, when I was married," Eliza said calmly, and lit the cigar.

43

"Where's Mary?" David demanded.

Eliza blew out a funnel of smoke. "Didn't you find her note? She's downstairs helping Mrs. Hardin fix up the table. She was worried you wouldn't get home in time. I must say, David, you might have shown us the respect to change your clothes. And both of you kindly take off your hats this minute."

Gay swept his off with a flourish. "Excuse me, my pet."

"You say she's downstairs helping Mrs. Hardin? What's the idea? What's this doing here?" David tapped his boot against the trunk.

"I bought it." Eliza drew competently upon the cigar. "Gay and I were married yesterday in Watertown. We are going to Oregon. I needed another trunk. Upon the whole, I am inclined to embrace this vice of the weed, of course in private. There is a soothing effect and it is a pleasure to watch the smoke."

"You won't get a rise out of me," said David. He sat on the trunk, looked at Gay, at Eliza, and contemplated his hat in his hands between his knees. "Going to Oregon, uh? And you two are married."

"Yes." Eliza's narrow hazel eyes gleamed at Gay with a fondness which David had seen before. She had long wanted Gay Thorne, and now she had got him. Gay's white teeth barely glinted under the black mustache he was twisting, and something of the same look gleamed back at her, with an alert and wary pride in it. Both of them were on their mettle, and it struck David that they were heading into a lifelong battle and ready to enjoy every minute of it.

Eliza was magnificent. What plans had been maturing in her head while she sat in her claim shanty listening to the wind, David could only surmise, or glimpse in flashes. It was plain that she had come west only because Gaylord did. Even ten years ago, David remembered, when she was seventeen she had upset their mother by refusing a good offer of marriage, talking then about woman's rights.

"What do the folks at home think about this?" he asked, and she replied, "I must confess that I have not consulted our parents."

She had not gone home when David put her on the train. She had gone to the Land Office in Watertown, where she had changed her homestead claim to a preemption and bought the land outright. Then she had gone to Fargo, to meet a banker with whom she had conducted some correspondence; she had mortgaged her claim for two hundred dollars more than it cost her.

287

"Buy your government patent, David," she said. "You can mortgage it for enough to get out of this country."

"That's right, Dave. Say, you owe me a bet!" Gay's smile flashed. "Told you I'd make more on my claim than you've made on yours. I'm getting out with better than four hundred dollars clear."

"Thanks to me," said Eliza capably. They had met in Denver. Eliza must have used that two hundred dollars to track him down in Denver. She had an offer from the banker in Fargo to put a nine hundred dollar mortgage on his claim. They had traveled to Watertown to buy his government title, and they had been married in Watertown. David felt a sneaking sympathy for Gay, until glancing at him again he saw how far Gay was from needing sympathy or help. Eliza needed none, either. It was as if live lightning flickered between them in that hot and shabby room, while below the open window nothing but dead dust stirred in the town.

"We're going to Oregon," Eliza said. "I always wanted to go to the real west, where chances are big." She did not mince words. "There'll be no more horse stealing. The only trouble was, Gay's not cut out to go slow and pinch the pennies. I have been employing my mind upon a study of the great natural wealth which Providence has bestowed upon the Oregon country. A gentleman of my husband's abilities will find himself in his element, I do assure you. Lands sakes! anybody with the gumption to take the risks, lawful risks, can make himself a millionaire!"

This did not seem impossible when she said it, the earrings swinging back against the intricate coils of her hair while cigar smoke preposterously came from her lips. In dark plum-colored silk, slim bodice, slim long sleeves, and regal puffs and lengths sweeping on the floor, she sat perched on the edge of the bed as on a sidesaddle, a huge bustle hitched up behind her. She was not wearing hoops; under the rustling silk the movement of her swinging foot and the points of her knees could be seen. She was daring, dashing, and sure, now that she had got Gaylord Thorne.

David thought, "Well, it's beyond me to figure out." He did not know what made people do what they did, want what they wanted. Eliza, anyway, had got what she went after. He had to admire that. Getting up from the trunk he said, "Well, good luck to you. I'll be stepping downstairs to speak to Mary."

Mary met him in a flurry, counting out plates around the dining room table. "My goodness, David, why didn't you change? Go right back out and put on your Sunday clothes quick. I brought my Sunday things in the valise to change into as soon as we get the pies out and put the chickens in. David, Eliza paid me fifteen dollars for the trunk and I'm spending eight of it for the supper, I've asked the Boles and the Insulls and the Wyatts and the Hewitts and us four make twelve. You don't object, do you? After Eliza sent to St. Paul for my roses, we've got to do something for her wedding. You could have knocked me over with a feather, but what's to do but put the best face on it? David, don't stand around! Hurry out home and do the chores and change your clothes."

It was a merry supper, and David ate two pieces of dried-apple pie and a piece of custard. Driving home late that night on the wagon, he said, "I'd hate to be in Gay's shoes."

"I wouldn't wonder if she makes him be somebody," Mary mused.

"That's what I was thinking."

289

"She's always been smitten on him, ever since we were all young ones," said Mary. "And he was smitten on her, only she couldn't pin him down. It was your getting back Star. I thought she was up to something when she left. She threatened him when she got him to Watertown, David, I'm as sure of it as I'm sitting here, she threatened she'd send him to the penitentiary for horse-stealing if he didn't marry her, and Gay admires nerve. It works both ways, he's got her as much as she's got him, and you can see how proud he is of her. I think they're a well-matched couple."

"Looks like it might blow up a rain," David said. He was appalled by what women are capable of.

44

Before morning the rumbling thunder broke with sharp flares of lightning. Coolness blew through the house and rain drummed on the roof. An evil-smelling, warm steam came up from the ground, but the relief of moisture in the lungs and on the skin, breaking the long ordeal of dryness, was so great that they got up to enjoy it.

The rain lasted less than an hour, barely long enough to dampen the surface of the ground. Still, they had some hours of refreshing sleep, and the turnip seed sprouted.

In September the winds, more variable now, were still warm. White piles of cloud floated dry in the softer blue. Leisurely the wild ducks and geese were flying south, lingering in the sloughs. David heard that Gooseneck was black with them. He would have gone hunting if he had had time. He did shoot jack-rabbits in the green turnip patch at dawn. Their fur was light, and the stunted weeds ripened multitudes of seeds. Another open winter was to be expected, and another dry summer.

Now that Eliza was gone, her claim held by some speculator in the east, all the neighboring settlers came in to cut her slough hay. David made no objection. The Fargo banker had paid more than the land was worth, for the legal mortgage papers on it to re-sell to eastern speculators. Everyone concerned was making a profit, and David saw no reason why near-by settlers should not profit by the hay.

He and Johnson traded works again and the stacks went up jovially. They were building the last stack by the stable, when looking up as he lifted a forkful David saw Johnson stab the tines down and let go of the handle. "What's the matter with your kid, Dave?"

Davy stood in the dead garden, finger in mouth, staring with petrified attention at something beyond the stable. David shouted to him; he did not move. It is absurd to be as frightened as David was; he knew that, while he was striding toward the boy, before he saw the two youngsters that Davy was staring at. They were little boys, perhaps three and nearly five years old, standing hand in hand on the plowed ground. He swung Davy up on his shoulder and called to them, "Hullo, bub! Whose young ones are you?"

They did not answer. David did not recognize them, and neither did Johnson. They would not come nearer, or speak, and at last David walked across the soft earth to them, annoyed by its working through the cracks in his boots. "What's the matter? Cat's got your tongue?"

They stood motionless, huddled together as they had

291

been, and tightly holding hands. When he was near enough to see into their eyes, David understood. He called to Johnson, "Come on over here, quiet. They're lost."

The look of a lost mind was in their wide eyes. From their calloused bare feet it was impossible to guess how far they had come, but the palms of their hands had been cut recently by grasses. Their legs and arms were raw with briar scratches, and grass seed was thick in their hair. The younger wore a short dress and the older a shirt and pants made of flour-sacks. Their skin was hot and dry, so they did not appear to be suffering from sunstroke.

"We better carry them to the house and give them a drink, first thing," David said. Johnson carried both of them ; their clasped hands could not be separated without using force.

They thrust their heads at the dipper, drinking so avidly that Mary took it away. "They'd make themselves deathly sick. You pull up the small pail of milk, David ; the one with the cloth tied over it." She fed them water from a spoon till David brought in the milk, then she fed them milk. She wiped their faces with a wet cloth. All her coaxing could not get a word from them, or a smile. They sat on the bench where she had put them, looking at nothing with those lost eyes and still holding hands. Their minds seemed completely gone. She said at last, "I declare I don't know."

"I'd better take the word to town," David said. Still it was plain to be seen from looking at the town that no alarm was out. Johnson suggested whiskey, and Mary gave them a good spoonful apiece. It seemed to have no effect.

"I declare I give up," Mary was saying. "I've a good

mind to put them to bed till morning, and then if — "

The older boy said suddenly, "Ma's sick."

"Where?" Mary asked gently. She had asked them a dozen times where they lived, who their parents were. The boy began to cry.

"The thing to do's to track them back," David said. It should be possible to follow their track through the wild grass or over plowed fields. He patted the youngster's shoulder. "There, bub, you're all right. Brace up and be a man. Come on now, tell us where your folks live, can't you?"

The boy tried to stop crying, but shook his head. He got out again, "Ma's sick."

David picked him up; he was a light weight for his height. "Well, come along and we'll go home. If your ma's sick, she's worrying about you, and your pa's out looking for you now. Likely we'll meet him on the way. How'll you like that, uh?"

The youngster was eager and hopeful. Used to a strong man's carrying him, he settled himself against David's shoulder and laid an arm around his neck. Johnson carried the other little fellow. They followed the tracks across the plowed ground and plunged into the wild bluestem, thick clumps three feet tall, ripe now and lodging in long billows. The disheveled furrow that the boys had made in pushing through them was not too difficult to follow.

The resistance yielding to the legs was hardly noticeable at first, but after half an hour of it David did not know how the youngsters had held out and kept on going so long. He and Johnson knew the settlers for three miles beyond his tree-claim. A number were bachelors who had gone east looking for jobs in this dry year. One sparse field of stunted wheat was not cut. The trail

293

in the grass went nowhere near any shanty. The youngsters were not tall enough to see over the billows of grass.
They had been able to see nothing but endless grass and
the sky.

They were frightened now. They hung on, dumb,
hiding their faces and constantly shivering in the sweaty
heat.

"See here, Dave, we're circling." Johnson stopped.
"This trail's going back east ahead here, or I'm a son of
a gun. How far you make us from your place?"

"Six mile, last section line. We're half to three quarters south of my south line, there's the railroad."

Hip-deep, they stood looking around them at the
wilderness of grass. They were aware of the sound of it
in the wind. It was an eternal and infinite voice beyond
space and time, unliving and not dead but without knowl-
edge of life.

The little fellow heard it, too. He crammed his face
smothering against David's neck and clutched him like
a kitten fighting against being drowned.

David's voice sounded hollow and too loud. "Well,
gosh, Johnson, they live somewhere! Let's plow along."

As they went on, he tried to reassure the boy. "You're
all right, bub. I won't put you down. I won't let go
of you. Tell you what, I'll keep on carrying you, see, like
this, if you'll tell me your name. A big boy like you,
you know your own name. Come on, now, speak up."

The boy finally whispered, "Jackson Baker."

"Well, that's fine! Baker, uh?" He exchanged a
look with Johnson; neither of them knew a settler named
Baker. "And you live in a claim shanty, uh? A
soddy?"

The boy nodded, but David could not get another
word out of him. There was no longer any question that

the meandering track circled. The sun had begun to cast shadows from the prairie swells. The grass continued endless, and when they ceased to rip through it they heard its monstrous indifference.

"How far north of here you figure we come west, Johnson?"

"Four to five mile." Unconsciously they stood close together. "They never made this in a day, Dave. Remember those young ones south of Brookings, lost eight days in the grass?"

"No wonder they're addle-headed. This thing's giving me the willies myself. What I can't figure is, why there's no alarm out for these youngsters before now. What say we cut north from here?"

"Where's papa?" the little fellow suddenly asked. David had told him they would meet his father.

They broke a way through the yielding grass which was wearing them out. No blade of the numberless millions opposed them, and their legs quivered near exhaustion from pushing through that nonresistance. Their throats were parched; they said to each other that they had been fools not to bring water.

The contours of the rolling land were plain in light and shadow when they came upon another trail which seemed to have been made by the youngsters. For some time they had seen no section-stakes; their only guide now was the sky. Though David still had a sense of direction, he would not have trusted it. Birds' notes became more numerous and clearer as sunset colors began to flare overhead.

"We better get back while it's light, and — You hear that?" A faint grating sound came from the southeast. Listening, they heard it again, across the wind. "You know any settler's got sheep around here?"

David shook his head. Both tried to shift the weights on their shoulders, but the youngsters clung in spasms of terror. Johnson had been leading, so David now went forward against the grass and in silence they waded doggedly toward the sound of the sheep.

They were soon able to make out, from the rises, a huddle of sheep beyond two horses and a wagon. The younger boy cried out for his mother, and the older one repeated, "Ma's sick." He pointed toward the sheep. "Ma's sick. We want papa."

The sun had set when they reached the deserted wagon. On picket lines, the horses whickered thirstily ; within the circle of their ropes, they had gnawed the grass to its roots. There was no campfire, no trace of anyone about. Tearfully the little boys confessed that their mother had told them to stay in the wagon. "We want papa. Where's papa ?"

They found the woman lying unconscious in the grass. She had given birth to a baby. They were both alive. David and Johnson laid them in the wagon, and hitched up. Johnson drove, and David brought along the sheep.

They were the most woe-begone Southdowns he had ever seen, twenty-four of all ages, their tear-stained faces no more than hide over bone and their wool matted with briars, burrs, and mud. David knew they had traveled a long way without enough time for grazing or rest, even before he hauled up a ewe that lay down, and lifted so little weight that he marveled at her staying on her feet at all.

45

Mary put the woman to bed in the front room and revived her with whiskey. She was feverish and out of her head. They made out that she had relatives in Indiana, whom she had tried to reach in time, and that her husband had been homesteading on the western ranges; the cattle barons had killed him.

In her fever she begged him to go back east. She cried out terribly against the killing of their sheep; her screams made you see the mounted men riding them down, the horses squealing and trampling and riders mercilessly clubbing the innocent sheep. She kept saying, "Oh, give up, let's give up, it's no use, all cut to pieces again, barb wire costs so much, give up and go home, let's go home, I want to go home, let's go back east." Once she said quietly, "They killed him. I knew they would. Poor folks don't have any right to live on this earth."

After a long night's sleep, the little boys turned out to be cheerful little fellows and bright for their ages. The five-year-old did his best to find ways of helping David. He pulled several bushels of turnips, slow, but sticking manfully to the job. The baby was incredibly small but a perfect little girl except that her fingernails and toenails had not yet grown. She was a seven or eight months' baby. Mary spent hours feeding her with a finger dipped into a warm mixture of milk, water and sorghum, and later taught her to suck a twist of rag.

"My goodness, David, what we have to be thankful for!" Mary said. They found nothing in the wagon but bedding, half a sack of flour, a few clothes and cracked dishes, tin pots and pans mended with bits of rag drawn through the holes. There was not a cent of money and no letters, no address of the woman's relatives. They knew only that her husband's name had been Baker, and David never learned, or did not remember, much more about her.

297

He put sleigh bells on the old ewe and let the flock graze. At night he herded them inside Gay's fence. Since all the bedding was in use in the house, he was sleeping in the straw stacks and he kept the musket ready to defend the sheep if coyotes attacked them. One morning Mary told him that Mrs. Baker's fever was broken. "I see no reason now why she shouldn't get well."

David saddled Star and rode to town to see Jake Hewitt. He estimated that a fair price for the twenty-four sheep, in their condition, would be about eighty dollars. Wire would cost thirty, and posts twenty. He must have a Southdown buck from the east ; say twenty dollars, and five for express charges. He said, "I can handle it, Jake, on a hundred and sixty dollars. There's not a man in the country can beat me raising wool and lambs."

The banker's fingers played thoughtfully with his watch charms. "I don't know, Dave. I want to let you have the money, but it's not good banking to loan up to a hundred per cent, and you say yourself the sheep are in bad shape. There's diseases that'll wipe out a flock practically over night. It's not my money I'm risking, you know ; it's my depositors'. I'd rather make you the loan on some other security."

"There's the household chattels such as they are." David took in Mr. Hewitt's reaction to that and added reluctantly, "And my team of Morgans. They're clear." As he spoke, he remembered that Dobbin was not paid for.

Jake Hewitt jollied him a little. "Heck, Dave, you're the bloated plutocrat around here. That team's good for a hundred and sixty dollar loan any day, will be for three, four years to come, way you take care of 'em." He made out the mortgage. "Bring that in with your wife's name and yours on it, and you'll get the cash. Don't mention it ; glad to oblige you any time I can !"

He had to wait two days before Mrs. Baker was strong enough to talk. Autumn weather had set in, with blustering winds and low clouds. Dashes of sleety rain came on gusts which parted the sheeps' fleeces. Not all the flock could crowd into Gay's small shed. He feared that the exposed ones would have pneumonia, and tearing the bunk out of Eliza's shanty he crowded nine sheep into it.

For nearly a whole morning he sat in the front room talking to Mrs. Baker, while the young ones played about. She had graying carroty hair combed back thin from the drained face on the pillow. He wanted her to feel welcome to stay until she got her full strength back. It was a long way to Indiana, with winter coming on, but he could not advise her to sell her team and wagon and go on the train. He said, "We've had a dry year here and feed's so high it's out of all reason, nobody's wintering stock through that don't have to. You'd have to let your team go 'way below what they're worth if you can keep 'em till spring." He said finally, "If so be you want to sell your sheep, I'd make you an offer for them."

Mrs. Baker was glad to sell them. In the kitchen he talked to Mary while she peeled potatoes. He said that this was the only chance he saw to get ahead. There was no sale for turnips this year. Every sign pointed to another dry summer, with not much prospect of making anything to speak of from the wheat crop. It was taking a risk, to go deeper into debt, but maybe with sheep he could pull out.

Mary listened without a word, until he had no more to say. Then she wiped her hands, took the paper and read it carefully from beginning to end. She brought the

299

ink bottle and her small pearl-handled pen and wrote her name, "Mrs. David Benjamin Beaton."

She put away the ink and pen and went on peeling potatoes while he blew on the writing to dry it. He said finally, "I appreciate you signing this."

She began scooping up the potatoes from the rinse water and dropping them into the kettle. "I don't know's I ever told you, David, I made up my mind the winter Davy was born, back east and you out here snowed in, that if ever I got back to you I was going to stay with you through thick and thin. No matter what happened. You better not go to town till after dinner, these potatoes'll be ready inside twenty minutes, they're so small."

The fence posts, piled by the stable, were frosty in the mornings when he took them one by one in mittened hands to sharpen them. In chill winds he dug the post holes and drove down the posts. He needed a maul for that, but made up for the lack by putting more muscle into blows with the blunt end of the ax. He set the posts around twenty-five acres behind the stable, including both bluestem and buffalo grass. Mrs. Baker with her children drove away one frosty morning before he had all the posts set. He had been up almost all night, shaping and setting wagon bows and stretching the canvas over them for her.

He had to hire Johnson at seventy-five cents a day and dinner, to help him stretch the wire. With a borrowed wire-puller Johnson held it stretched taut from post to post, while he drove and clinched the nails to hold it. They put five strands of tightly stretched barbed wire around the twenty-five acres. It was a good fence when it was done ; the posts, lined up by eye, were straight and true, so that the whole line of them down any side of the pasture would disappear behind either corner post.

Beating his hands together and stamping his feet, Johnson said, "How you going to shelter them sheep?"

"Don't you worry! I'll shelter 'em!" David clinched a second costly nail with accurate blows. "Right! Grab a hold there, you lazy son-of-a-gun! Pull!"

Johnson knew as well as he did that the two small ox-stalls vacant in the stable would not hold the sheep. The truth was that David had not quite faced the question. He could always buy lumber on time at three per cent a month. Going back and forth about his work, he constantly saw Gay's frame shed and shanty. Even when they were out of sight he could see those good, wide, weathered-gray boards. Good rough-finish pine lumber, half an inch thick, was standing there.

He had never longed for those boards when they belonged to Gay. But now that no one owned them, now that only some eastern mortgage-speculator held a mortgage on them, he thought of those boards while he worked, he thought of them at mealtimes and suddenly in church he put them out of his mind. He knew how his light crowbar would pry them from the studding with hardly a squeak of bright nails which would not be too badly bent to be hammered straight and used again; he knew how the gray roughness of those boards would feel under his hand and how the nails would drive again into their seasoned texture. They were rather badly warped, but with care and an accurate eye they could be used again without splitting. One day he saw Mr. Peters cast a measuring glance at them, and he felt a hot jealousy.

Mr. Peters had come over to look at the new fence and the sheep. He gazed at them with ungrudging admiration. "By golly, Dave! You're stepping right along!"

301

He had reached home a few days before, with little to show for his summer's hunt for work. Times were not good in the east, though most crops had been abundant and he had never seen such a year for fruit; the orchard boughs were breaking under the weight of it.

"Well, with luck and good weather we'll be having some fruit one of these days," David said. Daily watering had kept alive all but one of the nine little trees in his house orchard. Mrs. Peters and Nettie had pulled through alive three apple trees, a quince, a peach and a cherry. They should all come into bearing in three, four more years. Next year they would have gooseberries and currants; Eliza had brought the plants from his father's berry patch last spring.

"It's a great life if you don't weaken," Mr. Peters agreed. He took a turnip from his pocket and ate it while he looked at the sheep, tossing them the paring. Though he had come at the end of the noon hour, David noticed that on his way home he pulled and ate two more turnips while slowly crossing his turnip patch.

After supper that night David went to the stable. He took the crowbar and the unlighted lantern. Avoiding the lamplight shining from the kitchen window, he crossed his turnip patch and set out to Gay's shanty. It was a night of wild clouds blowing across a frosty crescent moon.

In Gay's shed the sheep were restless. Drafts blew through its cracks. The woolly sheep, once quieted down and huddled together, were still warm enough there, but they must have snug shelter soon. David put the shanty between himself and his house, and was about to light his lantern when a dimmed light came around the corner.

Mr. Peters stood there, holding a crowbar and a half-darkened lantern. For a moment neither of them

302

spoke. The light shining upward left blackness in the hollows of Mr. Peters' cheeks above his wildly blowing beard, and brought out only the rim of his eyesockets and bristling eyebrows. His canvas coat, patched upon patches, flapped like a scarecrow's. His teeth showed in something like a snarl. Not giving way an inch, he said, "See here, Beaton. You got a floor."

David had a feeling that the man was dangerous. That was absurd; they were old friends, and there was nothing to fight about. He said, "Well, Peters, you want to help yourself to a floor, I'm not objecting. What I'm after is a sheep-fold."

They set about taking the shanty apart. They pried up the plate and slid off the roof in one piece. They took out the window casings and the door frames, ripped off the sheathing and with their hands wrenched loose the tipsy studding. David said, "Well, there's your floor! Take that side and I'll take this, and up she'll come!"

It was a twelve-by-twelve floor of six-inch boards, caked with dirt and chewed-tobacco wads, but the under sides would be clean. Seasoning had left wide cracks between them. The crowbars took hold and the boards pulled up their nails from the framework of joists. The joy of destruction, the crumbling of the shanty under the wild sky, made David feel again like a boy out in the lawless night of All Hallowe'en. "By golly, let's not make two bites of a cherry! I'm going to hitch up and haul this!"

Careless of racket and of lantern-light, they divided that wealth of boards. They loaded the wagon, and hauled the roof, the floor boards and joists, the door and the windows with their casings, away across the prairie to the straw-stacks by the Peters' stable. Mr. Peters came

303

back to help transport the rest and pile it behind David's barn. Nothing was left of the shanty but the mark on the grass where it had been, and the well. Mr. Peters took the well-rope and the rusty tin pail.

"No need of the fence standing here around nothing," David said. "I'll divide it with you fair and square, soon as I move my sheep, but I figure I got to have most of the shed."

"That's all right with me, I got what I wanted." Mr. Peters tightened his muffler and picked up his smoke-darkened lantern to walk home. "You know, Dave, I've tried to live upright all my days. I don't say I didn't backslide that time we made the sled for the young ones ; it's been on my mind some, since. And you'd think I'd be ashamed of this night's work. But by Jerusalem, I've done my damndest to provide a decent living for my family, and this winter they're going to live on a floor ! Whoever the easterners are that put money on spec into land mortgages out here, they've got floors. So far's I'm concerned, they can whistle for this one ! I'm going home and sleep like a youngster at Christmas, and I recommend you do the same."

"Put 'er there !" They shook hands on it.

David built against his stable a roomy sheep-fold, twenty feet by twenty. It was an open framework patched together, with a low lining of boards around the inside to keep the sheep from nibbling away the straw stacks that he piled over it. When he was done, the only lumber that showed from the outside was the solid board door to the south. On the coldest day that winter his sheep were cozy-warm inside the thick walls of straw.

Before Thanksgiving the Peters' family moved into their front room, twelve by twelve, with a board floor, a shingle roof and two windows. The old soddy made a comfortable kitchen in which Nettie and the young ones slept. Mary did not say one word about the disappearance of Gay's shanty and shed, and neither did Mrs. Peters.

46

Molly was born in February, during the children's blizzard. This was not the great Children's Blizzard which came six years later and killed or crippled so many school children throughout the whole prairie west; it was a small local matter. Jeremiah Boles had advised against keeping the town school open after Thanksgiving, when all the small country schools were wisely closed. But he had been overpowered by friends of the teacher who wanted to prolong her job and by parents whose children did not want to lose any chance of schooling.

Nettie, Flora and Lucy were leaving the doorstep when David reached the shanty that morning. Charley was already trudging away, carrying their dinner pail. It was a bright, clear morning, with less than six inches of snow on the ground and the temperature ten degrees above zero. All the girls waved red-mittened hands and David called out a cheerful "Good morning!" as he pushed toward them, slanting across the pressure of the wind.

Mrs. Peters left the floor unswept and began at once to bundle Billy into his wraps, but every movement seemed as slow to David as the effort to move in a nightmare. He could hardly wait to take the youngster against his shoulder and grip Mrs. Peters' arm with his other hand, and he fairly lifted her along the three quarters of a mile to his house. She laughed at him, and they did find Mary all right, still on her feet and smiling.

305

The blizzard struck at eleven o'clock. Mrs. Peters was in the kitchen at the time, scraping the skins from boiled potatoes which she was going to warm up for dinner, and David was teaching the two little boys to twist hay. Outdoors was a bright glitter above frost patterns spread upward from the bottom of the panes and sunshine came through the south windows. With no warning, the light went dull gray and the blizzard hit the house.

The knife fell clattering from Mrs. Peters' hand to the table and the floor. She said, "Oh God, if that fool eastern teacher will have sense enough to keep them in the schoolhouse."

Respect for a prayer kept David silent a moment. Then he said, "Nettie's there ; she's got good sense."

That was the only help he could offer. Any infant in the school knew more about blizzards than the young lady from the east who had only book learning, but the teacher was in authority. Would Nettie dare take away from the teacher the terrible responsibility for the lives of all those young ones? There was the problem of fuel ; David remembered seeing only a small pile of coal by the schoolhouse. The demand for coal was so small that winter that Dixon at the lumber-yard was ordering only half a carload at a time. No one could say how long a blizzard would last, and without fuel the children would all freeze to death in the schoolhouse.

Mary's face on the pillow showed that the same fear was in her mind. Reckless of the cost of kerosene, David lighted the lamp. "Let's have some cheerfulness here !"

"Turn it down a little, that's light enough," she murmured, troubled by the waste. She reached out her hand and he took it, holding it tighter when it grew clammy from her pain. He pushed back the lank bangs

306

from her damp forehead. When she could unclench her teeth she smiled. "I'm all right. Everything's fine, David. We oughtn't to worry, it don't do any good; Nettie's sensible. There's nothing to do but take whatever comes and keep on bearing up under it. We've got a real comfortable house, David. I'm glad you built on this front room. We've had good times together, haven't we?"

"We're going to have a lot more," he said stoutly, but his mouth shook in spite of all he could do. The fear that had got into his mind made more unreasonable fears; he knew they were unreasonable but he could not overcome them. The blizzard raging around the house cut it off from any help, in a loneliness where anything might happen. He wished he had called the doctor.

In the kitchen he pleaded with Mrs. Peters. "Can't something be done? Don't you know any way to make it easier for her?"

"She'll be worse before she's better," Mrs. Peters said quietly. "She's having an easy time so far, everything's going along natural."

He was ashamed before Mrs. Peters' quietness, knowing what was in her mind; all her children but Billy, and no way of knowing what was happening to them. It shamed him to remember Billy's birth, as he sometimes did during that long night in his own warm and lighted house.

This time Mary wanted a girl. He managed to tease her a little about that, sometime near midnight, while she rested against his supporting arm and he held to her mouth a cupful of eggnogg to keep up her strength. "You get this over quick, and I won't argue, any more, you can have your girl baby."

"I'm sorry you mind so much but I'm glad you're

here. I missed you when Davy was born. He's all right, isn't he? He's safe? What are you keeping from me?" The blizzard made her mind wander a little.

"He's sleeping sound as a log. I'll bring him and show you."

The baby girl was born about two o'clock, not breathing. Mrs. Peters slapped the dangling limpness again and again. She blew into the silent mouth. Silence became horrible, stronger than the fiendish yells of the blizzard. Mrs. Peters snatched up the baby and smacked it, the head swung mute on the thin neck. "Cold water, quick. Real cold. No, in the washbasin." David dumped the water sloshing from the water pail. Mrs. Peters plunged the lifeless baby into it.

Breath came screaming, and caught back into a long squall of anguish. Swiftly Mrs. Peters wrapped the living creature in her apron and sat down before the oven. "Now if I can keep her from turning blue again. It's good and hot here, thank goodness, but put more hay in." Holding the child on her knees thrust into the oven, she began to smear her with lard from the tin cup on the stove. "She'll live, listen to her."

"Well, you've got your girl, mother," David said to Mary. Their daughter's bitter crying pierced the noise of the blizzard. Mary listened to it in drowsy bliss.

"Now if only hers are safe," she murmured.

Mrs. Peters went quietly about the work, day after day. Now and then David tried to say something encouraging to her, though he knew he could say nothing that she had not thought of. The house was warm and pleasant when he came back to it along the rope, after doing the chores. He brought in the old harness and mended it by the stove in the front room where he and Mary could talk, and carefully over wrapping paper

308

spread to protect the floor, he rubbed oil into the worn straps with his hands. Both he and Mary kept up a cheerful pretense that there was no reason at all to worry about Nettie and the young ones.

"They're sitting somewhere this minute, just as snug as we are," Mary often said.

The blizzard ended in mid-morning on the fourth day. Mrs. Peters put on her wraps as soon as she heard the wind blowing steadily, and David stopped only to shut the drafts and to set Davy on the bed where Mary could keep him from going near the stoves, before he set out with her. Less than a foot of snow was blowing over the hard-frozen ground, and their only difficulty was walking through the force of the wind. Before they reached the shanty they saw Mr. Peters making his way along the railroad track toward town. They saw no searchers setting out from the town.

David would have gone for news himself, but he could not leave Mary with the new baby in the house where fires were burning and accidents might happen. He scraped the frost from the south window and kept a lookout. It was impossible to conjecture why Mr. Peters did not bring home the girls and Charley, when at the same time there was no search party to be seen. Not until two o'clock did David see Mr. Hewitt's pung coming swiftly from town, and then against the dazzle of the sun he could not be sure who, or even how many, got out at the shanty.

He was putting on his wraps to go and inquire, when Mary called that someone was coming. Johnson's team passed the windows pulling a home-made cutter and Nettie was out of it before David could open the door. He called to Johnson to put his team in the stable, and shutting the door he began to help Nettie out of her wraps. She was laughing, red with cold, bringing the sparkling chill of outdoors into the warm house. "We can only stay a minute, how's Mary?" she asked hoarsely while he unwound her muffler. "Which is it, Mary, did you get your girl?" she tried to call out.

"Come in and meet Miss Nettie Mary Beaton!" Mary answered. "Oh Nettie, we've been sick with worry. Tell us about it, what did you do, what happened?"

"Nothing happened, we're all right, we spent the whole time in a straw-stack." Nettie's voice was a stage-whisper. "Lucy and Charley frost-bit their feet, I can't think how, they kept telling me they were warm enough and of course we couldn't see anything, but they thawed out with no trouble and Mr. Hewitt took them home, he's taking all the country young ones home in his pung. David! Mary! I'm almost sure of getting the town school next fall! Oh the blessed sweet thing; she looks like David, doesn't she."

The teacher, Miss Lancie James, had dismissed school as soon as one of the primer pupils saw the blizzard coming. She had told them all to run home as fast as they could. That would have ended her teaching school in that town, even if she had not said after the blizzard ended that she was going back east to stay. Of course not one of the pupils obeyed her. But there was not coal enough for more than a night and a day and Nettie was not sure that they could outlast the blizzard by burning the benches. She thought they had time to reach Mr. Hewitt's house, at least. He had more fuel and his house was weather-boarded.

She helped hustle them into their wraps and lined them up, holding hands. They ran for it, and they were so near when the blizzard caught them that she still thought they could reach it. But after three or four

310

minutes she knew they had missed. Every child was perfectly obedient and Miss James was so frightened that she would do anything she was told to do. She stood still at the end of the line while Nettie led it in an arc from side to side, and it was possible to be certain that they were going straight forward, as long as Miss James knew her right hand from her left and signaled when the line was in front of her. So they went on until Nettie walked against a straw stack.

The little ones were beginning to give out then, and she would not go any farther. She worked into the stack and they all helped her hollow out in the center a large enough space to hold them. They put the small children in the middle and huddled close together to keep all the warmth they could. Then they simply stayed there. That was all, except that until they judged that the first day had passed, the older boys took turns staying out in the storm so that if a search party came to the stack it would not miss them.

A search party had in fact been out with ropes and lanterns until after midnight of the first night. Jeremiah Boles had led it, and he had reached the empty schoolhouse. Strangely enough, the straw-stack was his; it stood less than thirty feet from the stable where he did his chores twice a day during that blizzard. He had given up his children for lost, when they were so near him.

Every child came out of that straw-stack as soon as the blizzard ended, alive and well. They had not even caught cold. Several of the middle-sized ones had frost-bitten feet, but curing those was only a matter of time. Nettie and the other older girls had grown hoarse only from singing and telling stories to keep up the spirits of the little ones in the cold and dark.

"And Mr. Boles and Mr. Wyatt as good as promised me the town school next fall," she whispered happily, sitting on the edge of Mary's bed. A four months' term, at twenty-five dollars a month, and so near that she could live at home.

Johnson sat in the rocking chair on the other side of the stove. He did not rock but kept the chair still, tilted forward on the tips of the rockers. His mended and half-soled boots were solidly planted apart on the floor and his arms rested on his knees. The short, wool-lined jacket which he wore under his buffalo overcoat was clumsily patched. He kept his eyes mostly on his cap in his hands; he sat there full of joy and pride in Nettie but his eyes became hungrily wistful when he looked at her.

It would be a long time before he could afford to marry. Likely he would not ask a girl to leave a house with a floor, to move into his soddy.

47

Almost from the first, Molly was a delight. She was small and dainty, but always lively and amused. Her head was so beautifully shaped that David could hardly keep his hands off it, and the curling wave of her auburn hair caught on his rough fingers like silk. She had large, dark blue eyes that looked sidewise roguishly; her nose was tip-tilted and her mouth quickly became firm and clear. Her tiny fingers, pink and white as porcelain, took hold of her father's huge forefinger with a warm sureness that melted all through him, choked his throat and made his knees weak.

312

That year was not as hard as it might have seemed to an outsider. The drought was not disappointing because they had expected it. The first shearing of the sheep was wool so dirty, so full of burrs and briars, that David was pleased when the little he sold brought money enough to meet the interest on the loan. Lambing was late ; one old ewe died and two lambs were stillborn, another so deformed that he killed it, but that thirty-two hours of work ended with twelve buck lambs which sold for thirty-six dollars, and ten ewe lambs added to the flock. And there was always Molly, changing a little every day, adding a new charm sometimes between his leaving her in the morning and his coming in at noon.

Even while the hail, which for two years had missed them, was slashing across the scanty field of wheat on the first morning he took the binder into it, he held Molly warmly wrapped in his arms and she was laughing. The thunder, the lightning and the noise on the roof did not frighten her. He said when the cloud went on, trailing a good downpour of rain across the slough which did not need it, "Well, mother, we'll harvest some crop, anyhow enough to pay for threshing and meet interest and taxes. Things are never so bad but what they could be worse !"

The well gave out while the threshers were there. He had been pulling all the water out of it every evening, till the last pailfuls they carried to the garden and the trees were thin mud, but every day it had filled again nearly to the previous mark. Haying, cultivating the tree-claim and trying to save the garden by hoeing, he had not had time to deepen the well and he thought it would last another week. Mary met him with a tragic face when he came from the stable at dawn on the day the threshers were coming. "Father, look." The water in the water pail was cloudy with mud. There was not more than two feet of water in the well.

There was nothing to do but go ahead with the threshing. He could not pay another man to take his place on the machine, or to deepen the well. Three more of the small orchard trees died, and fourteen in the windbreak could never be entirely revived though their twigs had some life in them until September. He dug the well fifteen feet deeper and bought another length of rope. But they were lucky; farther west there were settlers digging two hundred and fifty feet to reach water.

"Droughts go in threes," he said, when all signs pointed to another dry year. "I don't know why it's so, but it is. You tell me the answer to anything you're a mind to pick, except you say that that's the way God made it, and I'll tell you why droughts go in threes. Why does grass grow? Answer that one. All right, I'm telling you that year after next we'll need web feet."

"All signs fail in dry weather," Cliff Wyatt remarked. "Maybe we'll be drownded out next year."

"You fellows are so goldarned cheerful," said Dant Macray, "I'll just raise you a couple. Maybe there won't be no next year."

"Hallelujah! Amen!" Lafe Garner shouted out. He twanged a kind of music out of one of the hardware-store saws and sang,

> Oh, them golden slippers that I'm going to wear,
> A-climbing up them golden stairs!

A young fellow came out from the east that winter and started a singing school. He buttonholed David one Saturday afternoon in Boles' store, and put it to him that he had nineteen subscribers at a dollar apiece for two

314

months' music schooling, a lesson a week for eight weeks. He had the music books full of new tunes, and a tuning fork, and a diploma from an Academy of Music. He was boarding at Jake Mostar's, for two dollars and a half a week, and if he could get one more subscriber he could barely make out to stay in town for the eight weeks ; if not, he would have to give up the whole idea. "I appeal to your public spirit," he said. "All up-to-date towns nowadays have a singing school. Is this town going to be behind the others ? I don't believe it, no siree sir ! I can see you're a public-spirited man, Mr. Beaton, you'll help support a fine big singing school in your town this winter, or I don't know what I'm talking about !"

David's father had pointed out to him long ago that men who appealed to public spirit practically always had their own axes to grind, but he liked the idea of a sing-ing school. It would make a jolly winter. He was fol-lowing Mr. Peters' example of eating sparingly at table and filling up on raw turnips between meals, but he handed the singing master two dollars, for Mary and him-self.

From the old sled runners that he had used on the wagon box and some hoarded boards from Gay's shanty, he made a small sleigh, with a box behind the dashboard to hold Molly, and a space under the seat in which he put ropes. Every Friday evening for eight weeks they went to singing school, cozily warm under plenty of quilts, with the hot flatirons at their feet, hot baked po-tatoes in their pockets, Davy between them and Molly snugly sleeping in the straw-filled box.

Clint Insull used the railroad's coal to keep the waiting-room warm, and from nine o'clock to ten they sat on the benches, singing the new songs that the young sing-ing master lined out. At ten o'clock they came gaily

315

home, beneath a frosty moon or small stars, singing under their mufflers while the sleigh bells chimed.

> Oh, if ever you get into any such scrape
> Through being too timid or bold,
> Recollect, my friend, whose fault it is,
> And blame yourself if you're sold.

Wide awake under her blankets and veils, Molly was singing too. Before she was a year old, she could distinctly say, "Papa," and "Mama," and several other words, and she could walk. Davy was already proud of her. Carefully he led her by the hand, and kept her away from the stove, saying, "No, no, baby mustn't."

They were teaching the sturdy little fellow to take care of his sister. For a few weeks that winter he looked to them for praise when he helped or guarded her, but by paying no attention to him they soon broke him of that. He was good natured and beginning to be independent. It made the heart swell full, to see those two little ones together.

"I declare," Mary often said that winter, "we certainly are blest in our health and in our children."

48

Wool was selling for thirty-five cents a pound, that spring, and David felt that at last he was beginning to get on his feet. The March sunlight tingled through the cold winds with the peculiar feeling that comes from a dry-weather sun, and dust was blowing from the fields before he finished his spring plowing. But while he hustled the harrowing, the seeding, the planting of the corn and the garden, he looked forward to shearing the sheep.

He should have had a place to wash them. There should have been a clear stream, and plenty of soft soap, so that he could have thoroughly sudsed and rinsed each sheep before he sheared her. He must have a large, sunken, water-tight trough large enough to run the flock through sheep-dip, but he could not buy the materials to make it until he got the money from the wool. He had not yet been able to pay even for the sheepshears. Next spring he would have that trough, and use it for washing the sheep.

One by one he caught them and laid them on the shearing bench, and expertly with the large shears he clipped away at the fleece, over the tender belly and in the ticklish hollows under the legs, and on the throat, close to the pink skin to get every inch of wool, yet quickly careful not to cut it when the sheep struggled. He turned the sheep from side to side, clipping over the curve of the ribs and the legs, around the neck under the ears, till at last he let the shorn animal spring baaing from its fleece left in one unbroken piece on the bench. He rolled the fleece neatly and tied it, and caught the next woolly creature. His hands grew soft and smooth from the oily lanolin in the pure white of the inner wool, and a pain like a toothache settled in the back of his neck.

Eight pounds of wool he sheared from each sheep, and one Saturday he came home triumphant, with fifty-six dollars. There was enough to build the sheep-dip trough, to buy the sheep-dip, and to pay something on the grocery, the hardware, and the blacksmith bills.

"You see what sheep'll do, mother!" he said to Mary. "Next year, with the lambs growing up, we'll more than double that, and pretty near pay off the loan at the bank. This flock's going to pay for itself in another year or two,

and from then on it'll be paying a profit." He plucked
Molly from her clutch on his leg and tossed her. "Oopsy
daisy !" He caught her, laughing, and held her in the
air to hug her between his hands. Then seeing that Davy
perhaps felt left out, he sat down and took them both on
his knees.

A sharp cry from Mary cut through their chattering,
"David !"

The letter in her hand was from his mother. Her face
made him think that his father, Alice, Perley, one of his
brothers in St. Paul, was sick, or dead. She caught her
breath. "They're coming to visit us. Your father and
mother."

"Well — "

"David, I never exactly lied to them, but — but I —
They won't expect — Every letter, your mother's asked
how we are getting along, and I always wrote her we're
doing well, and — She's asked if we needed anything
and I always said, No."

He looked at the house, the two poor rooms, meagerly
furnished ; the unpainted shelves against patched muslin
walls. He saw his barefooted children, Davy's little shirt
and pants made of faded pieces from tails of his own
worn-out shirts, Molly wearing one of Davy's old short
dresses, patched. He could see the whole place as if
with his father's eyes ; the small sod house with rusted
tin chimneys, the low stable of sods under a sod roof and
the gray straw-stack behind it under which his sheep were
sheltered, the poor field of wheat and the yellowing
corn-rows unfenced on the prairie. Hired men were better off. His father hardly knew a shiftless ne'er-do-well
who lived like this.

"I don't believe the muslin will stand another washing." Mary was looking at the walls.

"Mother, we've got to pay for Dobbin, somehow," he said desperately. "We've got to."

"Yes," she said. "But how?"

He went to see Jake Hewitt. "Mr. Hewitt, I'm kind of up against it for a little cash. It's a personal matter. Will you let me have a hundred and fifty dollars on my household chattels and the sheep?"

"Come in and sit down, Dave." Mr. Hewitt had a small office at the back of the bank, with one window looking out between gardens and stables at the prairie. It had a tall desk and two chairs in it. His fingers played thoughtfully with the watchcharms hanging from the heavy gold chain across his vest. "Aren't you getting in rather deep?"

"Well, I wouldn't exactly say so, Mr. Hewitt. I'll prove up next August on three hunded and twenty acres of as good land as there is in this country. My sheep are coming right along, I ought to have better than fifty ewes next year, some buck lambs to sell. This drought won't last forever, you know."

"Let's see, four hundred and twenty you owe us, isn't it?"

"Yes sir, and I've never failed to meet the interest yet."

"Taxes paid up?"

"Every cent."

"It isn't that you're not good for it, Dave. I just don't like to see you getting in so deep. You're behindhand at the stores, too, aren't you?"

David turned his ragged hat in his hands. "Well, yes. Around a couple of hundred dollars, all told."

"You're carrying over a hundred dollars a year in interest, then. These short-time rates'll eat you up. They're too high, I think myself. But the storekeepers are hard-pressed, too. You can't blame 'em. We ought to fig-

319

ure out some way to get you in a better position, Dave. My business depends on how you homesteaders get along. You've no idea the troubles I have. Take those two Garner boys. Wouldn't you've said they were square?"

"Square as a die." Dave emphasized it.

"That's what I thought. Well, I loaned 'em forty dollars again on those two yoke of oxen, and what did they do? They lit out between two days. Here last week I had to chase 'em to Yankton and beyond, 'way down across Nebraska to Missouri, and clap a writ on those oxen to get back that forty dollars. Before that, I was all the way to Denver after another fellow, and had to take his team. It didn't square what he owed the bank, either, not to mention my time and expense. People are lighting out of here in all directions and leaving their debts behind 'em. You have no idea what a job it is to keep a bank going through hard times, and I hate to think what would happen in this community if I didn't keep it going. I just mention it to show you. I've got as much real interest in your making a go of it on your claim, as you have in being able to come in here when you need a loan."

"I been figuring, after I prove up this fall, I might mortgage my half section for enough to take up all these scattered debts," David said. "Have it all in one lump sum, and one interest-date to meet after harvest." A dart of suspicion from the banker's eyes startled him.

Mr. Hewitt shook his head. "No, I'm not in that business, Dave. You'll find bankers that are, but I'm not one of 'em."

"You mean you wouldn't lend me money on my land?" David was incredulous.

"Not a cent. No security's any good that a bank can't realize its money on if it has to. And I'm not peddling

320

western land mortgages at fancy prices in the east and keeping up interest payments on 'em from the proceeds of selling more western land mortgages. That's not my notion of sound banking."

David remembered Eliza's saying that he could mortgage his land for enough to get out of the country, and he understood the sharp glance that Jake Hewitt had given him. He said slowly, "See here, I've spent five years getting this land, and I'm staying with it. Are you telling me it's not worth the dollar and a half an acre the Government'd sell it for ?"

"I'm only saying I won't lend a penny on it. What it's worth — Well, it's worth to you whatever you're making out of it, and it's always worth what you can sell it for. You can't sell anything that's being given away or abandoned. But land values are pure speculation, Dave ; they always have been, in the U.S.A."

Having hit bottom hard, David's spirits rebounded. "By golly, that land of mine's raised two big bonanza crops — a crop of grass and a crop of debts. Before I'm through, it'll raise me a third one. How about that hundred and fifty, on my household chattels and the sheep ?"

"I'd rather not see you go in any deeper, Dave. I advise you not to. But I'll stretch the limit and let you have this hundred and fifty if you say so."

"Thanks, I'll take it," David said.

49

Back east it was the time after the corn was laid by and before the rush of early haying, when farmers could take a few days off to do odd jobs about the place or even to go fishing. Lambing was past; David had assisted into the world during forty hours of anxiously harried work fifteen ewe lambs and fourteen bucks. He was groggy from lack of sleep, for besides the unbroken hours of lambing he had used every daylit minute outdoors and had worked at night in the house.

"It don't look so bad, mother," he said that afternoon while they hurried to dress.

"It looks real nice," she answered.

More than eighty dollars' worth of lumber, fitted, sawed and nailed by lamplight, lined the kitchen neatly, cased all the doors and windows, made a shallow clothes closet in the front room and a pantry in the kitchen. He had spent no money for white lead and color, but the fresh boards had a pleasing yellow hue. Down cellar he had squared and smoothed the earthen walls, repaired the bins, and Mary had whitewashed them. She had made window curtains from the flounces of a white muslin petticoat and trimmed them with the knitted lace from those destroyed sheets. She had done marvels of making-over and piecing-out to dress the children prettily for everyday without buying one yard of new material.

The back doorstep was new; so was the well rope. On top of everything else, he had dug nightly by lantern-light in the muddy well while Mary more and more hurriedly pulled up the dripping pails, until they had lowered the well another twelve feet. Emerging muddy to his very hair, he had said, "We've got to quit digging this well deeper."

"Why? What's wrong?" Mary asked.

"When we get rain again, it'll hold so much water that it'll flood over and wash us away." That got a laugh from her.

Even to his father's eye, the place would look at least

322

well-kept. He had used the mowing machine to cut the wild grass from a square around the house and stable, and with the scythe he had trimmed down the edges left against the sod walls, through the windbreak and small orchard and along the sheep-fold fence. The yellow-green corn and starveling garden rows could not be charged to lack of cultivation. The pig was clean in her pen, the hens ruffling in dust-baths were red-combed and bright of eye and feather, fresh straw was in their nests and their roosts were scraped and whitewashed. Both calves this year were steers and had been vealed, but the two cows looked fairly well, for grade cows. The lately-shorn sheep and their lambs were healthy, though they would be the better for more feed than the drying pasture. No one could say that he had not done his best.

Star and Dobbin were brown satin in the old harness that disgraced them. The wagon could not be tightened up so that it would not rattle, and the two seats tipped on sagging springs. That day he saw even Mary with new eyes, and her worn face gave him a pang of suspicion that she, too, was always a little hungry.

They ate enough at this season to fill their stomachs, but there was somehow a craving not satisfied with bread and potatoes, eggs, or even a Sunday chicken dinner. What he craved was pie and cake, jellies, preserves ; it seemed that she wanted more green stuff from the garden. There were hardly two messes of withered peas that year, the lettuce shot up seed-stalks as soon as it leafed ; radishes were wizened and so peppery that they burned the tongue. All root-crops were tasteless and woody, sending their sap to leaf and seed, and the meagerly blossoming berry-row let fall its green fruit and put its hope in new shoots from the roots.

He set his frilly baby-girl, grave-eyed in her little bonnet, on her mother's starched lap, and tossed Davy shouting into the wagon box. The little chap clambered onto the seat himself and took his place in the middle, his stockinged legs and small new boots sticking straight out. David took the lines and let Davy hold their ends. "Well, here we go ! Who are we going to see ?"

"Grandpa and Grandma !" "Gwampa, gwam-ah !" They made a chant of it, riding along the shadeless road in the vibrant heat of a still day. Davy twisted and squirmed to see every shanty, bird, and tall weed they passed, until David spoke firmly to him, but from the first Molly sat motionless, her eyes fixed upon the ears of the horses turning forward and back.

The town that day looked strange to David. He saw the leaning barns, the straw-stacks, the gardens gone to weeds behind the weathered shanty-backs of the stores, and the paint flaking from the street side of their tall false fronts. He saw the crudely boarded-up windows of the empty buildings. There was no shade ; discouraged saplings fought to live in weeds between the glaring dusty street and the uneven heights of grayed board sidewalks. David had known that the town was only two blocks long, but it shocked him now to see the fact. He saw the footpaths straggling eastward past the livery stable and scattered claim shanties, and westward along the board wall of the lumber-yard and beyond Mr. Hewitt's painted house to the schoolhouse and church in prairie grasses.

Train smoke was already adding nearer puff to puff above the low snout of the train emerging from the three-mile cut. The long steel rails came together to point to it with an increasing tenseness. Boots lounged along the platform ; mechanically David nodded, lifted his hat in answer to hats lifted because Mary was with him.

324

"How are you folks this warm weather? In to meet somebody, Dave?" That was Cliff Wyatt, noticing their good clothes.

"My folks coming for a visit."

"You don't say so. Well, that's fine. Hi yuh, young fella?"

"No, Davy, the other hand," Mary said. When they were alone, she rustled carefully down to straighten his little shirt. "Now, Davy, remember what you're to say when you see grandma?" Later she said, plucking at Molly's skirts to arrange them, "Maybe I'd better take her, father. She's pushing her bonnet crooked against your cheek. She'll have finger marks on your collar if you don't look out."

"You look after Davy," he said. The engine was already whistling. Molly nestled soft against him, sure of his great power and wisdom. The enormous monster loomed terrifically roaring and he felt the small bonnet crush in panic beneath his ear. Black engine wheels cranked themselves past beneath the blistering red face and shoulders of the fireman, then small wheels grinding fast under brick-red box-cars, against the sky the brakeman applying his muscles, and crashing along its length the train was in. They had come. They were there. This was the moment, no longer awaited, but now.

Under his mustache he licked his lips; his mouth was dry. Faces hung on vague plush seat-backs looked down from dust-blurred windows of the passenger coach. Mary's rustling quickened. "There they are!" and Davy swung a little sidewise, pulled by the hand she held.

An elderly, stocky man lowered himself from the car steps and turned to assist down them a plump, fussy, little elderly lady, bright-eyed and chattering.

David's step checked, not so long as it takes to catch

325

the breath. In this miniscule of time, his vision changed and he saw his mother embracing Mary. He stepped up smiling, and man to man shook hands with his respected father. "How are you, father? Glad to see you. Have a comfortable trip?"

Davy, after all, extended his left hand and confused by this mistake he said, "Good afternoon, grandma," to his grandfather. Amid the laughter, James Beaton lifted the boy up and closed an arm around him in a way that went to David's heart. The graybeard and the youngster looked at each other closely and James Beaton said, "You favor your father, sonny, when he was knee-high to a grasshopper."

They took to each other at once. Davy settled on the old man's shoulder, and while David was shepherding them at their own slow pace toward the wagon, he heard his son ask, "What makes your whiskers that funny color, grandpa"?

He knew that his father's shrewd eyes were taking everything in, and shaking the lines along the team's shining backs he told him bits about the country and the claims they passed. He described a blizzard minutely and also gave him some idea of a cyclone. His father noted the evidences of drought ; he had lived through several notable ones in his time. They had hardly begun to talk when the rattling wagon turned westward and David said, "That's my place. You can see it from here."

His mother, on the back seat with Mary and the young ones, exclaimed. "But my land, Mary, wasn't you saying you don't raise any flowers? The whole place looks to be covered with flower beds."

It happened that one of the great masses of wild roses, at that season in bloom all over the country, lay up from the edge of the slough in the wild grass that David had not cut. But his mother's eye was caught by the square patch of sunflowers planted for chicken feed, and the oblong of mixed colors to the right of it.

"That's the sod roof of my stable," David explained. The blossoming weeds growing so thickly upon it perhaps took brighter colors from the sunset beginning to flame over the enormous sky. "I get up there and cut 'em before they start to seed the place."

"I've used thatch in my time," his father said. "But I don't know's I ever saw a sod roof."

David lightly slapped the lines on the willing horses. "We'll be home inside ten minutes and I'll show you one, father."

50

In the five years of living on their claim before they proved up on it, both Mary and David often said later, the best time of all was the time his father and mother came to visit. They stayed three weeks, and they had not begun to wear their welcome out when they went home. Though they had every confidence in Perley and Alice, and Perley had a hired man to help him in the haying, still they grew restless to see with their own eyes what was happening on their farm, and anyone could understand that. No farmer ever knows what will happen if he turns his back.

James Beaton pitched into the haying and the wheat harvest like a good one. His age was weighing down his steps, and he had a gold-headed cane which he often carried though protesting that he did not need one, but his arms were as good as they had ever been. With

Johnson on the third pitchfork, the stacks went up in double-quick time. The wheat ripened early that year, a light and low-grade crop, and David went into it with the binder while his father and Johnson finished putting up the bluestem. He caught the threshers at the start of the season, and got his grain into the market before the price fell, so that he came out with enough cash to meet interest and taxes.

It was a pleasure to see with what respect the threshers listened to his father, and a pleasure to step into the stores with the old man on Saturday afternoon and introduce the crowd to him. Jake Hewitt cordially asked him into the office and listened to him for an hour while men who came in on banking business went out to come back later. David enjoyed accommodating his steps to his father's slower pace and tapping cane, and slightly pausing at the changes of sidewalk levels. Their talk was always interesting. David was surprised to discover how much his father knew.

On each of the three Sundays James Beaton hired the two-seated livery hack with canopy to shade it, and the best team Luke Fagarty owned. Mary put up a lunch, and as soon as services were over they set out directly from the church to go driving. That team could cover forty miles between eleven o'clock and dark, and did it. They went as far as Blue Heron Lake, and into the rolling, almost hilly country southwest of Gooseneck, and north to Indian Slaughter. Such Sundays as these enlivened the whole summer and would always be remembered. They showed what a difference was made by having some money to spend for pleasure. Even at the time, Mary and David realized that their deprivations now were storing up such good times for the future.

"Ten years from now," Mary declared one Sunday, while in the shady hack they were eating the good lunch of fried chicken, hard-boiled eggs, bread and butter, with bread-and-butter pickles and jam which David's mother had brought as presents from her cellar, "when Davy's fourteen years old, we're going to have a top-buggy and a driving team. And you'll stay home, Davy, and take care of the stock while father and mother go gadding."

"Can I milk the cow?" Davy asked, in spite of her efforts to wipe his mouth.

"You can milk, maybe twenty cows, son," David said.

"What will Molly do?" Davy persisted.

"That's enough, son," David silenced him. The boy's grandmother took his face between her wrinkled hands and said, "Molly'll sit in the parlor and sew a fine seam, and live upon strawberries, sugar, and cream!" Davy's mouth opened; he did not know what a parlor was, nor strawberries, but a look from David kept him silent.

"I wouldn't wonder if you would," his father said slowly. "Though I don't know's my judgment would agree with yours about the length of time."

"Two good crop years'll put us on our feet, father," David said.

"There's bad years in between, son. I figured on twelve years when I started out, but it took us nearer twenty."

That was the last Sunday. They went home on the east-bound train, Wednesday. Tuesday evening after supper David and his father strolled along the wire fence looking at the sheep and went out to the picket lines to unhobble Dobbin who had caught his foot in a loop of the rope. The long summer twilight was still in the sky, though the evening star was out and the prairie seemed level as a table in the dark. They came back past the sunflower patch, and noticing that several heads were bent and ripened, David took a gunny sack from the tool shed and cut the ripe heads to put in it in order not to waste the hen's next winter's feed. His father sat on the wagon-tongue while he did this, and after he had put the sack in the shed David set one foot in the wheel and leaned on his knee.

They were companionable there, saying nothing, watching the sky darken and the stars come out. Now and then David flipped his jackknife blade from half open to straight out and back again, feeling the pleasant stiffness of it and the click.

"I don't know if your mother wrote Mary I got your check for Dobbin," his father said.

"I was some time getting around to it, but better late than never. He's a good horse yet."

"Yes, he is. In round figures, how much would you say you're in debt, son?"

"Well, I don't know's I've said, nor meant to. But since you ask me, round figures, nine hundred dollars."

"I don't know where you get it from, son; it must be your mother's side of the family. You know she had a swashbuckling uncle went to California with Kearney, that time they built the road to travel on, ahead of them into unknown country. Now Beatons are independent, but they don't take risks. It's in the Beaton blood to come along cautious. We're the backbone of the nation, as the politicians say. You're the first Beaton ever put his head into the jaws of a new country to open it up." Humorously he said, "I guess I'm responsible, I married your mother."

"It's a good country." David set his foot on the ground and put his closed knife in his pocket. "I've been on this claim five years come August, and today it's not worth a hoot in Hades. I started with as good as fifteen hundred dollars and I put five years work on top of that and sunk it. I couldn't sell out today, every jot and tittle I own, and pay over half what I owe. But it's a good country. I'll be right here, father, when this farm's worth something."

"I wouldn't wonder," James Beaton mildly remarked. "I wouldn't wonder at all, son. Fact is, if I was a betting man I might go so far as bet something on it. The Beaton comes out in you. We're pig-headed." He got to his feet, put his hands in his pockets and walked toward the house with the deliberate and heavy steps that made David feel like helping him and consciously refrain from doing so. The old man now was getting along near seventy.

"As good a time to speak of it as any," he said. "I want you should know, my will's made out. It gives every one of you children an even share of the property that's left, when so be your mother and me both are gone."

He stopped and looked up at the stars. "Don't know's I ever expected to see stars so big. Seems as though you could reach up and pick 'em like apples. But always quivering, I never could tell the weather by 'em."

He went on slowly and from force of habit scraped his clean boot-soles on the edge of the back step. The open house was dark, and in the front room the women were talking and the rockingchair rocking. Against the pale oblong of the front doorway the chair swayed back and forth with a shadowy woman rocking a child.

"Your mother and me been talking it over and made up our mind," James Beaton said. "So soon as we get

331

home, I'm going to send you two thousand dollars and charge it against your share of the estate. I don't know's you noticed it when you was to home, but ever since you young ones was born to mother and me, I wanted you to have an easier time than we did."

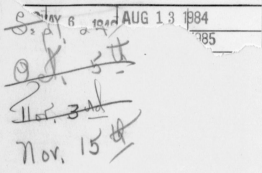

AUG 13 1984

985

Nov. 15